THE PRETTY GIRL: NOVELLA AND STORIES

THE
PRETTY GIRL

NOVELLA
AND STORIES

DEBRA SPARK

Please direct all inquiries to:
Editorial Office
Four Way Books
POB 535, Village Station
New York, NY 10014
www.fourwaybooks.com

Library of Congress Cataloging-in-Publication Data
Library of Congress Cataloging-in-Publication Data
Spark, Debra, 1962-
The pretty girl : novella and stories / Debra Spark.
p. cm.
ISBN 978-1-935536-18-5 (alk. paper)
1. Short stories. I. Title.
PS3569.P358P74 2012
813'.54--dc23
2011050999

This book is manufactured in the United States of America
and printed on acid-free paper.

Four Way Books is a not-for-profit literary press. We are grateful for the assistance we receive from
individual donors, public arts agencies, and private foundations.

This publication is made possible with public funds
from the National Endowment for the Arts
and from the New York State Council on the Arts, a state agency.

Distributed by University Press of New England
One Court Street, Lebanon, NH 03766

We are a proud member of
the Council of Literary Magazines and Presses.

[clmp]

Page 319 serves as an extension of this page.

for Laura

CONTENTS

THE PRETTY GIRL

PART ONE

I

All the houses had paintings. That's what Andrea remembers. That all the houses that she visited as a girl had paintings and that all the houses belonged to her family. She didn't get invited to other people's homes. And on the rare occasions that she did, the homes seemed strange. They were decorated with wallpaper—jelly jars around the cornice of a kitchen— or basketry. She remembers a friend whose mother pinned a whole nation of cornhusk dolls up the stairs, just where there might have been family photos. But her family liked a picture. There was a painting of a dead rooster at one relative's house and a lion with a lion in its stomach at another's. Her own bedroom had a small print of a little girl walking with a turtle. These pictures kind of made Andrea wonder. But they didn't make her wonder the way The Pretty Girl did.

The Pretty Girl was the name Andrea had given to a painting that belonged to her Great Aunt Rose. She was Andrea's great aunt because she was her grandmother's sister, and she was called Little Rose (though not by Andrea), because Andrea's grandmother had a cousin who was Big Rose, and because there was a baby Rose somewhere, whom people called Rosebud. Aunt Rose didn't live in a house but on the seventeenth floor of an apartment building in New York City. Actually, it was the sixteenth floor, a fact that had mesmerized Andrea as a girl. Aunt Rose's building didn't have a thirteenth floor. Back then, people thought thirteen was bad luck, so they skipped it. Even as a girl, Andrea knew this was foolish, but she sometimes believed thirteen was dangerous anyway. Just to be safe. Seventeen stories was so high up that if you stood on Rose's balcony—and the balcony was why she had such a small apartment, because in New York that's the way it was; people who got a big balcony didn't get a bedroom, or that's what Rose had told Andrea—you could throw your milk over the edge and never really see it hit the ground, which was what Uncle Jonathan once did with his drink. Only it wasn't a drink of milk. It was a chocolate egg cream, because that's what people drank in New York. Again, this wisdom from Andrea's elders. It must have been, she later realized, a martini he was tossing over the balcony. Or a Pink Squirrel. Or an Old Fashioned. People drank things with such names back then.

The painting of the pretty girl was inside Aunt Rose's apartment. She wasn't really a girl, but a laughing, young woman with two raspberry-colored gloves, which she held in one hand. She seemed to be looking at whomever was looking at her, and saying, "Oh, you silly. Go away."

For years, all visits to the relatives started with a ritual touching of the important items in the house. At Grandma Sophie's Long Island bungalow, there was a cookie jar in the shape of a barefoot boy in blue pants. Andrea had to rub the smooth red porcelain of his hat and call, "Hello, little boy! Hello!" before she ran to look at the toad statue in the garden. When she had done *that*, she knew that Ohio and the Midwest were truly behind her. Though sometimes she also had to go sniff the garage, which smelled like something new and plastic that she couldn't identify. And sometimes she also had to look at the sachets and folded rain hats in the top drawer of Grandma Sophie's bedroom dresser. At the other grandma's, Andrea had to run her fingers through the bowl full of hotel soaps. And then her grandfather would call her into the little kitchen to look at the mug that said, "You asked for a half a cup of coffee." It was a joke mug, round on one side, flat on the other, as if a woodsman had snuck out of a storybook to ax the mug in half. (That's the kind of thing a New York woodsman would do if he was bad. If he was good—her grandpa used to tell her—he would just slice bagels.) At Aunt Tova and Uncle Jack's, there were three green stone seals sitting on coffee tables and a funny orange chair with a button that elevated Andrea's legs so quickly that she launched her feet into the air over and over, as if she were on a carnival ride instead of a chair. At Aunt Rose's, there was nothing to touch and really only one thing to look at—and that was The Pretty Girl. And she didn't even really want you to look at her. "Oh, go away, you silly."

No one Andrea knew lived as Rose did in an apartment with mint green walls and furniture that was black and dark coral— the same creamy pink as the nail polish that her grandmothers wore. But even so, with the exception of the painting, there wasn't anything that you could call personal at Rose's. All the relatives were neat, but Aunt Rose didn't have anything to be neat with. She had a table with an ashtray on it, but no one smoked. On one of the shelves, there was a TV set that Andrea's mother had bought. There seemed to be a general feeling that Rose needed entertaining, perhaps because she was single. Andrea supposed if she were married, she could just tune in to her husband. Next to the TV, there was a little embroidered picture that Andrea had stitched (of a tree with oranges on it). In the cupboard sat a cereal box and water crackers—both sealed in Ziploc bags to keep roaches away. Curlers rested in a basket on top of the laundry hamper in the bathroom, but Aunt Rose wore a wig—that was the only scary thing about her, and it was because she didn't have much hair. She wasn't sick. There just wasn't enough hair on her head. Which was weird, Andrea used to think, as if baldness were gauche, not something that Rose, always concerned with being appropriate, would succumb to. She dressed very nicely. Everyone used to say so. Rose didn't have a lot, but everything she had was of the best quality: wool suit sets, button-up dresses, and silk scarves that she pinned to her jackets with a brooch. Nothing very girly. Legs showed. Chest, arms, and neck didn't. You never had to be embarrassed with Aunt Rose; you never had to consider the swaying heft of her breasts or the sounds she made in the bathroom. That was the thing with Aunt Rose; she was perfect. Only she never married. No one said this was a tragedy, but clearly they felt it was. She must be—Andrea remembered thinking at the time—very, very lonely.

The whole apartment was shaped like an L. In the short arm of the L was a small couch that turned into a bed at night. Guests sat on a black couch in the long arm of the L. A small folding screen with photographs (mostly of Andrea and her sister and cousins) offered a partial shield between the part of the L that was a bedroom and the part of the L that was a living room. There was a separate kitchen, the size of Andrea's bathroom at home, and one closet, right by the front door. Each dress in the closet hung in its own garment bag, and below the garment bags were neat stacks of boxes with shoes and handbags.

What would you guess about the person who lived in this apartment if you didn't know Aunt Rose? You wouldn't guess a thing.

But if you saw The Pretty Girl, you might have other ideas. You might think you'd like to be a pretty girl yourself. She wore a dark brown dress with a flared skirt, and the whole picture had the waxy brown sheen that Andrea associated with old paintings. You couldn't really tell where she was standing. Basically, she was standing in a lot of paint, but a lot of paint that gave Andrea the feeling of a place she'd like to enter. As far back as she could remember, Andrea had two ways of looking at The Pretty Girl. One was the normal way, where the things she most liked about the painting were the prettiness of the girl, and the look on her face, and the raspberry color of the gloves against the brown of the painting. There was a small bit of light that hit The Pretty Girl's left forehead, as if there were a small square window high above her. The other way Andrea looked at the painting was as if it were no painting at all, but an opening into another world, one that only she, only Andrea, knew about, and one that she could climb into, just by willing herself over the painting's heavy frame and into the world of The Pretty Girl.

In Andrea's own world—and particularly at her home in Ohio—everything was very light. There were no mysteries—no messy basements to explore, no boxes of forgotten treasures, no strange closets. She had seen everything there was to see in her parents' house—the yellowy hat of her mother's diaphragm in its blue plastic case, the old college yearbooks, the photo her father had taken of a girlfriend he'd had before Mommy. Sometimes Andrea might find a small sample-size shampoo hiding behind the stacks of toothpaste boxes—Andrea loved samples!—but otherwise there was nothing unknown. When Andrea imagined herself into the dark painting, though, everything was a surprise. As soon as Andrea arrived, she and The Pretty Girl ("Oh, you've come," she always said, so technically *that* wasn't a surprise) would walk into the recesses of the painting to get tea at a little shop, and then The Pretty Girl would show Andrea where she worked. (It was a dress shop, Andrea decided, and though dress shops in real life were very boring, The Pretty Girl's dress shop wasn't, because the other shop girls always had funny stories to tell, and, at the end of the day, men would come and spirit the shop girls into the excitement of a New York evening.)

Sometimes Andrea would try to make herself think that the world of The Pretty Girl was really just the next-door neighbor's apartment, that the frame around The Pretty Girl was just a frame around a hole in the wall. But that didn't work. And another thing that didn't work was thinking of the painting as both a painting and an entry into another world. The Pretty Girl was like one of those figure-ground exercises where you saw an hourglass or two faces, but you couldn't see both things at once. Or Andrea couldn't. She could only look at things one way, and it took a great deal of effort to switch things and see the other image that was also there.

You couldn't touch a painting. Everyone knew that. But just like the boy cookie jar or the hotel soaps, The Pretty Girl demanded something. She had to be looked at. It wasn't till Andrea had looked at The Pretty Girl and stepped once out onto the balcony to scare herself with how high up she was, that she knew she was really at Aunt Rose's. Unlike the things in her grandparents' houses, the painting seemed to acknowledge Andrea, but not in a good way exactly. In her fantasies, The Pretty Girl was Andrea's friend, but in reality there was something about The Pretty Girl's face that seemed to dismiss the very attention it demanded. And, even as a child, Andrea knew the only person who could dismiss attention was the person lucky enough to get it.

Everyone had paintings, because everyone was cultured. Even though Andrea lived in Ohio now, both of her parents had come from New York. Plus they were Jewish. Which meant they knew about art and books and didn't play sports, because sports were really for stupid people. That's what her parents said, at least. Andrea's mother could look at an all-white painting at the museum and say, "That's really interesting," and if she wasn't Jewish, she might have just thought it was a lot of white. When Andrea made her own all-white painting for art class and gave it to the art teacher at school, the teacher told Andrea that she should go back to her desk and paint some more. So she wasn't Jewish probably.

All of which didn't explain why one day, when her parents were complaining about how cheap one grandma was, and how they might have to take a loan from Grandpa, and how the other grandma would fart into her chair and not say excuse me, because she thought no one in the world had a nose or a set of ears except her, their complaints turned to Rose. Normally, Rose escaped the litany of family criticism. "You're our favorite!"

Andrea and her sister had confessed one Passover when the rest of the family was gathered downstairs and Rose was upstairs, unpacking her white suitcase, pulling each item carefully out of tissue paper. Rose had smiled at the compliment and said, "Oh, really," as if it were the craziest thing she'd ever heard. But Rose *was* their favorite. She was so easy to get along with. She didn't make demands, even good demands—like the grandpa who asked you to listen to his favorite classical music records, or the other grandpa who wanted to tell you his jokes, or the grandma who wanted to give you new clothes. Rose gave small presents—stickers or a single lacy cookie (what a relief!)—instead of the big-ticket items (sleeping bags, jewelry) that the other relatives gave. Rose's presents weren't valuable; they were just fun. And the parents, Andrea guessed, felt the same way about Rose till this one day, when her father and mother were sitting at the kitchen table with their bills. They'd worked through all the family members with whom they felt aggrieved, when her father said, "If Rose would only sell that painting."

"I know," Andrea's mother said bitterly.

"We could ask?" her father suggested.

"No, we can't ask," her mother said, exhausted, and her father nodded and wrote out a check.

How could they be mad at Rose? As improbable as it was, Rose was why Andrea and her sister existed. Though Rose was her mother's aunt, she had worked as a medical transcriptionist for Grandpa Saul, her father's father, a doctor at St. Vincent's. Rose had introduced her mother to her father, so she was the reason Andrea was even in the world. People worried so much about death, but they never thought about the small odds of having a life. Andrea loved Rose for being so easy, and never fighting with her parents, and for increasing her odds.

II

It took Andrea one semester of college to find her way to the art history department and Marshall Malcolmson. And from then on, if any close friend asked her why she'd become an art history major, she'd tell the truth: "I got a crush on the professor." He wasn't really a professor but a teaching assistant, but even people who weren't similarly smitten called him "God TA." He always dressed in pale suits and had a way of tossing his hair out of his eyes that made Andrea shiver. He seemed like the smartest person in the world. On the back page of her class notebook, she kept a list of all the books he'd told her to read, the museums he'd told her to visit, and even the restaurants he'd told her to try. He lived with his girlfriend in a row house south of campus. Andrea knew that, and yet her crush persisted.

Andrea was not, like the object of her girlhood affection, a pretty girl. She was a large woman with a mannish, square face and horsey teeth. Her blondish hair unfolded in frizzy waves that weren't quite curls, and that she couldn't quite bother to tame, because of the psoriasis that attacked her at the scalp and under the corner of her ears, and sometimes along the line of her chin and folds of her nostrils. It hurt enormously to put a brush to her head. When things were particularly bad, it looked like she was trying to shed her own face. Or like there was a boiled ham under her face trying to get through. Andrea never wore anything too revealing, because she wanted to keep the raw patches on her arms and legs covered (and this even though the doctor told her the sun would do her some good).

But Andrea didn't quite mind about her looks. Or she minded (because how could she not?), and certainly she minded about the skin disease, but mostly she believed what her mother (also not a handsome woman) once told her: it wasn't so lucky to be born beautiful. It was better to be forced into developing some attractive trait to win people over. As a young woman, Andrea's talent was her interest in things. Art history, music, literature. College might have been an institution invented just for her. She loved to learn.

And Marshall clearly was interested in her interest. Andrea was never quite sure if he shared her romantic feelings, but she was a favorite of his: he called her dorm room to chat, asked her to go to the Walters, invited her to join him at restaurants for dinner. If the various requests had been paced differently, Andrea would have assumed Marshall's attraction. But he rang her every eight weeks or so. If he had a desire, it surely wasn't pressing. Still, once she'd taken all the classes Marshall taught, Andrea's life revolved around these encounters. She dressed for them as she'd previously dressed for Marshall's classes. (Dressed in outfits bought by her grandparents that she otherwise had no occasion to wear: tweed suits, wool pants with sweater sets. Her grandparents lived in another decade entirely, one where college was a matter of raccoon coats and girls in headbands instead of a matter of sweatshirts, all-nighters, and casual sex. But it turned out Marshall lived, in part, in that decade, too.)

Andrea daydreamed conversations with Marshall for weeks ahead of time. After they'd been together, she'd turn over their actual conversations for hints of Marshall's affection or to register her own failures and successes in the cleverness arena. Surprisingly enough, Marshall often *did* ask her the sort of question that got one of her daydreamed conversations started. There wasn't ever going to be anything in her life, she thought, that she'd like as much as talking to Marshall.

And, of course, he never brought his girlfriend to these

dinners. That had to mean something. And he always kissed her goodbye. (On the cheek, though.) Still, Andrea had heard a rumor that Marshall's girlfriend was a dancer. A dancer—who could compete with that? Andrea's own stomach strained against the seams of her tweed pants. She was settling into an adult fat that seemed to run in the family—heavy hips, prominent stomach, plumpness all around. "This is what I need to do," a girl named Sisa once said while a group of friends were sitting around the dining hall. She'd taken a Bartlett pear from her tray and trimmed its dumpy bottom. How embarrassing, Andrea had thought at the time. You weren't supposed to confess openly your obsession with your figure, but privately almost all her friends would have admitted to wanting to trim the pear of themselves. Andrea started swimming laps at the pool and reprimanded herself harshly for failing to give up her nighttime snacking, for consistently ending a day of salads and fruit with a pint of ice cream. But what did it matter? A dancer. The situation was clearly hopeless.

Once, over dinner at a Japanese restaurant near campus, Andrea asked Marshall what sort of paintings had hung in his house when he was a boy. (His boyhood a fascinating mystery to her. He'd boarded at Jesuit schools from a very early age. His mother was dead. He never talked about his father. For years, he'd played—though this was so unlikely as to be completely ridiculous—in a rock band.)

"Paint by numbers."

"Really?"

"Yes, I think so. I can't quite remember." Marshall came from somewhere in New Hampshire, but every now and then his accent sounded vaguely British.

Andrea couldn't imagine forgetting a detail of her childhood. She was younger than Marshall by eight years, of course, but even so.

"And you, what about you?"

"Oh, lots, well, there were lots of things." She paused to let the waiter slide a neat tray of sliced fish in front of her. She'd never had sushi before Marshall brought her to this closet-like restaurant. She'd actually been a vegetarian—not on moral or political but on pure gross-out grounds. She didn't like the idea of having, say, dead bird for dinner. But overnight, Marshall had converted her to the rosy pinks, mild tans, and pale oranges of sushi. "My parents actually had a Georges Rouault print—a limited edition of a nude. My mom was pretty proud of that. But I never liked it. It seemed . . . " It seemed too labial, but Andrea couldn't imagine saying that to Marshall, and it wasn't even the genitals that seemed vaginal, it was as if the entire nude were somehow constructed in double folds. She shook her head, then remembered Marshall telling a class that John Ruskin never consummated his marriage, that he was disgusted by his wife Effie Gray's body, and that the rumored reason was that her pubic hair freaked him out. All those Greek statues had given him a different notion about what the female body must look like. His marriage night was a complete shock.

"It seemed what?"

"I forgot what I was going to say," Andrea said, toying with her chopsticks, the raw bite of Japanese horseradish in her nose, "but, let's see, there was actually a pretty good drawing that my grandmother did. A still life. No real imagination in it, but very, very good technically. And, well, in my bedroom, there were those National Portrait Gallery reproductions, those laminated prints with the little hook in back. Do you know the ones I mean? Anyway, there was a Fragonard above my bed. It was a woman viewed from the side. Her hair was in a chignon, and her face was cast downward into a book. She had a yellow top on. The painting was just of her upper torso. *Girl Reading a Book*, it was probably called, only we didn't call it that. We called it 'Andrea's painting.' I really lived in that image as a child. I somehow got it in my head that there was something about the Fragonard painting that was peculiar to me, that I looked like the reader in the picture (though I don't), that I shared important attributes with her. You know, I liked books!"

Marshall smiled at all this. He sat hunkered forward at the restaurant table, as if waiting to catch the next sentence she lobbed over.

"At the end of high school, the top ten students had little bios about their accomplishments in the local paper. A stupid thing. But everyone took it seriously. The journalist came to interview us, and we waited for the Sunday edition when the article ran. In my bio, the writer said that I had 'the look and manner of a gentle lady scholar.'" Andrea stopped to laugh. "But the thing was, when I read that, I thought, 'Yes, *that's* how I would describe her,' meaning not myself but the woman in the Fragonard."

Later, Andrea wished she'd told Marshall that the fantasy wasn't hers alone, that even her sister once said, "I always thought she *was* you." But then Andrea was glad she hadn't said that to Marshall. Maybe it would sound narcissistic. And then she wondered why she went on and on about the Fragonard in the first place. Why didn't she just tell him about The Pretty Girl?

She loved when Marshall called. Such a thrilling violation of teacher-student etiquette for *him* to call *her*, so the air was already charged the day, late in her junior year, when Marshall ended a phone conversation by saying, "I've got something to tell you. I don't want you to get upset." She immediately did get upset. Upset and interested, for what could he possibly have to say that would upset her, save that he didn't like her? She flashed on a conversation that she'd had with her roommate earlier that very day, when her roommate had said, "You really can't tell anyone this but—" and Andrea had interrupted to slap her playfully on the wrist and say, "Oh, all my favorite conversations start with those words. . . ."

"Well, the thing is, you know how I've been going down to New York regularly?" Marshall began.

She nodded into the phone. He had a very part-time job at the Met. It was one of the things that made him special.

"They've offered me a full-time job working in the education department, so I'm going to move to New York." He'd finished his Ph.D. at Johns Hopkins. There was no reason for him to stay in Baltimore.

"Oh." She felt crushed. She wasn't a sad person, but all the same she thought of herself as a drowning woman who'd lived by swimming to the life raft of his attentions. She wondered what she should say. She thought of how she used to go to the Charles Village bagel shop, because she had once bumped into him there. She used the rowing machine at the gym because once she'd seen him in the rowing room. She couldn't just strike out into the water with nothing to swim to. "Congratulations," she said exuberantly, for part of what she liked about Marshall was that he made her feel better than she was. And part of being better than she was involved acting, at all times, like a measured, unemotional adult. "That's good."

"I just wanted you to know. I didn't want you to be upset, and

I'll be back in Baltimore to see my dissertation advisor, so we'll still see each other. Probably as much as we do now. I'll call you when I'm in town."

"Thanks. That'd be great." This was disappointing and enthralling. What did he think he was to her that he'd worry that she'd be upset? "Sure," she added. "And then I'm in New York practically every other week to look in on my Great Aunt Rose." A lie, actually, though she did visit once a semester.

"I didn't know you had an aunt in New York."

"In Chelsea."

"You're kidding. That's just where I'll be living. I've got a rent control flat right near the monastery there. Do you know that place?"

"I think," she said, though she didn't.

"It's so peaceful there. Don't you love it there? And a great aunt, where does she live? London Towers?"

Andrea blinked, though she was on the phone, and he wouldn't see her surprise. "No, right next door. In those high-rises for old people. They're called . . . I forget what they're called."

"Well, that's lovely. So farewell till then."

"'Farewell till then,'" her sister, Megan, parroted back when Andrea confessed the conversation. "'Flat!' Lord, he sounds ridiculous." That had been the general feeling of Andrea's roommates as well, but Andrea couldn't help it, these little anachronisms made her love him even more.

Sometime later—before the summer, and also over the phone—Marshall made it clear that he and his girlfriend had broken up. Amicably, he suggested, because he was moving away, and because (it seemed to Andrea) he would never do anything any other way.

*　　*　　*

During her senior year, on weekends and breaks from college, Andrea arrived in New York excited by what she'd always loved—bunking with Great Aunt Rose and then rising early to explore the city—and even more excited now at the chance to see Marshall. He always decided what they would do—a brunch out at some place that artists of the thirties once favored or a visit to the Frick. "There's this man I'm interested in," Andrea confided to Aunt Rose. "Ah," Aunt Rose smiled, and she wouldn't let Andrea out of the house for her date with Marshall—even though it wasn't really a date—till she'd ironed her skirt and re-pinned her hair. In turn, Andrea collected Aunt Rose anecdotes for Marshall—Jewish things interested him, Jewish great aunts even more so. In the telling, Andrea presented herself in a semi-caretaker role in relation to Great Aunt Rose, though this was patently not the case. Who was crashing on whose sofa, after all? That said, Andrea did arrive at Rose's door with presents (flowers or a box of baked goods), which Aunt Rose appreciated with such vigor, one would think she'd never been given a gift in her life.

Rose was fastidious. Her apartment (despite its horrible colors) was immaculate. She swept her balcony daily and scrubbed the filth from the tabletop there, though Andrea had never seen her—not once, in all these years—actually sit out on the balcony. Rose ironed all her clothes, both after she'd washed them and again before she wore them. She had long been fascinated by Andrea's story of her college roommate, Carla Winston, who once bought a two-hundred-dollar dress, and then wore it with a pair of ripped stockings. "Just imagine!"

Rose had said, genuinely shocked by both the price tag and the sloppiness.

Marshall liked this story and asked for more.

So Andrea told all the usual stuff: Rose liked only the best of things—full cream butter, rich chocolates—but in tiny sizes. Rose had lived briefly in the Chelsea Hotel, but this was before the Chelsea Hotel was the Chelsea. (Andrea wasn't quite sure what this even meant. She'd been told once but had forgotten why the Chelsea was considered cool. Some poet or rock star had died there, she suspected, but that would have happened decades after Aunt Rose had boarded there.)

Finally, Marshall asked the natural question, "Did she never marry then?"

"Never. I don't know why." It was the big mystery of Aunt Rose. Why she never married, how she handled her own loneliness. Andrea couldn't imagine actually asking her to account for her lack of a partner. Andrea's mother had assured Andrea that Rose had had more than her share of men, that (yes, yes) she had had lovers. But Andrea couldn't imagine it. In her head, she had a little map for Rose. It was in the shape of a star and it allowed Rose to go east from her apartment to the grocers then south to the bakery then north to Macy's and west for the cleaners . . . that was it.

Marshall and Andrea were in the back of a taxicab, heading for a gallery in SoHo, when Marshall asked the question about Rose. There was a brief silence, as Andrea thought about the map she'd draw for Marshall's movement through the city, what pattern it would form. A big oval—uptown to work, downtown for art—with little spurs in the southern part of the oval. (He seemed to have lots of friends in the Village.) As she sat drawing her map, she had the vague feeling that it wasn't the speeding of the taxicab that was making Marshall lean in her direction. He might actually be thinking of kissing her. But she couldn't comport her face in the right way for a kiss. A solemn and ridiculous expression fell over her features. How embarrassing. She turned abruptly toward the window, and then looked back and said, "Rose hates people who are fat."

Marshall laughed.

"No, she really does. 'How could she let herself get like that?' she's always saying of old friends." Outside, the park was whipping by, then bookstores, a store called Fendi, and farther south a relic of Andrea's own childhood—a Chock Full O' Nuts coffee store, a chain that used to fascinate Andrea for being so ubiquitous and for featuring giant photos of baked goods in its windows. *Don't talk*, Andrea instructed herself, thinking of Rose's own maxim that one never learned anything if one's mouth was moving. But she was nervous and couldn't stop. (*Why?* She *wanted* Marshall to kiss her.)

"There's this really obese woman with two huge daughters who just moved into the apartment at the end of Rose's hall." They were some sort of crooks, Rose had decided, for her high-rise was subsidized for old people, and they were not senior citizens. One day, the fat neighbor started to fight with her daughters in the elevator, and Rose came rushing back to the apartment, crying (and half-laughing), "I thought they were going to hit me!"

Rose's own slim figure, bordering as she aged on real frailness, gave her moral authority. "That woman," she often pronounced, meaning the fat mother, "is so stupid. She thinks . . ." and here Rose always paused, for the foolishness of the thought astounded her each time, "that she can get from her apartment door to the trash chute and back with no one seeing her." This was shocking, because the woman consistently made the dash in her monstrous bra and panties. What a ghastly sight!

The taxicab turned a corner, and Andrea held tightly to the seat. She was afraid of sliding into Marshall. She thought of him all the time, but his leg, just inches from hers, seemed impossibly dangerous. He tossed his hair out of his eyes and then squinted out of the window to see what street they'd just passed.

"Did I tell you about when Rose met Carla?"

"No, that I'd like to hear."

Carla Winston had been Andrea's college roommate since freshman year. She came from a fabulously wealthy family with a ten-room apartment on Central Park South, right above a pink ice cream parlor, full of stuffed animals, where Andrea's grandparents used to take her as a girl. Andrea knew she had to engineer a way for Rose to see Carla's parents' place; it was so extraordinary, with its Tibetan rugs and lilac silk sofas. Not to mention Carla's dad's art collection. "The sex and violence gallery," Carla said. Wryly? Ruefully? Andrea was never sure what Carla made of her father's taste for vibrant, violently painted, and often violently imagined scenes. Andrea kind of liked them, though, the quick anger of the brush strokes, and the daring of hanging everything salon-style, one painting on top of another, instead of in the neat center of the wall, as Andrea's mother would have done. So one weekend, when Carla had plans to visit "the City," Andrea went, too, arranging to stay at Carla's, but not before she stopped in with Rose and pleaded weakness. She couldn't possibly carry both her bags over to the Winstons'. Rose would have to help.

"Oh, Aunt Rose, Aunt Rose," Carla's mother cried when Andrea and Rose arrived—just in the middle of the Winstons' dinner.

They stepped past the front hall—with its big bouquet of fresh flowers on a table that seemed to be dusted as soon as a mote of pollen fell—and into the living room. "Sit, sit, sit," Carla's mother said, gesturing to one of the lilac loveseats. "We're sorry!" Andrea cried back—this seemed the way of conversation at the Winstons', an exclamation point at the end of every sentence, something Andrea was coming to associate with all her college friends' parents. "We came at just the wrong time!"

"No, no, no," Carla's mother said emphatically. Andrea caught sight of Carla's brothers slinking out of the dining room at the far side of the apartment. No doubt they feared what was to come: a little tête-à-tête between Carla's mother and Rose, the kind of double-X-chromosome event they never liked to attend. Carla came into the living room, too, and said, "Dad's just finishing up."

"Please finish your dinner, we don't want to . . ."

"Now, Aunt Rose," said Mrs. Winston. "We've heard so much about you. . . . "

"Oh, you have," Rose said. She was trying to be arch, but she sounded uneasy. Andrea turned to her. The wealth of the place scared her. Andrea had been stunned, too, when she'd first seen the apartment. It had all seemed so unreal. Like a movie set. Still, it felt lucky just to get to see it. Later, Rose would say, "Those are people who can't like Jews," as if the fact (and she was sure it *was* a fact) were less about their proclivities than permission. Those were the people who didn't have permission to like the Jews. "That's crazy," Andrea said, but Rose wasn't convinced.

Rose looked to her left. There was a painting of a head on fire. Flames seemed to come from deep within the space of the painting and shoot forward to the surface. The face was one long scream. Rose's eyes scanned the rest of the room and then alighted back on the burning head.

"Would you call that . . . modern art?" Rose asked Mrs. Winston.

"Well, yes, yes," said Mrs. Winston, who was unfailingly gracious and seemed to understand Rose as something of a . . . well, not quite a joke, but someone to be humored, someone not quite intelligent enough for her circumstances at the moment. "I suppose you would. I suppose you would call it that."

"Well," Rose said emphatically, "I. Don't. Like. It."

Marshall burst into laughter when he heard this. Later, it would become a huge joke between Andrea and Marshall, a catch phrase they pronounced about everything they disliked, always saying it as Rose had, with each word a separate statement, "Well. I. Don't. Like. It." For now, Marshall just shook his head in amusement.

"You know," he said before he left the taxicab that afternoon, before handing the driver enough money to get Andrea home, "I have *got* to meet your Aunt Rose."

"Oh." Andrea wrinkled her nose and shook her head, as if to say, "No, you don't."

"No, really, I'd just love to."

But she didn't want him to meet Rose. She had already made too much of the nonexistent romance, and what if Rose didn't really understand, what if she said something that gave Andrea's misrepresentation away?

Only there was no way to stop it. The next time she was in the city, Marshall said, "Let me pick you up at your aunt's."

Andrea and Rose prepared as if for a prince, not because they did anything so grand, but because there was such a sense of moment, as Rose arranged two little platters of olives and fetched a dusty bottle of sherry from under the kitchen sink. Neighbors had been informed of the visit. Men were always an event on the seventeenth floor. The only man who actually lived there was the neighbor's son, who had Down syndrome—a sweet-faced, middle-aged fellow whom the women seemed to acknowledge primarily when they needed a window unstuck.

Andrea felt jittery—she kept imagining she had to pee, when in fact she didn't—as Rose considered what dress she should wear.

"He won't even be here but a few minutes," Andrea reminded her. She had done everything to prepare Marshall and Rose for the briefest of encounters.

"I know, dear," Rose said. And then to herself, "The blue dress, then."

Finally, the intercom buzzed.

"Oh," Rose said and hurried into the kitchen to press the button that allowed her to speak with visitors downstairs. "Come on up," she called in her gravelly old-lady voice, and then they waited, Andrea imagining each clunk of the elevator as it passed a floor as her own telltale heart. *I'm guilty. I'm guilty. I'm guilty. Of what? Of pretending I have a beau.* What a ludicrous thing to do.

The front doorbell rang. Andrea put her eye to the door, took in the sight of Marshall bent around the globe of the peephole, with the length of the hall looming threateningly behind him. He was wearing an olive-gray suit and stood nonchalantly, wrists crossed in front of his groin. "OK," Andrea said, under her breath, and moved back, so Rose could open the door.

"Come in," Rose said by way of welcome, though he couldn't, for all three of them were crowded in the doorway.

"Here, let me." Andrea pushed behind Rose and back into the apartment.

"Marshall," Marshall said and shook Rose's hand.

" . . . right on in. I know you two want to go get dinner, but stay for a short chat, will you?"

"I'd love to. Andrea speaks of you so often."

"I can't imagine what she'd have to say."

Rose led Marshall to the black living room couch and took up a position across from him in a hard-backed pink chair. Andrea sat at the far side of the sofa. It was as if they were a quarreling couple, come to fight it out before a therapist. Though what *would* they fight about, if they ever made it to couplehood? There would be a laundry list of things Marshall might not like about Andrea, but he would be too polite to say, and what of Andrea, what would make her turn to protest?

"Lovely apartment," Marshall said, swiveling his head around. "You must have quite the view."

"Would you like an olive?" Rose said. "Or something to drink?"

"My God," Marshall said.

"What?" Andrea said.

He had turned to look at The Pretty Girl. "Do you mind?" he said, rising to examine the painting.

"Not at all," Rose said.

"Who did this, if you don't mind my asking?"

"I don't mind your asking," Rose said. "His name was Sam Auerbach."

"I thought so. Good Lord, you've got a Sam Auerbach."

"Special, isn't it? Andrea's always liked it. Haven't you darling? Ever since you were a girl, you've fancied my painting."

"And how . . . well, how did you . . . or where did you . . ." Marshall stopped to look closer.

"You know the painter?" Andrea said, for it had never

occurred to her in all these years to ask who painted the picture or even where Rose had acquired it.

"So you've had it for some time?" Marshall continued.

"Well, I don't want to tell you, since it'll give away my age, but I think I've had it fifty plus years. Something like that."

"And you got it . . ." Marshall's voice rose into a question, but Rose shook her head.

"Where did I get it? Well, let's not talk about that. Andrea here tells me you work at the Metropolitan. No wonder you like paintings. Exactly what do you do?"

"Education, mostly. Right now I'm helping with a catalog for a fall exhibit. But you have to forgive me, I'm so curious about this painting. Did you find it in a gallery? I seem to remember that Auerbach was represented by—"

"Who's Sam Auerbach?" Andrea asked.

"A policeman, actually. A policeman-painter, of all unlikely combinations. He was famous for his portraits—like this one here—of women's faces emerging from the dark. This is the first full figure I've ever seen, but the way I knew it was him was these brush strokes." Marshall pointed to the dark brown paint that surrounded The Pretty Girl. His voice had the same professorial air it did in the classroom, and Andrea saw that this tendency—to lecture, to explain for the masses—might wear thin eventually. It might be what she'd finally object to in Marshall. He wasn't, in the end, enough of a democrat.

"It was a gift," Rose said. "I'm afraid that's all I can tell you of its . . . provenance? Is that the right word?"

Marshall nodded.

"Andrea tells me you're going to eat at Thompson's."

Marshall continued to bob his head. For dinner, he'd picked one of the wood-paneled private clubs he favored, as if he were already a middle-aged Republican—another reason none of Andrea's friends liked Marshall.

"Actually," Andrea said, patting her watch as if it had just beckoned her, "we should . . ." She stood.

"Well, that was a short visit," Rose said, "but say you'll come back."

Marshall rose and gamely said, "I'll come back." He took Rose's hand and leaned down to kiss it.

"Oh, well," Rose blushed, "what a gentleman."

Marshall opened the door to the hallway as Andrea turned for her pocketbook. When she looked back, she saw Marshall gasp and then slam the door shut again. He collapsed against it. "Are you all right?" she cried.

"Oh, oh," he said, hand to his chest.

"What? What?" He couldn't speak, but then she saw it was from laughing. "That woman. That woman. Your aunt's neighbor." Andrea put her eye to the peephole and saw a large, naked woman with a garbage pail scurrying toward the end of the hall.

If the painting was so special, why not write about it? She had to analyze a twentieth-century American painting for her senior seminar. She had the idea of doing this paper—it would be the final one of her academic career—on Wallace Stevens, the insurance man, and Sam Auerbach, the policeman. She wanted to compare the way their jobs affected their art, mostly because she'd come to a point—spring of her last semester in college—when the idea of a nine-to-five job seemed as terrible as it was inevitable. But Professor Harwich said no, the idea was too sociological. She was supposed to analyze a work of art, not speculate about matters that were outside the critic's realm. So life was outside the art critic's realm! How crazy! But when she complained about the matter to Marshall, he said, "Well, I agree with Harwich." She flushed with an emotion more complicated than pure embarrassment—thank goodness she was on the phone!—and for a brief moment she hated Marshall.

Not long after, in early May, she went to New York. More of a legitimate trip this time, because Rose and she were planning to go out to Long Island to celebrate Rose's sister's, Andrea's grandmother's, birthday. But that was on Saturday. On Friday, Andrea met Marshall for dinner. It was their typical night together—his questions, her answers, Andrea's delight in his apparent interest in all she had to say, her mental recording of whatever wisdom he chose to share with her—but just after dinner, as he hailed her a taxi and before she turned to duck into the cab—a skill she learned from Rose, who was appalled at how she used to roll herself in and out of cabs, instead of sitting neatly on her butt and sliding herself in—he kissed her goodbye on the lips. It was no accident—the lips heading for the cheek and meeting a mouth—but a firm kiss. Sans embrace, sans tongue, as if it were a proposition for Andrea: what did she think of this? But it happened so quickly that she didn't have a chance to respond. When she stepped out of the cab on 23rd Street, she was in a floaty daze, and the mica, if that's what it was, in the sidewalk pavement sparkled about her, an enchanted path to Rose's door. Or maybe it was broken glass that was twinkling around her; she'd read somewhere that this was how the city recycled millions of bottles. So there it was: Marshall left her charmed by trash.

Once upstairs, Andrea went over to The Pretty Girl. What was it Marshall had said about the brush strokes? She looked hard into the painting's background, as if she were finally, after all this time, really going to get to go there.

"I was thinking of writing about your painting for my art history class," she called to Rose, who was busy straightening pots in the kitchen.

"What's that?"

"Remember how Marshall said he knew about the painter of your picture and that he had something of a reputation? I was thinking it would be really great to write about this painting for my senior seminar." She didn't have to bring in autobiographical details, after all. She could just analyze the painting itself. Say something about how The Pretty Girl's affectionate disdain was achieved with two quick brush strokes for the cheeks but there was a more belabored effort for the mouth and eyes.

"No, you don't want to do that, dear."

"But I do."

"No," Rose said, "what I mean is that I don't want you to write about my painting."

"Oh," Andrea said, surprised. She was used to her aunt being charmed by her every suggestion. Dinner at the Chelsea Square, the diner across the way that had paper placemats with pen and ink drawings of cocktails? Of course. Shakespeare in the Park this weekend? Brilliant.

Why wouldn't Rose want the painting written about? This was Rose's vague self-effacement, the oh-don't-worry-about-me manner that she brought to family gatherings and to her dealings with her neighbors on the seventeenth floor. *I'm not an issue. I'm not something to be contended with.* Why not let her painting have the spotlight—if only the irrelevant spotlight of Andrea's brief attention?

"Well," Andrea said, for she put the activity of challenging her aunt in the category of levitating through the ceiling into an eighteenth floor apartment. *Just not do-able.* "I'll find something else to write about."

She looked back at the painting, the wispiness of The Pretty Girl's reddish-brown hair, loosely gathered in a bun at the nape of her neck.

Could The Pretty Girl . . . could it be stolen?

But that thought was so ridiculous, Andrea instantly dismissed it. No one in her family had ever done anything that wasn't aboveboard.

Rose had never learned to drive—why would she in New York?—but this failure always hovered over arrangements with Grandma Sophie, who was put out by having to fetch her sister for funerals on Long Island, drives to the airport, and other such things. It didn't help that Andrea and her aunt arrived late the next day, having taken the 10:20, instead of the 10:00 train as planned.

The weather was warm for spring, and Sophie was overdressed in a thick cotton pantsuit. She'd find a way, Andrea knew, to blame her own sweating on Rose. "We got out of the apartment a little later than we expected," Rose said carelessly as she leaned in to Sophie for a kiss.

"Because you had to have your bowel movement, right?" Sophie turned to Andrea. "I tell her, 'It'll come out when it comes out. It's not going anywhere else.' But she doesn't listen to me."

"Oh, really," Andrea exclaimed, in what she pretended was mock exasperation but was really the genuine article. "Do we have to talk about this?" Andrea flashed on a time when her mother had told her to stop using so much toilet paper. "You're wiping yourself too much," her mother had complained.

Andrea had responded, "Do you think there might be just

one thing in this whole world that is none of your fucking business?"—winning herself a slap across the face.

"I hate this family," Andrea had said. "I really do." A bunch of lunatics. That was another of Rose's virtues. She didn't always talk. She was the one member of the family who left things unsaid.

At lunch, Sophie and Rose were tender as ever with Andrea, but they sniped at each other. Little things. Who bought the better brand of cottage cheese? Who still read *The Forward*? Who knew there was no better paper than *The Times*? And, perhaps because Rose was so consistently patronized in these discussions—Rose didn't drive a car, ergo Rose was a child—Andrea couldn't help but take her side. *The Times was* better. Small curd cottage cheese *was* nicer. Alvin Ailey's dance "Revelation" *was* the most exciting thing ever performed on the New York stage.

"And what about the tickets we got you for *The Music Man?*"

"Yes, thank you, very nice," Rose said without offering up any commentary on the musical. So it was unclear if she'd ever used them.

"It's so good you have time to go to the theatre. Keeping this house," Sophie said and gestured around her, "and the gardens, I just never get time for that sort of thing."

Rose was retired—she had been retired for five years, because of a settlement that Grandpa Jack got for her, after she'd fallen on some ice outside a McDonald's. Her right wrist never quite healed, which was a problem, because of her work as a medical transcriptionist. Jack had convinced her to sue the McDonald's, claiming if the walkway had been better lit, Rose would never have fallen. Andrea suspected this wasn't true, but Rose won her case all the same. "I feel like an heiress," she had said at the time, though the settlement hardly made her rich. The settlement just made her retired.

Though Grandma Sophie had nothing to do with the matter, she had acted, ever since, as if she were Rose's benefactress. Rose resisted this suggestion at every turn, though she habitually deferred to Grandpa Jack, even when (as on the day of the lunch) he was out of town.

"It's so hot," Sophie finally said. "Let's go swimming."

"We don't have our suits," Rose said.

"You'll borrow mine. And I've got bathing caps." Sophie's flower-studded rubber bathing caps always cracked Andrea up, but the idea of slipping into her suit with its yellowing crotch and padded bra didn't appeal.

"We're not going swimming," Rose said. "Where would we go swimming?"

"At the Fishbeins'. I always go there."

Sophie intended to walk over to a neighbor's pool with two guests and jump in. She wouldn't phone to ask first. She was friends with the Fishbeins, and this was her way.

"No, I don't think so," Rose said.

"But you're hot. Aren't you, Andrea?"

Andrea smiled and kept quiet.

"Does Jack say we should go swimming?" Rose asked.

"Jack? Jack is in Arizona."

Rose had an odd habit of relying on Grandpa Jack's decisions in a way that made him seem like something of a suitor. Not that there was any hint of attraction between Rose and her brother-in-law, but there was a surprising and consistent deference. "Of course, men are smarter than women," Rose once said to Andrea, and Andrea had been stunned; everyone she knew thought just the opposite.

"I know where Jack is," Rose said simply.

"*Meshuga*," Sophie turned to Andrea to say. "Yes, Jack called up just this morning and said, 'Sophie, when you see the girls, you had better take them swimming.'"

"Oh," Rose said, as if it wasn't clear Sophie was joking, "then we'd better go swimming."

The next time Andrea and Marshall got together, Andrea refused his request to fetch her at her aunt's. It was the first time she'd ever said no to something he suggested, but he appeared unfazed. They had their normal dinner out, and when they were through, he asked her if she wanted to come up to his apartment.

"Oh," she said, "sure."

They walked to his building, not far from where they had eaten, and Andrea followed him up the steep stairs to his second-floor apartment and then stood awkwardly in the foyer till he motioned her to one of the chairs at his kitchen table. She looked purposefully at the dark chest hairs at his collar and felt repulsed. She had been up to the apartment before—a one-room arrangement with a tiny galley kitchen—and even fixed his toilet once when it wouldn't stop flushing. On those visits, she had quickly taken in details of the place (a bag of potato chips clipped closed on top of his refrigerator—how nice to see he had a bad habit!—the general neatness of the room, the odd scariness of the bed), but now she was too nervous to look. She wasn't a virgin, but she had presented herself as far more worldly than she was, alluding vaguely to former boyfriends, though she had no former boyfriends, just a few misguided three-night stands (as she and her roommates called them, for they were far too serious for one-night stands, and once they'd been brave enough to take their clothes off in front of a boy, it really seemed like they should do it again). Undressing with those boys had always felt like jumping off a cliff into the unknown, and Andrea wondered why she ever thought herself capable of it with Marshall. Finally, having stuttered through some desultory conversation, she said, "I guess I should go."

"You have to?" he said.

"I guess so." And now she *wanted* to go. She was so uneasy that being alone outside would be the relief that (in her fantasies) falling into his arms had been.

"OK," he said and stood, and it seemed to her that something very important had just not happened—though it could all be in her head; he could just be a friend; he could have not wanted anything to happen. Even now, nothing was clear. Still, it was true that things seemed to change between them after that night, that her romance with Marshall (now that it had formally *not* begun) was over.

Just before graduation, Andrea ran into Marshall on campus, and he was with a very beautiful woman, clearly a girlfriend. Andrea's jealousy was mixed with a curious remorse. How crazy that she had ever thought he'd be interested in her. She could tell stories till she was blue in the face, but she'd never look anything like the slim, perfectly complected Eurasian woman on his arm. When the girlfriend turned, her smooth, long black hair whapping against her back like a towel, Andrea wanted to cry. Andrea's mother was all wrong about beauty; beauty really helped a lot. How could someone who *majored* in art history— who did nothing but think about how things look—forget *that*?

III

It was Andrea's mother who made Rose move.

"She's too hard to take care of there," she said over the phone. Though what of that?

"She'll die in Ohio," Andrea protested. "She'll just die. I mean she's lived in the City her whole life." Already Andrea could picture the sort of antiseptic retirement community her parents had planned for Rose: meals as the highlight of the day; bingo as entertainment for adults who once knew the finer points of Aristotle; the natural world observed through the plate-glass window but otherwise as far away as the moon, there being convenient road access for middle-aged visitors to the community, but no walking paths, save for those who might want to circumambulate the parking lot.

"She'll have everything she needs at this place," Andrea's mother said, and then Andrea's father clattered on the phone.

"Leave your mother be. She has enough to deal with Rose in all of this." Her father had always spoken of Rose as if she were an impossible woman. He had a particular distaste for her eating habits—the way she'd eat pound cake crumbs but always decline a slice of cake ("No calories in the crumbs," Rose would enthuse, more than willing to make fun of herself), the regular trips she took to Macy's for her sweet cream butter—and her general enthusiasm for talking about food. Andrea's father managed to make her seem, for all this, like a three-hundred-pound glutton instead of the slight woman she'd always been.

It was another fall that had made Rose suddenly such an issue. She'd broken a hip this time around, and something needed to be done.

"I could go stay with her for a stretch," Andrea offered—though, in fact, she only got three weeks a year off from work. Nine to five, she worked for a historical society just north of Albany. She gave a nod to her education in art history by spending another ten hours a week working for a small, not-for-profit art gallery in Lake George. ("You're—what?—actually anti-profit?" her father had said when she'd spit out the words "not-for-profit gallery," this being what everyone said when describing the gallery, there being some difference—though she'd not yet divined it—between this word and the word *nonprofit.*)

"Don't be ridiculous," her father snapped. "That is just ridiculous. This is for us to take care of."

"We suggested three places," Andrea's mother put in, "and I think she really liked the last one, she . . . "

"That's enough, Cecile," Andrea's father barked.

Andrea was quiet. What a sin! For they weren't arguing about what to do with Rose. This was the Battle of the Two Versions of Aunt Rose, the War of the Roses, and Andrea was letting her parents' version—Rose as a hypochondriac, Rose as selfishly devoted to her own petty comforts, Rose as a whiner—win out. Andrea's parents hated this Rose (if, indeed, this Rose existed), yet they didn't (or at least Andrea's father didn't) have the generosity to appreciate the other Rose.

When Andrea called Rose to see how she was doing, what she thought of this whole plan, Rose said, "Your father knows best."

"My father does not know best."

Rose was silent. A buzzing came over the line.

"Rose," Andrea called into the phone. "Are you there?"

"What are you talking about?" she said, genuinely confused, an edge of panic in her voice. "Of course he does."

So once Rose had healed well enough to imagine travel, it fell to Andrea to take a train south from Albany, just thirty minutes from Saratoga Springs, where she now lived, and help Rose pack up the Chelsea apartment. Goodbye to youth, and goodbye to a free place to stay in the city.

But there was nothing to pack. Andrea's childhood perception of the absence of things at Rose's held true. Her parents had generously hired the sort of moving company that wraps lamps, carries out hanging clothes in a portable armoire, pads all furniture, and places vases in boxes of Styrofoam peanuts. Rose and Andrea had only to box up the little things—the contents of the kitchen, which took all of fifteen minutes—and the odds and ends from the living room. The Pretty Girl was to go with the moving company.

Rose sat amicably at the tiny rolltop desk at which she had always paid her bills. She was going through a small stack of papers that she had saved over the years, and though Andrea was the only person she'd probably see today, she was dressed in a suit and stockings. Andrea kneeled by her, on the now dingy beige carpet—it actually seemed to be shedding, like an old dog—and rearranged items in a box.

"Did I ever show you this?" Rose said, extending a piece of paper.

"What is it?"

"From when I lived at the Charley Arms. They used to print up a little newsletter for guests."

At the bottom of the mimeographed sheets, above a wavering ballpoint blue line were these words: "... and now the lovely Rose Fine has joined our ranks. Overheard in the halls of the Charley Arms: 'Now that Rose F. is moving in, this place is finally getting a little class.'"

"Hey, that's nice. How did they know you?"

"What?"

"Oh, never mind." There seemed no polite way to frame her question, but she wanted to know how the residents of the Charley Arms would have known Rose in advance of her arrival.

For in these lines, there was the suggestion (wasn't there?) that Rose was a known quantity. That the fact of her beauty somehow preceded her.

"A fellow by the name of Smithy wrote this. He was living at the Charley Arms when I moved in. He wrote the newsletter, and that bit about me was a compliment. Or maybe a kind of a joke."

Rose unfolded another paper and said, "And how about this? Did I ever tell you I once wrote a short story?"

"You read it to me! When I was in college. I still remember about that train ride where you bump into some famous rabbi, but don't know he's a famous rabbi."

Andrea remembered the story as lengthy, but Rose held only three typed pages in her hand. Over two decades ago, someone had told Rose the story was good, and so she had held onto it.

"What else have you got there?"

Rose unfolded her birth certificate. She was born right here in the City. She extracted an envelope with her social security card. Then pulled out a smudged index card.

"A recipe for blintzes!" Rose cried out. "This must be from my Aunt Joy. I didn't know I had it. She used to flour all the tables at my mother's house and then make enough for the whole neighborhood. We weren't allowed to help. You should ask Sophie about it. Blintz day! Sophie and I had to wander about in the streets, so we'd be out of the way. Think of it now, telling a child to go play in the street for the day!" Rose slipped the card back into her small stack, slipped a paper clip around the papers, and said, "Well, that should do it."

But how could this be it? The whole of Rose's life, so neatly packed, with only these slightest of reminders of a childhood, of a past? What was here to mark Rose's talent for buying children gifts? What here made it clear how inspiring she was to a young woman starting out on life?

Rose! Andrea wanted to cry out, for she felt everything that Rose had been denied all these years and only more losses to come. Two of the elderly women on Rose's hall—Rose's dear friends, who had always rushed over for hellos when Andrea had visited during her college years—had died, and where Rose was going, it wouldn't be the arrival of the lovely Rose at the dinner table that would be noted. It would be her departure via the retirement home's "Progressive Care Unit."

IV

"How do you like it here?"

"It's lovely," Rose said and sounded like she meant it, only Andrea didn't believe her. "Next time you come, you come on Sunday. They have a big brunch. And butter. Real butter."

Andrea demurred. In her new life, Rose's old habits—her attention to food, in particular—had all been perverted. Now she had a habit of chewing, and then spitting out what she ate, so a pile of partially masticated apple skin and bacon fat sat in a tannish heap on her breakfast plate. What a car accident of food! Andrea couldn't keep her eyes safely off it. Rose's delicacy—the admirable thinness that Andrea knew she herself would never achieve—had turned to brittle frailty. Her bones broke and broke. Rose didn't need a walker, but she refused to take a step without one. "She can walk," Andrea's father would declare, irate, after her visits.

"She's just frightened," Andrea's mother would say, but then Andrea's mother wasn't the one who had to lift Rose, bride-style, and carry her through the doorway of their home. Andrea's mother wasn't the one who drove all the way out to the retirement home to get Rose for Sophie's funeral, only to discover that Rose wouldn't go to the funeral. She was too scared to make the walk from the retirement home to Andrea's father's car by the curb.

All the others of Rose's generation had died gracefully. Sophie shrank cheerfully to the size of a child and then just quieted down, as if she needed silence to consider her own body. A sponge saturated with blood, she spent her eighties spontaneously bleeding. "No, no," she'd reassure others. "Doesn't hurt at all," as blood oozed from no discernible wound on her forearm. Before his death, Sophie's husband, Jack, embraced a provisional belief in God, after a lifetime of passionate atheism, but he, too, went quietly. The other grandfather (Andrea's father's father) shooed relatives out of his hospital room. It was nice to see them, but dying was something he preferred to do alone. And the other grandmother admitted her fear, but as if it were a foolish thing, to be scared of death, after all this time. They died in their seventies and eighties, but Rose failed to show for her own appointment with death, as if a lifetime of tardiness (another trait that had always irritated Andrea's father) had at last served her in good stead. Rose turned eighty-eight, eighty-nine, ninety and then someone lost count, and there was an argument about whether her birth certificate was even correctly dated in the first place. The best anyone could say was that she was probably ninety-two.

In her apartment at the retirement community, Rose's furniture was arranged in exactly the same way it had been in New York. The Pretty Girl still hung on the wall. The furniture still clustered around a glass-topped coffee table. The new place had a separate bedroom for Rose, but the same small kitchen as in New York, only Rose rarely used it. She took most meals in the dining hall.

Andrea visited, usually at Thanksgiving and Passover, but things were different. It was hard for Rose to read, so they didn't talk books anymore. There were splots of dried toothpaste in Rose's bathroom sink, and she'd given up wearing a wig. The uneven terrain of her skull was a shock, though no more than the housecoats that she now wore instead of suits.

Of course, Andrea was different, too. For one, she'd married, and her husband, Joshua, joined her on her visits, perching himself on the old black sofa (its springs now shot, though Andrea remembered it as a comfortable place to sleep, back in college) and failing in general to understand what was so special about the bald old woman, who kept telling him (six times, her memory was going) that she'd once seen a fox walking down New York's 23rd Street.

Otherwise, in the confines of her apartment, Rose was much like she'd always been. Solicitous. Would Andrea like a chocolate? How was Andrea's job? Andrea was such a smart girl. How was the weather in New York? Did Joshua like sweet cream butter? Rose just loved it.

But things were different when Rose was in one of the retirement home's care units. Sometimes what sent her there was no more than her desire to *be* in the care unit. (A cough, a dry throat, and she'd call down to the unit and ask them to come pick her up.) But once she strained so hard to go to the bathroom—her rumored morning obsession being apparently true—that part of her own bowel came dropping out of her. She kept pushing it back in for about a week, when it occurred to her that this might be something to mention to the doctor. After a quick operation to restore things, Rose was shipped from the hospital to the retirement home's care unit. There, Rose was a horror show. She yelled at nurses. She pushed the call button on her bedside. Once, and then again. And again. And again. After twenty-four hours, a nurse simply disabled the device. A light glowed permanently above the door of her room, but no corresponding beep signaled in the nurses' bay.

And why should they help? When a nurse did arrive, it was to a querulous demand for the toilet or to a wail, a true wail, a sound that started as an old woman's moan and then became louder and louder till it was the shriek of a madwoman. This Rose (the Not Rose, as Andrea came to think of her) chided you for not visiting more or for not staying longer when you did visit. This Rose said, "Well, *that's* unusual," about the new pleated dress Andrea wore one visit. This Rose had something to say about the nurse who used an exaggerated baby voice to ask, "Do you want to go to the bathroom?" This Rose was having her turn, it seemed, finally having her turn, and though she'd been denied a husband and children and, then, her sister, Sophie, and her brother-in-law, Jack, and her New York friends, she would not be denied this: her chance to be a patient, fussed over, worried about, bathed, patted, wiped, and fed. The center of attention. Now that she was getting some of it, she wanted it all, all the time. "Nurse, Nurse, *Nurse*," she'd call at any figure passing by the doorway of her room. Finally, Andrea's parents got a call. Rose was too difficult. They couldn't keep her anymore. She'd have to find a different care facility.

Only no facility would have her.

The War of the Roses, it seemed, had been won. Andrea's version of Rose had lost out. Only in her head, Andrea couldn't believe this Rose was Rose. Andrea's Rose was polite; Andrea's Rose had waiters, back in a certain Chelsea restaurant, who still remembered her as their favorite patron; Andrea's Rose charmed by stepping out of her role as an unfailingly polite person and saying, "I. Don't. Like. It." Andrea's Rose was something to aspire to. She hadn't had an important life, in the conventional sense, yet she had been important. Andrea pulled a page from a college journal—something she'd kept all these years for its novelty; she didn't keep a diary now—and showed it to Joshua, so he might know something of what Rose had once been:

She defines not what I want to *be*—unmarried, alone—but what I am interested in. The big world, the big, big world, where routine never becomes a cage, because the routine itself is so interesting.

How heartbreaking our youthful resistance is. Andrea wanted to reach across the years to her college self and give her a hug. For good effort. "But then maybe it wasn't so interesting, after all," Joshua said. "Maybe it was just how you'd romanticized New York, when you were young."

"But," Andrea started. *Could he be right?* "No, it *wasn't* just New York. It was wherever Rose went, like when I heard about a trip she'd taken as a young woman to Switzerland—she'd gone with a girlfriend, and it sounded like some Henry James novel—or when I heard about the B&B where she always rented a room for a week in the summer. Something . . . some glamour . . . I know it's hard to see now, but some glamour always attached itself to her. Maybe just the glamour of being a working girl in New York, in that era."

"Working girl," Joshua snickered.

"Not in that way," Andrea said. "You know what I mean."

But maybe he didn't.

At any rate, you could win a war and still be displeased. Andrea's parents panicked, when they got the call from the retirement home. They couldn't possibly have Rose living with

43

them. Andrea's father's heart, Andrea's mother's arthritis. They weren't so young themselves anymore. The retirement home finally agreed to keep Rose . . . for a price. Only the family couldn't afford the price.

"Well, that is that," Andrea's father said. "We've got to sell that painting."

V

It fell to Andrea to take the painting to be appraised. Not that she wanted to see the painting sold, of course, but if they could get real money for it, and if the money meant good care for Rose, then she wouldn't get all sentimental. People were more important than things. On that, Andrea and her parents were in agreement.

Andrea started with a friend in Albany, who referred her to a Hudson art gallery that specialized in early twentieth-century paintings.

"Well," said a young (a young-*sounding*) woman over the phone to Andrea. "You can bring it in, and we'll give you a verbal appraisal for free. We can generally do a written appraisal for a hundred and fifty dollars. It all depends on how much information you can supply us with."

"Oh, let's see, I know it's by . . ." But all of a sudden the name of the painter flew out of her head. "I know who it is by and . . ."

"Is he dead? You know we only deal in dead artists."

"Really?"

"Or once in a while, you know, if the person is eighty-nine or something, why quibble?" Andrea gave a snort of a laugh, before it occurred to her that the girl did not mean to be funny. "Is it framed?"

"Yes."

"And it's a painting, so it doesn't have a dust paper on it."

"Actually, it does."

"Well, you might start by taking that off, since there might be some information there. Like is it signed? Front or back? Are there any labels or inscriptions? What's the provenance of the painting? Its condition? Was it ever cleaned or repaired?"

"Oh, Lord, I just don't know. And the owner. She's an old woman. I don't think she can supply any of this information."

"Well, all this is what we need to determine value. Then, we either find the painting itself or something similar in sales or auction records. And it's a little like real estate. You see what something similar sold for in the area."

"God, I don't know where to start." But even as she said this, it occurred to Andrea that she *did* know. Some years back, at one of the gallery openings, she'd met Dana Chandler, a conservator— or a woman who used to be a conservator till she got so allergic to the chemicals that she got allergic (or so she claimed) to the world. Not long after they met, Dana moved to Baltimore. *Don't go*, Andrea had wanted to cry, even though she'd just met the woman. This always seemed to be the way, people with whom Andrea could imagine intense friendships leaving for other places. In her middle age, Andrea pined for friends the way she once pined for men. But everyone she knew was too scattered for friendship, too busy with their jobs and kids, their desire to work out or read—at the very least—a book sometime before the end of the decade. At any rate, Dana now ran a company that transported art—a high-end U-Haul, essentially—but the job put her in touch with much of the art world.

Andrea tracked down Dana's number, feeling, as she did, an awful lot like her mother, who was an expert at making worlds move without ever removing her ear from the phone.

"Oh, yeah," Dana said, once Andrea had asked her question, "I know what to do. Take it to my friend, Howie Corn. I can't believe you have never met him. He works for a lab up near you that the state runs. They're responsible for all the art in the state parks. He's a little bizarre, but you know all conservators are a little bizarre." She laughed, as if her own form of bizarreness was just this—to announce something peculiar but not spell it out. "He can probably look at the painting and give you some information. Maybe look at it under ultraviolet light and see if it's painted over something, or just whatever. He's got to be the smartest person I ever met."

Howie Corn talked fast. "Un huh, un huh, OK, bring her on in. You can come this afternoon, if you'd like." He seemed focused on something else as he listened to Andrea's explanation of her situation. He gave her directions, explaining that the conservation center occupied former textile buildings near the state park. Andrea knew the park, for she'd hiked there a few times. Actually, she'd hiked there on her first date with Joshua, though they'd rarely been out in the woods since.

Joshua was in the City, pricing some marble for a rich client who was redoing her kitchen. Andrea was already planning to go to the Albany train station to pick him up, so it was easy enough to go to Howie's. She popped The Pretty Girl into the backseat of her car and headed out, feeling duly embarrassed about all she hadn't done—unframed the painting herself, removed the dust paper. But her general unhandiness with screwdrivers (reason number one for marrying a carpenter, she used to joke) made her think she shouldn't touch The Pretty Girl, that the most routine of efforts would cause the surface to flake or the canvas somehow to crack.

The drive took Andrea south along the Hudson. She imagined she was driving toward some charming historical property, ill-used but quaint brick walk-ups, but when she arrived she found ugly factory buildings, a whole complex of bad taste. Built, no doubt, in the seventies. (The decade of her teen years! A black hole when it came to good judgment, clothes, music, and anything even remotely attractive.) Andrea wended her car through three parking lots to what looked like a mall-side medical office building. This was Howie's lab.

Or so she thought. There were only two other cars—an old Toyota pickup and a blue Subaru—in the giant lot by the building. Perhaps she had made a mistake? But the door to the building opened, and across the hall to the left, where he said it would be, another door gave way to a room with several large worktables and a light board along one wall. Clearly, some sort of studio. Howie, however, wasn't around. Andrea stepped from the room back into the hall, flashing on the vague panic she used to feel in junior high school when she found herself alone in the institutional hallways, bathroom pass in hand, and the usually crowded corridors with their shiny floors feeling suddenly like a secret place where she might be permitted any wildness.

At length, a man with a dustpan appeared at the end of the hall. He approached, walking briskly and somewhat jerkily, as if he were a toy that had just received a fresh battery. As he came closer, Andrea could make out the words on his T-shirt ("Who Let the Dogs Out?"), the salt-and-pepper of his bristly mustache, and the slight stubble of a scalp shaved to hide an emerging bald spot. He entered the room without acknowledging her, walked over to the light board, and started to sweep up a puddle of white dust. Above his head hung a plate, lit from behind, so that its cracks were apparent.

"I'm looking for Howie Corn," Andrea went back into the room to say.

"Yeah, that's me," he said quickly and flatly. He looked simultaneously scornful and eager, as if he couldn't wait to insult her.

"I spoke to you an hour ago, about a painting."

He sniffed, half-friendly. "Yeah, well, I didn't think that was a growth under your arm. Let's have a look." He extended his arm toward the painting, which she had wrapped in a large green trash bag. He slipped the painting out of its bag and held it, arms extended, before him. "It's not bad."

Andrea nodded, as if in agreement with his judgment. Her own fondness for the painting had . . . not exactly waned, but been compromised ever since Joshua first saw it. This was on the afternoon when she'd first taken Joshua to meet Rose. While Rose was in the bathroom, Andrea had pointed to the painting. She was about to tell Joshua about her feelings for the painting, when he said, "Nice painting, save for that weird thing with the chest."

"What?" Andrea had said.

Rose was still in the bathroom, but Joshua would have spoken freely even if she had been in the room; that was why people found him so much fun (he could be outrageous) and why, too, he had his enemies.

"What're you talking about?"

"This . . ." Joshua said and pointed to a fold in The Pretty Girl's coat. "It's supposed to be a scarf, but the perspective's all messed up. It looks like her chest is jutting out at a weird angle."

And the thing was, though Andrea had looked and looked at the painting for her whole life, she'd never seen the flaw, but once Joshua had pointed it out, she couldn't look at The Pretty

Girl and not see that there was an anvil sticking out of her chest.

Now, Howie Corn said, "Fucked up this coat though. It looks like she's stuffed a giant triangle up her shirt."

"I know," Andrea said, somewhat wearily.

"So, let's see," said Howie. "Do you know who this woman is?"

"No, I don't."

"You don't know?" Howie said disapprovingly.

"No, the painting belongs to my great aunt. I know it was a gift. And I know the painter was . . ." She paused, and then all of a sudden there it was, the name she couldn't access earlier. "Sam Auerbach."

"Who?"

"Sam Auerbach."

Howie shrugged. "Never heard of him." He propped the painting on the wall behind a large table and then went to get a magnifying glass. He examined The Pretty Girl's face and said, "And you're sure you don't know who it is?"

"Quite sure."

"No idea?"

"None whatsoever."

"Huh," he said, again with an air of great disappointment.

"Well, this Sam Auerbach . . ." Howie turned the painting over. "Weird," he said. Without even asking, he tore off the dust paper behind the painting. ("She jumped at the sound," Andrea thought, as if she were doing the voiceover for the soap opera of her life. "She jumped at the sound, as if she'd been struck.") "Did he sign it? I don't see his name."

"No, I was just told."

"Mind if I pop this out of its frame?"

"No, of course not."

The majority of the room was tidy—no art on the tables and

only the cracked plate on the light board. But on the counter that ran around three sides of the room—the fourth wall had windows—there were all sorts of supplies, scraps of lumber, bits and pieces of magazines, liquid-filled containers, paintbrushes, squeegees, and crumpled bits of canvas.

"What you're going to want to do," Howie said and then stopped. "You have *no* idea who this is?"

"Well," Andrea said. "I suspect it was done in New York in the thirties or forties, and I've always had the idea that it might be Henry James's sister."

Andrea just pulled this out of a hat. She had no idea if Henry James had a sister, or indeed when Henry James lived.

"So I tell you what you're going to do. You contact the National Portrait Gallery, tell them that you think you have . . . no, that you *know* you've got a picture of Henry James's sister, and see what they can do for you."

"OK," Andrea said hesitantly. Why would he be encouraging her to lie?

"You obviously never had this cleaned."

"No," Andrea said. "But how do you know? It's so obvious?"

"Well, if you cleaned it, you'd make sure that you could at least see that demon back there." Howie pointed to the dark area to the left of The Pretty Girl's head.

"What're you talking about?"

"This." Howie looked at Andrea. "Don't you see this monster in the background?" Howie's forefinger made a small circle. "It reminds me of that Goya painting. What-the-fuck-is-it-called? You know, and that whole idea—I'm going to forget who said this, too. It's the goddamn drugs I'm taking."

Andrea smiled stupidly.

"'Without the background, there is no foreground.' It's true here, too—without that demon in the background, this woman doesn't even really work. That flirty look on her face, it somehow only works because of the sense of the demons behind her."

"I just don't see it."

"Well, you do see this eye, don't you?" There was a small bit of paint that *could* be an eye. Andrea had always read it as part of the atmospheric background of the painting, the texture of the brush stroke.

"If you had someone clean this painting, trust me, you'd see the monster. As for pricing this thing, I can't really be of help, but I can tell you if it's been repainted, or if there's something underneath. We can look at it underneath ultraviolet light and then X-ray it." He moved the painting over to the side of the room. "Actually, I'll tell you what. If I can keep this for a week or so, you come back, and I'll tell you what I've found out."

Andrea hesitated. "Just leave the painting?"

"Well, I'm not gonna steal it. You want a voucher? I'll give you a voucher." He reached over to the counter for a yellow Post-It note and wrote, *Good for one painting of a girl with red gloves.*

Andrea smiled.

"Feel better now?" Howie said.

"I feel better."

But, of course, she didn't feel easy as she left the lab, motored along the river, and then around Albany for the train station.

"Baby," Joshua said as he stepped off the train and took her into his arms. "I heard. I'm so sorry." At first, Andrea thought that what he'd heard had to do with the painting, but when he noticed her confusion he said, "I called in for messages and heard on the phone machine."

"Heard what?"

"About Rose."

"What about her?"

"Oh, baby," Joshua said, and later Andrea would think of his kindness in this moment, for in two weeks' time he would file for divorce, "your mother called. I heard that Rose is dead."

VI

"You've got a talent for interesting men."

Andrea laughed. "I do, don't I? For getting them, not for keeping them."

"Actually, I don't count your ex as an interesting man," Carla Winston said. Andrea and her old college roommate were hiking along the Ausable River in the Adirondacks. Carla had come to comfort Andrea about the breakup, but Andrea abruptly needed no comforting, for she had just met Ray Davis, a college librarian, whose life's greatest joy seemed to be spending lazy weekends in bed with Andrea.

The end of her marriage (though it was still not officially over, there was still the paperwork to come) was a real puzzle to Andrea—Joshua coming home and saying that he didn't want to be with her anymore, that she was fat and didn't shave her underarms. "I can shave my underarms, if you want me to," she'd said, thinking, at first, that he was joking, and then stunned when she realized he wasn't. Although why stunned? She was his third wife, and he was known around town as a good time. And as an asshole. Only Andrea hadn't managed to realize about the asshole part till just recently.

Now, Andrea told Carla the divorce was the most painful thing that had ever happened to her.

"Not really," Carla protested. "What about your Aunt Rose dying? You loved your Aunt Rose."

"But I didn't expect Joshua to go away, you know."

"What does poison ivy look like?" Carla said.

Andrea looked down and laughed. "That's a sassafras bush. That's not poison ivy."

Andrea understood why Carla didn't like Joshua. Even during the brief two years Andrea was married to him, she knew why people didn't like him. But, fresh as she was from the wound of the split, Andrea still appreciated him. Joshua was one of those bear-like men who take what they want—which meant he could be an oaf, but he also had the courage that comes with unequivocally expressing desire. Her new guy, Ray, didn't have that particular courage. Most nice people didn't have it, but Andrea admired it all the same.

"This is so lovely," Carla said. "I don't know why I don't get out of the city more." The two women walked in silence, and then Carla started to laugh. "Remember, remember that time your aunt came to visit my parents, and she said that funny thing about the painting. What was it? 'It's no good.'"

"I don't like . . . oh, Jesus," Andrea interrupted herself. "The Pretty Girl. My aunt's painting!"

"What? What? Did she leave it to you?"

"No, no. My aunt left everything to my mother. What's today's date?"

"August 16th."

"Shit. Oh, shit. I was supposed to get the painting on the 10th. I had it out here, because I was supposed to get it appraised. And I left it at this lab to be looked at."

"Well, it's still there, right?"

"I can't believe I completely spaced out on the appointment. I'd been worrying and worrying about the painting, because I left it there so long. The lab was only supposed to keep it for a week, but then I went away for the funeral and then the guy from the lab was out sick, and then our schedules wouldn't match up. And of course everything was going on with Joshua. All this time has passed. I've been wanting to get the painting, just thinking about it and thinking about it, and the day comes, and I don't go. It's ridiculous."

"It's OK. You'll go get it on Monday."

Andrea stopped walking and shook her head. "Yeah, if I can get out of work. I can't believe this."

"Well, you've had other things on your mind."

"Yeah, but, oh Carla, I feel as if I left my *daughter*. And you know 'I had other things on my mind' is not exactly an excuse if you accidentally leave your daughter at daycare for two months."

"Oh, I don't know about that," said Carla, who had two kids. "And anyway it's not like someone's going to throw it away. It's probably just stored in some corner."

Andrea nodded. How could she have been so offhand? Her own mind—always given to slippage when it came to the practical details of life—never failed to astound her. Did her Alzheimer-like lapses portend a terrible future? If so, there was no child to direct her through that ocean of confusion. (Though already Ray seemed inclined for kids, as Joshua had not. *Oh, Ray*, Andrea thought. Three weeks into their romance, and he was already thinking of her as something permanent.)

"Andrea," her mother had said at Rose's funeral. "Promise me I'll never end up like her." Andrea promised, knowing that her mother was thinking of all Rose's final humiliations, but especially of the day she found Rose in a urine-soaked bed, one that she'd been lying in for half a week. (Some retirement home community! They hadn't even checked in on Rose when she'd failed to show up for dinner for three days straight.) And what could the family do? Andrea's parents visited once a week and then edged guiltily back into the flow of their own lives.

"Andrea!" Carla insisted. "It's oh-*kaay.* You'll call on Monday, and it'll be fine."

"You're right," Andrea shrugged.

"Of course I am. Sure, you left your daughter at daycare for half a year, but you're going to pick her up and take her for an ice cream. You're a model parent."

On Monday, Andrea didn't even bother to call. She drove straight back to Albany. "Hi," Andrea said, sticking her head into the lab, and Howie lifted his head from some project on the table and said, "Oh, it's you. I've been waiting for you."

"You have."

"I certainly have. What do you make of this?" He walked to a corner of the room and pulled The Pretty Girl from a rack. The frame was gone, and, maybe because Joshua was gone from her life, Andrea abruptly felt a surge of affection for the picture. The Pretty Girl's face looked fragile and knowing, as if she'd somehow apprehended the great irony that her fiscal worth didn't matter anymore. Now that Rose was dead, no one needed to sell The Pretty Girl. "Look at this." Howie lifted the painting to her, not so she could see the surface but the strip of canvas that wrapped around the painting's edge, before it was stapled to the back. "The return," some painters called it.

"Words," Andrea said and stepped closer to read the block letters: ROSE, THOU ART SICK.

"Good God," she said. "Why would someone write that?"

"It's Blake. From the *Songs of Innocence and Experience.*"

Andrea had to sit down. "I know that, I know . . . ." She read the words again. "Could I use your phone? It'll be long distance, but I've got a calling card."

"Of course. Are you all right?"

"I'm all right. I'm just wondering . . . . See, my aunt, who owned this, her name was Rose."

"Ohhhhh," Howie said, understanding and growing interest merging in the exhalation. "Well, look at this." He turned the painting over and showed her a signature that had been hidden by the frame. SAM AUERBACH in block letters. But there was no date. Howie put the painting down and reached for a phone. "Don't bother with your calling card," he said, extending it to Andrea.

As she dialed, Andrea looked at the painting, now resting on the table before her. Could it be *of* Rose? Andrea had seen photographs of Rose as a younger woman—one of her at a cocktail party, another in some unknown kitchen—but none of her much younger than fifty. By the time Andrea knew her, Rose was beyond looks. She was old.

"Mom," she bleated into the phone.

"Hey, honey."

"Mom, you know Rose's painting. Is that a picture *of* Rose?"

"Of course, didn't you know that?"

"No, well, how would I know something like that? You never told me."

"Didn't I?"

"No, never. I'm shocked, quite frankly." Because The Pretty Girl had met such a terrible end? Yes, it was that as much as realizing that Rose had been *this* lovely, and that she'd chosen to display a youthful version of herself (with a secret, punishing dedication) in her living room. "Look, I'm sitting here with this fellow who's just unframed the painting, and you know what's written on the side? Someone's written . . ."

Howie interrupted her, "The artist has written." He tapped

the block lettering of the return and then turned the painting over and tapped the block lettering there.

"The painter, I guess, has written these words: 'Rose, thou art sick.'"

"It's from a Blake poem," her mother said.

"I *know* it's from a Blake poem. Mom, doesn't that . . . aren't you, I mean, surprised? Why would a man paint a picture of Rose and then write something like that on it?"

"Oh, who knows?" her mother said, completely uninterested. "You know, artists. They're all crazy."

Here it was, finally, a mystery in the family, though there was everything in her mother's manner to suggest it was no mystery at all.

"Don't you want to know?"

"You make such a big deal about things, really. It's crazy." Andrea flashed on her father's angry response to a genealogy search she'd tried to do a couple of years back. When she'd sent a tentative note off to a Rutterman who seemed to be related to her family, he went crazy, as if she was opening herself up to the known extortionists who listed information with genealogical institutes.

"Well," said Andrea. "I want to know."

"What you should do," said her mother, "is sell that painting. My mother always said it was worth something."

"It's not mine to sell."

"I just gave it to you," her mother said. "Why don't you pay off your car?"

VII

It was September, the first autumnal day of the season, an exciting crispness to the air—though why exciting? Everything was dying, no? Still, who didn't feel it, the terrible poignancy of fall? "It's the angle of the light," Alex Auerbach said, nodding at the trees and the sheep pasture before him. "It always makes me nostalgic. I hope you don't mind," he added, pointing to the door behind him—this was the cheese cave, a square green door that opened into the side of a small hill. It was where he'd told her they should meet.

Alex Auerbach made artisanal sheep cheese on a farm west of Portsmouth, New Hampshire. He was also Sam Auerbach's son. When Andrea had first called to say that she was the niece of Rose Fine, Auerbach had said, "Are you *really?*" in a tone that suggested he was, if not pleased, definitely interested. Certainly that he knew who Rose Fine was. This was a surprise—for why should he know of a woman his father had painted once, over seventy years earlier? The bigger surprise was what came next. "Well, if you are her niece, I had better meet you, hadn't I?"

"Hadn't you?" Andrea echoed.

"I guess I had," he said, which was how she came to be visiting a New Hampshire sheep farm on a late September day. In her bag was a folder with a handful of clippings about Sam Auerbach, the public outline of his life, significant enough to have merited an obituary in *The New York Times*, though not (it was true) a very long obituary:

SAMUEL K. AUERBACH, PAINTER, 52, DIES

To some, Samuel K. Auerbach's portraits of the young women he met through his work as a policeman—initially orphans and prostitutes, but later women of means and culture—were aesthetically unadventurous, out of step with the times in which the artist had his heyday. In fact, they represent a latter-day allegiance to his first teacher, Robert Henri, and the portraits of his virtual contemporary George W. Bellows. Auerbach's social realist paintings of city life had a Manichean simplicity for which he was often criticized, but his portraits, characterized by a schematic but sure brush stroke and a Sienese palette, have a compelling ambiguity and complexity. Though early in life he studied at the New York School of the Arts, he followed his father and grandfather into the New York City police force. Although his career there was not typical, he never abandoned it fully for the life of the artist. He died Friday, after a short illness, at his home. He was 52. He is survived by his wife, Eliza; his sister, Mrs. Clara P. Nardin; and his son, Alex Auerbach, of Boston, Massachusetts.

Nothing about this obituary—or the handful of images and similar bios—that Andrea had managed to pull off the Internet or from microfilm at the university in Albany satisfied her curiosity. Nothing explained the words on Rose's painting; they only made Andrea's curiosity more focused. How, given that Aunt Rose was neither a prostitute nor a woman of means, had Sam Auerbach come to paint her? The question gave her the courage to make a few calls, to find that Eliza and Clara were now dead and that Alex still lived, though no longer in Boston.

"We'll meet in the cave," Alex had said to her over the phone, when they were still arranging the terms of her visit.

"I'm sorry?" Andrea had said.

"Oh," he had laughed. "My cheese cave. It's built into the side of a hill here, and my office is inside. It's such a busy time of year it's hard for me to leave the farm."

Now Alex was directing her into the "cave," which consisted

of a small room, with two windows behind which was a temperature-controlled room for the waxy rounds his farm produced. On the phone, Andrea had pictured Alex as a patrician man—tall, elegant, and white haired, living out his retirement on a picturesque (but none too productive) farm. In fact, Alex looked like the lovechild of Mark Twain and Mrs. O'Connor, the dumpy Irish woman who used to babysit for Andrea when she was a girl. He had a huge white mustache, curly white hair, and—though this wouldn't be a Mark Twain quality per se—a pinkish, almost piglet-cute face, though he was probably in his late sixties. He wore janitor's gray pants and a white T-shirt, over a stomach that looked as if it was only now giving way to a small pillow of fat. The farm itself was clearly no gentleman's retirement occupation. Before he shook Andrea's hand, Alex had had to pull himself away from the side of a FedEx truck and then finish a discussion with two employees who wore white coats and plastic bags on their feet.

The office itself was a messy affair, with papers falling from shelves, cartons by the wall, and curling faxes—some sort of agricultural bulletins—thumbtacked to the wall. Upside-down on the floor was a sign that read *Sheep Meeting*, and Andrea tried to form a little joke in her head, something she'd tell Ray about the image she had of sheep in a boardroom, but then nothing truly funny came to her.

"This is the time of year when we get almost all our orders. So we're a little crazy around here."

Andrea nodded.

"Listen." Alex cleared his throat, in that masculine, ready-to-get-serious way. "If you don't mind, before we begin. Are you really Rose Fine's niece?"

"Well, no," Andrea allowed.

"I thought not," Alex smiled, as if relieved.

"I'm her grandniece. She was my mother's aunt. My mother's mother, my grandmother, was her sister."

"Your grandmother?"

"Yes, my maternal grandmother. Her maiden name was Sophie Fine."

"So you're here because you want to know about the circumstances of the painting."

"Yes, like I said on the phone. And I thought you might want to see it." Andrea felt how false this sounded. After all, would she have driven four hours just to do a stranger a favor?

"I would. Like *I* said on the phone."

"It's in the car . . . . I should have . . ."

"And here I've just got you settled." He held out his hand to the door in an "after you" gesture.

"I was twenty-two when my father died," he began as they stepped outside. It was sunny, but in the minutes they'd been inside, the cloud bottoms off to the east had bruised. It would probably storm.

"I'm so sorry. That's so young to lose a parent."

"Yes, well, it was. It was all very hard."

"I read in the paper that he'd been ill."

"He had MS, so . . . " Alex stopped himself. "I did get a chance to really know him before he died. I think I did. You know, young men and their fathers. But we talked pretty well, and because he knew the disease would . . . "

". . . kill him?" Andrea flushed. How rude to have finished his sentence for him, and with these words!

"No, no," Alex said and stopped. They were standing next to Andrea's car in a dirt clearing between the two gentle hills that formed Whistling Valley Farm. Sheep grazed in fields on both swells. Alex's frankness was appealing, though there was something decidedly unintimate about his manner. He looked down at the ground. "The disease didn't kill him. He shot himself. Or maybe a friend did it for him. He didn't want to live like that."

"Oh, God, I'm so sorry, the papers didn't . . . "

"No, they wouldn't." He looked up and gave Andrea a wry smile. "But I guess it was an open secret. Not so open we didn't get his insurance money, but, otherwise, people knew."

"I'm just so sorry."

"Well," he said, as if shaking the sad event off, and gestured to Andrea's car. "Let's have a look."

Andrea opened her trunk, removed the painting, and handed it to Alex.

He took the painting gingerly, studied it for a while, and then said, "So this is her."

"By the time I knew her, she was an old lady, but . . . "

"She *is* beautiful. I guess I knew that, that she'd be a real beauty."

"But look at this." Andrea took the painting gently from his hands and turned it so he could see the words.

"That's my dad's hand all right," he said.

"But why do you think he would have written that?"

Alex looked at Andrea and then ran his tongue over his teeth. "You . . . ," he started, and then put the painting back in the trunk and closed the door. Andrea had thought he'd want to look longer. "Let's go back into the office."

"Alex," a worker called from a small white shed on the other side of the clearing where Andrea's car was parked.

"Not right now," Alex said, raising his hand, as if to hold the question off, but also, it seemed to Andrea, because he was upset.

Once they were sitting back in the office, Alex cleared his throat and said, "Listen, you seem like a nice person. And it isn't my way to . . . I'm sixty-seven years old now, and I know your generation and my generation, we handle things differently. It was hard for a man of my generation to go to a psychiatrist and talk about his troubles. It's different for all of you. You do it like going to the dentist, routine care. Now, none of it bothers me. I can see you don't know what I'm talking about, and I'm not the sort of man to reveal other people's secrets. But I'm also not the sort of man not to speak plainly."

A bit of Andrea's lunch rose in her throat, and she swallowed it back down. She had already half-guessed Rose had been Auerbach's lover. "She had lots of boyfriends," her mother had told Andrea when she was a girl, and once, when Andrea was in college, and concerned about these things, her mother had snapped at Andrea's indirect line of questioning and said, "Yes, yes. She had sex. It's not an invention you kids just came up with. She had sex, for Christ's sake." ("Oh, yeah," her father had chimed in wryly, "this sex thing. It's been around for a long, long time.") After that, Andrea had felt much better for Rose. Why, then, had Andrea never asked Rose about that life, that time of boyfriends—for she'd always known she couldn't, that it would be obscene to ask, that somehow she had brought nothing of that life with her into her years in the Chelsea high-rise.

"Your aunt, Rose, and my father had a daughter that they gave up," Alex said.

"They *what*?"

"Un-huh. A child. And I know it doesn't sound like the story could go this way, but it was Rose who didn't want the child. My father asked Rose to marry him, but she wouldn't. She wouldn't, even though she was pregnant, and, you know, it's not like now:

there weren't even *illegal* abortions to be had, back then. Not as I understand it. Maybe someone would try to hurt themselves—I suppose that trick has been around since the beginning of time. But she didn't stoop to that. She had the baby."

"She had it and gave it up for adoption?"

"No, she didn't give it up for adoption. She gave it to her sister. She had a sister who was married and couldn't have kids, and she gave the girl to her. Her sister raised her daughter as her own."

Andrea was quiet, processing this material.

"So," Alex continued, "my father left her. He left Rose. After all, what sort of woman gives up her own child?"

Alex fell quiet. She had to respect him for this, though she felt angry, at everything dark he seemed to be saying about Rose. At length, she said, "Are you sure this is true?"

"I'm positive."

"You're talking . . . You're talking about my mother. My Aunt Rose only had one sister, and that was my Grandma Sophie, and Sophie only had one child, and that was my mother, so you're talking about my mother?"

Alex nodded.

"Did your mother know?"

"About the child? Yes, my mom knew. She's dead now, too. She knew from the start. He waited to tell me till just before he died. I think other people . . . if they know their parent has given up a child, they . . . it . . . it doesn't make them feel very safe. When I learned about my father's daughter, my dad took great pains to make it clear that he wouldn't . . . well, you know, that it was Rose who didn't want the child. He didn't want me to think he was the sort to abandon his child. He didn't want me to be afraid."

A protest rose to Andrea's lips, but she forced it away.

The demon in the background of the painting. If it really existed, had it been intended not as something The Pretty Girl was opposed to, but as something she was? Rose? How improbable. And then Andrea almost laughed. Watch her mother act unruffled at *this* information! Or maybe she already knew? But that was impossible. Her mother didn't keep secrets. She was famously bad at it. And there was nothing Andrea could find, as she did a quick scan of her history, all the hugs and kisses between relatives, to suggest that her mother thought Aunt Rose was anything other than her aunt.

Andrea supposed she should be shocked or repulsed, that her whole picture of Rose should shatter, and that she should be down on the ground, trying to piece the shards together. So Rose *was* selfish, so her mother had been injured, so Sophie *was* more long-suffering than Andrea ever supposed. Andrea knew she should feel all this, that she should be reconstructing her whole sense of history, reinterpreting every piece of her childhood, analyzing every complicated interaction for its hidden meanings. She should be doing this. She should! She should not be giving a silent victory cheer: To Rose! For not missing out, for having a life!

PART TWO

I

Hannah Krinsky could speak English, all right, but her writing was terrible. Which was why Rose Fine wrote letters from Hannah to Sam. It wasn't a Cyrano sort of thing. It was just some help. People said Rose was a beautiful writer. She thought they meant her penmanship—she had a long, loopy hand, very elegant, and she never spilled ink—but Hannah said they actually meant the way she expressed herself.

Dear Mr. Auerbach,
My friend Hannah Krinsky knows only two smart boys, and you are one of them. She knows you like to paint and to read books, and who wouldn't like a man who likes these things? She thinks you should know that she knows how to drive a Model T Ford, as she has been making deliveries for her Uncle Sol's grocery business since she was thirteen. Even so, she sometimes dreams about acting

in the theatre. She is no fool, though (this isn't her telling you this, but me), and will do what she has to do to keep a family fed.

Sincerely,
Rose Fine

Dear Mr. Auerbach,

My friend Hannah Krinsky thinks you are smart enough to be a lawyer. But where you are going to get the money to go to law school she doesn't know. My parents (this is me Rose Fine talking, not Hannah Krinsky) married each other when they were fifteen. Their parents arranged the whole thing. That they figured out how to love each other is a crazy thing. When I say crazy, I mean miraculous. Go see if parting a sea is any more difficult. Hannah is herself fifteen, and she knows a smart boy when she sees one. I'm wondering, Mr. Auerbach, if you know a smart girl when you see one?

Rose Fine

Rose was talking about Hannah, when she asked this question. She loved the dare of it, even as she wrote it, but she wasn't flirting herself. Rose already had a boyfriend. Lenny Smallens. He had her a little dazzled—the way he'd wear overalls without a shirt when he was working—but her mother and her married sister, Sophie, worried. It looked like they could tell, just from the way Lenny said, "Your daughter'll be home early tonight; don't you worry," that he wasn't really planning to take her for a walk. And he wasn't. Rose's life with Lenny was her biggest secret—a small, separate room that she couldn't occupy while occupying the rest of her life, for no one she knew did with anybody what she did with Lenny. Only somehow Sam walked right into that life and decided to grab her out of it.

She started working before she left high school. Her first job was with Doctor Parsons, who had an office near Delancey. Sometimes Doctor Parsons asked her to do a letter, but mostly Rose just answered the phones, made appointments, and sent out the bills. That sort of thing. There was a nurse who worked with the doctor, and once (when Rose went back to use the bathroom), she heard the doctor say to the nurse, "It's a mess. What she's done to herself." And she knew they were talking about a woman who'd come in without an appointment, three rivers of blood running from her skirt hem to her ankle. "She was a girl, the first time she came here," the doctor added, and then, seeing that Rose was in the hall, he'd bobbed his chin, so the nurse would shut his door. Rose pitched forward and held her own stomach, as if it were she who was in trouble. Then, she closed the door on that thought and went back to her filing. That very day, when she stepped out of the office, a packet of letters for the mailbox in her hand, an umbrella poised for opening—the day had turned to misty rain—a young man pulled the door open for her, and said, "Hello, Rose Fine."

She stepped back, startled. "No, it's OK," he said quickly. "I mean, I'm Sam Auerbach."

"Oh, Hannah's boy," Rose said. Hannah had pointed him out once at services, but then he'd just been a black skullcap bobbing below her. She'd figured he had dark hair, nothing more.

"I wouldn't say that."

He was ugly. That was Rose's first thought about him. He had soft red lips and a short, sparse beard. Though he was a thin man, the softness gave the impression of fat. What made him ugly exactly she couldn't say, except nothing fell together in a pleasing way. He was balding—one of those boys who starts to bald before he's come of age—and had a left foot that turned in. *Turned in weakly*, Rose thought, and let herself dislike him, though she couldn't help but thrill at the notion that he'd come right to the office building to see her.

"I like your letters," he said, falling into step beside her.

"I write them for Hannah," she said.

"I know. You're a nice person to help her like that." He seemed to sense her disdain. The light for which Rose had been waiting changed, and she started across the street. "Well, good night," he waved and turned back in the direction from which they'd come.

Dear Sam Auerbach,

Hannah Krinsky meant no offense when she sent the comment about being a lawyer. She understands that yours is a family of policemen. And she has since learned of your enrollment in the School of Arts. She has never heard of a Jewish policeman, but she hasn't heard of a lot of things. She is very interested in art, because who but a Philistine isn't interested in art? She would like you to know that she is ready to be a student of the world. If you will accept it, she sends this challah. (A mini-challah. Isn't it dear?) She baked it herself. I have also eaten her rugelach, which she meant to send, too. It is delicious. Only her brothers ate it all up.

Respectfully,
Rose Fine

It felt strange writing this letter. Even that mention of her own tongue tasting the rugelach seemed too personal.

Sometimes, at school, during lunch, if she was particularly hungry and if her head was hurting—which it often did when she was hungry—she'd imagine a large rugelach, the size of a small cow, floating above her head. As the teacher talked about Jack London's *The Call of the Wild*, she'd unroll the sweet, eat it flaky layer by flaky layer. Still, she shouldn't refer to herself in Hannah's letters.

Sam Auerbach wasn't in high school, which was part of the reason for the letters. As Hannah had finally learned, he had a job at the police station, and he studied painting at the New York School of the Arts, which meant he was gone all day and most of the night. A scholarship boy, Rose supposed. He was "infected" with art, his mother said proudly. But then something happened. His teacher died. Sam took it very hard. He didn't go out for a stretch, and when he did, he sighed, large, expressive exhalations that might have seemed like a joke, if you didn't look at his face. The boy was suffering.

"What should we say to him?" Hannah said. They were in her family's flat on Orchard Street, the smells of chicken fat wafting in from the other apartments and a distinct stench from the back alley below. Just a few buildings away, where Rose lived, there was a bathroom on every floor, but here there was just one outside privy for the whole building. It made Rose a little sick.

"Sorry for your loss?" Rose suggested.

"I know, but that never sounds very sorry, does it? I *am* sorry for his loss."

"We'll say that then."

Dear Sam Auerbach,

It sounds like a cliché . . . it is a cliché . . . to say that

Hannah is so sorry for your loss, but the cliché hides real feeling. Hannah Krinsky grieves with you.

Sincerely,

Rose Fine

One day, he came to the office. Rose looked down at the schedule. She only worked afternoons, so the other girl might have put in his name.

"I can't find you," she said to Sam, taking in his face more fully than she had before. Was there a way to think it attractive? "Did you make an appointment?"

"I don't have an appointment."

She looked him over, tried to guess what was wrong, but he wasn't coughing or sweating out a fever or pressing a forearm to his gut. Still, if you carried a grief for too long, it could manifest itself physically. Hadn't she seen that with her mother, whose headaches became so pronounced in the months after her father's death? "The doctor won't see you, unless it's an emergency." The frightened face of the girl with the bloody legs came back to her. "I'm sorry. It's just his way." More than once, Doctor Parsons had complimented her on her gentle manner with the patients in the waiting room.

"I'm not here for the doctor. I'm here to see you."

Heat rose to her face. A still wind tickled her lips. Her skin—the surface of me, Rose thought—felt preternaturally sensitive, as if poised for a blow.

"I need to tell you something."

Rose nodded, as if to say she would listen, but she couldn't quite look Sam in the face. She focused on his shoulder, the wrinkles in his shirt.

"I saw you with Lenny Smallens. And you need to know

about that sort of boy. You have to stay away from that kind. He doesn't mean any good for you."

"You saw me?"

"On Hester Street. He was giving you a kiss goodbye."

"Oh," Rose said, for she was thinking that he'd somehow seen the roof of Lenny's family's apartment building, a spot behind an air shaft, where Lenny always took her in good weather, and once, actually, in a thunderstorm, because he said he just "had to." This was before he'd become the custodian over on Stanton Street. Then he had a key to the basement boiler room. He wasn't going to wait till he married, he said, to move out of his family's apartment. He'd take a job, as soon as he found one, that came with a room for the super. They were in the gray basement room when he said this, the boiler looming like a boat in mist behind Lenny's head. "Won't that be sweet?" he said, leaning in to kiss her. "My own place." He tugged at her waistband, slid his hand under her skirt, up her leg, over her stomach and down. "And you can visit whenever you want."

Whenever you want, she thought, not quite bitterly. Why would he want super's rooms? She'd be out of school, soon enough, and between them they'd have the money for a place once they married.

"I'm trying to tell you," Sam whispered now, "that boy isn't . . . You're too good for him, you see? You don't have a dad—." Her head snapped up. She *knew* her father was dead; she didn't need this boy telling her. "—and I just think you need someone to tell you what a father might. I'm just telling you."

She looked down at her desk.

A man waiting for the doctor approached the desk and said, "Is this young man bothering you?"

She shook her head no but didn't look up.

"I'll be going," Sam said—not to Rose, but to the patient standing next to him—and Rose heard the creaks of the floor till he reached the door. She didn't look up when she heard the door swing shut, not even to say "thank you" to the man who had tried to help her.

Dear Sam Auerbach,

Hannah Krinsky still thinks of the loss of your beloved teacher. Again, she sends her sympathies. She didn't tell you this before, because she didn't want to add to your burdens, but her baby sister died when she was twenty-four hours old, so she knows your sorrow. This is what she wants me to tell you. So I'm telling you.

Sincerely,

Rose Fine

After that, Rose told Hannah she couldn't do any more letters. School was coming to a close, and she had to find another job to supplement her work at the doctor's. There was a pathologist who needed a typist, and she was giving up the letter writing for Hannah, so she could type the man's autopsies. She could do seventy-two words a minute, which covered, it turned out, a lot of death.

A week later, as if he'd read the final note from Rose as a sign, Sam Auerbach was back in the doctor's office. He had blue paint on the tips of his fingers.

"You'll show me what you paint some day," Rose said. It wasn't a question really. "And where," she added. She hadn't planned to say it. Of course, he would read this the wrong way.

"You have to end it with him," Sam said. Not a question, a plain fact.

When Rose told Lenny, he cried, and because he cried she said that no, no, she didn't mean it. She was still his girl.

"I haven't been good to you. I haven't," Lenny blubbered.

"No," Rose said. "No, no," for he had been there, two years earlier, when her father died—his heart doing what hearts do when they shut down—and he'd sat shiva with the men and then come to see her. He had been good to her when she needed him. And then she had done what she had done with him, had done it and though she had no category for thinking of it this way—because no one talked (not even Sophie, who would just smile and say she was ready to talk, whenever Rose needed) about men and women—she had liked it. She *had* liked it: the dizzy thrill, the mess, the flattering (always flattering) sense of Lenny's need for it all. And yet there were things: Lenny never took her to meet his friends, Lenny didn't ever want to go out someplace with her, not even somewhere free like the park, Lenny wasn't (it seemed sacrilegious to say it, if only to herself) all that bright.

"Give me another chance," Lenny said.

"No, no, you don't need another chance," Rose said, holding his head in her lap, as if he were a baby. "I don't know why I said it. I was just confused."

"You didn't end it?" Sam was incredulous.

Rose shook her head.

Sam looked down with regret into his own soft hands, as formless as the jellyfish Rose had once seen buried in the sand at Coney Island. Lenny's hands were rough with small calluses and broken blisters. "Well, I guess I can't see you until it's over," Sam said. They were sitting on a park bench, Sam having overtaken her after work and led her to this spot.

"OK," Rose said. He would punish her with his absence— she knew that was what he thought—but she felt relieved. The matter was through.

But it wasn't, for a month later Sam actually dared to come by her mother's building to insist that she end it, that Lenny was using her. Rose whispered at the doorway of the flat, "I can't yet. I can't yet. I'm sorry," and her mother called (from the back room of the apartment), "Who's at the door?"

"This is the last time I'll come," Sam said, again as if his own absence were the worst punishment he could imagine. And he didn't come again, but he seemed to manage to show up in places where Rose was—once at the market, another time at the butcher's—and he gave Rose a long look that managed to be disapproving and loving at the same time. It was clear, his eyes said, what Rose needed to do; she only needed to be brave enough to do it.

So, finally, down in the boiler room, she thought, "OK. It's time."

Lenny said, "Rose, don't leave me."

"Will we marry?"

"You know I can't marry you, because—" but the reasons he came up with were no reasons at all. Rose thought of all the times she couldn't follow the train of Lenny's thought, how she drifted while he talked, and how these long gaps in her attention never seemed to mean anything for their conversation. He just went on and on.

She avoided Hannah, of course. And then when it was all decided, she went home and said, "Mama, I've met the boy

I'm going to marry." She meant it. Sam was everything she'd been raised to admire: he was smart, he was artistic, he had a real job. Rose's mother, Zimmie, was glad to say goodbye to Lenny and to find that he hadn't so damaged her daughter's reputation that a man with higher aspirations wouldn't come along and claim Rose. Rose had her affectations. Rose had things she wanted. If they married, before Sam found all this out, all would be fine. And then Zimmie could move in with her older daughter, for while Rose was still at home, it didn't seem like a good idea. Sophie and Rose loved each other, but Zimmie couldn't bring Rose into Sophie's household. The two girls had always fought. Sophie didn't like Rose's distracted manner, her fussiness over food, her vain carefulness in dress, her routine tardiness for appointments ("You've always got to make your late arrival"), and on and on. Rose found her sister bossy and pedestrian. Once Rose even said she wondered how Sophie had tricked Jack—who already was on his way to making himself into something, having gone straight from high school to law school—into marrying her. Sophie responded by refusing to talk to Rose for the better part of a year. But the girls had reconciled of late. It actually seemed to help that Sophie hadn't been able to get pregnant. It gave Rose a reason to feel for her older sister, though otherwise, of course, the childlessness was a tragedy. When Zimmie talked about Abraham and Sarah and miracles, Sophie would just start to cry.

But Sam Auerbach's arrival wasn't all good news. It got around the neighborhood that Rose Fine had stolen Hannah Krinsky's boy. She was pretty—that Rose Fine—and could do things like that. And then Lenny Smallens, that *schlemiel*, started telling stories about Rose, as if she were some common tramp. He was jealous, anyone could see that, but still people talked.

II

Part of Sam Auerbach's appeal was that he wasn't a known quantity. He'd grown up in Queens—which might as well have been the moon, for all anyone traveled there—before his family took a flat on the lower East Side, where everyone else had lived, for so very long. He was Jewish, and he even went with his parents to synagogue. Still he'd say, to anyone who listened, that he wasn't sure he believed in God, but he was sure about art. Art, he said, was a way of seeing beyond the surface of the usual to the real.

He really said things like that.

Sam took Rose to the school where he was studying. There was a large open staircase, and Rose followed him up the stairs, through cluttered studios to a lecture hall, and then back downstairs, a destinationless tour that interested Rose nonetheless. These were the rooms he haunted after work. Once she joined him at a crowded evening lecture, and a tall man sitting next to Sam (his name was Smithy) turned to Sam and said, "If a bomb dropped on this room right now, think what would happen to the future of American painting." They thought a lot of themselves, the students did, but still they liked what they were doing. What a thing that was. Rose knew people who liked earning a living, even when it wasn't much of a living. She knew people who were proud of their efforts, but who could say they enjoyed cutting shoe leathers or pressing clothes or sewing the same seam on a garment, over and over again?

Everywhere Sam went he was unusual, because he and his father and grandfather were the only Jews on the police force. Sam was the only policeman at the art school. And even though he was a policeman, he didn't do what Rose thought policemen did—walking the neighborhood and apprehending bad boys. He had an office job, he explained to Rose. It was in Brooklyn on Bergen Street, and she'd never seen it, but she imagined it as a large fortress looming over the street.

"You can't have light without dark," Sam told her. "Art school is the light." His job was the dark.

"Why?" she asked. "Why is it the dark?"

He shook his head. "You don't want to know."

They went to museums and met his friends from school for coffee, late at night. They went to a weekly gathering at an apartment on 17th Street, where no one was Jewish and someone even asked Sam where his horns were. She wasn't trying to be mean. She really thought Jews had horns. Sam hadn't gotten angry. He'd laughed. "You have to laugh," he said, "at how stupid people are." But most of the people at the 17th Street apartment weren't like that. Some of them were even journalists. Once a playwright came, and they all took turns reading his play about a coal miners' strike. None of them had ever met a coal miner, but they approved the spirit of the story.

It was at the 17th Street apartment that Rose formally met Smithy, the friend she'd overheard at the lecture.

"Ah, the lovely Rose Fine," Smithy said, taking her hand. "The lovely Rose Fine finally shorn of the unlovely Lenny Smallens."

Rose looked at Sam for a clue to how she was to respond to this. They were still at the entrance of the apartment, having not yet been waved into the small room, furnished with a single couch and table, where guests always gathered.

"Yes, here she is," Sam said, pressing her back lightly to encourage her to step into the apartment. "And you," he continued, "are back from the ends of the earth."

"I am." Smithy turned to Rose to say, "I've been in far-off Vermont."

"Close the door," someone shouted, and another person cried, "Smithy!" and pulled the man away.

As always, people sat on the floor in sociable clumps. They were waiting for Polly (who lived—all alone!—in the apartment) to announce what it was (a play reading, a recitation of a poem, an organized debate about the latest efforts of Margaret Sanger) that she had planned for the evening.

"Hey!" Sam called, clapping a man on the back, but then he turned from the friend and whispered something to Rose.

"What?"

"I want you to know about Smithy. Three years ago, his fiancée died. Tuberculosis. He's not over it. None of us are. But you should know, just in case. Not that you'd say anything, but you know."

Rose looked past Sam to where Smithy was standing, drink in hand, with Polly. Polly ashed her cigarette, and the cinders hit Smithy's hand. "Ouch!" he said and reached up to give Polly a pretend slap on the face.

Sam turned his head to look and then huddled back with Rose. "Something about the circumstances of the death has made Smithy very attractive to women."

"Oh," Rose said, having no sense of the man's attractiveness herself. Smithy wasn't Jewish—you could tell that from his looks—which immediately put him off the map of Rose's real consideration. Still, she could see how other women might feel otherwise. He was tall, with big eyes and an open, boyish manner.

"He was trying to find some measure of comfort in the country."

Rose nodded. She didn't like the country much herself. With the woods and the mud, she never knew quite what to do. She came from farm people, way back, but seemed to have inherited nothing from them.

"Portia," Sam said.

"What?"

"That was her name. Portia."

Sam steered Rose back to Smithy before much more time had passed.

"So, buddy," Sam said. "How's the work?"

"You know, you know."

They chattered on, about people Rose didn't know, so their words didn't mean much, though the men seemed delighted. "Oh, yes," Smithy called at one point, in reference to a professor's name that had come up. "Did you see the review of his show? Harris Benjamin wrote it!"

"Yeah?" Sam said.

"Well, Benjamin's dead, isn't he?"

Sam laughed. "Not yet."

"Oh, you're kidding. I'm thinking Zizek's work is so great that Harris Benjamin doesn't only come out of retirement to write it. He comes back from the dead."

"Yeah, you gotta admire a guy whose work inspires so much loyalty," Sam said, though later, he admitted, he felt odd about the conversation. Joking about death, after all, when Smithy had a real grief, still fresh in his mind. And there was Sam's sadness about his own teacher who'd passed away earlier in the year.

Rose liked these evenings out. Or she thought she did. It was a pleasure to listen to Sam talk. He had an idea about almost everything. But now that they were finally together, she preferred being alone with Sam. Especially on Sundays, for they quickly fell into a routine of devoting the day to long walks through the city. Sam had a sketchbook, and Rose walked beside him as he went from place to place finding things to draw.

"I like her," he said pointing to a large woman with a pram in the park, "because her face looks like a boulder."

Or, "See that man's back! He's curved like a shrimp."

If Sam saw another man out sketching, he always gave him a short sharp nod of acknowledgment.

"Do you know him?" Rose asked, the first time she saw him do this.

"No," Sam said, "but I feel he is my brother." Rose flushed at this, a small part of her finding his words foolish, perhaps because she knew how noble Sam felt as he uttered them.

By Sunday evening, what with all their walking, Rose felt both pleasantly tired and hungry, though usually she felt meals came too often, and that most people ate far more than they needed. Usually she and Sam spent Sundays with her mother, but one Sunday, when her mother decided to go to Sophie's for dinner, Rose made Sam a special meal: stuffed chicken, kasha, green beans. And for dessert, an apple cake.

"Oh," Sam kept saying during the meal, "oh oh oh," not appreciating the tastes as much as the woman capable of making such things. He loved her.

And he loved himself for loving her. Rose didn't quite formulate that thought, but she saw his pleasure in loving her, the vague note of self-congratulation. He wasn't pleased by her exactly, but with himself for winning her heart. Rose Fine—a beauty and a cook, someone who liked art. He could bring her with him everywhere. Well, everywhere but the police station, but everyone had a part of his life that didn't sustain him. And it wasn't that work didn't sustain him, for he had a natural affection for anyone who worked hard and then had his efforts threatened by toughs and bigots, the whole manipulative underside of the city. It was just that his job wasn't "the" thing. That was his painting. And Rose.

Rose was his true love. That's what he thought. She was his Portia, the lost girl for whom Sam mourned, but of whom he'd always felt a little jealous. There was something so perfect about the Smithy-Portia union, something that transcended not just what women and men achieved (which was usually a whole lot of nothing), but what people could be together. Portia had been an art student, too, though a fairly tortured one. She painted beautifully, when she painted, which was practically never, and when he thought of her now, he thought of something Smithy once told him: that she liked to take long, hot baths, almost too hot to bear, and Smithy would talk to her while she did so. (Outside the bathroom door? Inside? Smithy never told Sam, and Sam didn't ask.) There was nothing they didn't talk about: God, love, the size of the sky.

Once, Sam called Rose by the wrong name.

"Portia," he said.

"What?" Rose's head snapped to attention. They were in the art school's lecture gallery again. Rose had said she'd like to come along and hear another professor. "What did you say?"

"I said, 'Rose, do you see if Smithy's come in?'"

He was lying, and Rose wondered if he knew he was lying.

"You called me Portia," she said. It made her feel ugly and dead.

"I did not."

"Oh," Rose said, for she wasn't in the habit of disagreeing with men, but when he didn't pursue this, didn't ask her why she imagined he said such a crazy thing, she knew that she was right.

She was three months into her relationship with Sam when he said this, and she had figured out some things. First, some men waited. Lenny had said it was just a big lie that men waited for marriage, but some men *did*, for all that Sam had done, so far, was kiss her. Kiss her passionately, it was true, and he'd run his hands up and down the length of her back, but that was all. Second, that Sam thought he loved her, but that what he wanted was to win her so she would adore him. It wasn't exactly the same thing. It was what men expected from relationships, but it wasn't exactly the same thing.

"I want to paint you," he said, one day in late fall.

"Me? Oh, no." The idea was too embarrassing. But he convinced her. He said, "When I paint you, I won't be painting you. I'll be painting me. My whole being can't help but come out on the canvas." He paused. "If I do it right, I mean."

He had a good friend who had painted a picture, one that later became famous, of a woman washing her hair—out in the bustle of the street—and he had some idea of repeating this. But that picture . . . Rose blushed. Sam's family was better off than Rose's, and Rose saw what Sam pictured all too clearly— the Jewish girl in the city shtetl. No, no, she wouldn't agree to that. So she put on the clothes she wore to the office, the good dress and gloves. "You can paint me in this," she said. He laughed, as if she were putting on airs.

"I'm not!" she insisted. "I dress nice for the doctor's. I always do. It comforts the patients. You think if I wore what I wear to do the wash they'd feel as if they'd come to someone who knew something?"

"OK," Sam said. "You can wear that. You've given me an idea."

She went to his school after Saturday evening services. Sam occupied a corner of an upstairs studio. It was a shared space, but few students kept the hours Sam did—none of them worked on Saturday nights—so Sam was alone with a room full of abandoned canvases. "I'm here," Rose called into the room, and Sam started. "Sorry, I didn't mean to scare you." He'd lit a lamp for his canvas, but otherwise left the room in shadows. It wasn't spooky so much as sad. He positioned Rose so the streetlight—shining through a small window, high in one of the studio walls—filtered onto her face.

For five Saturdays, she sat for him. Then he said it was enough. He could work without having her in front of him. She'd shaken her rose-colored gloves at him. "You're crazy! Now you need me; now you don't."

She was playing around, but he stared at her very seriously, and said, "That's it."

"What's it?"

He sighed, the big, heavy, shoulder-wrenching groan that signified (Rose now knew) that he was feeling something important. He still hadn't let her see the painting he was working on. "You know," he smiled, "I have an idea of you that I need to put down here, and I can't let you see it, till I've put it down."

Rose nodded, as if Sam had answered her question. But hadn't he said a painting of her would really be a painting of himself?

One night, on their way home from a Sabbath dinner at Sophie's new place, a row house in Bensonhurst, Sam said, "At the cheder in Queens, the boys used to lock me in the rabbi's study." Their bus had passed by the synagogue in Brooklyn, and apparently this was what called up the memory.

"Children can be so cruel," Rose said, and then, "You know what I remember from being a girl is how we used to hide in the crawl space under the front steps. It was full of spiders and who knows what down there. I wonder we didn't get scared. Sophie and I did it and told each other stories. We were very close then."

Sam was quiet. The pattern of the raindrops on the bus window seemed to have caught his attention.

"Should we stop for coffee before we get back?"

Sam nodded. There was a diner on 9th Street that made French toast out of raisin challah, and Sam liked to go there. She took his arm when they stepped off the bus—they often linked elbows when they walked—but tonight he shook her off.

"Is something the matter?" Rose asked, as they sat at their favorite table in the diner. It was off in the back, in a bright little alcove away from the stools and counter. She couldn't quite figure out what had happened, for Sam had been lively at dinner. Sophie had whispered, "You've got yourself a good one," when she hugged Rose goodbye.

"No," said Sam, but it was the kind of self-indulgent no that really meant yes.

If it had been Lenny, not Sam, across from her, Rose would have slipped her foot out of her shoe, and then—if the chairs of the diner were positioned for concealment, and if her own chair was at just the right distance from Lenny's—into his lap. "Oh, Rosie," Lenny would have said, and his mood would lighten.

With Sam, though . . . They had kissed, Sam's open-mouthed wet kisses a little disconcerting, and Rose never quite able to stop thinking of how damp his mouth seemed when he spoke, the explosion of spit he seemed to swallow with any word that started with "b" or "d." Still, "Men all want the same thing." Hadn't she heard that a thousand times, though it didn't quite seem to be true? She took off her shoe, let her stockinged toes feel their way over a crumpled napkin and a sugar cube to Sam's shoe. He flinched at her touch.

"Sorry," she said and drew her foot back. And women, she thought, all women wanted what? But why was she even feigning curiosity? She knew the answer to that. They wanted someone to provide for them.

"You can't make up for things by that sort of thing; no matter what you've done in the past." Sam's voice was uncharacteristically cold.

Rose looked at him. If she'd reacted to his tone, she'd have been angry, but this wasn't her way. "What're you talking about? What's the matter?" She was gentle, as if addressing a hurt child, as if genuinely eager for information.

The waitress set their coffees down in front of them. Rose knew Lenny had been talking about her, but still Sam's manner surprised her.

"Why are you angry?"

"I just can't believe what you did back there."

At dinner, Rose had joked and said, "This boy, he only sees in pictures," but she had meant it as a compliment. Rose thought further. It had seemed like a nice dinner. Sophie had asked Sam plenty of questions about his art. Jack had mused about how he and Sam worked—in a way—together. Since he was a lawyer, they were two parts of the great system trying to set things right, to make people feel better about the problems that beset them.

Now Sam was quiet. Finally, he said with difficulty, "I tried to tell you about something that matters to me, and you have nothing to say."

"I'm sorry. I don't know what you're talking about."

"You just started talking about yourself, after I told you about being locked in the rabbi's study."

The rabbit's study, she thought, thinking of how she and Sophie used to tease a cousin of theirs who wanted to be a rabbi. *You want to be a rabbit when you grow up?* they'd both say. *What kind of rabbit?* "What did you want me to say?"

"Well, to ask me about it, of course, instead of just talking about yourself."

"I'll ask next time," she said, bemused. This seemed so ridiculous, as if he were desperate for a fight, no matter that he didn't have a cause. "Tell me now."

"It's too late."

"OK," she said simply. "I'll ask you about it later." She felt proud of herself, as she said this, as if she'd effectively quelled a child by playing along. But Sam's mood didn't lighten, and instead of making her feel sympathetic—or even angry—the exchange made her ashamed of Sam. What had his life been like—how easy had it been, she meant—that he could afford to be upset over something like this?

He respected her. He seemed to want her to know this, but, in truth, the respect came across as timidity. So the next time Rose and Sam were alone in his parents' apartment, his hands at her back, his mouth to hers, she reached up under his shirt, her hands moving onto the warm stretch of his belly and up to his . . . He pulled back. "Rose," he said, taking her hands into his. "I don't think we're ready for this."

She felt chided, like a schoolgirl, and didn't say anything. She

DEBRA SPARK

turned from him and wished herself back home, in bed, where she wouldn't have to consider what he now thought of her.

"What happened," she said cheerfully, "at work today? We had a very busy day at Doctor Parsons'."

"That so?" he said absently, and Rose had her most serious stab of worry. She and Sam were a mistake.

They had been together, an item, for eight months, when it happened. She had been in one of those moods that came over her. "Is your time of the month coming?" her mother used to ask when Rose would sink into one of these funks, but it was invariably not her time of the month. Her time of the month might still be two weeks off, but she felt a sort of angry desperation, as if something needed to happen, something very particular, though she didn't know what it was, and it had to happen tonight, for if it didn't, she didn't know what she would do. Only it never happened, whatever it was, and if she managed to get herself to sleep, without too much angry crying, she would be back to herself, and whatever had come over her would be all right, for a stretch. To a degree, she knew what she was hoping for. Something special. Something very, very special, and when she would get in one of these moods as a younger woman, she'd undertake some project in the kitchen—bake something fancy or settle on a new sewing project. But now, after work, she was usually too tired for baking and sewing, and, anyway, neither a cake nor a plan for a new dress would satisfy her. She was eighteen, the age (she supposed) when those things lose their luster.

Sam had taken Rose off to yet another artist's lecture, and, instead of enjoying it, she'd felt annoyed at all the unfamiliar words the painter used. They'd gone back to Sam's parents' place, only it was so late that his parents had already retired to the back room. The place only had two rooms and a small side kitchen, but that made it bigger, by a room, than Rose's mother's apartment. Later tonight, after Sam walked Rose home, he would make the couch into a bed and go to sleep.

Sam had been pleased with the lecture, and he chattered away about it as they walked south to his parents' place. Inside, he put water on for tea and then drew her to the sofa for an embrace. He kissed her passionately. The usual. It didn't seem right not to be more physically drawn to him. For Rose, in all these months, had never quite gotten over her feeling about Sam's appearance or the wetness of his mouth. Soon the night would be over, and whatever it had promised, as she'd been walking home from work, people closing up shops and calling out their good nights, would not have been fulfilled. She felt angry. Not at Sam exactly, but herself, or the self she wished she were. Sam's hands ran along her back, and Rose decided— although it wasn't even a decision—to push him backward onto the sofa and climb atop him, and when he grabbed her wrists and said, "Rose, we aren't ready," she kissed his mouth shut, till he loosened his grip on her wrists, and pushed her up and said, "Rose," before tumbling her over onto the floor and pulling her shirt (finally, finally) out of her skirt and working his hand up under her buttons and toward her bra. She helped him undo the bra, the big cotton weight of it, and he sighed heavily into her ear, "Rose." It seemed she had won some argument they'd been having ever since they'd first started seeing each other, and now that she'd won, everything in the room was dissolving—the heavy brown dresser against the yellowing walls, adorned only with Sam's framed high school diploma, the blue vase in which Sam's mother never put flowers. "Oh, Lord," Sam whispered. "Oh, Lord. Oh, Lord." He'd let himself lift her skirt and push her underwear away, and then she'd guided a single thick finger of his into her. "Rose, Rose, Rose," he said. They had been right to wait. This was more passionate than anything that had ever happened with Lenny. Rose actually thought she was on the verge of passing out. Sam wasn't ugly. He was beautiful, and she reached up and undid the zipper to his pants, and he let her, all the while whispering, "Shush. Shush," for she must have been making sounds, and, of course, his parents were asleep next door. But he didn't know what to do next. He poked between her legs. He didn't know what Lenny did. He didn't know, it occurred to Rose, anything, certainly not where to put himself, and she didn't want to direct him, to let him know that all the rumors were true. But then he was in, and it was over, and she pushed him abruptly off her.

"A safe," she cried. She was just about to suggest it, when he'd done his business.

"What?" His hair stuck up wildly above him, like a torn flag in a hurricane.

"Oh, no."

"What?" he said. "What is it?"

She slipped out from under him and ran into the kitchen for a rag. How could he be so stupid? She reached up under her skirt and started wiping herself with it. "Oh, no. Oh, no."

He followed her, pulling his pants back together, the wet log of himself inside. An idiot, Rose thought. "What did I do?"

"What's today's date?" Rose calculated in her head. "Oh, no," she cried again. "Oh, no." She'd heard about people who did crazy things, douched themselves with cleaning powders. The plain fact was she wasn't exactly sure what a douche was, how she'd get one if she wanted one. The pharmacy? She scrubbed herself furiously. "Maybe it'll be all right," she told Sam. She said it again, later that night, as he left her by her building on Orchard Street. This was in September. By November, she wasn't willing to see him anymore. In January, she disappeared.

Or it looked like she disappeared. She was really only up in the Bronx. Her mother had eight sisters, and it was to the youngest of these—Aunt Zipporah—that Rose went. There was the requisite yelling before she went up there. "You'll have to marry him." "How could you do this?" "To think, it was the Smallens boy we worried about." But Rose was firm on one point. She wouldn't marry Sam Auerbach. She was going to marry for love, and she didn't love him. She wasn't even sure she liked him. She went to Jewish Family Services, and arrangements were made for an adoption. About this, however, she was persuadable. "Adopt? What adopt?" Sophie said. "You'll give the baby to me."

III

Rose stayed up all night, doing crossword puzzles, her eyes and throat always poised for a sob. Everything was ruined, but there wasn't anything really there to be ruined. It was just her, and it was all pointless, pointless. She didn't quite think of herself as having a life within her, even when the little elbows started to travel across her belly. She didn't think of much at all. During the day, she worked at Rubens, the neighborhood grocer. She was diligent and quiet. No one would have recognized her as the same gracious girl who'd reassured patients in Doctor Parsons' office. At six months—when even Zipporah's big dresses wouldn't conceal her state—she left the job. She helped Zipporah out with the household, but otherwise stayed in bed. She couldn't think past the day of the baby's birth. At first, in the most abstract way, she thought of keeping the child. "You can't do that!" her mother had cried. "You're not fit to be a mother. The evidence is . . ." She pointed at Rose's stomach. "*That's* the evidence." A girl fit to be a mother would never have gotten herself in this situation in the first place.

When she had a month to go, her family, with the help of Jewish Family Services, arranged for her to be sent upstate. North of the Bronx, the world turned to Indian territory, a rough wilderness that made no sense to Rose. If she ever wondered how her mother, who rarely went north of Houston Street or south of Canal, had been able to travel with Sophie over an ocean to meet a husband whom she barely knew and from whom she had been separated for three years, she had her answer. When you had to go, you went. Your predilections didn't figure in.

It poured the day Rose left, the sky doing her crying for her, so she could sit stone-faced in her train seat, her shoes damp, a wet ruffle of fabric decorating the bottom of her skirt. She balanced her arms on the swell of her belly, let her cheek rest against the glass windowpane. She was through with her family. She was through with men. She was through with everything. She had the baby in her belly to deliver. There was money in her wallet which would run out. After that, she assumed she'd die. Where her imagination ran out, her life would, too, and it was all of no consequence to her. She was scared, and the fear occupied every corner of her body. When the baby was born, the fear would expand, she would explode, and be dead. She actually liked children, but that fact seemed entirely unrelated to what was going on with her.

"You'll excuse me," a voice said, and she looked up to a man with an untrimmed, graying beard and a dark hat. "The train is full," the man said. "So if you don't mind." He gestured to the seat by her side. Chasids didn't trim their beards—Rose couldn't remember why. But other men? They really should. A ragged beard aligned them with the unwashed, the crazies, the rag and bone men of Victorian novels. It made them old before their time, and this man (if not for the beard) might have been any age between twenty and fifty. His face was unlined, at least, and the curves of his chin and nose were soft, almost boyish.

"Of course not," Rose said of the seat and pulled herself up out of her slump.

The man tucked his hands under the dark legs of his suit and sat, pushing a small bag behind his calves.

"Headed up north, too?" he ventured.

She nodded.

"To where, if I might ask?"

She said the name of the station on her ticket.

"I'm going there, too." He smiled politely. "To speak to some friends of mine. And you?"

"For . . ." She stopped. It was a habit of hers to sit with the back of her hand in her lap, her fingers curled. She didn't want anyone to see that she didn't wear a ring. "For some care," she said.

"I see," he said, nodding at her stomach. "Congratulations to you."

"Thank you."

"What friends?" Rose said, surprising herself. She didn't plan to get engaged in discussion, but then the prospect of conversation *was* comforting. She had long ceased to be a good companion to herself.

"I have some friends, and we have decided to meet to discuss our dreams."

Rose flashed on the dream she'd had the night before. It

involved going to an apartment where Lenny Smallens now lived. (Not where he truly lived, but where the dream said he lived.) The place was full of mice, and for some reason, Rose had gone there barefoot. As soon as she stepped into the flat, she felt the form of a desiccated mouse stick to the bottom of her foot. And then she saw three rats, walking atop the cushions of Lenny's brown sofa. She stared, unable to turn her head from their ugly lope, but she knew if she nodded toward the couch to let Lenny know there were rats in his home, he'd only yell at her.

"I had a terrible nightmare last night," she said. "I'm just remembering it now."

The man laughed. "I didn't mean that kind of dream. My friends and I are getting together to talk about our daytime dreams, plans we have for a community out in the woods. All Jewish," he said, bobbing his chin toward her, as if to say he'd divined her religion. "My name is Lev, by the way."

"Rose," Rose said and held out her hand.

"I'm sorry you had a nightmare. And in your state. What was it about, if I might ask."

"Something silly. I went to an old friend's house, and . . ." She shrugged. "It doesn't matter."

Lev nodded. But after a pause he said, "Sometimes I'll tell a friend my night dream just to make the dream . . ." He held up his hand in a fist, as if he were at a rally, and then let his fingers fly open. "Just to scatter the bad thoughts like so much milkweed in the air. Not that you need to tell me. But if you'd like, I'll listen."

Rose thought of her father, who used to come sit at her bedside, after one of her girlhood tiffs with her mother. He'd talk very seriously to her, as if she were an adult, though in the years when she fought most ferociously with her mother, she was only twelve or thirteen. Somehow he always managed to cajole her up out of bed and over to the kitchen to mutter a sour "I'm sorry" at Zimmie.

"Well, that's kind of you," Rose allowed. "Like I said, I went to the house of a man named Lenny, and he . . ." Her throat clogged with tears.

"That's OK, my dear. You don't need to tell me."

But Rose found she wanted to, so she cleared her throat, as if it were just dryness that had made her stop, and told the whole dream, mice and rats and all. At some point in the many hours it would take them to reach their destination, Lev would notice there was no ring on Rose's finger, and what would he think? Probably that this Lenny character had gotten her in a bad way and left her to deal with the consequences.

"A strange dream, and when you awoke, do you remember what you thought?"

"Well, I thought," Rose began. Then she stopped herself. What she had thought was that she was so undesirable that the Lenny of the dream didn't even want to go back with her to the neat apartment she kept with her mother, the careful home where there were never any animals, where everything was always bright and in order. Living in a place like Lenny's, horrible as it was, was better than marrying Rose. Of course, the whole narrative didn't really make sense, for it was Rose not Lenny who had broken off their relationship, but Rose felt the injury of her dream profoundly. "I guess I didn't feel very pleased. But then, who would?" Rose finally said.

"This Lenny," Lev said. "Not much of a character, is he? That he'd prefer this sort of life to something better?"

"Perhaps not," Rose said, feeling that Lev had given her a

small gift, a different way of interpreting things. It wasn't that Rose wasn't good enough, but that Lenny wasn't good enough to make a better choice. "Perhaps not," Rose said, more firmly, almost brightening. She felt a sort of grief for herself and took pleasure in the emotion. She *did* feel like a rejected woman, abandoned to her fate, though if a jury were to hear her argument, how much sympathy would they have? "You broke it off with Lenny Smallens," the prosecutor would say. "You broke it off with Sam Auerbach." And she'd present her small bag of evidence. "I never met one of Lenny's friends, not once, in all the time he saw me. And he never gave me evidence that he planned to marry me."

"That's just one fellow," the prosecutors would insist.

"Sam Auerbach," she'd say, "it's true, he said yes to who he wanted me to be, but he never said yes to who I was." What crazy distinctions for a girl in the 1920s! Whoever did she think she was?

"Well," Lev said, and he reached his hand over to pat hers. Rose drew her hand back instinctively, a quick jerk of shock. *Don't touch me.* But this was crazy. Men didn't have designs on pregnant women. This man hardly seemed to be capable of designs, anyway. His manner was so gentle. She awkwardly returned her hand to her knee. And now he knew, of course, that she didn't wear a ring on her left hand. Lev didn't react to either of her movements, or his new knowledge. He let his hand continue its slow descent, and when he finally reached her fingers, he patted her knuckles lightly. "You'll be fine, my dear. You'll see. It will all be OK in the end."

And who was he? To tell her this?

"Thank you," she said, in what she hoped was modesty, and the two rode largely in silence till their station.

*   *   *

It was still light when the train clattered to a stop, though Rose could feel the dark hurrying to come on. She had the sense that days, not hours, had passed, though she hadn't slept on the train. Distance and time seemed like one and the same thing, the train bringing her nearer to a moment from which thought retreated. Only a sense of humming dread remained.

"May I help you down?" Lev said, as he stood to get his hat.

"Please, no," Rose said. "I mean, I think someone is planning to board to help me."

Lev looked at her skeptically, which made sense, for, in fact, she thought nothing of the kind. "Peace be with you," he said finally with an air of sadness that, she saw now, had been behind everything he'd said to her.

"And also with you," Rose said automatically. He headed for the train door. It seemed he'd divined her embarrassment and was kind enough to leave her with it, even though a man wasn't supposed to leave a pregnant woman alone with a weight to lift.

A young man, sitting behind Rose, offered to carry her bags. Rose nodded, said, "Yes, please."

Outside, the air was chilly. A large woman in a voluminous gray skirt held a sign that read *Cranley Lying-In*. Did people at the station know about Cranley? Rose ducked her head as she pushed toward the sign, the young man in her wake. There was a bustle to her left, though, which caught her attention. Rose turned to see a host of Chasidic men in their penguin garb kissing the suit of her seatmate.

"Who is he?" she turned to the young man behind her to ask.

He shrugged, but a man called over, "Don't you know? Reb Lev Mirsky himself!"

Rose wasn't all that religious, but the famous rabbi she knew, refugee of—where wasn't he a refugee from?—and a great lover of men. His spiritual father was the Baal Shem Tov, and his mother, too. There was no gentler man on earth. That's what people said. And Rose! She thought he'd just been a man on a train.

Some facts, had she told them later, no one would believe. One, she only gained fifteen pounds with the pregnancy. Two, she didn't think, not really, that there was a small person inside her. She felt the baby move, of course, but she'd felt lots of things move inside her body, and those thumps and whines never meant Life. Three, she really thought she was in the Cranley Lying-In. No one told her that was just what they called the place to the women (either poor or unmarried) who had children there. The real name of the place was the New York Home for the Feeble-Minded.

The first thing she saw after the taxi pulled through the gate was a row of deformed children—ten or twelve years old—all tied with white bedsheets to wooden wheelchairs. To prevent them from falling over, presumably. The sheets formed big festive bows at the chair backs, and the chairs themselves sat on an immaculate white porch, which ran along the front of a brick building. Rose had the idea that the unadopted remained at the hospital, atrophied, and became these poor unfortunates. Her taxi passed by the children and made its slow way up a hill. To her right and left were more brick buildings, about ten in all. At the crest of the hill, there was a building constructed of field stone. It had a circular section that rose into a turret and a square section with a peaked roof. Rose had never seen anything like it, save in storybooks where a moat and fortress would have also been part of the arrangement. This was Cranley Lying-In.

The building itself had been the home of some railway baron whose children had all died. So it had been left for medical purposes. Within twenty-four hours, Rose saw how the grimness of those children's deaths still clung to the place. The forest surrounding Cranley kept the building in darkness, even during the day, despite its being built on a high spot. Behind the building's kitchen, a low black metal fence contained three small graves, and there was a great deal of talk, during Rose's first night, of the three ghost children with their nasty, desiccated teddy bears who would appear at the foot of a woman's bed the night before she went into labor. It wasn't the children's fault that they had died. Their mother had something—some virus, some strange cough, and the children had been sent away, so they wouldn't catch it. But then the mother felt better, and she had the children brought to her, and they all died of whatever she had. She'd killed them with love. That seemed to be the message, and the other women in the hospital—the poor but legitimately pregnant—lay in bed considering the horror of their own hearts.

From this, at least, Rose was relieved. Her sin was too little love. At least that seemed to be the consensus—a woman who would give her child away. The nurses didn't let any of the mothers walk about much, so what little sense of the place Rose had came from that initial motorcar journey from the train station to the room she shared with three other pregnant women. She'd been led, at first, through a grubby back corridor that gave into a kitchen, and then out of those stark rooms into a whole different world: a grand front hall with stained-glass windows and a statue in the middle of a small pool of water. A tremendous stairway—it put her in mind of the stairway back at the New York School of Arts—led up to a landing, from which a gigantic stained-glass window rose. She hadn't fully taken in the images—she only had the vague idea they were secular and pastoral, for she didn't experience that minor sense of offense that she felt whenever she saw a cross—before she was hurried up the rest of the stairs to a large living room cluttered with books. "You can read these if you like," said the shy nurse who'd been charged with bringing her to her room. And then she was in a small room with dark wood paneling and green drapes. Jewish Family Services was paying for all this, and so far she didn't know what accounted for her relative luck. She didn't know anyone who slept in such fancy circumstances. The bed was just a cot, the table workaday, the chairs plain and wooden. Whatever could have been sold out of the house—from drapes to sofas—had been removed, but you couldn't sell a stairwell, or the indoor balcony that was in one of the other wards, or the nickel bath fixtures and marble sinks throughout the home. All the patients had sore backs from bad mattresses, but the grandness remained.

Cranley was her home, and whatever happened to her in her future life, this building, alternately nightmare and fairy tale, would be part of her past.

The doctors believed Rose was lying about the day she'd been impregnated, that she was really farther along than she admitted, so every morning the pleasantly indifferent nurses gave her a liquid to drink—it tasted like bad orange juice—to make the baby come. Only the baby didn't come. The drink did make Rose rush to the bathroom, however, and from her days at Cranley on—not just for the rest of her stay, but for the rest of her life—her bowels were in a constant uproar. It wasn't just Rose, though. No babies were coming, it seemed, that season. The wards were silent. Everyone was overdue.

"What," she said tentatively to a nurse one day, "if I want this baby?" It was a new thought, and she almost hoped to be contradicted. The nurse's name was Shannon—an Irish woman with tight gray curls and a broad jack-o'-lantern face. When she'd first seen Rose's reddish-brown hair, she'd whispered to another nurse—but loud enough for Rose to hear—"It's a shame she's not Irish, with hair like that."

Shannon gave her a piece of paper with a line down the center. She said, "Here's what you'll do. On the left, put down what you can give to a child. On the right, put down what your married sister can give to the child." All the nurses knew the circumstances of the upcoming adoption. They didn't seem to think it strange. Mothers often raised their illegitimate granddaughters. A sister raising her sister's child? That was a little more unusual, but not unheard of. Rose looked at the paper. She didn't even lift her hand to the pencil Shannon extended toward her. The only thing she could think to put down on her side of the paper was "myself."

A month into her stay, there was an unexpected run on legitimate babies, and as Rose seemed so determined not to have her child, despite four weeks of the orange drink, she was brought to a basement room in one of the brick buildings to make space for the delivering mothers. The brick building's basement was where old women with dementia were kept. The hospital, Rose had finally learned, specialized in all sorts of female extremity. In Rose's room, there was a woman who had lost her legs and screamed throughout the night. There was another who'd been restrained in her bed, for she kept insisting on getting up, at strange hours, to pack for a trip. A third woman woke in the middle of the night for the express purpose of dumping a pitcher of cold water on another patient's head.

When it was time for screaming herself, Rose didn't, though she knew all the jokes about women screaming during labor. At first, she wasn't sure what was going on, and then a quick flood of liquid soaked her sheets. It was evening. Hours passed before the pain intensified. The nurses seemed to have vacated the building; the lunatics by her side were no help. And anyway, she couldn't have screamed if she tried. She was too frightened for yelling.

After the delivery—which the doctor almost missed—the nurse Shannon came in and mopped Rose's brow and said, "Well, I'm sorry about all that. We'd've come if we knew you needed us." Now, a sheet was strung up at Rose's waist, and the other nurses were cleaning up the mess around Rose. "You'll be OK. You'll be OK," she said, as she wiped down Rose's arms.

"Where's the baby?" Rose whispered.

Shannon took Rose's hand and placed it in the warm shell of her own two palms. "Now, you listen to me," she said firmly. "You'll go back home, you'll meet someone and marry and have your own children. You're still young yet. This was a terrible accident, but now everything will be OK."

"No, no," Rose said, her voice rising into the high, insane squeal of the old ladies in the basement. She'd finally found what she wanted to say, back in the train, when the old rabbi patted her hand and told her that everything would be OK in the end. She'd wanted to agree with the rabbi then, but now she saw how wrong agreement, even with a holy man, would have been.

"What, dear?" Shannon said, but now she was tired, having offered the wisdom and compassion she had.

"I won't marry," Rose said. "Of course I won't. If I marry, then I'll have children, and if I have children, someday someone will stop me in the street and look into my carriage and say, 'Ah, what a love, what a pretty girl.' And then they'll ask me: how many children do you have?"

Shannon's thoughts turned to her own troubles. Her bathroom ceiling had been leaking when she left for work that morning. There had been ice under the eaves. Now that the weather had warmed even further, who knew what awaited her, after her shift?

"They'll ask me how many children I have," Rose called, irate, to Shannon. No one paid attention to the old crazy ladies in the ward, and the louder the women yelled, the more they were ignored. Rose knew that, and still she demanded, less of the nurse than of the whole building above her, with its floors and floors of mental suffering, psychic limitation, and wholesale derangement, the only architecture, she imagined, that might ever have an answer for her, "And how, *how* will I answer that?"

THE REVIVED ART
OF THE TOY THEATRE

What We Know

London, 1862. Sometime during the night of December 2, an intruder entered the Theatrical Print Warehouse at George Sherson's Circulating Library on Fairfield Street. The vagrant declined to take any money, so on waking, Mr. Sherson was, at first, unaware of the damage to his property. Later in the day, some boyish tittering drew his attention to the corner of his shop. There, on a sheet of drawings of Annette in *The Maid and the Magpie*, was . . .

We cannot say that we didn't know that in the very shop where George Sherson entertained boys of all ages with his prints for the toy theatre—his character drawings for *Bluebeard*, *Timour the Tatour*, and *The Maid of Genoa*, his scenes of isolated hilltops, harridans' cottages, and multi-turreted palaces—that there was another business going on. We never partook ourselves. But we felt—we were led to feel—that the pornography trade should in no way diminish our respect for the very real talents of this first great producer of prints for the toy theatre. We were, at any rate, unable to keep our children out of the shop. Unable to keep the boys away. It was always a boy's game. The girls might be placated by the promise of a doll. The boys, though, would save the coins we fished from our pockets and then go to the shop for their one-pence plain and two-pence colored, the drawings of stage characters that they would take home, cut up, color (if they'd bought the plain sheets), and then mount to use in the theatres that we had bought for them the previous Christmas.

They were always in dramatic poses—the characters of the miniature theatre, one hand outstretched—up or down—to indicate grief or woe or surprise. And thus, in *The Maid and the Magpie*, one saw "Annette with handkerchief," a hand raised to someone in farewell; "Annette with letter," a hand poised in shock; and "Annette fainted," no hand raised save that of the man who bore her away. One knew—if one went to the theatre and who didn't go to the theatre?—what that letter said, why Annette's cross bobbed from her body as she waved a farewell, why Annette fainted. Even the boys knew, if they bothered to skim the playbook that came with the full set of characters for a given production. But why ruin a story by reading it?

Certainly, the tittering boys, on the morning after the intrusion, weren't looking at the playbook. They weren't manipulating wires through slits in the stage floor, so they could slide characters on and off stage. They were engrossed in Annette's un-handkerchiefed hand, stroking a male member, in Annette fainting at the sight of a naked man drawing a woman onto his lap. Someone had crudely inked the images onto the blank parts of a sheet of drawings that Sherson had pinned to the wall.

Sabotage, Sherson thought. Someone trying to expose his secret business to the law. He could be jailed for his trade. He knew that, even if the jailers were some of his best customers. He was lucky the children and not their mothers had found the prank. But who? Who would do this to him?

A Likely Suspect

Smugglers carousing. That was what Harper Donovan was engraving onto a plate when Sherson called. A long wooden table, steins of beer with foamy heads like so many lambs drunkenly collapsed atop their glasses. One smuggler tipping back in his chair. Another tipped so far back he'd fallen on the floor, his legs stuck up in the air—an unfortunate beetle, unable to right himself. Still another face-down in a puddle of liquid. Beer? Saliva? Blood?

"Sir," Harper said curtly to his former employer.

"Yes, well," Sherson allowed. It had been some time. Walking over to Harper's place, Sherson had been irate. But now that he was here, he couldn't quite summon up the nerve to accuse Harper, though the sight of the man—a skeleton garbed for the poorhouse—enraged him. Was he trying to reproach Sherson by starving himself? Well, *that* wouldn't work. Sherson didn't hire men because they were skinny. Or cold. And Harper, who'd bent back over his work as soon as he'd acknowledged his former employer, was shivering. Cold ashes from the hearth skittered about the floor like ethereal mice; even the vermin at Harper's seemed bound for the next world. Rather than bend for the labor of a fire, Harper was warming himself by wearing two coats and a pilling winter scarf around the neck that (in warmer weather) was always full of razor nicks. Sherson took the sweaty sheen of Harper's face as more ostentation. Only he, only Harper, a virtual knight of trouble, could suffer from both hot and cold at once.

"So who is this for?" Sherson asked, looking at the engraving.

"I don't have a buyer yet," Harper allowed, not raising his eyes from his handiwork.

Sherson wasn't surprised. Hadn't he parted company from the artist himself? Though Harper was talented—perhaps the best in Sherson's stable—he'd ceased to be reliable. At first, like the other artists, he'd visit the theatre regularly, go to dress rehearsals, finagle an opening-night ticket. Then he'd draw the characters in their signature poses. He'd sketch out the stage sets, draw a whole theatre, if necessary. He'd always taken a bit longer than the other artists, most of whom drew figures ahead of time, using the play merely to suggest how to clothe the actors, what props to put in their hands. Otherwise, Harper was good. A good and fine artist, and he didn't complain, as the others did, when Sherson signed his own name to their work. He understood—or must have understood—that boys bought a name they recognized, that Sherson was a name that everyone recognized.

Sherson bent over a small dagger that one of the smugglers was picking from the pocket of his neighbor's jacket. A wench carrying a tray of mugs scowled at a smuggler with his hand to her backside.

Something occurred to Sherson. "What play is this from, anyway?"

Harper shrugged.

"What's that supposed to mean? You don't know?"

Harper said, "Did you come here for a reason?"

"Where were you last night?"

Harper looked up. "Ah me," he said, as if he'd just remembered he'd been born a gentleman (which he hadn't). "Was it dinner at the Shersons? I completely forgot."

"Answer the question."

Harper placed his tool on the table and said, "There's a potato in your beard."

Sherson reached up to the gray frazzle at his chin, but dropped his hand quickly before he discovered whether part of his breakfast *had* caught in his whiskers. "I *know*," he said testily of the potato. "I put it there. In case I get hungry later."

Harper nodded, as if at the reasonableness of the claim.

"Potato. No potato. Answer the question."

"What's the question?"

"Where were you last night?"

"I was here. Where else would I be?"

"Can you prove you were here?"

Harper pointed to the ashes stirring at his feet. "Ask my landlady."

The Landlord's Wife

She had a soft spot in her heart for Harper. A soft spot, even though she imagined he made fun of people like her—doddery (to his mind) women with soft spots in their hearts. She brought him little things to eat. A portion of the nightly stew, fruit (if they had some), the end of a loaf of bread. But she didn't think he ate her gifts. In the old days, he'd hired her, once every two months, to clean his room, and she'd found a bowl of stew under his bed, some bread crusts surrounded by droppings. They looked like so many flaxseeds, but they were clearly from mice. If she'd given him something lavish—a lemon cream tart—she knew he'd be dyspeptic for days, but she guessed that this was what he had a taste for: lemon tarts, almond paste cookies with a dollop of cream, anything from the Viennese bakery. Still, his idea of himself didn't allow for his tastes. Which was why he got sick, she supposed, just to prove he didn't really want what he wanted. He used to be gone from his rooms all the time, but of late, he was always there, working. He'd never been on time with the rent. And the last two months, he'd forgotten to pay altogether. Which she would have forgiven, only she had her own bills due. And a husband, not as charmed as she by Harper's manner. Harper used to come down, now and then, to their table. Her two sons loved him. They couldn't believe he was an adult, though he looked like one. "I don't know why you let me rent your place. Such a worthless tenant," he'd say. "I barely make my keep," he'd confess, if another guest were at the table. "I go watch the stories." He'd gesture out the window, in the direction of the theatre. "And then make my little drawings. You wouldn't want someone like me, working at the bank." He would point at his face, as if the flaws there were apparent. "It would frighten depositors away."

"He made Three-Fingered Jack," one of her sons might interrupt at this point. They had just been looking through the Poury Walk shop window the other day and seen Harper's latest creation. It didn't matter what Harper said about himself. They thought he was a hero.

And the landlord's wife's guests, either they'd join in with Harper's self-disregard or try to argue him out of it. Which was why, in her heart, the landlord's wife thought she was special to Harper. She didn't do either. She paid no attention to his words. She asked him about what he'd drawn that day.

The Ersthauser Dozen

Twelve bell towers with twelve clocks with twenty-four spindly hands telling the time. Twelve churches. Twelve parks. From outside town, from across the river where cacophonous cowbells filled the Swiss countryside, twelve spires—a mountainous line graph—carving up the Solisturn skyline. And twelve brothers, of course. The Ersthauser dozen with their twelve toy theatres. When the brothers were children, the theatres sat on drawing tables and in the corners of bedroom floors. As adults, they had other, more public-minded ideas about their playthings, a general (though not quite universal) sense that their theatres should be shared with others. For half of the brothers, the default location was their place of employ, so now one theatre was in the town hall, another was at the apothecary, and still another was in the guesthouse lounge. There was one in the toy store window, one at the university library, and one at the funeral parlor, its figures assembled for grief. Two others found homes in the town's public parks. One in a little knoll in the woods, logs split to form benches before the tiny stage and even children's backs aching at the prospect of a performance. Another in the hollow of a statue's pedestal—right near the park's water fountain, which was a virtue for plays that required strong weather or a sudden, population-decimating flood. The rest were privately housed. There was one in the attic of the reclusive Ersthauser's home, and one in the living room of his gregarious brother, and another hidden, no one—save its owner—knows where, and one in the youngest Ersthauser's youngest son's bedroom. They came from England, the toy theatres, purchased by a thespian uncle, who'd played the part of King Lear for so long on the stage that it took some convincing for the boys to believe their uncle wasn't mad, that he could see quite well when they were getting set to lob walnuts at his head.

Appearances

It was far too late for him to be anything but an artist of theatrical portraits, but this was not a good life, not for him. He didn't have the strength of character for his own profession. For a while Harper had worked for everyone: Sherson and Greene and simply everyone, but one by one they'd fired him. The same complaint: they didn't like his little extra flourishes; why couldn't he just stick to the story line? They hadn't remembered that Juliet, in *Romeo and Juliet*, had a flute. Why would Juliet have a flute? And then the arguments: Well, why wouldn't she? The girl might have had a talent, no? Even at that young age, something other than the boy to occupy her, night and day? Music might have been a consolation to her. Hadn't music, throughout the ages, been a consolation to men and women, young and old? "I don't need this," Sherson had said, when they discussed the flute. "I really don't."

Work had dried up before, and Harper had despaired—this was the one and only thing he knew how to do, the one and only world that interested him. Then something would happen, and Harper would have a new assignment. And that was the good part, the new assignment. There was always the excitement of a fresh project and the pleasure of going to the play. It was, everyone said, a world of appearances, and they didn't just mean the show. That had always been a source of pain for Harper, for even back in the days when he had all the work he could want, when Sherson called him before all the other artists to sketch out a play, there had been the problem of dressing for opening nights. Since early adulthood, Harper had cringed at the sight of his reflection: the cauliflower knob of his nose, the constant pus-filled eruptions of his skin. He'd asked the landlady to take the mirror out of his flat, so when it came time to go to the theatre, his tie was often askew, his collar half anchored under his suit jacket, half rising in salute to his chin.

Once at the theatre, Harper indulged in his own form of vanity.

He gave a chummy hello to the ticket taker, an acknowledging nod to the usher. He didn't want people to think he was a member of the audience, though he entered through the lobby like everyone else. And then he'd chide himself for his behavior. *Hubris*. Why did he care so much what others thought? Once a play began, what did it matter? The lights would go down, the curtain would open, and he'd feel ... well, what he always felt, which was that he'd arrived, that this was where he should be.

Other Possibilities

If not Harper, Sherson thought, then maybe Glenna. She'd been so offended by Sherson's portrait of her in *The Ship She Sails* that she'd come into the shop to complain. "My head," she said, and she'd gestured to her neck—the engraved version of it—"it's all ..." And she flopped her head over in imitation of the imitation. It was true, of course, but she'd played a sickly orphan in *The Ship*, unsuited to even calm days at sea. Her head *was* always lolling back on her chair. "I don't look very pretty," Glenna said.

"Nooo," Sherson agreed. "But then it isn't you. It's ..." He flipped through the playbook, trying to find the name of the character.

"Oh, very amusing," Glenna said. "That's very clever." She pulled her threadbare coat tightly around her body. Outside Sherson's shop, the cold rain had deposited a thin layer of ice on everything.

She pulled at her coat again. Sherson could imagine her tugging so tightly that she'd disappear entirely. Like a toy that folded in on itself, then in on itself, then in on itself, till it was ... as the magician who performed out by Braxton's sometimes liked to say, before he displayed his palm, empty of coins ... all gone.

But it couldn't have been Glenna. Glenna's way wouldn't be to deface Sherson's shop. Glenna's way would be to vanish.

Childhood

When he was a boy, Harper had smacked his head on a fall from a horse. Now, he could barely recall the years before the injury, remembered only tests with baffling instructions, rooms full of chiding nurses and disappointed schoolmasters. He told people that he'd never been young, that he'd arrived on earth as a forty-year-old man, though, in fact, he'd not yet reached that age. His parents were dead. His father, a shopkeeper, faded out when Harper was thirteen. A long illness, though Harper never knew the exact nature of the disease. Now, at any rate, there was no one to contradict Harper's version of the past. Of course his mother (before her death) had told him stories. About this, about that, about the time she'd first taken him to the theatre and how he'd insisted on traversing the stage after the show. She had thought he'd turn and perform, make up a soliloquy on the spot—he'd been a lively child—but he'd wanted to see what was behind the set. It had been some landscape, a forest, maybe, with trees extending into the distance. There was a diaphanous cloth draped over tree limbs to suggest moss or a swampy fungus. Harper's desire to peek behind the trees reminded his mother of how he'd once tried to scratch a museum painting, how he seemed to think a flap there might open on to something else. Also of how he believed there was another page in between each page of his books, another toy cabinet behind his toy cabinet. Harper had sensed that his mother couldn't decide if this was childish or heartbreaking, but he supposed she thought it portended no good for a boy whose financial circumstances would require him to settle and settle. As an adult, he'd have asked her what she thought. But she'd died. Died young, Harper realized once he was almost past the age she was at her death. His mother: a flap that would no longer open to reveal anything more.

Rumors

"W.B.," carved right under the sole of the Harlequin's foot. The Harlequin balancing on the letters, as if he might skate away on them. And the rumor? William Blake. William Blake was an artist of the Juvenile Drama. Yes, *that* William Blake. "Tyger, tyger, burning bright." He'd died decades ago, but perhaps a relative held a grudge, perhaps a relative thought that it was Sherson who'd forced Blake to sign his engravings with the cryptic "W.B.," a way to deny Blake's handiwork, to pretend that someone else—Worley Berdman, Warren Butts, Wesley Blackman—had done the engraving. There was no telling what people might do when they weren't allowed to sign their own work.

A Kiss

Once, while tending her garden, the landlord's wife looked up and saw Harper behind the house, kissing a woman goodbye. The landlord's wife turned quickly away. It had startled her— his face, the utter absorption in it. She had never thought him a handsome man, but she could see how a different woman might feel otherwise. She glanced back. His cheeks were slack with pleasure, his lips startlingly sensuous. Nothing avid in the kiss—which was what she had so liked about her husband's caresses, back when they first started courting—but love, there was a complete sense of love in that kiss, the way his lips slid off the woman's and nuzzled in her neck. Perhaps this was what it would be like when her boys found wives. The landlord's wife would feel pleasure at their pleasure, but a vague nervousness at seeing them in an adult mode, and so far from her. She felt despair and happiness in equal parts as she pulled up the weeds around her tomatoes. He had found someone; wasn't that lovely? Now she was truly alone. In some essential way, she was always going to be alone.

But then, the landlord's wife never saw the woman again. She'd wondered and even tried to ask Harper about the woman. He only said, "I'm through with all that. That part of my life is over."

"Surely not," the landlord's wife said. "You're young yet," though it was a thought she'd had about her own life.

Competition

The business was difficult. People didn't believe that—children's toys, after all—but it was a constant competition. First, to sell the theatres, and then to sell the characters and scenes for a given show. Some boys already had all the plays, so when a new play was produced, Sherson hurried his artists to the theatre and then back to their engraving plates. And Sherson moved swiftly himself, going place to place, checking all the plates before he allowed them to be printed. There were props, too, special effects. One was fighting all the time in this business— no one understood that, but it was true, fighting even against the boys themselves, their terrible habit of growing older.

Which was why Sherson had gotten into his sideline business. Pornography. A new word. It still sounded strange to him. *Pornē* and *graphos*. Meaning: the writing about harlots. Something to keep the money coming in.

Old Smith sometimes stopped by Sherson's to pick up supplies for his stationers shop. Boys could buy straight from

Sherson or Green or one of the other manufacturers of toy theatres, or they could get the sheets at the stationers.

Children were scared of Old Smith. They often left Sherson's shop when he came in. Sherson would have left, too, if he could. He didn't like Smith, especially disliked his willingness to carry sheets from Sherson's competitors. But business was business. "Boys," Smith complained of his own establishment. "They come in, but they have no intention of buying. Pry open those fingers, and you'll never find a coin. They think my shop is a museum. That's what they think."

"We're all theatre here," Sherson said. He meant it as an insult, because his shop didn't deal in pens, ink, and cards. Sherson sold the theatres, the scenes, and the coloza oil for the footlamps. He sold fire pans for volcanic eruptions and exploding ovens for blowing up the mill in *The Miller and His Men*. Sherson didn't care how long a boy wanted to riffle through a playbook or examine characters before he bought. Sometimes it was a hard decision for a boy; did he want red, green, or blue fire? And if a boy didn't buy, he'd surely tell some other child about the prints, and that child would have a parent ready to make a purchase. You had to be clever in this line of work.

"I know which ones to keep my eye on," Smith said. "That Robert Stevenson. Robert Louis Stevenson. Seen him?" Smith held up his hand to indicate the boy's height—which was about Smith's waist, also about Smith's shoulders, since the man was rather stooped. "Up to no good. I know which ones."

Work

Sometimes, while Harper worked in his rooms—the chilly night air leaking in around his windows, his toes numb though his face felt florid, a loose shutter banging in the alleyway, its *tat tat rat-ta-ta-tat* a nervous second heartbeat, louder and more insistent than the reliable drum of his own bloody instrument— he'd find himself trying to calm himself by reciting, "Gamboge, Prussian blue, carmine, black." These were the four colors artists used on engraved plates. He thought of the boys who bought the already colored pictures as lesser creatures than the ones who bought the plain. Boys should color them themselves. Show some imagination. But then Harper liked working with colors. Not so much laying the blue over the carmine for a king's robe or for the jewels of some pirates' treasure, but using the gamboge and black for the scenery—all those caves' mouths to darken, those mysterious forests to color so as to suggest inns or cottages, or castles with pillowed, airy maiden bedrooms, behind and beyond.

To comfort himself, he made up lists. First, of all the plays he'd already engraved. *The Old Oak Chest. My Poll and My Partner Joe* and so on. Then, of all the plays he'd done this year. There weren't many. And then of women. All the ones who'd ever made a gesture that suggested, yes, they would have him. And then . . . then he'd go to sleep. Since Sherson fired him, it had been harder and harder to get out of bed in the morning. He hadn't had the money for rent in two whole months. Now, he might have to take a job as a dresser, down at the theatre, and then that would be that. When would he have time for his engravings?

When he told his troubles to the landlord's wife, she said, as if in sympathy, "Well, people have to have a job, don't they? Everyone works."

He hated her. That's what he said, later that night, when one of his friends asked him if he'd ever had any feelings for her.

"That woman? I hate her." Then, he shook his head and laughed, "No, no. It's just I can't see her that way. I've always thought of her as my little sister."

"I didn't know you had a little sister," the friend said.

Harper looked at him, puzzled. "I don't."

Competition

A group of villagers started meeting each morning outside the apothecary to make the rounds of the Ersthauser toy theatres. Not all of them. There was the hidden theatre, so that couldn't be visited, and there was the funeral parlor theatre, which seemed too grisly in its appointments—all done up with collapsed cardboard figures and even a flap under the stage which you could lift to see the dead rotting in their boxes. The reclusive Ersthauser wouldn't let anyone up to his attic, so that was a third theatre that no one could see. But the other nine. They became part of a route—a morning constitutional—that the villagers traversed, before they headed off for their own days. It was just as well there were only nine theatres to visit, since people spoke of the nine stops—always approached in the same order—as stations. It wouldn't do to have twelve stations.

The villagers' purpose, initially, was to gossip as much as anything else. Or perhaps that's not fair. Perhaps they welcomed the chance to admire their town, its early morning freshness, the twelve compact plazas, each of which led (if one ascended an alleyway staircase or darted between two residences) to another plaza, as if the whole town were a giant house, and its plazas were the house's rooms, and its buildings merely the rooms' walls.

At first, the townsfolk walked by each of the theatres as they might pass the illuminated window of a house: with only a vague awareness of what went on in the interior. But one day, the town hall toy theatre looked different. One of the Ersthauser brothers had bought a new scene for his theatre. Overnight *The Terror of Jamaica* had become *Robin Hood*, and the brother, in a playful mood, had added a few extra Merry Men, plump archers of his own devising. That day, the townspeople spent so long admiring the Merry Men's hats (so many thimbles and fabric bits) that they never finished their rounds. And the gregarious Ersthauser brother—who always looked forward to the villagers' arrival—decided to improve his own theatre, trick up *Three-Fingered Jack* with something new to ensure his neighbors' curiosity and thus their continued presence at his door.

Which is how the contest started. Not for the best toy theatre, but for the best set and characters, and not for something purchased from some stationer's in London—no more *Jack Sheppard* or *The Smuggler*. A set for a story of their own devising.

Whom They Hired

Harper Donovan. He'd once been an artist for the Juvenile Drama, so he knew the theatre, though not quite from this angle. Still the stage manager thought he'd be a good dresser. Better than the boy whom they'd just fired, the one who'd torn two jackets as he tried to work an actor's arm into a sleeve. The actor said that it wasn't the jacket he was concerned about, but his arm, which had been practically twisted out of its socket. There might be a lawsuit against the theatre in the works. That's what the actor said.

Harper Donovan . . . at least he didn't look like a man who had the strength to wrench a man's arm out of its socket.

The Landlord's Wife

They argued, of course, about the rent, but her husband gave in. Years ago, when she fell on the ice, Harper had been the one to find her in the alley with her broken leg, and her husband always appreciated Harper's kindness from that time. They both loved him, in their way. She didn't know why she'd never—not once—had a romantic thought about Harper. They were about the same age, and her husband went for long periods when he seemed to have no interest in her. During that time (and, in truth, for months after), her thoughts often alighted on this one and that. But not Harper.

Still, she wondered about *his* desires.

They were out for a walk at Harper's insistence. He said she looked like she needed an airing.

"Oh, sure, like an old feather bed. Well, you're right," she said. "Get me out in the sun."

It was an ash-metal gray day. They walked down to the park, where she had strolled when her younger one was little. Her older son hadn't liked prams. They were off on their own now, most of the day. At school and then they'd taken shop jobs.

"How's Beulah?" The woman with whom he'd been spending time. Not the woman of the kiss, but someone else. She was very pretty—blonde, cheerful, but with a dark sense of humor. She had some aspirations for the theatre. In the meantime, she worked for a producer for one of the stage companies. She wanted to act, but she had—this is what everyone said—more of a sense for things behind the scenes, which meant she was good with money.

"She's good. She has a chorus role in a new operetta, so I don't see as much of her."

"Well, that's nice for her."

They were quiet. Under their feet, the path was slushy from a recent snow. The Office of Parks had sprinkled sand on the roads and walks, and the dirt had mixed with the snow, so the ground seemed like a large bowl of pie dough, over-mixed with cinnamon. The thought made the landlord's wife gag, as if someone had just instructed her to eat the whole park.

"Do you ever think to marry her? She's such a nice girl. And funny." But sad, the landlord's wife thought. She had the edge that comes from not marrying in time.

"Oh, no, you know me. I can't marry. I'm just . . ." Harper shook his head. Before Beulah came along, he'd been alone for a long stretch and had played the part of the lonely bachelor. Actually, if he'd been in the theatre—not as an artist but as an actor—you might have said he overdid his role. Too much grief at being alone, too much emphasis on the pain of the unwanted.

And what did he know of it? For loneliness, the landlord's wife thought, marriage really couldn't be surpassed. So why did she want to push it on Harper?

The Club

As we say, we never partook of Sherson's secret trade ourselves, but sometimes—say, down at the men's club, when the fellows were handing around samples of these things—we might see something. A pop-up book once, with . . . well, it's easy enough to imagine. Clever, we supposed, but why not put these talents—those little tabs that could make things come and go—to better use? We might have chuckled, to be good sports, and because when you hadn't paid your club dues in a few months, you didn't want to draw attention to yourself. The club was nice, with its leather chairs and sandwiches, but, in the end, the people there . . . the people there were despicable.

The Apothecary

Years ago, the Ersthauser brother who became a druggist went on holiday to Italy. One afternoon, while his wife was napping, he'd gone down to the café by the train station. He couldn't make out the menu, so he'd asked the waitress if she spoke Swiss-German. She didn't. French? "No," she'd snapped, and she seemed to think he was some sort of fool, for thinking she'd be amicable about the whole matter. He asked for a wine and then pointed to the menu. He didn't know what he was asking for; he just wanted the waitress to get away from him. If he'd had more courage, he'd have left the place. She brought a pitcher of watery white wine and a raw mushroom on a plate. "So there," she seemed to want to bark, when she set the absurd-looking fungus by his glass. What exactly had he done to anger her? He noticed a run in the back of her stocking as she walked away. A man at a neighboring table blew his nose into his coat sleeve. There was something seedy about the café; he didn't know why he hadn't realized this before. Some time earlier, he'd noticed a sign indicating that two of the café's upstairs rooms were for rent, but it occurred to him now that this would be an odd place to take a room, given that trains came and went all night. Suddenly he had an idea about what must be going on in this café. He never returned, though when he passed the station, he always glanced in the café's direction, took in the cut of the women's dresses and the nature of the men, smoking their cigarettes at the tables. And he never quite forgot the strange feeling he'd had that day in the café, as if he were living in two worlds at once, two worlds that were normally laid one atop the other, so he couldn't see the one world for the other. Only on this one day, the day at the café, the worlds had misaligned, the slip of one peeking out from under the hem of the other, and he'd seen how things truly were.

When it was time for the druggist to design a stage set for the Solisturn contest, he made a café. In it, there were several tables with men scattered about. Behind, stage right, he placed a building with two upstairs rooms, balconies off both. Shabby curtains were visible through the windows. Behind the building and trailing off stage left was a train station with a small newspaper shop. A man and his young wife step off the train with their luggage. Above, a woman at one of the balconies observes the young couple. The husband looks up, catches the woman's eyes, and starts. She has plans for him. There is no reason for him to think this, but he does. This woman has plans to ruin him.

Suspicion

Harper's eyes were weak. In the distance, he could make out a gray smudge floating over a body, a disembodied spirit that eventually resolved itself into Sherson's head with its unruly beard, twitching eyes, and ashy complexion. A blue-purple bruise that never seemed to heal, a thumbprint-sized wound, stained Sherson's forehead. Once Harper dreamed his landlady was testing produce at the market, her thumb and forefinger gently dimpling the fruit, when she pulled out Sherson's head, pressed the flesh, and said, "I don't think this one is quite right."

Harper fought an impulse to cross the street to avoid Sherson. When their paths finally met, Harper managed a hello.

"You!" Sherson flinched, like a man abruptly woken.

"Me," Harper said. "What of it?"

"Did you come into my shop one night?"

"One night? Why would I come at night?"

"Because . . . because . . ."

Harper hovered on the edge of curiosity. He had never known Sherson to have trouble bringing words to his lips. "Often in error, but never in doubt," Sherson had once laughingly said of himself, when the two men were on better terms.

"Oh, never mind," Sherson huffed. "I'll find the truth out soon enough," and he continued his purposeful lope down the road.

The Lounge at the Guest House

A scrim hangs in front of the stage. When light hits the scrim from the front, it is opaque. On the fabric someone has painted an elaborate scene: a cozy library with handsome wood paneling, dark green upholstered chairs, and lamp-lit students concentrating on books. When light hits the scrim from behind, the drop becomes transparent, and the audience sees through the library windows to a forest covered in deep snow. Two paths cut neatly through the woods. One goes off stage right. . . . The other blends into a path painted on the stage's backdrop. At the end of that painted path, there is a small, painted cottage lit against the darkness of the wood. Toward the front of the stage, a boy, rucksack slung over his back, heads away from the audience. Something heavy is in his sack, and the boy bends under its weight, in an attitude that suggests he is in a hurry to get to the house in the distance.

Repeat Performance

He could be repetitive. At any one time, Harper had a handful of stories he told about himself—usually stories in which he played the part of the fool. The landlord's wife heard him repeat stories, word for word, first to her husband, then her boys, and finally her friends. Once, it was about how he'd been out by Drury Lane, and he passed a man he knew because he'd engraved his likeness for the toy theatre. "Hello, Pancake!" Harper had said cheerfully, because he was in a good mood. He'd just gotten some plum assignment from Sherson.

Pancake didn't respond. He was a bald man with a thin, carefully tended beard.

"It's me, Harper," Harper said, as if expecting to be recognized.

"I don't know what's the matter with you," Pancake said in a hushed whisper. "My name is J. M. Nolan. It has always been J. M. Nolan." And then he'd hurried away.

Harper flushed. Too late, he realized, he'd called the man by his character's, not his given, name. What was the matter with him? Harper actually remembered asking J. M. Nolan to ink his name onto a piece of paper, so he could engrave it on a plate. *Pancake as played by* (and then in Nolan's own hand) *J. M. Nolan.* It was how all the character sheets for the toy theatre were done. With autographs. In deference to the toy theatres' antecedents, since the character sheets had started out as theatre souvenirs.

The Pancake story. The landlord's wife had heard it six times. So, like an old married couple, she and Harper made an agreement. In her presence, he couldn't tell a story more than five times. Now, when he started on an oft-repeated tale, she held her hand up, fingers extended. To indicate the number of times she'd heard the story. How many more performances he had left.

Only now that Harper had stopped telling his stories altogether, the landlord's wife felt bad about her impatience, for there was nothing she could do to get him to come down and talk with her. He was always up in his room, engraving, though everyone said he'd lost all his commissions, every single one, even from Sherson, and once you lost Sherson, Harper had told her, you were done for. No one else would hire you. The man had that kind of power.

"That man?" the landlord's wife had said at the time, not quite believing Harper. "The one who goes about in a bed cap?"

Harper nodded. Sometimes Sherson *did* wear a bed cap during the day. But it didn't matter what the man looked like. His commissions meant everything.

The University Library

Smugglers carousing. That's what the Ersthauser brother who was a librarian came up with. A long wooden table, steins of beer with foamy heads like so many lambs drunkenly collapsed atop their glasses. One smuggler tipping back on his chair. Another tipped so far back he'd fallen on the floor, and his legs stuck up in the air—an unfortunate beetle, unable to right himself. Still another face-down in a puddle of liquid.

Boys

It was Robert's birthday. His uncle said he'd get him a play for his theatre. He'd get him *Hamlet*. But Robert didn't want *Hamlet*. He wanted *Aladdin*. If his uncle got him *Hamlet*, Robert would show him. He'd color all the characters, cut them out, paste them to cardboard, and then tear that Ophelia's head off. He wanted nothing to do with any *Hamlet*.

His uncle said he'd like to help him put on the play. His uncle started in with his old "To be or not to be." Which shows how much he knew. No one ever performed with the miniature theatres. No one he knew. That wasn't the point.

It was raining—it had been raining all week—so Maxwell came over with his new sheets for *Twenty Thieves and Twenty*

Knights. When they had the characters ready, they put them into Robert's theatre—even though his theatre still had the set for *The Old Oak Chest* in it. Robert slid a thief over to Maxwell's knight. "I've got the jewels and the girl, and I'm not giving them back."

"Yes, you will," said Maxwell's knight, his sword already extended for an easy victory, "you will."

They played on, Robert growing increasingly irritable. Sanctimonious knight. Robert knew the girl actually liked him—liked the thief—better. The thief had a mustache and a smart hat.

"I won't," Robert said, and when he thrust his thief forward on one of the slides in the base of the miniature theatre's floor, he must have pushed Maxwell, for all of a sudden the boys were tussling.

"Rascals," his mother said, when she came in to see what the commotion was all about. Robert was still angry with Maxwell when Maxwell was sent home for tea.

"No more playing with the theatre," his mother said. "You and Maxwell always end up with these terrible scenes."

Mornings

That kiss—the one she'd seen so long ago, between Harper and the woman, whoever she was—came back to her in the mornings, in the hour after her husband left for the bank and before she rose for her own day. Her thoughts circled back to a specific moment of the kiss, the moment when Harper's lips slid off the woman's lips. The fullness of his lips in that moment, their romantic sag, before they edged back to the woman's skin.

And then her thoughts stopped. She didn't want to think of Harper that way, though she did want to think of that moment, that kiss, and what it would be like to have that kiss for herself. Her love life, she was coming to understand, was all in her head. It had nothing to do with her body. There were lots of things she was going to think and never do. That was what it meant to be grown up, to not suppose thoughts were possibilities.

The Knoll in the Woods

A simple set. A fallen log out in the middle of a clearing where two lovers meet. The Ersthauser brother who owned this particular theatre was married, and he'd never strayed from his wife. He didn't want to, and yet he was aware that all the stories that interested him were of clandestine romance. What story was there to tell, in the end, except the story of forbidden love? And where did that leave him, with his own relative pleasure in his entirely sanctioned marriage?

A Print a Day

For the past two years, Sherson had been so busy, he put out a print a day. And he didn't see any sign of business slowing. A few days after the break-in, one of the artists in his stable, a John Braham, had come in with drawings for *The Pirate King*. But they were no good. First, "the virtuous heroine" didn't look like Mrs. Cooke, the actress who portrayed her on stage. She looked more like a certain woman, popular at one of the men's clubs, till she died of syphilis. Sherson said as much to Braham.

"What do you mean?" Braham said tightly.

"She looks like a whore."

"I got *that*," said Braham. "Why do you say that? There's nothing here," he gestured to the engraved plate, "to give you that impression."

"Well, it's the impression I have. So . . . do it again."

A man who was going about town, interviewing toy-makers for a little history he was putting together, came in later that day to talk to Sherson.

"It's not a business to make friends in," Sherson admitted. "I've learnt that. You have to be tough. I have to be tough. Tough as old meat." New artists would sometimes appeal to him for work, and he'd take their portfolios and never look at them. He didn't mean to be hard-hearted, he said, but there were only so many hours in a day. "I'm doing a print a day now, and you know," he said. "I'm one of the very first to make the prints for the miniature theatre. Before me, it was the lottery cards. No artistic value in that at all. Yes, I'm one of the very first ones."

"He was one of the first producers of theatrical prints. He seemed," the interviewer wrote in his history, "very proud of the fact, for he repeated it, a number of times."

The Park

A naval scene. Rigged up so that at just the right moment, the park's water fountain could be directed through a series of hoses to produce a tremendous storm and wash the ship right off the stage.

The Theatrical Warehouse

A tall man with the thin, awkward movements of an albino flamingo came into the shop. "What can I do for you?" Sherson asked.

"Just looking," the man said, and his eyes flitted over the theatres quickly, and then glanced up to the shelves with the playbooks.

"Something for your little boy?" Sherson suggested.

"Yes, no, no, I don't have a son," the man said.

"A daughter, then?"

"Well, no . . . do you just sell the theatres here, then?"

Sherson hesitated. Since the break-in, Sherson didn't know whom he could trust. But then this man seemed so nervous. "Someone from the club sent you?"

The man waggled his head. Sherson said, "I think I know what you want." And he reached under his front counter for a small pack of cards that had, of late, been particularly popular.

The Landlord's Wife

Her husband was more irritating when Harper didn't come to visit. His lacks all the more painful. If she said, "Oh, I'm so tired," he'd say, "I know, honey. I know," in the very same absentminded manner he might have told a secretary at the bank to go away, he was busy just now. "I know, honey. I know." And she'd want to hit him. Conversation was like this with her husband. She'd say something, and he'd say something back, and then there'd be nothing to say. He had a way of stopping all conversation and inquiry cold.

But he was a good man. Moral. Handsome. Well-liked for his amicable manner at the bank and the club. He'd been kind and playful with their boys, when they were little. They both had liked to chase him around the couch. Back then, the older boy had a way of putting his hand up in the air, almost as if he were a pirate saying, "Oh ho," and this was the signal for the landlord to drop to his knees and crawl around the couch. Cooking dinner, the landlord's wife would hear her boys laughing and laughing on the far side of the room, and even though she knew about life, had grown to adulthood herself, she wondered what it was *exactly* that would steal this pleasure from her boys in the years to come.

The Youngest Ersthauser's Youngest Son

The youngest Ersthauser commandeered his youngest son's theatre for the contest. But they worked together on the set. For a long time, they were stuck for an idea. Père Ersthauser thought of times when he'd gone to the theatre, and the curtain rose, and he'd been instantly disappointed by the set, the suggestion about the story to follow. A military camp on the outskirts of Bohemia. He didn't want to see a story set there. A cramped household interior, poorly furnished. Ditto on that tale. Finally, his son decided what the set should be. A whale's belly. He'd just read Jonah. "Maybe," the father suggested, "we could do the ship, the one that Jonah's thrown off of?" But his son wouldn't hear of it. He wanted a belly—a floor full of half-digested octopi and sharks. Red walls and just beyond the walls, the constant, anxiety-provoking *lub-dub, lub-dub* of the whale's heart.

Work

He had one of the landlord's sons run over to the theatre and say he was sick, so he didn't go in, that first day of his job as a dresser. He *was* sick, in a manner of speaking. The landlord's wife came up with a bowl of soup. "Can I get you anything?"

He shook his head no. He knew he should be embarrassed. His room was a mess, plates piled high on the dresser and the room's one table. He'd cut himself while doing an engraving last night, and there was a smear of blood on his sheet.

The landlord's wife flinched when she noticed it, as if it were something dirty from a woman.

"It's nothing," he said. "I'll clean it."

She seemed on the verge of speaking, but then she didn't say anything.

"So you've found work," she finally announced cheerily.

"It's not work. It's not really work."

"Well, it'll bring in some money. That's good, isn't it?"

"Oh, you'll get your rent, all right."

She looked hurt. "I wasn't thinking of that. I didn't mean that."

It was his turn to look hurt. She meant well. He knew she did, but he wished she'd just leave him be.

The Sociable Brother

A large, tall hall with two stories of long windows, opening up to balconies on the second floor, private gardens on the first floor. Stage left, a drive leading up to the hall's entrance, and stepping out of the carriages, finely dressed men and women. Inside, a large ball. Dozens of people in attendance. But not "ordinary" people. They are all poets or musicians or artists. Stage actors and actresses. And when they come into the hall, they don't come to dance or eat or drink, as much as to see what they can make with their talk. Out of their conversations come ideas for symphonies, frescoes, and epic poems. One character looks a bit like Giotto, another like Homer, but these are men and women of the present day, all right. A well-known author arrives. Accompanying him: the characters of his novels, so authentic that one bleeds real blood from a tiny cut on his hand, something he got—he tells guests who ask—from an engraving tool. He and his companions seem unaware of the crowd's surprise to see them, moving about the hall, like living people. They seem entirely insensible to the sharp divide between fact and fiction, the line between this world and that.

There was a boy, a son of one of the cousins of the Ersthauser brothers, who had been visiting Solisturn for the winter. Each morning, he'd gone with his relatives to visit the theatres. He'd seen nine in all and had heard townspeople talk about a prize for the best theatre set. As far as he could tell, the prize was going to be a blue ribbon, which didn't seem like much of a prize. He had his own favorite. The smugglers. So now that he'd seen the theatres, he wondered, out loud, when the puppet shows were going to start. The adults laughed. Someone patted his head and reminded the others that he was from far away.

No one, it turned out, had any intention of beginning. There were no puppet shows to come; the lives the sets suggested were far richer than the stories any one of the villagers could imagine.

Dinner Conversation

It was the first time he'd spoken to her sharply. But not the last. She came up to invite him down to dinner.

"No thanks."

"Oh, come on. It'll do you good. And we haven't had a chance to talk in so long."

"All right," he said.

She went down to finish cooking the meal. He came some fifteen minutes later, but he didn't speak.

"You all right?" her husband said.

He nodded. "Just tired," he said.

"Because you're in the house all day. You need to get out of the house," the landlord's wife said. "We should all go for a walk after dinner."

"How do you know what I need?" Harper said.

Her husband was silent, but he must have been shocked, because she felt his palm under the table, the reassuring squeeze he gave her skirt—his hand not quite pressing hard enough to reach her leg.

The Reclusive Ersthauser

The reclusive Ersthauser made his own set, for he had heard about the competition, though he didn't invite anyone to see his creation. He was reclusive for a reason. He had dark, untenable desires, and his set was of a London men's club, a place that seemed respectable, with its leather chairs and formal waiters distributing sandwiches on silver platters. But there were back rooms at this club, where bad business went on. There were women for sale by the hour, and, once in a while, there would be pictures of men with men. The reclusive Ersthauser's set was strange, as if seen not from the audience's point of view, but from the side of the stage, as if a stage manager or dresser was viewing everything. Looking into the theatre, one saw the sides of chairs and tables. One saw the backdrops, which were so richly painted on one side, and so completely blank on the other.

The Landlord's Wife

She had dark desires of her own. She was only coming to realize it. Sometimes she thought she'd do something dramatic: walk into the woods and lie down and go to sleep and never get up. She didn't go to the theatre often, but when she did, the romances angered her, making her aspire, as they did, to things it were best not to aspire to. Not because these things were unattainable, but because they were ridiculous. It was lowly to believe in melodramas, yet she did, even while she didn't.

And, of course, she had a real sense that the theatre had stolen Harper from her, finally stolen him away, her good friend Harper, now so lost to his own disappointment, the landlord's wife didn't think he'd ever come back. But it wasn't the theatre, of course.

You couldn't be ruined by what you loved, only by what kept you from what you loved. It was Sherson. When she really thought about it, it was Sherson who had ruined her friend.

New York

The hidden theatre, with its futuristic set of New York City in the twenty-first century, is in America. Its curtain depicts the façade of an art gallery. Three stone slabs lead up to the gallery's door. When the curtain is raised, one sees a brightly lit interior space. On tables and walls throughout the gallery, there are toy theatres. In one, the stage's floor tilts toward the audience, so that were the set's furniture not glued to the floor, it would surely slide into the orchestra pit. In another, multiple flights of stairs lead to walls without doors. On each flight of stairs, a single running woman, her long hair a stiff banner beside her head, stares at something terrifying from which she flees. Only there is never anything behind these women. In other theatres in the gallery, there are jungle scenes or beautiful summer gardens or crowded restaurants. And many theatres show interior scenes of people sitting at desks in front of glowing boxes that contain pictures. Cords join these boxes to the walls, and there are numbers everywhere.

High on the gallery wall is a frieze of quotes, a single line of words that rings the room. The characters in the hidden theatre tire of holding their heads bent back at such a ferocious angle to read what's above them:

> "These childish toys are more to us than they can ever be to children. We never know how much of our imaginations began with such a peep show into paradise."
> —G. K. Chesterton

"I know of nothing to compare with it save now and then in dreams, when I am privileged to read in certain unwrit stories of adventure, from which I awake to find the world all vanity."

—Robert Louis Stevenson

"It is not for the theatre—not even the toy theatre—to curl the lip at rogues, for has it not always bred them, and perhaps necessarily so?"

—www.pollocks.cwc.net

There is a largely incomplete playbook that comes with this particular theatre. The opening page of the playbook features a short bit of dialogue. A child says his favorite thing about the gallery is the cheese. The artists in the gallery talk excitedly about the revived art of the toy theatre. But what happens next, when everyone (or at least all the artists' friends) has come to see the toy theatres, the playbook doesn't say.

The Landlord's Wife

Each month, the landlord's family had to do without the money from Harper's rent, so finally the landlord's wife took a job at a nearby guesthouse, helping with the meals and making up rooms. The guesthouse sheets were well starched and ironed, and it gave the landlord's wife a real pleasure to smooth such nice linens over mattresses. One morning, while she was pulling up a quilt, one of the girls gave her a nasty piece of news about the club, about the goings-on there.

"Is it true?" she asked her husband that night, and he said he had heard it was, though he never partook himself.

"In one of the back rooms, that's what I hear," he said.

She frowned. "So why do you go there?"

"I know," he nodded. "It's a despicable place, but I'm supposed to go. For the bank. Put on a good show and all."

He was well liked at the bank, but it was a middling sort of position he held, without any real power. It didn't pay enough, which was why they'd always needed the rent from the upstairs room.

"I'll tell you something else about that place," her husband said. "Sherson, you know the one Harper used to work for, he sends around some things for the men to look at. Dirty things. He does a whole secret trade in that, out of that same store where he sells the theatres. That's why I never wanted our boys to go into his shop. Must be a filthy old fellow, to sell that stuff out of a shop for children."

Unlike her husband, the landlord's wife didn't have a head for numbers or dates. She never remembered birthdays, and she needed to look at her wedding invitation to recall exactly how many years she'd been married. She had even, on occasion, forgotten how old she was, but, for some reason, she remembered the date of this conversation with her husband. It was the first of December, 1862, and she was thinking, as they talked, that this year, her sons would finally be altogether too old to be given toys on Christmas. And yet, much later that night, having pried open a window at Sherson's shop and hoisted herself up through the window and into the Theatrical Print Warehouse, she had stopped, candle (now lit) in hand. In the corner, there was a strange theatre—not really a theatre at all, but a stage set complete with dolls and dollhouse furniture. A section of the stage floor had been cut away to reveal a basement scene with dark figures. She brought the candle closer to make out the scene, then jumped. Something was in the theatre. She looked again. But it was only her eyelid, blinking closed. There was a mirror on the floor of the basement scene. All the dolls down there, under the stage floor, had been painted red. So it was hell. The mirror a joke, she supposed. She took note of the implied reprimand and then thought of Harper and of how Sherson had hurt him and of her own poor boys who really were men now. She placed the candle by the theatre and did what she'd come to do.

CONSERVATION

"It's him," Dana said from her spot at the window, and Tom rose to join her.

Jerome was not the person Dana remembered: clean-shaven and suited, blond hair cut to within a quarter inch of his skull, skin the pink-yellow of raw chicken. Now, in jeans and T-shirt, sparse hair cinched into a scraggly ponytail, mustache drooping over his mouth, he looked like some backwoods math professor, a man who'd traded equations for dope.

"God," Tom whispered. "That's *him*?" A question for Dana, though she'd only met Jerome once, back when she and Tom were first dating.

"Well, *you're* the one who would know." Tom saw Jerome only a week ago. How much could he have changed since then?

"Get the door," Tom instructed.

"No, you. He's your friend."

Four years ago, Jerome was a rising star at the network where Tom was a news producer. Then he dropped out, joined an ashram or something. He flipped. That's what Tom said. At the time, Tom took his departure personally. After all, he had brought the young man aboard and championed his ideas, which were invariably just cockeyed enough to work. He argued for Jerome's quick promotion out of booking into news, a trajectory (had Jerome continued on it) that would have resembled Tom's own rise to the top of the network. "The guy's brilliant," Tom used to say. "A real maverick." And he wasn't one to compliment. If you said someone had hidden talents, Tom laughed. He liked his talents right out in the open, thank you.

And now here was Jerome, on a Sunday evening in early September, halfheartedly ambling up the path to Tom and Dana's place, as if this might or might not be a house he cared to call on. Stalks of collapsing daylilies lined the brick walkway, and the windows by the front door featured construction-paper frogs that Benjamin, their elder child, had made at school.

Dana was in the stairwell at the station, that one other time she met Jerome, Tom having stopped Jerome (in mid-descent to the newsroom) while he was in mid-ascent (to the tape library). This must have been back in Tom's early flush of enthusiasm about Dana, just after the unemployed macrobiotic whom no one liked. What a thrill to be with someone who had her own professional aspirations. "Jerome," Tom said, "this is *Dana*," the stories Tom told about Dana implied in the way he inflected her name. And Jerome did what? Nodded, hurried on? Whatever it was, Dana felt embarrassed, though (as Tom insisted, or must have insisted, later) it was Jerome, not she, who should have felt odd. He shouldn't have been so impolite.

"Jerome!" Tom cried now at the door, raising his arms for an embrace.

Jerome extended his arm for a handshake, and Tom ignored

the formality, stepping back to say, "Well, come in, come in." In sweatshirt and jeans, Tom had the avuncular manner of an old sports hero, welcoming the renegade teammate back into the fold. Dana tried to do the math on Jerome's age. If he came to the station not long after college, and stayed five years, and left for four . . . . Well, never mind. He was clearly out of his twenties, but perhaps because of his slack posture, or the way he dug two fingers into his T-shirt pocket for something (cigarettes?) that wasn't there, or the slide of his pants off his non-existent hips, he had the aspect of a younger man.

"Let's sit, and I'll get you something. Can I get you something? Like some tea? We've got mate tea."

After all this time, Tom had discovered Jerome working in the kitchen at The Lotus Seed, a health food store with a four-table café and a constant, inexpensive buffet of baked tofu, steamed kale, brown rice, and the like. Both men had conditions—arthritis and asthma in the case of Tom, severe eczema in the case of Jerome—that they were trying to regulate through diet. They avoided alcohol and foods that made them mucousy. They knew the benefits of bromelain, boron, and acidophilus.

"OK," Jerome said to the offer of tea, and Tom disappeared into the kitchen. From upstairs came the sound of the kids, bumping down a slide they had formed out of old sofa cushions.

"So, you're The Wife," Jerome said, joining her on the couch.

"That I am," Dana admitted. Perhaps he didn't remember that they had met once before?

"And you do something. . . ." This wasn't quite as rude as it sounded. He was trying to remember.

"I do do something. Sometimes I do."

Jerome grinned. "Sorry."

"I'm a conservator."

Jerome placed his hand behind his right ear and pushed his earlobe forward.

"Conservator," Dana repeated.

"An artist?"

"Sort of halfway between artist and scientist. I patch up old pictures."

Jerome nodded his head while rocking it side to side, as if he found this funny.

Tom came back with mugs.

"Thank you." Jerome took his tea with both hands and then held it to his chest as if the mug were a little furnace.

"Well." Dana stood. "You two must have a lot of catching up to do."

Jerome raised his eyes, bemused. "Whose pictures do you patch up?"

"Well, at the moment nobody's. The chemicals were making me sick, so I've had to take a break. But I do have a job, if that's what you're asking. I work part-time at the Museum of the Astonishing Mind."

"The what?"

"It's a . . ." There was never a quick way to explain the Museum. "It's a workshop for outsider artists. Generally people who are developmentally disabled or in some way mentally ill. I help the artists. And we have a gallery out front."

Jerome reached into the neck of his shirt to scratch his back. She sensed that he didn't want her around. Which didn't surprise her. There was a charge that bordered on the sexual between Tom and the people he employed. They wanted his attention; they wanted their stories on air. The brief exchange about her employment was a digression in the business of the evening, which was . . . well, who knew? It wasn't about a story.

"So maybe I'll stop by sometime," Jerome called, as Dana was leaving. She smiled vaguely. Both her father and her husband were important men within their fields, and Dana had long ago made peace with the attention they received, the way it nudged her just out of most people's consideration. If people paid attention to her, it was normally to get at the men in her life. "Yes, I'll definitely come for a visit. I'll make a day of it. First, your place. Then . . ." He made a woop-de-doo loop with his forefinger. "The Institute of the Incredible Kneecap!"

"I'm sorry?" Dana said.

"Or maybe the Ankle Atelier. Or the Great Groin Gallery. I've always meant to go there."

"Was it good to see him?" Dana asked, when Tom finally came to bed.

"I guess. He's funny, isn't he?"

"I thought he was rude."

"Nah. He just doesn't see things as other people do."

And yet he saw Dana as a housewife, amusing herself with a part-time job while the kids were at school. That was clear enough.

"He hasn't been in touch with anyone else over at the station. Doesn't want to. 'Greasy socialists,' he said." Tom's own voice twisted into the slight mocking tone she already recognized as Jerome's. "Why—he kept asking me—should he go back?"

"So?"

"So what?" Tom said, a touch of irritation in his voice. He didn't like to chat once he was in bed for the night. He liked to sleep.

"So, how was it? Did you learn anything more about what happened to him?"

"No, why should I?"

For a man in his job, Tom was strikingly uncurious. Dana wondered if his colleagues ever hated him for this, the way he dismissed a line of thought by refusing to pursue it.

"Never mind."

"Don't get angry."

"Well, I *am* angry. It was just a question."

"It was just a question back."

Dana huffed. This could spiral out of control. Someone might drive off in a car in a few minutes.

"Oh," Tom said, conciliatory but also annoyed that he had to offer something else. "I forgot to tell you. When the kids came in . . ."

"I'm sorry. I tried to keep them away."

"No, it's OK." He began to laugh. "Jerome asked Sarah what she wanted to be when she grew up. And she said . . ." Tom waited a beat. "'A giraffe.'"

Her marriage, Dana sometimes felt, was an argument about the relative merits of what you did in the world versus how you lived in the world. On the side of the former were Tom's unfailingly interesting colleagues, men (and sometimes women) who'd invariably just returned from Baghdad or Sarajevo. On the side of the latter was Dana's perfect pleasure in her kitchen, where she was now making lentil soup. The kids were down the street at a birthday party, the afternoon light cut through the room, the trash can formed its long, regal shadow, and Dana remembered how, as a girl, she'd study dust motes in a light beam and think she was finally getting a handle on how everything in the world really was, all that was really *there*, if she'd just still herself and *look*.

The doorbell—comically loud—jolted her back into the

world. For a time whenever it rang, the kids staggered backward and then collapsed on the floor. "These sound waves," Benjamin explained, after his first pratfall, "are really rough."

"Oh, hello." Dana's voice wavered. Such a surprise to find Jerome at the door. She'd assumed it would be a neighbor kid, selling magazine subscriptions.

"Just thought I'd come for a visit."

"Oh." She couldn't remember the last time someone stopped by unannounced. "Tom's gone, I'm afraid. In Canada, on a story, that CEO of Graphic Maps, you know, the pedophile." The story was in all the papers.

Jerome peered behind her. Did he think Tom was back there?

"Not that you aren't welcome to come in." She stepped back, making way for Jerome.

"Actually—" Jerome palmed the back of his head, the very caress Dana gave her kids before they went to sleep. He squinted. "I wasn't looking for him. I was looking for you."

"You were?"

"Want to go swimming?"

"Swimming?"

"Tom says you love to swim."

"I do." Under what circumstances might Tom have revealed this? It seemed too minor for even desultory conversation: My wife likes artichokes. My wife swims laps at the Y.

"So . . . there's this spot I found. On the Gunpowder. If you want to."

She knew the Gunpowder, a river north of her home, had hiked there once.

"Well, I've got to get the kids at four."

Anyone else would have heard this as a no, but Jerome looked at his watch and said, "Great. That gives us plenty of time."

*　　*　　*

He drove. An ancient Ford Fiesta, so rusty that the passenger-side floor offered a dime-size view of the road, tar lightening into gray and eventually the dusty tan of a dirt road. The strangeness of the outing lifted with the beauty of the day—warm, but not oppressive, a light breeze, pumpkins dotting fields as they turned off the highway. The season would end, but here it was: one last chance for a summer pleasure.

"So." She turned to face Jerome fully. He was bleeding just behind his right ear, the skin there chapped and angry. "You have a twin, I heard." Tom mentioned this before Jerome's previous visit.

"Yes. That I do."

"Do you look alike? I know twins don't like that question."

"Hmmm?"

"Do you look alike? You and your twin?"

"I wouldn't know. I haven't seen him in years."

His manner warned Dana off asking how come. Her shorts felt tight over her bathing suit bottom. She did not really want to stand in the equivalent of underwear before Jerome. She might have weighed this disinclination a bit more, before she agreed to come. The dirt road grew rocky, but Jerome didn't slow for the change in terrain. "Can I ask about the time you were away; what you were doing?"

"I don't see why not."

It would be matronly, of course, to suggest he slow down.

"So . . ." Dana said leadingly.

"Let's see. For a while, I traveled in the South Pacific. Later, I was a Buddhist monk."

"Really?"

"Well, I wanted to be a nun, but they wouldn't let me."

Dana laughed.

"And I went to Switzerland after that."

"Why Switzerland?"

Jerome smiled, as if grateful for a question he was willing to answer. "I heard about a choir that sang in a Romansh church there. Boys' voices. The beauty, people said, was beyond compare. I didn't know what such a thing would sound like—beauty beyond compare. Not something you usually trouble yourself with in the news business; there's all that tragedy and scandal to get to first. So I went to hear it. Only I went in the wrong season. The concerts were given in the summer, but I stayed, because I met a shepherd who needed help with his flock." After a moment, he added, "I learned how to make cheese and then I came back here, because I'd left without finishing something."

"What was that?"

"I don't know."

This was a little Zen koan for Dana, or so she supposed. It didn't make her curious. It irritated her. As koans did. There was something smarmy and self-righteous about the impossible puzzle, though what she knew of Buddhism otherwise attracted her. She'd like to practice a little non-attachment right now and not feel so bothered by the conversation. Jerome and she were having a silent tug-of-war, though about what she couldn't say.

Jerome turned the car into a narrow road, a tunnel of trees ending in a small clearing. There was no beach but a dirt path that cut between the foliage and then led steeply through shrubs and down to the river.

"I'm not going back to the network. I do know that. I'm not interested in that sort of probing anymore. And no more news.

I don't read papers anymore. No TV." He laughed. "After all those years of being so plugged in, it's a relief, I tell you."

This confession thawed something in him. Or maybe it was stepping out of the car, pulling off his T-shirt for the heat of the sun. She disrobed on her side of the car, he on his, emerging in yellow swim trunks to say, "This way." He started toward the path. Dana took some comfort in the slight cushion of flesh at his abdomen. Some evidence of... what? Excessive desire? Occasional laxness?

"And you?" he said. "Tell me about this astonishing conservation work."

"Oh." She waved her hand at his back as if to dismiss the topic. The truth was, now that Benjamin was five, and Sarah was four, she might not return to work. She had never truly been certain that her reaction to the chemicals in her lab—it had started with lacquer thinner and turpentine—wasn't a sign. She was altogether too consumed with the business of knowing and being known in the art world. (When she first got sick, she still commuted to her job at the National Gallery. If she worked in Baltimore, people would forget her, or, worse, confuse her for a mere restorer. At the time, such things mattered to Dana.) "It all turned out to be a little more bureaucratic than I bargained for, though once I got to do a Renoir, which was how I met Tom."

"Is that so?" He turned, cocked his head in the "do tell" posture of a girlfriend.

"He came in to produce a story on the restoration. I was telling the reporter—Harry Terry, do you know him?"

Jerome climbed up on a rock that bordered the river and said, "Don't think so."

"Well, I was telling Harry about how you're supposed to match the technique of an era, when a cameraman interrupted.

'Ask her if she'd piss on an Andy Warhol. If she had to.' Harry rolled his eyes. 'Andy Warhol's piss paintings. It's a legitimate question,' the cameraman kept saying. Finally, Harry turned off his microphone.

"'Sorry,' he said to me, then handed the microphone to Tom and said, 'You fire that guy, or I'm quitting.'"

"And?"

"Tom fired the guy. On the spot." He was courageous, in his way, had that cowboy-reporter thing that always attracted and intimidated Dana. You got the virtue—if it was a virtue—if you married it. You didn't need to have it yourself.

Jerome dove into the river. "It's deep," he called out, when he emerged, shaking water off his face. "It doesn't look it, but it is."

Dana stepped gingerly in, waiting till the water reached her waist to dive under. The water was cool and clear, the river's muddy appearance just an effect of the riverbed. Something— maybe a trout?—slicked by Dana's leg, and she went under again, began to swim. She did love swimming, almost more than anything, and a river swimming hole was the best: the water's skin against one's own skin, the childlike pleasure of neutralizing sound by floating on one's back, the illusion that the water (because it moved) was fresh. And talk. There was no pressure to talk when you swam. "Oh, God," Jerome said as he dipped in and out of the river. "Oh, God." It made her think of some Chekhov she read in college, some story where men bathe in a pond together, and one old man can't stop saying, "Oh, God," as he splashes water over his face. Or something like that. Jerome looked like an emaciated walrus, water streaming down his hair (still in its ponytail; she wondered if he ever let it down) and through his mustache, over his now slick back. He glided over to Dana, put his finger to his lips, and whispered, "Look." Downriver, a stately blue heron stood motionless on the bank.

They pulled themselves from the water, some forty-five minutes later. Dana needed to get home for her children. "I came back to Baltimore," Jerome began, as if he now knew her well enough to answer the question she posed earlier. "Because I need to learn how to be around people. I kind of forgot how."

"Hun."

Tom. They spoke every day, even when he was on assignment. She could picture him running his hand over his high forehead, as if still surprised by the retreat of hair from his face.

"I fell asleep." She could smell the river on her skin, her pillow slightly damp from her hair. "God, it's only eight."

"How are the kids?"

"Fine. Fine. Asleep." She felt groggy and distracted. "They went to Leif's birthday party, came home exhausted."

"Glad you got a break."

"I made soup." Her voice was tight.

Why did Tom always assume she vacationed during her non-parenting time? And yet, hadn't she? Today, at least? She didn't want to tell him about her outing, as if this would contradict a message she never could convey: when *he* was parenting, she was paying bills, cooking, folding laundry, buying food.

"Right. Well, I'll let you go back to sleep. I'll try to get you in the morning. OK?"

"OK."

At work the next week, Dana was helping Susan McFlarrety choose colors for a sixteen-foot-long scarf, when she looked up and saw Jerome, standing next to the loom. Susan—a squat woman, given to butting her head against walls—followed Dana's gaze and then turned to Jerome and cried, "I made this!" She held up the scarf, which promptly unrolled, like a medieval scroll, to the floor. Susan protested when workers at the museum encouraged her to make items of a more practical length. Jerome lifted the scarf's corner, carefully considered the weave without offering the cheerful, high-pitched praise of most visitors to the museum.

One-armed Kylie approached Jerome and said in her slurred voice, "What's your name?"

"Jerome," Jerome said gamely.

"Jerome." Kylie rested her head on the pillow of his chest. "I love you, Jerome."

"I love you, too," he said automatically, glancing at Dana, "but you understand this can't be an exclusive relationship, right?"

Kylie wandered back to her button collection. She'd spent the morning deciding and then redeciding which buttons she wanted to glue to the frame of an unfinished painting. "I'm too *tired* to paint," she had announced theatrically earlier in the day. And the staff let this disinclination to effort stand. At any one time, half of the twenty clients were merely drifting through the museum's six small rooms.

"I thought I'd come see you," Jerome said to Dana. "Maybe take you to lunch."

The workshops themselves—with their loony, life-size puppets staring out each window, their lopsided sculptures decorating the minute front lawn—occupied a corner house near a dilapidated shopping district. Nearby, the only place to eat was Jenny's Pub, a dark grotto, even at midday, serving things like nachos and potato skins. Jerome—committed to sobriety, denizen of the tofu ether—probably never went into restaurants like this.

"What can I get for you?" a waitress said enthusiastically.

"I'll have some tea," Jerome said.

"A bowl of minestrone soup."

"Did you see the specials? We've got shrimp poppers for $6.95 today."

"I think we're set," Dana said.

"And there's a chocolate mud pie dessert. You won't want to miss that."

"Like I said."

Dana turned from the waitress to Jerome. "Well, this is a treat. Getting to go out and all." He waited. He seemed eager, as if ready for Dana to be quite interesting, the evidence of her conversation so far notwithstanding. She should hazard something about the artists with whom she worked, the curlicue track of their minds, the images they obsessively repeated. "My husband," she began instead, not sure of how she planned to finish her own sentence. "He . . . He thinks quite a lot of you."

"I suppose I've always wondered what he thought of me."

"He thinks you're brilliant."

Jerome laughed dismissively.

"And now the brilliant man encounters a shrimp popper." She meant this as some frank reference to herself—you got political analysis and a thorough comprehension of world history from Jerome; from Dana, you got a restaurant that offered shrimp poppers. But she saw instantly that it must have sounded like she was asking him to contradict her with praise.

"In fact," he said slowly, hand rising to the back of his neck, his stare overly direct, "I had some popping in mind."

She flushed. What was *that* supposed to mean? Something crude?

Dana hadn't liked being single, back when she still lived in upstate New York, or in her first years in Baltimore, and she hadn't quite lost the desire to be pleasing to men. She'd developed a mildly flirtatious manner in her twenties and thirties, and she fell back into it, even now that she was married and had two kids, and found the whole spectacle of her flirtation humiliating. There was a slight pause while she processed Jerome's words; then she answered with a campy, mock enthusiastic, "Well, *that's* what we like to hear."

And so began Dana's crush. Which went as crushes do, harmlessly at first, with Dana enjoying her brief encounters with Jerome at The Lotus Seed, her awareness that she dressed more nicely when she went shopping there. And, too, with her trying to gauge his interest. Was it an accident that he visited when Tom was out of town? That hand that brushed hers as he rang up her Lotus Seed purchases? Just a hand, or something else? It was all very high school and dumb, and she could hold her thoughts and the silliness of those thoughts together in her head without much agitation. But then, something . . . didn't quite change, but her internal narrative heated up. She imagined Jerome kissing her, the slight sag of their bodies into one another, the relief of the kiss, the kiss as confession. Jerome pulling her into a bed, the specific hotel where she would meet him, and the ruse that would get her there, the train of the life she wanted chugging alongside the train of the life she should live.

All of it fantasy. She was as loyal as a rock. Put her somewhere and, barring an avalanche, she stayed.

At night, there was the possibility of switching this longing to Tom, of reversing their current sexual dry spell. "It's not that I'm not interested," Tom said, once home. The kids were asleep, but as Dana began to kiss Tom's neck, he pushed her away. He needed to unwind. He wanted a beer and to watch part of the ball game. Dana couldn't blame him. There had to be a small part of the day when you weren't answering another person's demands. She'd had her own stretch, after the kids were born, of being too tired for sex. And it wasn't like she had lots of energy now. By the time Tom came to bed, Dana was invariably asleep.

The bells of The Lotus Seed's wooden door clanged behind Dana. She grabbed a basket and looked around. No Jerome stocking produce at the front of the store, no Jerome at the cash register, no Jerome stirring a pot of something behind the back counter.

She shopped anyway. She liked this place so much better than the supermarket, the small comfort of the vegetables' claim to be organic, the musty yeast smell, the row of "healthy" cookies. It didn't really bother her that it cost more.

A door at the back of the store banged open and shut. Jerome coming from some basement storeroom. "Hey," he called, "I've just been thinking of you." This admission gave her the requisite thrill. "Can you sit?" He pointed to the café tables, empty now that it was 3:30.

"A little bit. I've got to get the kids at 4:00."

"Mind if I take a break?" Jerome turned to ask a tall, skinny white girl with Rasta hair and a pierced nose and lip.

"No problemo," the girl said leeringly, giving Dana an appraising glance.

"So," Jerome began, as he sat, "I was just over at the Baltimore Museum of Art looking at paintings and thinking how much I'd have liked to have you with me, explaining things. I was looking at all that Dutch stuff, those still lifes."

"Oh, yeah, they're meant as moral directives. Like fruit, youth is luscious. It too will rot. All things must pass. All that vanitas stuff."

"Thus the skulls next to the grapes. Yes, I think I got that."

Dana felt vaguely deflated. She'd never have guessed how the still lives were meant to be read if she hadn't been told, back in college. "And contemporaries would have gotten all that symbolism, too."

"Unlike us. We're left to trod through the muck in our fluffy slippers."

"That's us, all right."

"Well, listen. I stepped up to one of the paintings, close, when the guard wasn't looking. There was something reflected in the shine of the apple, a window from behind the viewer, or something. I couldn't quite tell. So I stepped up and touched it." Jerome tapped the air with his finger to illustrate.

Dana jumped at this, as if it were she, and not the painting, he had touched. "You shouldn't. . . ."

Jerome gave her a wry look.

"Well, you *shouldn't*. There are oils in your finger that can really damage—"

"Thanks, Mommy," he said, snide, and Dana felt what she never felt as a mommy—a desire to hit him. "The thing is," he added, hunching forward, "a bit of the paint came off on my finger." He looked down at the pad of his forefinger as if at paint still there.

"It's flaking."

"That's it! That's what I wanted to ask you. What do you call that, if the paint comes away. I left a note in the museum's comment box that said the painting was chipping, but I knew that wasn't what I meant. So how do you fix that? Could *you* fix that if you tried?"

"It *used* to be that you removed the painting from the stretcher and put it on a new canvas. But if the damage isn't that extensive, you use adhesive to prevent the painting from flaking more."

"Makes sense. You want to figure out how it can stay together, before you imagine some deception."

"And certain people don't paint the flaking parts. They leave them blank and just try to stabilize what's there." Dana looked at her watch. "Gotta go."

They stood for a farewell, a hug and kiss on the cheek having become standard between them, as it was with most of Dana's friends, but then she bent her head and briefly brushed his shoulder with her lips. She hurried for the door, instantly ashamed. It wasn't really a kiss. Oh, how she hoped he wouldn't register the gesture, that he'd think (but, of course, this was a mother's thought) that she was merely wiping her nose. "I love you," Dana always said to Sarah, "but I am not a tissue."

It started stupidly, as their fights always did. Tom and Dana were driving to Philadelphia, a city Tom knew but that Dana had never visited. The occasion was the second wedding of Dana's old college roommate. Hennie—a friend from work—agreed to babysit, and she managed to act (bless Hennie) as if Tom and Dana were doing her a favor, giving her time with their wonderful children. Not that Dana was for arguing against her kids' virtues, but really.

"Well, she *is* lucky," Tom, said shortly after they drove off. "She'll never have any herself."

"She still might."

"Not likely."

But that wasn't what started the fight. What started it was a traffic jam. Dana dozed, and when she woke they were in the middle of it, backed up (from the looks of things) for miles. Tom cursed. There was a cocktail party that night. All of Dana's old friends. The wedding wasn't till lunch tomorrow.

"It's OK," Dana said. "If we miss it, we miss it. We'll still get there for the wedding."

"Just . . . fuck," Tom said, hitting the dashboard. "Fuck, fuck, fuck."

Dana's father had rages over traffic, and she and her sisters used to sit—very good and very cowed—in the backseat, as their mother said, "Your father needs some quiet now." The old bad daddy gets what he wants, no matter what. That was the lesson of Dana's childhood. The famous man rules.

"Your manner isn't moving the traffic." Dana struggled to keep her voice even. "It's just making it a drag for me to sit here. We could talk, or something. This could be an opportunity."

"*You're* the one who's been sleeping."

She was quiet, then said, "So what're you working on at the station?"

"This and that."

"Like what?"

"Well, we're going to do a report on that new drug-resistant staph infection. Maybe as part of the flu coverage. Three babies and a college student have already died of it."

"How horrible."

"It's not horrible. It's a good story."

"I mean the deaths, for Christ's sake. How horrible about the deaths. Losing a child to a stupid infection. I'd never get over it."

"You think I would?"

"No, no, never mind." This was impossible. She could not get engaged in a conversation with her own husband. All they ever managed to do was trade anecdotes about their kids' cute behavior. "I saw Jerome yesterday."

"Yeah?"

"I was getting some stuff at The Lotus Seed. He seems really interested in my conservation work."

"That guy is a lost cause."

"What, may I ask, makes him a lost cause?"

"I think that's obvious."

"That he doesn't work for you anymore?"

"No, no, he doesn't need to work for me, but he gave it up. He gave everything up to live like some college kid, clerking at a store and reading his philosophy books. He can't possibly be happy doing what he's doing."

Jerome might stop by, it occurred to Dana, while Tom and she were away, and he'd meet Hennie. Dana could picture him, arm above his head, propped against the door frame, his ready-to-talk posture, and Hennie saying something outrageous and then laughing her laugh, a beat too long and loud, a shade too antic, but appealing all the same, and Jerome leaning down, cupping her chin for a kiss.

"There's more than one way to live a life."

"Did I say there wasn't?"

"Yes, yes, you said there wasn't. You say it in everything you do. You . . ." She broke off, her voice choked with angry tears.

"What's gotten into you?"

"Oh, fuck off, would you? Just fuck, fuck off."

He was silent.

"The happy couple," she said, "off on their romantic weekend."

In the morning, before the wedding, a group of Dana's old college friends met at the Barnes. Dana had seen the prints that were finally released of the museum's collection, but the place itself was a surprise: a big Matisse painted high on the wall of the first gallery, an unfamiliar Seurat nearby, the strange order and symmetry of the paintings—if a picture of an apple graced an entrance to a room, a picture of a pear adorned the exit. House museums were Dana's favorite. She loved the Frick in New York and the Gardner in Boston. The artwork was almost irrelevant to the whole experience of the place, the daydream of Old World wealth and social customs into which the building invited you. *It must have been like this. And this. And this.*

Tom and Dana had gone to bed angry—no sex, of course—and been tensely polite on the drive to the museum. Once there, Tom stomped ten yards ahead of the others. Eventually, Dana lost sight of him altogether; he was moving so quickly through the galleries. In the end, she found him sitting on a bench by the exit.

Under these circumstances, a wedding ceremony would surely be excruciating—all that talk of respect and mutual affection—and it was. Twice, Dana left her lunch table to sniffle in the bathroom. She shouldn't have married Tom. She shouldn't have. She had not a thing in common with him. And yet, he was the bargain she'd made with herself. And why?

But the question was entirely disingenuous. She knew why. She wanted kids. "All those years," she joked to her friends back in Albany, "what I thought I wanted was a guy. What I really wanted was a four-year-old." Benjamin and Sarah's snuggly affection; it was worth everything.

"It's OK," Tom said when she came back to the table the second time. "It's OK. Whatever happened, let's just move on from that now." His voice was placating, somewhat wheedling, and she hated him afresh. He reached over and gave her hand a double squeeze; he had done the same before the justice of the peace when they married, the only secret part of the ceremony, and the gesture had become their code for love.

"I don't know what I'm doing with you."

Tears sprang to his eyes, and she felt equal parts shame and satisfaction in seeing she'd hurt him. "Dana," he whispered, but everyone at the lunch table was lost in conversation and wouldn't have heard anyway, "sometimes you really say terrible things."

"Any visitors?"

"Huh? This weekend? No. Were you expecting someone?" Hennie had plaited Sarah's hair into a row of neat braids, each ending in a handmade bead. That had been the project for the weekend: making and painting beads. Benjamin wore a necklace of them, which he refused to take off.

"No, I wasn't expecting anyone."

Tom came downstairs, Benjamin in his arms, wrapped in a towel. Tom was singing, "And then the water drains out of the bath. And then we go downstairs and find pajamas. O where O where O where are the pajamas? In the laundry room. Oh, in the laundry room." He stopped in the kitchen to say to the women: "Our Life. The Musical."

Tom's sweetness made her feel worse. They had apologized to each other on the drive home, said they felt sick—physically sick—and they did. They always did after their fights. For at least a week, they'd be careful with one another—and Dana would try to abandon the notion that one should be able to talk easily with one's spouse—but then they'd fight again. None of it would stop the affair—the affair in her head—from growing torrid. Jerome and she would have the ferocious, sweaty sex of her twenties, the pre-Tom sex. And why not? If you took a poll, wouldn't most people admit to surviving this way, through their imaginary lives?

She pictured herself asking Jerome this very question, saw him nod as if in agreement and then say, "Sure. Most people who are incarcerated."

"I finally found out what happened to Jerome," Tom said, the next night, as he undressed for bed. "His brother died. That's what happened four years ago. His twin killed himself. Because he thought he was a failure at business. Which, I guess, he was. But Larry"—Larry was one of the morning news anchors—"says that's why Jerome quit. He didn't want to end up like his brother."

"My God."

"And here's another thing. He found out from the TV. A local news broadcast. The brother killed himself out in the woods, and I guess at first police thought there might have been a crime. You know, police have revealed the identity of the man who . . ."

"Jesus. His brother?"

"His *twin* brother."

"Well, that'd fuck you up. God, that's so sad. What about the rest of the family?"

"What about them?"

"I don't know. Are his parents still around? Other siblings?"

"I just *told* you all Larry *told* me."

There was a potential for their weekend fight to flare up again—and around this tragic news. Why couldn't he just talk like a normal person? If he'd said, "I don't know. I wondered about that myself," Dana wouldn't have an urge to throw the novel in her hand across the room.

*　　*　　*

It was cold. Dana sat by the window of a fancy coffee bar. She was in a tony neighborhood, near the Walters and lined with townhouses, not far from where Jerome lived. She had called in sick yesterday, her first day back from the wedding. And then again today.

Tom and Dana had been in and out of endless Baltimore row houses, back when Dana was pregnant, and they were looking to buy. Dana didn't want to forsake the city for the Roland Park suburb that Tom favored, but then every place they visited—no matter how handsome on the outside—was a mess inside: full of lead paint, exposed pipes, and dangerous wiring. "You can put in a bathroom. You can redo the walls," the real estate agent would always sing, but they couldn't afford the property in its terrible condition, much less take out an extra loan. And Tom's job paid well.

A man passed by on the sidewalk outside, a thin blond, and her head darted up. The Lotus Seed opened at ten. She guessed she was hoping to see Jerome on his way to work. Though she hadn't pictured past this. What would she do? Rap on the window and smile. He'd smile back and continue on his way. One didn't skip work for such things.

She leafed through *The Baltimore Sun* but couldn't focus on a single article. The hour of The Lotus Seed's opening came and went. The day suddenly seemed without possibility, and the responsibilities left to her (supermarket for dinner, the evening with Benjamin and Sarah) felt onerous.

She cleared her coffee cup, pulled on her coat, and stepped outside. The official start of winter was a few days off, though the leaves had long since fallen and been carted away, and everything looked bare and gray, as if the entire city—even the trees—were made of the drab formstone one saw over by Fell's Point.

Dana wasn't ready for her car, so she headed aimlessly up a hill. She'd make a short circuit, her exercise for the day, before driving to the airless Rotunda supermarket. She passed Sawyer Road and Houghton and then saw Bridge Street. 14 Bridge Street. That was Jerome's address.

He wouldn't be there, of course. He didn't get off work till six, and yet she walked down the street anyway. His building was what she expected—a brownstone with four names written on tiny pieces of paper in four different hands and taped under the buzzers. Four mailboxes, too. She opened Jerome's. It was too early for a mail delivery, but there was an envelope inside. *Jamie*, it read, and inside was a key. And no note. She could feel that.

Jamie was who? A girlfriend, come to visit for the weekend? A friend? Why had she supposed he didn't have someone? And why should it matter to her? For all her thoughts, she'd no more cheat on her husband than grow an extra nose for sport. She put the envelope back in the mailbox and headed back down the steps.

The street was empty. She was unreasonably tired. Fear and fidelity could look like the same thing. She knew that. What if she started crying? She turned back for Jerome's building with the idea of going into the foyer to hide her imminent tears. Not that anyone was on the sidewalk. She paused at the row of mailboxes and then took the envelope from Jerome's box. She was precisely not the sort of person who would open it and go upstairs. Which was why she placed her finger under the lip of the envelope and began to tear.

*   *   *

Jerome's apartment—the high attic apartment, as she had always supposed—was a one-room affair, with an orange counter separating the living area and kitchen, with its fake wood cabinets, dirty stovetop, and sink full of dishes. If Jerome was expecting a girlfriend, he might have washed a few glasses. Tom—in the rooms he kept before they were married—always put a vase of flowers on the kitchen table, if she was coming to stay. Despite the dirty dishes, Jerome's place was tidy. Picked up at least, with few clues to the man's personality. (And what did Dana expect? A lot of yoga mats?) There was a plaid couch— apparently a sleeper, as there was no bed in the room—and a single round table with a computer. A trunk was pulled between two armchairs to make a coffee table. On it, there was an art book—paintings by Marsden Hartley. And more art books on the bookcase. *Persian Paintings*, Albert Pynkham Ryder, *Celestial Charts: Maps of the Heavens*. Also a box of white envelopes. She took one to reseal Jamie's key.

High in the walls, the room's windows let in the same diffuse, cold light that had been darkening Dana's spirits since daybreak. If only the day would wake up. She went into the bathroom, stopped to pee there—the dare of it almost preventing her. But Jerome surely wouldn't notice that his toilet paper roll was a few sheets shorter in the evening than in the morning. Two pairs of jeans, shaped as if an invisible man were still in them, hung behind the bathroom door, and Dana found their forms unaccountably poignant. Men. Their small inadequacies when they lived alone. Briefly, she imagined washing Jerome's dishes, scrubbing the top of the stove, and leaving him wondering at the thief who broke into his apartment only to clean it up.

Inside the medicine cabinet: scissors, a razor, a stack of hotel soaps, and condoms. But why *wouldn't* there be condoms? He wasn't *still* a Buddhist monk; he could have a sex life.

Coming out of the bathroom, she started. There, on a table next to the couch—it must function as a bed stand at night— was her father's book, *The Male Nude in Modern Art*. Her dad wrote it back when Dana was in high school. She and her sisters had called him Professor Dick, behind his back. "My dad," they joked to friends, "he's got a Ph.D. in penis." Not that they didn't know to value art, even then. Their dad had a reputation in the art world, and there were some family trips to Europe, financed by his university.

Now, though, if one of the book's naked men stepped off the page to greet Dana, she couldn't have been more startled. Was it an accident that Jerome found his way to Dana's father's book? It was no longer in print. For some reason, the cover didn't depict a male nude, but spiraling lines on a light blue background. It might have been a math book, save for its heft and shape. (Dana remembered the consternation over the cover, her father complaining, "You'd think it was a secret. Nobody's wearing anything underneath their clothes." Were the times that prudish, as recently as the seventies, that they wouldn't put a male nude on the cover of a book *about* the male nude? Or maybe her father went too far in the image he picked. It would have been like him to insist his selection was right, no matter how shocking.) And Jerome . . . could he know . . . but he must know that Simon Kruger was her father.

She shivered. Was the apartment even heated? She picked up her father's book, brought it to the trunk and stood it up, as if it were a volume at a bookstore. Her ears rattled with something like panic, blood hurrying its way through the tiniest of passages, and she headed for the door. Downstairs, she dropped the key—now snug in its new envelope (though with no *Jamie* scrawled on the front)—back into the mailbox and turned for her car.

The spark of Jerome's smile when she next entered the store, the eager way he waved her to his counter, the heat of his cheek when they kissed hello . . . none of it meant he knew where she'd been. Or that he cared for her. He saw her and held up a warning finger. His cell phone (she was surprised he owned such a thing) must have buzzed in his pocket, for suddenly it was at his ear. "Yes." He put a finger in the other ear to hear. "No, no. Let me call you back." There was such a long list of things they never spoke of: she didn't know anyone in his life, had no sense of who might call him in the middle of the day. Today, Jerome wore small wire-rimmed glasses, something she'd never seen him in before.

"Listen," she said, pushing her fingers through her hair. "I hope I'm not out of line here, but I heard about your brother, and I wanted to say how sorry I was."

"My brother? What about my brother?"

"Your twin brother and what happened to him, I mean."

"Oh. What happened to him?"

"I mean, you know, his death."

Jerome pulled his glasses halfway down his nose and looked over them. "My twin brother's not dead," he said, an air of something new in his manner, the door of his perfect attention slamming shut. "Unless you know something I don't know. Where'd you get that idea?"

On Saturday morning, perhaps to put salt in the wound of her own uncertain feelings, Dana told Tom that Jerome had visited while Tom was in Canada.

"Oh, yeah," Tom said tiredly, as if he knew all about it. They were sitting on the kitchen stools, coffee mugs in hand. In the neighboring room, the kids watched a video—"The People of Israel," a *Shalom Sesame* special. Tom and Dana didn't let the kids watch TV, but they fairly begged them to watch videos, knowing how much they might get done during the half an hour of a viewing.

"Do you ever get jealous of me?"

"No," Tom said reassuringly, missing her point entirely. "Of course not." Then: "I know about Jerome."

"You do?"

"Yeah, Jerome told Larry."

"He did?" A rushing feeling came over Dana, not unlike the watery emotion she felt (an acrophobe on the edge of a rooftop) when she propped her father's book on the trunk in Jerome's apartment.

"Yeah, I don't know how it is that Larry knows everything. At least, Jerome wasn't telling the truth when he said he wasn't going to be in touch with anyone at the station."

"Yeah," Dana said. They were silent. Tom's face was impenetrable. Whatever did he think about anything? Why didn't he just *react?* "So, what *did* he say?"

"Jerome?" Tom stood to fill his coffee cup. "Jerome said he made a pass at me."

Dana jerked her head back. "He . . ."

"Yeah, right. That's what I said to Larry. 'He what?' 'He made a pass at you,' Larry says. 'Wouldn't I . . . like . . . have to *be there?*

If he made a pass at me?' I say to Larry. 'Jerome didn't make any pass at me.' Larry just shrugs and tells me that's what Jerome said."

"And . . ."

"He never made a pass at me. For Christ's sake. A few weeks ago, he took my hand when I was telling him about how sick that stupid pedophilia story was making me. You know how it was the dumbest story, and I was pissed I had to produce the segment, but how it touched something in me in terms of my fears about the kids. Well, if someone said that to me, I wouldn't exactly be like, 'Hey, wanna go to bed?' But he did take my hand and say, 'That's gotta be hard,' and I said, 'It's OK. It's nothing. Don't worry about me.' And it's true, he dropped my hand, and said, 'Well, it's not like I'm making a pass at you or anything,' and of course, I said, 'Sure, yeah, I know that.'"

"Jerome's gay?"

"He's gay. I guess. That's what some people say. *He's* never said it. I don't know *what* he is."

Neither of them spoke for a moment, and then Dana began, "But he knew you . . . I mean he met me . . . ."

"Yeah, but plenty of gay guys are married. Remember that show we did on that? In fact, that was Jerome's pitch, way back when, that story. I think that's why I wanted him to meet you, when we were first dating. Maybe I thought something was up. That he wasn't just another guy trying to get attention for his stories."

Dana didn't know what to say.

"He's just a guy who likes to unsettle, who likes to play with what people do and don't know about him. I'm sure he has some Buddhist justification for it all, for playing with our idea of reality. I bet if you even knew for sure he was gay, he'd drop you as a friend. He seems to have some idea that he can't be known. He's too . . ." Tom searched for the word but didn't find it. "He's too 'something' to be known."

"Too brilliant?"

"Maybe so. And maybe I put him onto that idea about himself. I did think he was special. For a long time, I did." When she didn't respond, he said, "What's the matter?"

"Nothing."

"Really?"

"Yeah," she said, turning to face him fully, thinking he'd just spoken to her, that they'd just had a conversation, the way people do. He was forty-four years old. His father had been the headmaster of a private day school in Washington, D.C. He'd spent his entire childhood around privilege, but he'd joined the Peace Corps and gone to Yugoslavia, just before it fell apart. He'd been to Poland and Africa and the Middle East. He'd had coffee with Ariel Sharon and Bruce Springsteen. Bill Clinton and then George Bush waved hi when they saw him at news conferences. He never had a close female friend. He never wrote a love letter. He'd cried three times in his life, once at his father's death, once when he almost backed his car into a child, and once last week at the wedding, when she said that harsh thing to him.

He was defined in a way that she was not. He had what he wanted and was working with it. He had agreed to live his life, and Dana, on some level, hadn't; she still thought something needed to change. And why was that? The waning of her professional life? A poor choice of partner? A reluctance to grow up?

"The problem with relationships," Hennie once said, "is that we expect our partners to have all their own virtues and all our virtues, as well." How smart that seemed to Dana at the time, even though Hennie was dating a man whose name she wouldn't reveal. She just called him "The Dog Man," because he'd found her missing dog. That's how they met. Things were never good between Hennie and The Dog Man. But then Hennie added, entirely earnestly, "We really should do things on the kibbutz system: go to this one for sex, this one for conversation, this one for financial support."

"This one for Orioles tickets," Dana put in. The Dog Man sold beer at Camden Yards.

"Yes! Isn't it a great idea?" Hennie asked in her too bright way.

"Sure," Dana said and laughed, as if she had the emotional flexibility—and plain nerve—for such a thing, as if she understood how to step out of a marriage. And back in.

I SHOULD LET YOU GO

I

"Do you like it?"

"I guess," Ginny said.

"You don't like it," Cara said, not yet accusatory, as if she couldn't imagine that Ginny wouldn't like it, wouldn't find it (with all the expected changes in the apartment) charming in an eccentric way, more evidence of Cara's theatrical skills.

"Well, what is it?"

They were standing on the back porch of Ginny's—actually, now Cara and Ginny's—apartment on the top floor of a broken-down triple-decker in Cambridge, Massachusetts. Not "Harvard, Cambridge," Ginny was quick to point out. More like Somerville, Cambridge. Kind of a dump. Her street had actually scared her, when she first took the lease—a neighbor shrieking incomprehensible curses because of something, she never figured out what, she'd done wrong when she pulled her car up to the curb; a murder (a swim-by shooting, she now joked) in the pool at the projects around the corner—but she liked her place now, had missed it during her two weeks in the Southwest.

"It's an Indian," Cara said.

"Well, I got *that*," Ginny said. She weaved her hair into a French knot behind her head and then, having nothing to secure the effort, let the whole mess fall back down her neck. Jesus, it was hot.

"Like a cigar store Indian."

An Indian chief, in fact: chest high, with a massive headdress, buckskin clothing, and dark face, its fierce scowl edging into dementia.

"But is it supposed to be . . . funny?" Campy, she meant, some sort of a joke, a play on its own horribleness.

Cara stared at her.

"Just . . . Don't you think . . . I mean it's sort of offensive." Cara said nothing. "But . . ." Ginny rushed in to add. "But . . ." She couldn't think of a but. Not a but she'd say out loud.

There were other changes. Some of them expected. Like: the Czechs. Their belongings in Ginny's bedroom. Their economical foodstuffs filling the pantry shelf. Half bags of single-serving ramen noodles, taped shut for future use. Small plastic bowls of unidentifiable mush in the fridge. For the two additional weeks that Petra and her son, Marcus, were staying, Ginny would sleep on an air mattress by Cara's bed, a reversal of their childhood situation, when Cara (the younger of the two) was allowed to bring her ladybug sleeping bag over to Ginny's house for the night. They were cousins, but more like sisters, having grown up in neighboring houses in a Boston suburb. The truth was Cara herself was the biggest unexpected change:

in fourteen days, she'd bloated into obesity—the steroids having a field day with her face and torso—and there was something else wrong. She wouldn't say what. "Mom'll explain," she told Ginny dismissively, as if she couldn't be bothered to go into it. *Tell me,* Ginny thought with such intensity, she imagined the words forming a large cartoon bubble above her head. *Tell me, tell me now.* But she kept quiet. Cara could—Cara should—have her way. The cigar store Indian was going to stay.

And maybe it wasn't so bad. Maybe it was just that *everything* seemed off on her return. The sky too small, trees too close at hand. Outside, the world seemed colorless. Downright ugly. Inside, there was the disastrous pairing of her aunt's old pea-green refrigerator (the apartment was a "cold flat," which meant "Supply your own fridge") with the kitchen's worn red-and-white-checked linoleum, the tan paint on the wainscoting, and the striped wallpaper above. Rule (from what? A house and garden magazine?): colors you wouldn't wear together shouldn't be together in your garden or your living room. But what did it matter? For a long time, the only person who came to the apartment was a friend from college, who'd sit on a kitchen chair while Ginny made dinner. She was a decent cook. From the start, Cara had insisted that she was happy about moving in. Ginny would get Cara eating right. Big healthy salads. No more potato chip dinners.

When Ginny lived alone, the back porch was unfurnished. Once Cara came to stay—just two years ago, when Cara was twenty-five and Ginny was twenty-eight—the entire apartment filled with leftovers from Cara's parents' house. It would have been a terrible seventies flashback, with Peter Max fabric paintings and orange and purple furniture, if not for Cara's skill with needle and thread. She'd stitched coverings for the couch, added her various dressmaker's busts (two shapely women, one Pavarotti-size man) to the living room. (She'd been working as a costume designer in New York, when she got the news that forced her back to Boston and her doctors.) She'd plunked her parents' old kitchen table on the back porch, covered it with her collection of Fiestaware teapots, all turned into planters.

There were chairs out back, too, but on that first night home, Ginny took up her customary place on the porch: butt on the chipping gray floorboards, back to the gray vinyl siding, a glass of white wine with ice cubes by her side.

"So tell me about Petra."

Cara sighed and plopped into one of the porch chairs. "You'll see it's not like what we expected." Over the phone, Cara had already made it clear that the charm of Petra had worn off, though she adored Petra's three-year-old son.

And what had the cousins expected, back when they agreed to put Vaclav Havel's press secretary up for a month? Well, nothing really. Their thoughts hadn't got any further than a vague pleasure at being able to help out, at getting to meet someone close to Havel. The situation was this: Petra was supposed to attend a month-long seminar at Tufts University's school for international relations. She'd been given five hundred dollars to live on for the month, which wasn't going to get her very far in Cambridge. A woman Cara used to bump into in New York—Parker, now interim artistic director at the American Repertory Theater—knew someone at the burgeoning Prague Opera Company who knew about Petra's situation. Since the cousins lived within walking distance of the university (though it was admittedly a rather long walk), and since, for two weeks of the month in question, Ginny had work in New Mexico, it seemed natural enough to agree to put Petra up. Cara seemed to have taken a turn for the better and said she wouldn't mind the adventure of the visitors in Ginny's absence. Ginny was an art director, too, but for mail order catalogs. (She'd be doing a hiking catalog while out in New Mexico.) Nothing, at any rate, like Parker, whom Cara had described as a cross between Catherine Deneuve and a Gumby doll. Not an image Ginny could quite wrap her mind around. "Well," Cara had said, referring to Parker, "picture someone flat and blond and glamorous. With cat's-eye glasses."

"Oh," Ginny replied, dispiritedly, "do I have to?"

"I don't think press secretary there is like press secretary here," Cara said now.

"What do you mean?" There was a photo of Vaclav Havel under the Felix the Cat magnet on their refrigerator. Havel's eyes were the blueberry blue of an infant.

"Well, first, she's not the only press secretary. I mean: you'd wonder how a press secretary could take off for a month. I guess Havel has a few press secretaries. And it's not like she has any training. She was a tour guide before. I mean, her English is good, but otherwise . . ."

"But I thought that was the thing, the charm of the Czech government," Ginny said. "A bunch of writers who don't know a thing about politics. Artists running the government."

"Well, Petra's not an artist. She's just kind of needy."

Needy. Quite a put-down for Cara, who wasn't needy, not even when most ill. Each morning last winter, during the worst of her chemo, she'd had a businesslike manner about coughing till she vomited, quickly spraying the bathroom sink's surface with disinfectant, and then sitting down cheerfully to her breakfast—always half a dry bagel and a Diet Coke. "In what way needy?" Ginny asked now.

"Oh, you'll see, you'll see. I can't really explain it."

Ginny didn't see, not right away. The woman who came through the door later that evening was sweet. A blonde, straight hair cut to her shoulder, with girlish bangs. She was slim, wearing a slightly faded cotton skirt and a T-shirt with a tiny butterfly appliquéd under the scalloped neckline. Ginny was getting a tissue from the bathroom when she heard the front door open. "I'm out here," Cara called back into the house, and then a red-haired little boy charged past the bathroom door. "Ca-ra," he cried.

"He's in love with your cousin," Petra said right off to Ginny, knowing, of course, who the strange woman emerging from the bathroom was. They followed Marcus onto the porch.

"Under the sea," Marcus shouted and threw himself into Cara's arms. Cara pulled the boy to her lap. "Under the sea."

"His first words in English," Cara smiled.

"It's *The Little Mermaid*," Petra said, but Ginny hardly needed the explanation. Cara had bought the Walt Disney video, because she'd liked the movie. Another piece of evidence, as far as Ginny was concerned, that even though she was only three years older than her cousin, they lived on opposite sides of a sharp cultural divide, one that put Cara, for all her love of serious theatre, in the camp of those adults who knew all the Brady Bunch episodes by heart, who thought Mr. Potato Head was a hoot, who weren't ashamed to own a Pat Benatar album. In college, Ginny had gone to Memphis to spend Christmas break with her then-boyfriend. "If you don't go to Graceland," Cara had said, knowing Ginny wasn't inclined, "I want a divorce."

"This little boy," Petra said, mussing her son's hair, "has seen that movie thirty-five times."

"Thirty-six," Cara said, as she stood to cue up the video for him in the living room.

"I think I have something to tell you," Petra said, when Cara reemerged from the apartment.

Cara cocked her head.

"Ernest is coming for a visit."

"Oh," Cara cried, "that's great. When?"

"This Friday. The people from the program . . . we're going out on a boat in the harbor on Friday night, and he said he'd meet me after. It's near the . . . what's the word I want. You know, where fish . . ."

"Aquarium."

Petra nodded. "But I have a favor to ask . . . ."

"Sure," Ginny said quickly, aware that she had a rather adolescent desire to reassert her place in this apartment, to gain some fast intimacy with Petra and her son.

"Can you watch Marcus on Friday? It'll be too late to take him."

"Yes, oh, sure," Cara said.

"I'll put him to bed, so it'll only be if he wakes up."

"No problem."

"And maybe Ernest won't come anyway," Petra said, a bit mournfully.

"But," Cara said, "you just said he was."

"Yes," Petra allowed, "he says he'll fly in after work on Friday."

"But," Cara said, "this is good news, right?"

"Who's Ernest?" Ginny put in.

Ginny knew from Cara that Marcus's father was out of the

picture. Petra and he had been married, but then, early on, Petra had found out something dark about her husband. "He liked doing it with little girls or he was having an affair with his brother. Something like that," Cara had said on the phone, while Ginny was pulling on her hiking shoes, getting set for the day's pre-shoot trek. "I didn't care to find out the specifics. Anyway, I think they were only married a few months. At least, she got Marcus out of the deal."

"Ernest is . . . ," Ginny said leadingly.

"The crush," Cara put in. "Petra's love interest."

"Five years ago, I was giving a tour. I used to work as a tour guide, and he stayed to talk to me after. We've sent letters ever since, but I can't say he's interested."

"You don't fly up to Boston from Florida if you're not interested," Cara said.

"Really?" Petra asked, as if this weren't a self-evident fact. Petra was at least ten years older than Cara, but clearly Cara had taken the parental role in this relationship. Not that Cara spoke from direct experience. She was twenty-seven, and, so far, had never had a boyfriend. Losing your breast at age twenty-one did sort of complicate things. "At what point," she'd once said to Ginny, "am I supposed to say, 'Hey, buddy, one of these isn't real'?"

"Really," Cara said now. "You're golden."

Ginny allowed herself to hate Petra for a second. The kind of woman for whom men bought plane tickets. Ginny had had her share of boyfriends—was even currently and somewhat halfheartedly seeing Joe Langlais, a mechanic who worked down the street—but as yet, no one had ever actually plunked down a major chunk of change for the pleasure of her company.

"Oh, well." Petra waved her hand as if wiping the conversation away. "I better go check on that little guy." She turned for the short hall that led back into the apartment.

"Ugh, she drives me nuts," Cara said, when she was gone.

"She's not that bad."

"She's got that helpless thing, though. She takes good care of Marcus, but otherwise, she's the little girl."

"Oh, I guess," Ginny said, not yet sure if this was a fair characterization, but sensing that it was, that there was something in her own waffling reaction to this last exchange that proved Petra was the kind of person you wanted to protect and criticize, all in the same breath.

On Friday night, the night of the harbor ride, when Marcus first woke, a little disoriented at not finding his mother with him in the big bed, the cousins said they were having a pajama party in the living room, and he should come join them. He padded out, ate a small handful of popcorn, and played with a dancing chicken toy. "Under the sea," he finally said, rather plaintively, and Cara cued up *The Little Mermaid*. After ten minutes, he was asleep, and Cara scooped him up and back to bed.

"He was patting my shoulder blades, as I carried him," Cara said when she returned to the living room. "I think he was trying to burp me."

The second time Marcus woke it was one o'clock, and the cousins had turned in themselves. "Mama," they heard. "Mama," an edge of real panic in the boy's voice.

"It's OK," Ginny heard Cara whispering in the next room. "Mommy will probably be here in a few minutes." But the boy wouldn't stop calling out.

Ginny went in to offer her own reassuring words, but Cara

waved her away. "He was just starting back to sleep," she hissed. Ginny retreated for her air mattress. Sometimes, even now, Cara's harshness could make her gasp. When Cara came back to the room, it was 1:30.

"She's never stayed out this late before," Cara said, sitting on the edge of her bed. The streetlights gave her bedroom a silvery glamour, touched the computer screen and the edge of a chair draped in blue jeans, like a benign moonbeam. It wasn't so hard to imagine the cousins' exchange as the first scene in a movie in which the next scene was the cousins' adoption of the poor little boy whose mother disappeared into the endless night.

Ginny said, "Oh, I bet she'll be back in a few minutes." But by 2:00, both cousins were worried.

"What should we do?" Cara finally said, sitting up, a hulking shadow.

"Don't worry," Ginny said, starting for the phone by Cara's computer. "I'll take care of it. You go back to bed."

"Fuck you. I'm not going to bed."

"Well, I'll try Tufts," Ginny said. "Just to see when the boat docked."

But no one at the Tufts switchboard had ever heard of the international conference or its members who were visiting Boston Harbor that night. Ginny was transferred and transferred. Then the line went dead. "Idiots," she crabbed at the phone and dialed again.

"Let me have the phone," Cara demanded, holding out her arm, but Ginny shook her head no. So imperious, she thought, and then tried to calm herself. Why did she care? Eventually she was put through to someone who said, "Oh, the van got back here around 11:00."

Ginny looked out the window, but no cars were coming down

the street. "Maybe they went . . . I don't know if she really liked this guy, maybe they went and got a hotel room."

"No," Cara said, emphatically. "Trust me. She wouldn't do that."

"Well, why not, she's a grown woman. She . . ."

"No," Cara said, angry this time, as if she'd had it with Ginny and the way she lorded her sexuality over Cara. "I know her. She wouldn't."

At 3:00, they rang the police station to ask about reports of accidents, and then, shortly after, Ginny started calling hospital emergency rooms. She was on the line when Cara—stationed at the bedroom window—called, "Hold it, hold it. It's her." There was the sound of the front door closing and then feet on the stairs. Cara opened the apartment door to Petra, looking as freshly showered and powdered as she had hours earlier, when readying herself for her evening. "Hello," she said cheerfully. She held out three silver Mylar balloons, the whole of the landing, with its six-foot, yellow eighth note (something from a New York City Opera set) bent around their surfaces. "We bought everyone a balloon." She didn't seem to think it surprising that the cousins were awake in the middle of the night.

A man trudged in Petra's wake, a gentleman apparently, not being invited upstairs for a drink, but walking his date *all the way* to the door. Not really crush material in Ginny's eyes. He was somewhere in his forties, bearded and graying, not fat exactly, but pudgy around the middle, a thin man who'd gone soft. He wore a wrinkled gray suit, without a tie, undershirt sticking out from beneath his checked dress shirt. No hair on the top of his head, but a thick untrimmed muff above his ears that made him look a bit like a clown.

"I'd better be going," he said and put his hand to the back of his neck, as if he needed this sort of support to think clearly.

"We were so worried," Cara said, ignoring him. "And you'd better go see Marcus. He was scared. Where were you?"

"Oh," Petra said, "we were just having fun."

"But the boat docked hours ago," Cara said. This wasn't something Ginny would have pursued. You didn't ask a grown adult where she'd gone after dark. And yet, Cara seemed to have read the situation correctly, for there was something super-innocent about Petra's response, as if sexual dalliance weren't a possibility.

"Oh, I'm so sorry. We took a long walk. Over the bridges of the river. We didn't even notice the time."

"I used to row," Ernest said, as if this were why they had been looking at the river.

"He was showing me the boathouses for MIT and Harvard."

"Oh," Ginny said. "Were you in school up here?"

"No, not me," Ernest said.

"Ma-ma, ma-ma," Marcus called from his bedroom.

"The little guy," Petra said and turned to press her hand to Ernest's forearm. "Will you excuse me?" she asked, and before an answer came, she darted into the apartment.

"Well." Ernest smiled at Cara, sensing of course that she was the one to make up to here. "I'm so sorry we worried you. It's my fault, of course. I should have been paying attention to the hour."

Cara nodded, noncommittal, as he turned and made his way down the stairs. "Asshole," she whispered, when the thud of the downstairs door meant he was truly gone.

"So what happened last night?" Cara said, turning to Petra, who was putting a small teaspoon of jam in her oatmeal.

"Well," Petra began slowly, "I went out on the boat, of course. All around the harbor, and then when we came back, I saw Ernest, waiting for me at the end of the . . . whatdoyoucallit . . . She brushed her hand out in front of her to indicate a walkway.

"Gangplank, I guess," Cara said and shrugged. "*Is* that what you call it?"

Ginny shrugged.

"Well, there he was, and I thought he'd recognize me, but he didn't seem to. And I thought, well, if he doesn't recognize me, then that's that. So I walked off the boat and went all the way past him and still he didn't recognize me. So I thought I'd just better come home."

"Wait a second," Cara put in. "A guy flies all the way from Florida to see you, and you think you're going to blow him off because he doesn't *recognize* you?"

"Of course," Petra said reasonably, and Ginny had to suppose that something had been lost in translation.

"Christ Almighty," Cara said, and Marcus chirped, "Crisp Almighty."

"Go get your jacket," Petra instructed. "We've got to get ready to go." Marcus ran for his room but then let the toy trucks on the bedroom floor distract him from his errand. "All the other people from the program got back on the van, and even though there were only a few people left on the dock, he still didn't know me."

"Well, it had been a long time, right?" Ginny said. "Wasn't it five years?"

"And then finally he did say my name." Petra paused and smiled. "And that my hair had gotten much longer." She put the pads of her fingers to her hair lightly, as if it were he who were touching her. "The van went off, and then we went to that

Quincy Market and took the subway back to Cambridge. We walked over to the river and onto the bridges, then back again. And that was that. We took a taxi here."

"So . . . ," Cara said, waiting for the summary statement. What did she think about Ernest now? But her manner made it clear. She was smitten as ever.

"Well, why don't you invite him for dinner tonight, if you'd like?" Ginny said. "Joe'll be by. Maybe we can invite George." George was a friend from around the corner, owner of a local—and rather popular—Caribbean restaurant, a reliable procurer of good snacks, tostones, and sometimes even conch fritters.

"Crap," Cara said, and stuck her finger into her mouth, as if trying to dislodge something from her back teeth.

"That's attractive," Ginny said.

"Fuck you," Cara said, though Ginny had only been joking. "I can't swallow this thing. It's like something got stuck back here."

"God, I'm sorry," Ginny said, standing. "Do you want something to drink? I can get some water. Maybe some water will make it go down."

"No," Cara snapped. "I don't want anything to drink."

The news, Ginny suddenly knew, the news that Cara didn't want to go into with Ginny, the other night, could only be one thing. The cancer wasn't gone, not really.

It wasn't a great night for a party. Humid, the air a thick soup. Even moving one's mouth for conversation felt like too much of a workout. Still, Ernest showed up. And Joe and George.

Ernest seemed comfortable enough, though his arrival in a suit—in this weather! And he was from Florida!—seemed to suggest he was used to more formal gatherings. And older people.

"What do you do for a living?" George asked, after he'd deposited two platters from his restaurant on the table. Ginny wondered why she'd even bothered to cook. Who ate in this heat? "I brought some rum punch, too," George announced.

"Excellent," Ginny said, wiggling her fingers, like some craftily pleased madwoman. She loved George's super-strong rum punch. "This is so generous. Do you want some?" She turned to Ernest.

"Oh, no," he said. "I don't drink. Except for a sherry, now and then."

"We don't have that, I'm afraid."

"I'm happy with anything."

"Well, what would you *like*?" Cara put in, testily. "Some water?"

"Water's great," Ernest said.

"Hey, man." Joe emerged from the kitchen with a beer and gave George a slap on the back. "I haven't seen you in forever."

Ginny sat at the kitchen table with Petra and Ernest, while the others ate in the living room. "So what do you do?" Ginny said. "We never gave you a chance to answer."

"Business."

"What kind?"

"Oh, international."

"So when you were in Prague, when you met Petra, you weren't there on holiday?"

"Oh, no. That was before Prague changed, before it became fashionable to go. Before you saw Kafka mugs and Kafka key chains and Kafka T-shirts."

Ginny smiled.

"I'm serious. It's like that now. The people who go there now see the castle, and they walk over the bridge, and they think they've seen the true Prague."

"And . . . ," But Ginny didn't want to continue this conversation—there was something boring and slightly contentious in his manner. "Florida. Are you from there, or did . . . how did you end up there?"

"No, no. I'm from all over. I lived up here for a while. Down in the Square, in one of those apartment houses with the Harvard boys." He rolled his eyes, in the way that people always did around Cambridge. "Still I love that regatta. I used to row, you know."

"Yeah, I think you mentioned that."

"That guy's kind of weird," Joe said later that night, as he was readying to leave the apartment. Ginny had walked him out to his truck. She never stayed at his place—not a place really, but an upstairs room with a tiny kitchenette in one of the grand Victorians over by Fresh Pond Parkway. He had to walk through his landlady's house to get to his room, often stopping to open a jar for her or hear about the state of her impending divorce.

"Weird, like how?" It had been Ginny's impression, too, but she couldn't quite put her finger on what seemed off about Ernest.

"I don't know, just weird. Like, well . . . when I went upstairs, after you guys went for your walk?"

Ginny nodded. Earlier in the evening, they'd all had an after-dinner stroll, save Ernest, who wanted to rest, and Joe, who came down with everyone but, at the last minute, decided to stay, too.

"Well, I went back upstairs, thinking I'd cover up the food. And Ernest was gone. I thought, 'Hey, that's strange.' But I just got out the Saran and all. Then, I hear something in Cara's bedroom, and I went in there, and there he is. 'Can I help you?'

I say, and he says, 'No, no. Just needed to use the phone.' Only he isn't standing by the phone. He's across the room by the dresser."

Ginny grimaced and nodded in agreement. "Weird. And he's a little pompous, too, a little weirdly pompous, don't you think? Sort of a know-it-all about everything."

"Yeah, well. If Petra likes him, it's not our place to judge."

Ginny had a brief desire to hip-chuck him off the sidewalk. She hated this: stupidity masked as morality. "I don't analyze them. I just watch them," he'd once said, when Ginny had tried to get him to join some debate she and Cara were having about a movie. He made it sound like a virtue. He was a simple soul, who appreciated things, while the cousins talked and talked things to death.

"It is *so* our place to judge," Ginny said.

Joe huffed, and Ginny huffed, and had a sense that the relationship wouldn't last the week.

One night, when Cara was out at the movies, Ernest sat opposite Ginny at the kitchen table, as Petra told them about her mother's death. She'd had cancer. "And in the end," Petra said, looking down at her lap, her voice breaking, "she was just all full of these soft spots." Petra lifted her hand into the air to demonstrate. "Like an overripe melon. Just all soft. It was so horrible. My poor, poor mother, just all . . . " Petra seemed to be searching for a word, but then she skipped right over it and continued on: " . . . into herself. The progress of the disease it's just . . . like some rotting fruit, you know." She shook her head.

"You know," Ginny said, slowly, but then her question to Petra seemed ridiculous, so she directed it to Ernest, "that Cara has cancer."

"Well, obviously," Ernest said, pointing to his head, as if to indicate baldness or a headscarf.

"But she's in remission," Petra said quickly.

"Noooo," Ginny said, "I wouldn't exactly say that."

"Oh, my God," Petra said, "but she'll be fine, no? It would be too much for the little guy. I mean, he loves her so much, and I love her so much. And . . ." A spot below Ginny's breastbone suddenly hollowed out, as if someone had abruptly reached in and torn open a space there, because Ginny's body wasn't quite big enough, it turned out, for all it was going to have to absorb. Ginny pressed her hand to her chest, as if trying to hold something still. "Of course," she said, "Cara's going to be fine."

The air had a still, white quality. Even the fat purple grapes in the landlady's arbor, tucked improbably inside the backyard's chain-link fence, had seemed decidedly gray this morning, when Ginny stepped under the leaves, simply hoping for a little of the plant's green coolness.

Now, Ginny was washing Cara's head, with its patches of crusty, yellow skin. They were going to take Marcus and Petra for a farewell dinner at Ginny's mother's house. Marcus and Petra would sleep in the suburbs that night, and then Ernest would come in the morning to take them to the airport.

"Stamp out dry, scaly skin," Ginny said, and Cara laughed.

They were in the bathroom, Cara seated on the toilet lid, Ginny above her.

Marcus and Petra were making one final loop through the apartment, checking for belongings.

"It's so fucking hot," Cara said. Day twenty of the heat wave.

"Not that bad, not yet," Ginny said absentmindedly.

Cara slapped at Ginny's hand, the one with the washcloth. "Just get the fuck away from me."

"What's the matter?"

Cara was silent.

"What is it?"

"You *know*," Cara started to stand, but then didn't, "what *it* is. Just get the fuck out of here."

After the evening party, the plan was for Cara and Ginny to head back to Cambridge, but, at the last minute, Cara decided she'd just as soon stay with her folks till the heat broke.

"You stay, too," Ginny's mother said, but Ginny didn't want to.

"Come on," Cara demanded, but Ginny still refused, enjoying the small triumph of saying no to Cara.

The wrong decision, Ginny thought, when she reentered her apartment, for the place seemed eerie on return. Sooty and empty. So much gray dust on the moldings, so many water stains on the ceiling. Purposely abandoned. Was that it? Or only the fact that there was no one occupying the rooms. No Joe— they hadn't spoken since the night of the dinner party, so Ginny supposed they were off-again; no Cara, Marcus, or Petra.

It had been a whole month since she'd slept in her own bed, so she set to reoccupying her room. Stripping the sheets, moving her clothes. Dumping some of the leftover bits of food into the trash. And still this sense of being unsettled.

The phone rang.

"Hun?" Ginny's mother.

"Un-huh."

"Sweetheart, I've got some bad news. It's the real reason I wanted you to stay over, so I could tell you."

Ginny felt cold, the cold of panic. She looked up from the

phone. Something was off with the back door. It looked like it had been jimmied open.

"Oh, God," she said and pulled the phone cord into Cara's bedroom. She opened the jewelry box on Cara's dresser.

"Cara's going to have to have another mastectomy."

"Shit," Ginny said. Her eyes teared immediately. "Oh, shit."

II

The warehouse was dark, so they'd brought lights, enough lights to create the effect of sunlight falling on the caboose of the train. This was in Portland, at the Maine Narrow Gauge Railway, a dark, bayside building stuffed with antique trains. Actually the trains from the old Meadville railway, which Ginny had ridden as a child. Or maybe she'd just seen a TV ad for the place. It had sounded familiar, at any rate, when she got the assignment— which was a big one—as art director for a travel catalog. Now she was standing to the side as a photographer considered a lumpy duffel bag placed at the train's rear. It was black, so the challenge was to come up with a photograph that would reveal the bag's details—its many zippered compartments, its detachable shoulder strap, and so on.

There were a thousand sensible questions one could ask about the lengths to which they were going to create the illusion of daylight. The first being: why not just shoot outside? But the company wanted this particular train caboose, even though it had rusted into immobility years ago.

"Ginny," called one of her assistants, holding up a cell phone and waving it above his head like a flag.

"Hi," Ginny's mother said, her voice leisurely, as if ready for a long chat.

"What's the matter?"

"Nothing's the matter. I'm calling to wish you a happy birthday."

"I'm at work."

"I know, but you can talk."

No, I can't, Ginny almost said, but the truth was she *could* take a break just now. It was almost 5:00, and her work was more or less done for the day. She carried the cell phone out to her car.

"What're you doing?"

"Photographing luggage. Tomorrow, the models come and we'll do clothes."

"No, I meant for your birthday. You're thirty-one."

"Well, I *know* that. I didn't make plans. But the crew usually gets dinner out. There are supposed to be a lot of good restaurants here."

"I got you a pearl necklace."

"Oh, Mom, you didn't need to do that."

"I wanted to, to replace the one that got stolen." Ginny's apartment had been broken into last summer, on the day of the goodbye party for Petra, just before Cara took her final turn for the worse.

"Someone who knew what they were doing," the police had said, for the junk jewelry had been left behind; the pearl necklaces, Cara's antique charm bracelet, and Ginny's great-grandmother's wedding ring were all gone.

"And speaking of that . . . here's something interesting. Aunt Judy got a call from Petra." Judy was Cara's mother.

"Oh, yeah. What's up with her?" After they left Cambridge, Petra and Marcus had gone back to Prague for a few months, and then Petra had married Ernest and settled in Florida. "So much," Cara had said, "for those free vacation digs in the Czech Republic."

"It's a crazy story. Ernest flew Petra back home, for a treat supposedly, but then he called her in Prague and told her the marriage was over. She flies back to Florida to see what's going on, and he's cleaned the whole house out. Robbed her of everything."

"He *what?*"

"And there's more. Judy says, it turns out, he never really quite moved in with her. I mean, they were married—or Petra thought they were—and they had the house and all, but he didn't really stay there, most nights."

"That doesn't make any sense."

"I know. Completely crazy."

"So it must have been that Ernest. Who robbed us. Back then. Remember how weird we thought it was that he didn't want to come to the goodbye party for Marcus and Petra? Joe actually found Ernest in Cara's room once, saying he was going to use the phone, but he wasn't near the phone."

"Who?"

"Joe Langlais. That guy I was seeing back then."

"Oh," her mother sighed. "I can never keep all your men straight."

"Well, Mom, there haven't been that many."

"Whatever," her mother said. "Parker met that Ernest fellow, you know." Parker, the old ART director, who had introduced Cara to Petra in the first place, Parker who'd left the ART and was now running The New World Theater in Baltimore. "Parker said she thought he was CIA."

"Mom. *I* said that. Not Parker. I said he must have been CIA—the way he'd never say what his job was."

Her mother ignored her. A truth was more interesting out of Parker's than Ginny's mouth. "Anyway," her mother breathed now, "what's done is done."

"But Petra . . . I mean, what could you steal from her? I'd think a plane ticket back to Prague would cost more than the sum total of everything she owned."

Perhaps Parker had more of a line on the whole story. Not that Ginny could place a call and ask. Parker, whom Ginny had met only at Cara's funeral and knew only through Cara's descriptions—Parker with her cat's-eye glasses, her art object clothes, her tendency to find herself written up in the pages of magazines (the ten most fabulous women in Boston!)—she was beyond the Cadishes with their ordinary lives. Parker and her husband (a fairly well known movie star, it turned out) had caused a vague stir at the shiva; there was something in knowing that important people were taking notice of *this*.

At shiva, the night that Parker came, Ginny remembered hearing George—George who had loved Cara, who had always brought her all that soca and tuk music from his restaurant—saying, "You just want to say, 'You do know you're gay, right?'" He was talking to somebody about Parker's actor-husband. George had laughed, and Ginny remembered leaning into the room to say sarcastically, "Yeah, they're both each other's beards." But then she'd shaken herself. What was she doing? Cara was dead. Why weren't they talking about her? Why wouldn't anyone give Cara the attention she deserved? At her own funeral, for Christ's sake?

Cara had died young, and in that she was extraordinary—worthy of Parker and her actor-husband's attention—but Cara's whole family, they might get their ordinary, unglamorous hooks in, expect phone calls and attention. Parker knew better than to get mixed up with that. Parker had a plane to catch the night of shiva. Parker couldn't do as real friends did and return for shiva each night. Parker was gone, gone, gone.

*   *   *

But she wasn't. A month after the Portland shoot, FAO Schwartz flew Ginny to the Hands On Museum in Michigan. And there was Parker, shepherding a silent little boy (her own?) through an exhibit about peanuts. "I'm here for the festival," Parker explained.

"Festival?"

"Visionary Playwrights," she said flatly. She was wearing a lilac coatdress, and her hair had changed—it was slicked back into a little duck's tail above her neck.

"What's that?"

"Ohhhh—" Parker waved her hand in the air, as if it was too much of a bother to explain.

The women were silent, and the boy at Parker's side didn't have the good sense to tug Parker away. Above them, a funny contraption on the ceiling let go of a wooden ball, which sped along a clear tube before dropping into the wall and then along a clear maze down to the floor. The boy with Parker watched all this carefully, but with no apparent pleasure.

"Well . . . ," Ginny said, "did you hear about Petra?"

"Oh, *yeees.*" Parker's eyebrows arched up. "Strange."

"What do you think that was about?"

"About?"

"I mean, doesn't it seem that the whole ruse of duping Petra cost more than the sum total of everything she had? It just never fit together in my head."

"I suppose. I never thought about it." There was a hint of reprimand in Parker's voice, as if Ginny's question weren't stupid so much as boring, leading the women down a corridor of Norman Rockwells, when there was so much visionary art to be had in the museum of conversation.

And yet Ginny persisted. "Are you still in touch with her?"

"Me? No. She wanted to come live with me after Ernest ripped her off, but I said no. And then she must have gone back to Prague. I never heard."

"But your friends in Prague. They must have known."

"No, the whole opera project fell through. I'm not in touch with those folks anymore."

"God," Ginny breathed and then told Parker the story of being robbed last summer. Parker tilted her head in something like interest. At her side, the boy finally piped up, "Where's that ball?"

"Another one is going to come out in a second," Parker said, and as she did, there was the whirr-plop of a ball falling out of the ceiling and into the clear tube.

"We never really cared," Ginny added, "you know, about getting robbed. There was so much else going on then. Cara was going back in for surgery, and then they found this tumor at the back of her tongue, and well . . ." It was Ginny's turn to wave her hand in the air at a piece of information she didn't care to elaborate on.

Parker turned her head and scanned the wall, as if looking for a clock, but she didn't move.

"I just don't get the motive. Petra was a struggling single mother. Why pick on her? Or on Cara? Cara who in the last months of her life was extending herself to two strangers?"

Parker shrugged, twisted her mouth into a helpless I-don't-know grin.

"Don't *you* wonder?" Ginny said. She wanted the reasonableness of her curiosity to be confirmed. Or maybe for Parker to admit she'd had a role in bringing about both losses.

"Well, that's the thing about it," Parker said wisely if absentmindedly.

"The thing about what?"

"You just have to accept that the unknown is part of life."

How visionary of you, Ginny might have said. Or: *Fuck you.* Instead, she stepped back, gesturing to the boy, as if he were pulling Parker forward, to the wall maze and beyond. "Well, I should let you go."

A New England storm delayed all flights east, so Ginny and Kevin Mehta, a photographer from New York, found themselves with a free night in Ann Arbor. Over dinner, they decided to go to the university to check out the theater festival. This was the fourth time Kevin and Ginny had worked together, though the shoots had been spread out over the past five years. Every time they saw each other, Ginny was between boyfriends, and the two of them slept together, a bit of casualness that Ginny suspected was ordinary for Kevin, but was altogether unusual for her. She'd said as much to him the last time they saw each other. "I don't really have sex with my friends."

"Oh," he'd said. "Well, let's just go to sleep," and then they were in bed together, fumbling around. But when she next saw him (which was a few days ago, when the shoot started), he was, as always, cordial and friendly, there being nothing in his manner to suggest they'd ever touched each other. And Ginny followed suit, though she wondered why it seemed a priori ridiculous to suppose they would ever get *involved* involved, as Cara used to put it.

There were three plays being performed that night: on the university's main stage, in the black box theater, and (improbably, given the temperature) outdoors on the football field.

"Can we go to this one?" Ginny said, reading aloud from the newspaper. "*Folk Wisdom.* It says it's at the main stage. 'About youth, the world, and death.'" It was an original play, the paper said, written by Parker Martin.

"Sure," Kevin shrugged. Ginny liked him. Another man would have rolled his eyes at that description and observed that a Big Ten school like Michigan must have *some* team playing *some*thing tonight.

"Oh, good, because I sort of know the playwright from Cambridge."

It had been a long time since Ginny had been to the theater. She loved the frisson of excitement in the audience, the sense that you were going to an event, not just watching a story. And Kevin always made her feel rather special—his light touch at her back as he steered her past the ushers, the automatic way he slipped her coat off when they reached their seats. He grinned—boyish, excited, for all his worldliness—as the lights dimmed and then rose on two young men sitting on a bench in front of the curtain.

"Here we go," Kevin whispered.

At the intermission, Kevin and Ginny went outside so Kevin could have a cigarette.

Act I—"Youth"—had been about a group of hip students experimenting with some Fountain of Youth drug. The second act—which began with the word *World* projected on the stage curtain—was about depression, but it played depression not as the problem of an individual, but of the world itself. The point seemed a little strained.

"Want to stay?" Ginny asked, feeling apologetic about the play, as if it were her fault it wasn't better.

"It is pretty lousy," Kevin admitted and then smiled. "But how can we miss death?"

"You're right," Ginny said. "That would be terrible. We'd be . . . like . . . two hundred years old if we miss death."

"Plus your friend, if you see her, you won't want to confess you didn't weather it out."

"That's what I was thinking, though she's not really a friend. Just someone I know."

So back inside they went, to see the word *Death* projected onto the curtain, which parted to reveal a cozy contemporary apartment, decorated with rattan furniture covered with colorful throws, a place (with its Sienese colors—all those muted browns and mauves and greens) in which Ginny wouldn't have minded living.

"I'm just not going to take that part," a very pretty woman on stage was saying to someone on the phone. "I'm just not going to take it. Once you've done Chekhov, you don't have to take parts like that." There was a pause while the woman apparently listened to whatever the caller had to say. "Yeah, well, then, I'm a snob. So what? Listen, I've got to go. Kylie Marks is coming over." Another pause. "Yes, you do. Kylie Marks, costume designer. Talented young kid who's got breast cancer. She's coming for tea."

Ginny turned to look at Kevin, but his eyes were trained on the stage.

A buzzer sounded. The actress walked to a button on the wall. "It's me," called a voice, and there was another buzz. The actress straightened tea things on a table that sat stage center and then turned for the door. "Come in," she shouted. In walked a woman wearing a headscarf. Thin, pretty, presumably bald.

"Hey." The women embraced. "How's it going, Kylie?"

"All right. Well, all right, save my roommate. Jesus Christ, my roommate's driving me nuts. She's shtupping this stupid guy from down the street who fixes her car, and ever since she got back from the West, with her new enthusiasms for all things big sky, she's going on and on about how claustrophobic our place is, and then . . . And then . . . catch this? You know that woman from Prague who's been staying with me? The actress?"

Kylie nodded and went on, "Yeah. Well, she turned out to be a real character. Impossible, but my roommate's all buddy-buddy, like she's discovered the charms of the Eastern bloc. Which wouldn't be so irritating, but she's always staging these parties and dinners for us all. It's just un-fucking-bearable."

"Why don't you just tell her you don't want to go?"

"Me? Tell Miss Thin-Skin anything? Can you imagine? She'd just *flip out*. 'Oh, was I really bothering you? Was I really?' until I say, 'No, not really.' Like I need it. Like a dying woman needs this sort of shit."

"You're not dying," the actress said.

"I'm dying," Kylie said matter-of-factly. "I am . . . like, so outta here."

The act went on, though with Kylie as a minor character. A series of other people came to the actress's apartment—a FedEx man, a house cleaner, a playwright—all revealing sooner or later that they were, despite appearances, fatally ill. None of them was going to see old age, and the actress ended up seeming like the unfortunate one, having to survive old age all alone. In the end, she concludes, to a lover, that "we're not under death's thumb, but death is under ours. It's right here, all around us."

"Idiotic," Kevin pronounced the play, when it was all over. "I mean . . . you're not under death's thumb, because death is under your thumb? What kind of bullshit semantics is *that*? And that . . . what was that she was doing at the end . . . smushing an ant under her thumb?"

"What do you mean?"

"When she was grinding her thumb into the table, and then she picks it up and flicks something off? She kills something with her thumb, so . . ." Kevin gestured for Ginny to step before him into the slow-moving departing audience.

"I guess I missed that," Ginny said. She guessed she'd missed a lot of the play's end. Miss Thin Skin. *Could* Cara have felt that way about her? Could she have? Could all of Ginny's sense of the love between the cousins just be . . . just wrong? Could letting a robber into your home and feeding him dinner just be the tip of the iceberg when it came to bad judgment?

"Should we go backstage?" Kevin said, not sounding too enthusiastic about the idea, but he was a man, if nothing else, of propriety.

"No, no, I don't think so." But when they pushed into the lobby, Ginny changed her mind.

The room where Parker was—to all appearances—accepting fervent compliments from strangers and friends alike was a typical, untidy green room, recently subject to a snowfall of paper coffee cups. At least, that's what people kicked aside as they pushed past the costumes that fringed the walls. At the far end of the room, Parker half-sat on the edge of a cluttered old conference table.

"She's got her fans," Kevin whispered. "So add that to your list of wonders of the Western world."

Ginny hung back a bit, not quite wanting to join the dense circle around Parker, but then there was a little rustling in Parker's crowd, as if the group as a whole had taken notice of Ginny by the door, but had politely decided not to turn and stare.

"Maybe," Ginny said to Kevin, ready to change her mind again, and half-turning as she did, but then she realized what it was: Parker's husband had entered the room behind them.

"Oh," Ginny said and smiled. "This is . . . ," she started to say to Kevin.

"Oh, but I know who you are," Kevin said politely. "I saw you in *Happenstance*. Great movie."

"Thank you," the actor said.

"Kevin Mehta," Kevin offered.

"Sorry," Ginny shrugged and then the actor—Ginny couldn't get herself to remember his name—leaned toward Kevin. Ginny pressed her palm to her throat. It looked like he might kiss Kevin, but he stopped short of Kevin's ear and whispered, "I'm that . . ." He wrinkled his nose, and gestured over to Parker with a slight upward tip of his chin, "that woman's beard."

"Ginny!" Parker cried, at just that moment, as if they were old friends. "You came to my play. I didn't even know you knew about it. And I'm so glad you came, because I figured it out."

Ginny just looked at her and then said flatly, "What out?"

"Why, your problem. I've been thinking about it since I saw you this afternoon." Parker stopped, as if she was expecting a compliment, and in that moment some roses *were* handed from the people at the door to other admirers and then pushed into Ginny's arms, so she had no choice but to extend them forward, as if in thanks for the insult of the third act.

"Thanks," Parker said and turned to put the flowers on the table behind her. "Passports," she said, as she turned back.

"What?"

"Cara and Petra. He wasn't stealing their things. He was stealing their identities, their passports. That's worth something."

Ginny was silent and then said, "But I have Cara's passport. I've got it in a little . . . a little Godiva chocolate box that she saved for some reason. It's in there with some snapshots of her wrapping her arms around the neck of a Wild Thing. One of those huge Wild Things for the New York City Opera's production of . . . you know, that Sendak's kid story." Her voice was breaking up. Miss Thin-Skin. What could be worse than to enact the truth of the character's terrible words in front of their author?

"Well," Parker said. "That's probably just an out-of-date passport. That guy, Ernest, wasn't that his name? He probably left the out-of-date one and took the one that was still good."

Ginny didn't say anything. She could be right. Cara had been to England when she was eleven—they all had, for a family wedding—and then again in college. And if she'd planned to travel after, she might have gotten it renewed. In which case there would have been two passports in that chocolate box, but Ginny knew there weren't. She knew everything there was to know about all Cara's things, which had been carefully touched and evaluated and then reevaluated before they were kept or given away or discarded.

"Why else . . . not to be crass," Parker began, "but why else steal from a dying woman?"

Your play, Ginny could imagine herself saying, *your play was so mean to me.* Or: *But Cara couldn't have told you that. She couldn't.* Instead, she said, "But what about Petra and Marcus? He couldn't have taken *their* passports. He'd sent them out of the country, so they'd have to have their passports with them."

"True, but . . ." Parker waved her hand as if bored and then grinned a broad grin at someone she recognized behind Ginny, someone probably just now coming through the door. She looked back at Ginny. "Ernest was probably using Petra and her kid as a cover of some sort, an explanation for why he was traveling in certain countries."

"I guess that makes a kind of sense," Ginny allowed.

"It does," Parker said. "Doesn't it? So many creeps in the world."

"But . . . ," Ginny began, and as she did, someone pushed in front of her to give Parker a big hug.

"Kevin," Ginny said, reaching out for his forearm, and then quickly pulling her hand back. She didn't touch Kevin in public. "Let's go."

"What was *that* all about?" Kevin asked when they were back out in the now-empty lobby.

"Nothing," Ginny said. "It'd take too long to explain."

"OK," Kevin said, "then tell me this. What's with the beard comment? Hans Martin . . ."

"Yes, *that's* his name."

". . . said it to me again when you were talking to your friend." Kevin paused and then mimicked Martin, saying, "I'm that woman's beard."

"I guess . . ." Ginny rolled her eyes, but then realized. "I think he thinks I said something about him that I didn't say. Or didn't mean to say. I think they must both think that. Something I said when my cousin died."

They were well onto other subjects—an exhibit he'd liked in New York, a friend they had in common—by the time they were back at the hotel. They agreed they'd meet back at the bar for a drink but would first run up to their respective rooms to check their phone messages and so forth.

There were no phone messages for Ginny, and none on her answering machine back home. But she didn't want to get to the hotel bar before Kevin, so she decided she'd call Nan Williams—an art director-friend, someone who knew Kevin, too, from mutual projects.

"Hey," Nan said when Ginny identified herself. "Haven't heard from you in a while." She seemed genuinely glad to hear from Ginny, and Ginny realized that this was what she'd called for—or part of what she'd called for—for someone to acknowledge the pleasure of her company.

"Just called to say hi," Ginny said. "I'm out here in Michigan on a shoot. With Harvey Wilson, you know him?"

"Unt-ah," Nan said.

"And Kevin Mehta, you know him?"

"Oh, of course, Kevin Mehta. He's a charmer. Guy who'll sleep with anyone but only have relationships with Indian women?"

"Oh, no. I mean . . . I didn't know that."

"Oh, yeah. It's that whole Indian Brahmin marriage thing. I don't completely get it."

"Well," Ginny said, "how've you been? What's up with you?"

By the time Ginny got herself downstairs into the bar, she wasn't up for a drink. She told Kevin she was too tired, and given that the East Coast airports would be open in the morning, she'd better just get to bed.

"Well, hell," Kevin said, flipping a bill out of his wallet and leaving it with half a glass of whiskey at the bar. "You're right. I should turn in, too." He gestured with his chin to a TV in the corner of the bar. "News was just saying the storm'll be out to sea in a few hours. It's still ripping through now though."

In the elevator, Ginnie pressed the 3 for her floor, and then, when he didn't do it, the 5 for Kevin's floor.

"Well ...," Kevin said, and he tipped his head sideways. She could see he was waiting for her to ask him back to her room, and she let herself hold on to this little gesture of his, let herself acknowledge that, for the moment, he wanted to go to bed with her.

The door opened on her floor. She stepped out.

"I'll see you," she said and let the elevator door close between them.

Just then, back in Cambridge, a broken fence from the lumberyard next to Ginny's triple-decker was flapping in the wind. Later that night, it would break loose, and land on Ginny's car, driving a pole through her front windshield. Out on the back porch, Cara's cigar store Indian toppled forward, its plaster form cracking into three large pieces, exposing the thick metal piping around which it had been cast.

Two days later, when Ginny reached to pick up the Indian chief's head up, the plaster didn't break away from the piping, so she had to scoop her arms under the Indian's entire body. She hefted him up—a cracked and drowned boy—first balancing him on the front of her thighs, and then carrying him over the threshold of her apartment and through her kitchen and Cara's bedroom and the front hall. She would move, she knew. She would move away from this place, very soon. At the landing outside her apartment door, she rested him back on her thighs and then took a deep breath and edged herself to the staircase's railing, steadying herself against a fall. Down one flight, to the turn of the second floor landing, and then down another flight. At the building's door, she gasped. The weight was too much for her, but she took the five stairs to the concrete walkway, and then the final two steps to the large green garbage cans by the triple-decker's chain-link fence. The legs fell into the trash can, and the body folded over, in a crash, bits of plaster hitting the sidewalk. *Traitor*, Ginny thought, nonsensically. Of herself, she supposed. She had thrown Cara away! Or maybe not. She pulled her sleeve across her damp eyes—she would not cry here, out in the yard—and stepped back to study the statue. Paint (goldenrod yellow, hunter green, chimney-brick red), wire, and plaster. It surprised her, though she didn't know why. What, after all, had she thought it was made of?

CHOCOLATE MICE

I

When she was young, mothers—or her mother, at least—would speak of those bad girls, presumably pregnant, who left home at the first opportunity, but Monica wasn't waiting that long. She left before her first opportunity, using school break to escape. To run away: if you could call it that, since she had her mother's acquiescence, if not her permission, in the matter. Her father was irrelevant. A farming accident had paralyzed him, days after Monica's younger brother—her mother's second boy and seventh child—was born. There were no more children after that, which made clear, in a public sort of way, the full nature of the damage her father had suffered. Monica let her mother know that she would "just die" if she couldn't get away from the farm, and the fervency of her conviction must have convinced her mother as well. "Just don't get pregnant," she said, as if that were the source of all evils, and it made Monica ashamed to be alive, to be one of the seven reasons for her mother's unhappiness. But then her shame quickly turned to anger. Her parents. They were so stupid. Switzerland was the world's richest country, and even here, they couldn't make a living. Why had they had so many children when they couldn't afford them?

What Monica did first was go to Nice. She had studied geography in school, of course. Every Friday afternoon, her teacher produced the walking stick he used in lieu of a pointer and gave emphatic little taps to the classroom's browning map. Meanwhile the students passed around a book of color photographs, all curiously yellowed, so the message was clear: outside of Swiss borders, jaundice awaits.

At fifteen, which is how old she was when she left for France, Monica couldn't even say what it was in that book that attracted her. The name of the town had become an attraction in and of itself. Nice. Nee-isss. It was in her head, when she did favors for her grandfather, the one who had a particular affection for her and was stiff in the hips. She'd tie his shoes. *Ja ja*, he'd say, patting her on the head as if she were still six and then slipping two francs into her hand. She reached under his shirt and scratched his back, picking with her short fingernails at the scabby skin there. Five francs for that, for it was a favor that embarrassed him.

When she had assembled fifty francs—she thought of it as so much of her grandfather's skin under her nails—she hitchhiked to Nice. The final driver dropped her off in the middle of town. She had no idea what to do with herself. She hadn't thought beyond escape. The air smelled strangely briny, and a crab, a child's wind-up toy, scuttled nonsensically by her ankles.

Even back home, she hadn't pictured the rest, had secretly supposed the opposite of what she told her mother—that she would die *before* she got to Nice, because it seemed so impossible that she would ever be there. Now the town presented itself as an intricate puzzle. How to crack it open? Monica didn't know.

But she wasn't dumb, though her demeanor wasn't one of intelligence. She had a large, turnip-shaped head, with a sprouting of reddish hair at the top. Her features were broad, and she was always chewing on some part of herself—her bottom lip, her fingernails. When she was little, she sucked the hem of her dress. "Farm girl" was written all over her, though she didn't have the healthy tan one associates with a life outdoors. There was a certain thickness to her movement and appearance, a rough mannishness, despite the large breasts which she tried to flatten beneath a harness-like bra, stolen from an older sister's dresser.

In Nice, she needed to find a rooming house and, as they said about work for girls but not for boys, a situation. Neither, of course, was going to come to her in the middle of the square, so she picked the road that led off to her left and started walking. She had two shocks, then. The first was a body, lying in the middle of the road. There had been a shooting, a murder so recent that the dead man's eyelids still parted to reveal milky slivers of eyeball. But that wasn't the shock. The shock was the way people stepped over the victim, as if he were a large but unnoteworthy bump in the road.

The second shock was lunch. Monica stopped to buy a sausage at a cart by the park. She bit into it and instantly thought, "This is it. I am go-ing to die." There was hot pepper in the sausage, and she'd never tasted such a thing, never had any spices beyond the salt and pepper her mother added to potatoes and vegetables. Her tongue expanded and sent bolts of lightning crackling through her head. Her eyes teared, and she thought to spit the lining of her own mouth out. After that, she couldn't think for feeling. She ate the rest of the sausage anyway. She was hungry and didn't have money to waste.

In the end, she didn't find a situation or a room. She spent that first night, and the next six, on a park bench. She bathed in the loo in the back of a restaurant. She had to buy a coffee for the privilege and quickly saw her money disappear. Each morning, she bought a liter of milk and drank it all at once, her stomach bloating uncomfortably. On her second day, she bought a tin of Gauloises—blue, without the filter—because she found smoking them made her feel so sick, she didn't want to eat, no matter how hungry she was. Soon, the mere thought of the cigarettes made her lose her appetite, and she sold the second half of the tin. When the money from that sale was gone, a week had passed and she hitchhiked home.

"How was it?" her mother asked, and Monica shrugged. She was hoping to make her mother as irrelevant as her father, the cigar-colored man with gaps between his square teeth. What Monica might have said, but didn't, was there was nothing about the trip to make her feel she wasn't ready for Paris.

She got the idea from a young French couple, honeymooning for the entire summer in "spinach land," which was what she called her hometown in the flatlands of German Switzerland. She couldn't figure out why they'd choose to vacation here—in a converted room in what used to be a textile storehouse—that bordered the grazing pasture of her family's dairy farm. They loved everything she hated—all that stupid green, the constant clanking of the cowbells, the sudden silences that would descend over town—at noon and after 6:00—so if not for the carefully groomed gardens, you'd think everyone was dead.

Her friend Sonja met them first. Sonja's father ran a hardware store, and when the couple came by the shop to ask for help installing a phone, Sonja and her French-German dictionary helped decipher the request. Sonja couldn't believe Monica's good luck, to be so near this glamorous couple. The husband, tall and dark, dressed in long black shirts and baggy pants. He was a translator from Yugoslavia but had settled in Paris soon after meeting his painter-wife, Marcelle.

Before long, Sonja started to pattern herself after Marcelle, sewing herself a simple black dress and trying to train her long curls into the same slick ponytail into which Marcelle combed her straight dark hair. It was a hopeless project. Everywhere that Marcelle was straight, Sonja was curved. Even her cheeks, two cheerful red pillows, betrayed her.

One day, Sonja rang Monica on the phone and told her to bring ice fast. Monica arrived with a bag from the grocers, and Sonja selected two fat squares to rest above her eyes. She had plucked her eyebrows into tiny high arches, the very curves that made Marcelle look like a perpetually frightened cat, and, as Sonja lay on her bed, ice dripping down her temples, she pronounced the pain indescribable.

Soon enough, Sonja had the couple inviting the girls to the roof of their building for tiny glasses of grappa. Sonja had a gift for bullying her way into the center of things, and she always took Monica along. At street fairs, she pulled Monica to the most interesting tables. She took her up to the front row during concerts. "This is my friend, Monica," she'd exclaim at parties and then drop her voice to say conspiratorially, "She's a bit timid. What are we going to do with her?" And suddenly Monica was everyone's concern. How to solve the problem of *her*?

On the roof, Sonja and Monica would sip their drinks judiciously, considering first the sunset, then the stars. The honeymoon couple liked to hear stories about farm life. "What do you do up there?" Monica's mother asked, and Monica shrugged and said, "Tell them stories about our boring lives." Her mother laughed with her. The French really were crazy.

Not that Monica talked much. Sonja told the stories, while Monica's thoughts wandered. But she listened when the conversation changed, when the couple passed her the verbal equivalent of color pictures of Paris: Notre-Dame, Musée du Louvre, Tour Eiffel, Champs-Elysées, the Seine, the Seine, the Seine. It wasn't even that Monica had settled in her mind to love architecture or art or waterways, but that the sights—and the world she imagined buzzing around them—represented her chance for another life. If she analyzed it, she might have seen the contradictions. She was terribly shy, but she wanted to go where there were as many people in one block as there were in her whole town. History, in school at least, bored her senseless, but she wanted to see where everything had happened, and, for a reason she didn't understand, she wanted to do all this before Sonja.

But she failed in this. Long before she could do the requisite number of chores for her grandfather, the French couple had secured Sonja a place as an au pair.

On the day before Sonja left, the two girls went to the drugstore to have a strip of passport-size photos taken. They lingered by the cosmetics counter while the film developed.

"Oh," Sonja said, with pleasure, when the two strips were finally placed before her—but it wasn't her own image she was admiring. "Look at you," she breathed.

Monica's left eye, normal most of the time, had turned inward at the moment of the camera's flash. "You look like Gertrude Stein!"

And Monica saw she did—the rough short hair, the loose clothes. "Just what I told you," Monica said. "I'm too ugly for this."

"Oh, you," Sonja said and took one of the pictures of Monica. "I'm going to put it in my wallet, right now."

And then Sonja turned for home with dismaying ease. There was no formal leave-taking, and in the days to come Monica saw how, as the younger of the two, she'd never occupied the place in Sonja's heart that Sonja had in hers. Sonja had outgrown her, though she did send back a postcard with an encouraging entreaty: Monica should come visit as soon as possible.

Monica's mother said the French couple must have had the longest honeymoon on record, since they stayed in town for over two months. But it wasn't long enough for them to find Monica work, though they'd talked grandly about their ability to do so. Toward the end of their visit, after Sonja had been gone a week, Monica noticed how Marcelle's face always looked stained with tears. And during their final days in town, Marcelle seemed to have stubble, small black dots, under her eyebrows and even at her chin.

When they were gone, the landlord said they never paid the rent they owed and that they'd left the flat filthy: the walls covered with paint and, for reasons no one wanted to speculate about, urine in the bath.

Terrible, everyone in town said, and Monica agreed, until Sonja sent a second postcard. *When are you coming?* she'd scribbled, as if confused about what was taking Monica so long.

It took forever to find Sonja in the suburbs of Paris. Not because Monica didn't have the right address—Sonja had sent that—but because it was one thing to hitchhike from Switzerland to France, quite another to find some way to get to a very specific street, in a very specific neighborhood, unserviced by bus or rail.

In her first days in Paris, Monica used her Nice trick of milk and Gauloises, but even so she was hungry by the time she finally arrived at Sonja's doorstep. During her travels, everything she saw had reminded her of something she might eat. The cobblestones crisscrossed in just the way her mother's *rosti* did. The floors of buildings seemed stacked like layers of cake. A molding, especially if it was painted, might be jelly filling; a roof, so much frosting. Even shrubs reminded her of broccoli, a vegetable she detested but longed for now.

She'd gone to Sonja's place on the back of a boy's motorcycle, a bit of exotica Monica savored, because she knew Sonja would love it, the suggestion of romance, and even Monica had liked pretending, as the wind whipped through her hair, that she was the motorcyclist's girl, but then a bug flew up her nose, and she couldn't, for all her efforts, get rid of the sensation that the creature was still there. She didn't dare let go of the boy, but as soon as they had arrived, she put her finger in her nose, at just the moment when he might have kissed her.

He drove off, and when she turned to take in the house, she saw what her preoccupation with her nose had deprived her of: a tour of the area's lavish homes. She walked up the long drive to the house that matched the address on her postcard, the missive she'd folded twice, so it fit like a matchbook into the back pocket of her jeans.

She rang the bell and waited a full minute before the door was pressed open by a servant, a woman dressed in a maid's uniform, which Monica vaguely associated not with household help but the porn movies she had never seen. Monica explained who she was and asked for Sonja.

"*Enchuldigung*," the woman said, having caught the accent in her voice and knowing enough to say "sorry" in Swiss-German before continuing on in French. "Sonja left about a week ago." She lowered her voice to whisper, "She was dismissed."

"I . . . oh," Monica said, dumbly. She knew she was supposed to apologize for her error, turn and leave, but that just wasn't possible. She'd exhausted her little bit of money in getting here, and even if she had had the means to return to downtown Paris, where would she go? She stood still and gnawed gently at the right part of her bottom lip. She vaguely remembered reading a novel about a stupid girl, just like herself, refusing to ask for assistance, while she waited for someone to help her.

"Ay, come in," the maid finally said. She was a small woman with bright eyes and a long nose that came to a point and would have made Monica think of a weasel if the woman hadn't been so friendly. The maid introduced herself as Véronique, and as they walked down the hall, she asked Monica a series of questions: where was she from, how old was she, whom did she know in France, how much money did she have in her pocket? She tsk-ed, but not in a bad way, at each of the answers Monica gave. Then, she left her on a well-shined wooden bench in the hall, while she went to talk to "the lady of the house" about the visitor. But, she reported, when she came back, neither Madame nor Monsieur Morandi was well-disposed to Monica. Clearly, their distaste for Sonja was now going to lap, an ungentle wave, onto her friend. Whispering in the hallway, Véronique reported that the Morandis had reminded Véronique that they didn't know where Sonja had gone to— only that she was gone and their experience with her had not been happy. Véronique rolled her eyes as she disclosed this last bit of information. Given the hour, Véronique said, the

Morandis had agreed to let Monica stay for the night, but in the morning, she'd have to move on.

Monica nodded at all this, and then Véronique took her back to the kitchen. While the Morandis' toddler son decimated a bowl of macaroni and cheese, Véronique explained what *really* had happened, the true story of why Sonja had been dismissed. Madame Morandi had been polishing silver—a chore she never left to the help, since she felt they streaked things shamelessly. As always, Madame Morandi prepared herself for the task by leaving her wedding and engagement rings on the small porcelain tree ring, dotted with violets, which she kept on her dresser. Later in the afternoon, when she went up to get the rings, the engagement ring—the one crusted with an emerald and two tiny diamonds—was gone. The conclusion was obvious. Sonja—who was supposed to vacuum and make the beds in all the upstairs rooms—must have taken it.

Monica, quiet during this whole explanation, started to protest; Sonja would never steal. And it was true. Sonja had been horrified when Monica confided her own single theft: the pilfering of her older sister's bra, the sweaty undergarment, yellowing under the arms, that even now was flattening her out as effectively as any mummy's bandage.

Véronique held her hand up, not to disagree or agree, but to say, "True or not, it doesn't matter," for the ring was found. Sonja discovered it under Madame's dresser. Crying with anger, she presented it to Madame Morandi. Clearly, she was expecting an apology. Sonja told Madame Morandi that she must have dropped the ring. Véronique confessed she thought Madame Morandi believed Sonja, but it was too much—the loss of face and all—to admit it. She said Sonja had produced the ring only because she'd been caught. As she said this, Véronique reached over with a napkin to snap a cheesy noodle off the Morandis' infant's chin.

"So you see," Véronique said and shrugged. "She'll hire someone else for this little man." She reached over to ruffle the boy's hair affectionately.

Monica nodded. This was important information, but her eyes were trained on the box of chocolate mice that lay, open but untouched, on the table in front of her. She'd once seen just such a thing in the window of a shop, but had never known anyone to buy such ornate treats. If Véronique didn't offer her one, she knew she'd steal one later.

"Do you want one?" Véronique asked her and nodded toward the box. Monica bobbed her head once, while Véronique said, "But you haven't eaten. Let me fix you a snack." She turned to assemble a plate for Monica. When she placed it in front of the girl, she saw the box remained untouched. "But you aren't a child," Véronique laughed—the first time anyone had suggested such a thing—"if you want a sweet, go ahead and take one."

Monica popped a mouse into her mouth, let her tongue run itself around the mouse's cartoon features, the tiny yellow whiskers, the two red pinpoints for eyes, all of it so unlike (thank goodness!) a real mouse. Still, as the dark chocolate outer shell melted into the soft chocolate in the center of the mouse's head, Monica thought of Cleopatra, her family's cat, and of the terrible crunch of mouse bones.

Her table manners weren't good. She bent over the plate of curried rice and chicken and curved her left arm into a U, so she gave the impression of being two people—a large baby and the disembodied arm that was spooning food into that baby's mouth.

After Monica had cleaned two plates, Véronique seemed

to realize the girl would simply eat until Véronique stopped putting food in front of her, so she picked up the plate, and, as she washed the dish, said, "Before you go to bed, you need a plan for tomorrow." Monica nodded. The food had tired her out. "You'll get a job the way I got this one." She tugged at the skirt of her maid's uniform—it really was too short—then gave Monica detailed directions to a job board at a Paris university. Positions were advertised there, she explained, with the expectation that they would be filled by the industrious young women who had been smart enough to be accepted into the school in the first place. In the morning, Véronique said, she would give her the money for a taxi to the city.

The bedroom where Monica slept that night was like nothing she'd even dreamed of. It was under one of the house's gables but didn't have the feel of an attic cloister. The ceilings were draped with a rich, red fabric, and where the walls weren't slanting, there stood a dark brown dresser, a cosmetic table (illuminated by a lamp built into the base of the mirror), and a wardrobe. Her bed was a feather bed: essentially a giant pillow laid out on a box spring. When she lay down in it, she felt as if she were suffocating. The poverty of her parents' lives reached across the borders and seemed to slap her, a reproach for having all this, if only for a night, and Monica felt honor-bound, despite her distaste for her parents' life, not to enjoy herself. Still, her sleep was fast, deep, and sweet.

At the university, things were not as easy as Véronique had promised they would be. Monica found the job board with no problem. She even selected a few positions for which she felt qualified, but when she went to present the numbers of the listings to the desk clerk—since this was how one obtained the name, address, and phone number of the prospective employer—the woman asked her for her student identity card. Monica fumbled, said she'd left it back in her room, and the woman, suspicious, said, "Well, run and get it then."

"Yes, yes, of course," Monica stuttered and rounded the corridor, away from the job board and the clerk. Then she slumped herself down on a bench. Clearly, she had to find a girl to get the addresses for her, but this was the very sort of chore she'd always felt incapable of, the kind of chore that, if Sonja were here, *she'd* do with quick delight.

Monica sat sullenly on the bench for some time; she was not resolving on a plan of action as much as stewing over her circumstances. Then, a girl plopped down on the bench beside her. She looked to be part European, part Asian. Her face, Monica quickly remarked, was quite beautiful, but she was too heavy to be genuinely attractive. Her plump lower half was stuffed into black jeans, and she wore a pink slouchy shirt, torn at the neck, so one of her shoulders kept slipping out of the garment.

"Lord," she breathed in exasperation and then turned to Monica. "Hey," she said brightly, in a voice that was a little babyish. "I don't know *you*. You can be my subject." She pulled her left leg up onto the bench, so she made a triangle with her leg and her right thigh, and then she clasped her hands before her as if praying. "Saay, you'll do it," she said, bobbing, with a dovening movement, toward Monica. "I've got to interview five people I don't know for this *stu*pid project, and it seems there's only four people in this whole place I don't know." She rolled her eyes and then, as if to prove her point, called out to a few girls passing, "Ciao, Cécile. Hello, Mireille." People didn't respond, and Monica had a feeling the girl was getting her friends' names wrong. Then the girl leaned in close to Monica and said, "It's for psychology, of course. A questionnaire. It won't take long. I promise."

"OK," Monica said, adopting the student's exasperated enthusiasm, "but can you help me with something? I can't find my stupid identity card and the witch over there," Monica gestured with her chin to the end of the hall, "won't give me the addresses for the job board." Monica showed her the piece of paper in her hand, with the penciled numbers of the jobs she was interested in.

"Oh, sure," the student said. "I can get those for you. So, OK, here goes. What's your name and where do you come from?"

Monica told her the truth.

"Really? I'm Justine. I thought I was the only international student here. I'm from the States, though I was born in Korea. Well, the meat of this survey is all of one question—who knows why you need to ask the question of a stranger. Like a friend is going to have trouble answering this honestly, but there you are. Psychology. It's a load of crap. But an easy course. Everything they tell you is obvious. Which is why it's my major." She laughed. "No, that's not true. I find the human mind quite fascinating, don't you?"

"I suppose," Monica said.

"So, anyway, the question is . . ." Justine looked down to read from her notebook. "What is your field of study, and why did you choose this field of study?" Justine looked up. She lifted her pencil above her notebook in preparation for the answer. She smiled goofily and said, "Girl reporter."

Monica was silent. It wasn't that she was above dissembling, but that she couldn't even think of a lie that would suit her. Biology? Of course not. What were the other options? Philosophy? Literature? Physics? History? The depth of her lack of interest in all these things struck her. If only this were the Polytechnic, she thought, but it wasn't as if the answers that institution might provide pulled on her with any more force. She'd always had the vague idea that she would be famous, that, because she was unusual, she'd be singled out, but now it occurred to her that what had struck her as so special about herself—her desire to get away—might be the most ordinary of wants and that independence couldn't be an end in itself.

"So?" Justine prompted Monica.

Monica said, "I . . . um," and smiled in apology before falling silent again.

"Oh," Justine said. "Is it a crisis? This is just the sort of thing I keep hoping they'll talk to us about in psychology, but they just tell us about mice in mazes. Are you doubting your choice? 'Cause that's fine, I can put down, 'Confused,' and if the teacher says it isn't an option, I'll just say that all human responses are legitimate. 'Put this mouse in a maze,' I'll tell her. Huh—that's a good one." She stopped to scribble something on her pad of paper. "Now give me the numbers you want." Justine reached over to take the piece of paper that Monica had folded in her hand. She inspected it and said, "Let's see how many I can get out of her," and then she disappeared around the corner.

She was gone long enough that Monica wondered if she'd just continued down the hall, forgetting altogether to fulfill her end of the bargain, but she came back eventually, settled down on the bench, and said, "Bitch. She'd only give me one, but here it is." She held up her forearm, where she'd penned in the name and phone number. "Nineteen. The job where you get a room in exchange for housecleaning?"

"No," Monica said, "that wasn't one of the numbers I wrote down."

"No?" Justine said. "Strange. Well, I gave her the paper, and this was all she'd give me."

Monica nodded and copied the information down on her own piece of paper.

"Don't know why I do this," Justine said, holding up her inked arm again. "I mean I've *got* a pad of paper. Well, good luck." She stood. "And if you need to talk about your crisis, well, I'm very good with people." Monica nodded. "A pleasure and all that, Monica." She waved goodbye and went back down the hall, giving forceful "Ciaos" as she went.

Of course, Justine didn't seem to have a talent for people. She was a blowhard, but Monica saw there was a lesson to be learned here. Your desires were supposed to accord with your talents, and in thinking this, Monica felt hit, full in the face, with her own mediocrity. She was an OK student. She could sew a serviceable dress and milk a cow. When she baked, the results were tasty but somewhat heavy. When she sang, she was on key but unremarkable. And yet, as she thought all this, she saw that others were equally unremarkable, and yet they made their decision. They chose a life. But what should she choose? In her hand, the paper with the phone number had grown damp. She saw she'd smeared one of the numbers with her own sweat. She couldn't make out if it was a 3 or a 7, so she stood quickly and made her way to the phone, as if the rest of the paper's ink might disappear, as she sat, failing to make a decision.

The number was a 3, and the voice on the other end of the line explained the situation. She and her elderly father needed a live-in maid. There was a room off the roof of the apartment building that Monica could have. Her father and she lived a floor below, in a bedroom—which the father used—and a kitchen, where the daughter slept.

"As you can see," the woman continued, "we are not rich people. But we need some help."

"Yes," Monica said, cringing at the tone of apology in the woman's voice. What ever did *she* have to apologize for?

"Well, then, we'll have to interview you first. When can you come by?"

"At your convenience," Monica offered, and then: "I don't have any classes this afternoon."

Patrice was a strange-looking woman. She was in her twenties, probably, but wore dark-rimmed glasses and pulled her hair back in a bun. The effect wasn't—as one might expect— schoolmarmy; instead, there was a real drama to her. Her hair was black, and she wore bright red lipstick. When Monica arrived, Patrice was wearing jeans and a pretty kimono-type top. If Monica had seen her out on the street, she'd have assumed she lived like the Morandis. The truth was quite a bit less glamorous. Patrice said she earned a living by cutting hair in the apartment, but it was hard to believe that anyone would agree to such an arrangement. The place was a mess, a single dark room, cluttered with clothes and magazines and boxes. The "kitchen" consisted of a tiny half-refrigerator below a sink and hot plate. A shelf above the sink was lined with cereal boxes, their tops open, like baby birds' mouths, to the ceiling.

"We can give you the room upstairs," Patrice said. "And you can eat what's here, but there's never anything here." Monica had drunk her daily liter of milk before she came to the interview— to give her courage—but now it felt as if the liquid was souring in her stomach.

"My father's room is back here." Patrice opened a door and said, "Papa." A man with a long, yellowing beard turned around. He smelled horrible. There were flecks of something—oatmeal?—in his beard. He was sitting at a small table with several boxes on it. There were two small cots in the room, one also piled high with boxes, the other empty.

"So," Patrice said, "he needs to be bathed, and we need the place taken care of. It's five days a week. On the weekend, we take the train out to my brother's, and you can have off."

Monica nodded.

"So let me ask you some questions."

Patrice proceeded through a list, and Monica saw, quickly, that the answer to each question was "yes."

Are you Catholic? Do you really go to the university? Are you a hard worker? Have you done this kind of work before?

Satisfied, Patrice pronounced Monica hired and took her out in the hall to see the closet where the cleaning supplies were and then upstairs to see her room. They climbed a narrow staircase and emerged on a flat roof. It was starting to snow lightly, and though it was darkening outside, Monica had a view of the city, its twilight beauty, and knew she would not go home.

And yet the chore seemed impossible. She could not bathe the old man, could not see her way to handling—as Patrice made clear she would have to—his privates, washing away what he hadn't managed to clean.

"He loves his baths," Patrice had said. "It's the only part of the day he looks forward to."

But how could Monica do it? She'd grown up on a farm, and still this felt beyond her. Indeed, her farm girl past hadn't really toughened her up when it came to certain things: she didn't mind the smell of cow dung but couldn't handle the snails that freckled the strawberry field after a rain.

"Here," Patrice said, after she'd let Monica stare for a while at the city. The older woman took out a key and walked toward a small building with a green door. It looked like a tool shed that had been swept up by a tornado and dropped, randomly, here. Patrice opened the little building's door.

Monica poked her head in. The room was dark and, it seemed, moving. Something flew up at her, and she jerked her head back, called out.

"Ahh," Patrice said, exasperated. "Roaches." She pulled at a string in the middle of the ceiling and a single light bulb illuminated things. There was a sweeping sound, which Monica saw was no broom, but dozens of black bugs running to the corners of the room: under the single bed, and behind a tiny sink. It was the first time Monica had ever seen a roach. "You might want to clean up the room, before you move your things in," Patrice said. Monica had, in fact, already moved her things in, since everything she owned was tucked into the string bag at her back. "We go away this weekend," Patrice said. "We leave in an hour, so you could use the time to settle in. Monday will be your first day of work."

On parting from Patrice, Monica faked a trip to go get her things, which meant that she roamed around the neighborhood for an hour, noting the grocers and the Métro stop. The air was starting to chill, so she lingered by a warm subway grate for a stretch and then returned with the key that Patrice had given her and set to scrubbing out the rooftop room. It was awful. She couldn't believe how dirty the place was. Patrice had said she'd turn on the heat, and the pipes, as they clanged, sent out more of the prehistoric-looking bugs.

Monica dumped bleach and soap on the floor and scrubbed, while she batted the bugs from her. They flew, too. She used even more bleach, making a wet puddle in the center of the room. She pulled off her shoes and socks, hitched up her skirt over her waist. She didn't want to ruin her clothes. It seemed she was just moving dirty water across the floor. She felt like a washerwoman in some children's book. Her own two-handed scrub with the brush struck her as just this side of comical. This wasn't going to work. Finally, she put all her things on the mattress and pushed it up against the wall as if it were a Pullman bed. She started in one corner and began to work methodically back.

What did she want to do? she thought. "Well, not this," she might have told Justine. But even more than she didn't want to do this, she didn't want to wash that old man. If there were bugs here, who knew where else there might be bugs? She tried to put the thought from her mind. Instead the thought combined with the bleach to make her dizzy. She kicked open the door, and despite the snow, which had now created a two-inch-thick white carpet, a grand clean welcome mat for her dirty little garret, she was relieved. She'd worked up a sweat cleaning, and the cold of the night felt good. It was hard to judge the time, but she was nearing the end, working her way till there was just one dirty spot of floor, at the entrance to the room. On her hands and knees, she backed into the snow. She scrubbed the last little bit and then stood, barefoot in the snow. Her feet ached, but she walked quickly to the edge of the roof—to give the floor a chance to dry and to remind herself that this, this pattern of lights, was her reward for scrubbing the floor in the first place. When her feet could stand it no longer, she ran back to the door, and as she did a gust of wind slammed it shut.

"No," she said, out loud, and reached for the doorknob, but it was already locked. The keys were inside. It didn't even matter that she didn't have the money for a phone call; Patrice and her father had not left a number where they could be reached.

Monica jangled the doorknob. "This is my life," she instructed the door. "This is not a Charlie Chaplin movie," but it would not open. She tried kicking at the door with her bare foot, but only succeeded in bruising her toe.

She hurried into the apartment building. Already it felt as if her feet were bleeding from the cold. She could always sleep in the hall. She'd done worse, but it was unheated, and what money she had was in the room. An image of the old man's testicles came to her once again, and she thought she'd be sick. The job was the least of her problems now, but she felt with absolute certainty there was no way she'd be able to do it, that she couldn't wait through a cold and foodless weekend for such horrors. She walked down the several flights of stairs. On each floor, she considered knocking on a door and asking for help, but timidity overwhelmed her. If only Sonja were here, but, of course, if Sonja were here, she would never have gotten herself into this situation in the first place.

Finally, she walked out into the street and down into the Métro. A policeman stood at the far end of the platform. As she got closer, she could see him looking at her, taking in her bare feet. He made a funny sound—almost like a nervous giggle— and she saw he was not much older than she was. She would not, she told herself, cry, not in front of someone who might have been a schoolmate. But her perceptions were off. As she got closer, she saw he wasn't a boy but a delicate, long-limbed man. He had a look of stunned sweetness, like a child who has just woken from a nap.

The subway platform seemed to lengthen as she walked closer to the policeman. He seemed to be at a distance, though she could clearly see the stubble at his cheeks, the quick whisper he made into a box at his hand—was it a walkie-talkie?—and the way he stretched his arms out, forearms up, like some picture she'd once seen in church, when he said, "Mademoiselle?" It was a question, and it was a kind one. Still, Monica felt a noise in her head, a sort of clanging that was apart from the shriek of the subway on the far side of the track or the noise that was coming over the PA. The air of the subway seemed to be forming itself into waves and crashing down on top of her. She thought she might fall back and imagined the air, like water, would hold her if she did. The elements inside her were shifting, as well; her bones felt like they were filled with helium, and they were expanding inside the balloon of her body. Just as she reached the man, she thought what hundreds before her must have thought in his presence: "I'm never going to run away from anything." The thought didn't frighten her, till she saw how she'd make her failure complete. An image came to her, as crisp and clear as anything on a movie screen; it was a picture of herself, inking up the back of a postcard of the Eiffel Tower. *Sonja*, she was scribbling, *I'm going to be a policeman's wife.*

II

When she thinks of herself back then, fainting in front of her husband—for that is what she did, both fainted in front of the policeman and then married him—she doesn't know whether to laugh or cry at herself. How stupid she was, and how brave. She was such a mess of not-knowing. You couldn't even claim she existed, she learned later, when she went to university and studied the existentialists. They said you were the sum of the choices you made, or something like that. And what had she chosen?

In the midst of her barefooted swoon, when she'd had that image of herself writing the news of her engagement to Sonja, she felt a sudden constriction, as if she'd been sucked back to her point of origin. Her feet had felt planted in mud. She'd never leave the farm. She'd just move to a different field.

And, who knows? If, twenty years ago, she'd picked another subway station, walked up to a different man . . . but Monica tries not to dwell on this too much: the ways her life might have gone wrong.

They lived just outside the city, and each night, from their patio, she could see the lights that had so seduced her as a girl. She didn't expect surprises anymore, felt she'd had her share of them between the time she stepped over the dead man in Nice and when her marriage catapulted her into a sphere of wealth that made the Morandis' place look shabby. You didn't expect a policeman to be wealthy, and in her life's single clairvoyant moment, when Monica knew she'd marry the sweet-faced law officer, her vision was of drudgery, a continuation of the state of affairs to date, a sense that her life would always be about stupidity. But Victor Amédée's profession was mere play, something he was doing to upset his notion of himself as a privileged, spoiled brat. And he was privileged and spoiled, but no brat. He had a good heart and an unworldliness that shocked Monica. If he had fallen in love with her—and he insisted he had—it was with everything she didn't like about herself: her farm girl past, her lack of education. He'd never met someone before who knew how to slaughter a chicken.

Being the wife of a rich man, it turned out, was a profession in and of itself, so she didn't begrudge Victor the things he didn't give her. Like children—she'd never wanted them anyway—or passion. He was absentminded about sex. She had to remind him that, like dinner, it was an activity to be regularly engaged in.

Victor gave up enforcing law, soon enough. In Monica, he had what he had wanted out of *that* profession—a touch of the "real" world—so he could give up the hours and costume that never truly suited him, could agree, at last, to do what his parents wanted him to do: enter the family business, as (before long) vice president for Amédée Elevators. You didn't go up or down on the continent or in the States without putting money into the Amédées' pockets. The family was, as Victor himself said, piggishly wealthy.

Money didn't disappoint. Victor sent her to university, and then she was busy on her rounds. She attended charitable occasions and served on the boards of museums. If you had asked her if she was after money when she was young, she'd have denied it. But now that she had it, she liked it, saw how it gave her what she wanted: freedom and ease and, of course, the thing that she felt she most lacked when she was a girl, an idea of what to do with herself. Having come from poverty, she was a novelty in her circle. At first she resisted the way people seemed interested in her story. Then she gave up. Before long, there wasn't a person who knew her who didn't also know the story of how she'd met Victor. It became necessary, in a way, to embrace her past.

Of course, this didn't mean she went home. She sent money and called, but she didn't visit. It made her sick to think of visiting. Even with the money she sent, she knew everything would be the same there, and she couldn't bear it. The same stuffy downstairs room—it used to be the only heated one in the house—would be filled with relatives. People would be telling stories about the hen who refused to go into the henhouse or arguing about who should bring the cows to the upper pasture. Her mother reported that her father was drinking now and that she couldn't get him to eat anymore. He'd have his beer and, perhaps, a bowl of ice cream. His teeth were rotting in his head. His gums were so bad that the bone poked through. Still, he wouldn't go to the doctor, even when Monica said she'd pay for the visit. His only power in the world was in resisting what others wanted him to do, and he exercised it with a fury. Monica's Grand-Papa had died, of course, years ago. Her brothers had gone full-time into the Swiss Army, and her sisters had married and had children. Monica lost count of how many nieces and nephews there were.

What suited Monica so well about her marriage was that Victor and she lived fairly separate lives. They came together in the evenings for dinner and took weekend excursions, but they were apart for the better part of the week. She didn't feel the need to join him on business trips. He didn't feel the need to know every woman she had lunch with, every charity she wrote a check to. It was probably true that their separate worlds bored the other. Victor got tired of the city life and crowds that seemed, as a phenomenon, so unfailingly interesting to Monica. And Monica found the idea of being cooped up in an office for several hours slightly terrifying. Even in her years at the university, she couldn't study for more than an hour at a stretch. While studying for exams, she placed her books on the mantel of the fireplace, so she could walk around as she studied, even do a little dance with her feet as she read about Plato or Thomas Mann or supply and demand curves.

She rarely went to his office. He couldn't bear traffic, so he always took the Métro there and back. On occasion, if they were going out for dinner, she'd pick him up in front of the building, but she never went to help out with the typing or organize his papers, as some of her friends did for their husbands.

One day, though, she had to drop some papers by the office—something he'd left at home—and when she did, she had a bit of a shock. She passed by a storage closet, filled with manila folders, and the woman who was pulling folders from the shelves turned and looked at Monica just as she walked by. She was an Amer-Asian woman, pretty as Monica always found such women, but surprisingly overweight. Perhaps because she admired the elegant slimness of Asian women, she always noticed when one had what she took to be Western ailments: a heavy torso or acne along the cheekbone. Monica smiled and the woman smiled back, and Monica continued on, feeling vaguely unsettled. Then it occurred to her: Justine, the university girl who had once quizzed her about what she wanted from life. She was older, of course, twenty years older, but there was no question. It was Justine.

"The lovely wife," Victor said when he looked up to see Monica at his office door. Monica looked down, as if just considering the wisdom of her outfit—a black skirt and camisole with a sheer maroon blouse over the top. She'd turned out to be interested in fashion, after all, if only because it was a necessity in the circles in which she traveled. Still, she'd never managed to get rid of the chapped redness of her cheeks or the slump of her shoulders. She was in perpetual shrug.

"Victor," she said, without returning his greeting. "Who is that woman, the Asian one, who is filing papers out there?" She gestured with her head back through the corridor. The firm wasn't small, but there were no more than fifty people who worked on the floor.

Victor looked blank for a second and then said, "Oh. Big ass?"

Monica nodded.

"That's Claudia. She's been here forever."

The name didn't dissuade Monica from trusting her memory. Perhaps the girl—but she was a middle-aged woman now—had changed her name.

"You know," Monica started but shook her head. There was no way to explain the effect Justine had had on her that day at the university, and she dropped it. She went back through the office to try to find the woman, but she was nowhere in sight, and what did Monica think? That Justine would remember her? That was hardly likely.

Back home, Monica wondered why she hadn't tried a little harder to explain things to Victor. He probably would have understood. After all, wasn't this something that she and Victor had, at least initially, shared: a desire to get away from their own lives, a desire that so confused them they didn't know what they wanted to do with themselves? Witness his single year as a policeman and, before that, his trouble at university, his constant switching of areas of study till he finally dropped out. It was a bit of a joke between them that of the two, *she* was the college graduate.

In Monica's circle now, people spent a good deal of time dissecting their marriages and the marriages of friends. Monica couldn't quite settle into the custom. She wasn't a gossip, and she didn't feel that she had words to articulate her own situation. She supposed she loved Victor. He was undeniably good to her: a gentle man, a success in business. True, there was a nervousness to him that could be annoying. And some blue-blooded affectations that grated—like saying things were "marvelous," when he thought nothing of the sort. And he had a restlessness, an uneasy manner of jumping from thing to thing. At a party, he was best filling up the wine glasses, avoiding sustained conversation but having a chance to give everyone an enthusiastic hello.

There was a way, even after they'd been married for two decades, Monica had to admit that Victor didn't come into focus for her. She never learned to read his moods in a social situation, and when he reached under the table to touch her thigh, she didn't know whether he was affectionately patting her or warning her that she was saying something stupid.

For their twentieth anniversary, they took a trip to Lucerne, a destination that worried Monica, only because it was so close to home that her failure to visit her mother seemed criminal. As they rode lake steamers and took trams to high mountains, Victor said he couldn't see what Monica had against the country of her origin. He'd never seen any place so beautiful. Monica smiled at him. He knew that she had nothing against the country itself. It was actually nice to speak Swiss-German and to have to translate for Victor. She liked it when he felt in debt to her.

They took a room at a hotel in the center of things, by one of the city's famous bridges and right next to the stylish shops of the old town. Victor went off for golf one afternoon, and Monica used the free time to sit in the hotel's outdoor café and embark on *Anna Karenina*—she'd been meaning to read it for years. Occasionally she'd look up to take in the young people lunching on the banks of the river, the groups of pretty girls with their cartons of iced tea and bags of *gimfili*, and the boys who seemed too young for the early elegance of their female counterparts.

She wasn't making much progress with her novel, only looking down sporadically. Still, her state was as dreamy as if she were reading, so she jumped, quite visibly, when she heard a female voice call her by her maiden name. She looked up and there was Sonja, her girlhood friend. She had just been walking by. It took a moment for Monica to absorb her, to take in the changes in her appearance and register her own emotions at the surprise encounter. The women embraced, gave each other the air kisses—cheeks brushing three times—that were the custom of the region.

"What happened?" Sonja said, gesturing to the table where Monica had been sitting, for the café was known to be one of the best in the city. "Did you marry a king?"

"Almost," Monica said and quickly glanced down at Sonja's ringless hand. "And you? Tell me everything. Come sit. It's been so long since I've seen you."

Sonja stepped out of the thoroughfare and slipped into a chair.

"You look great," Monica said, but Sonja did not look great. She had lost a great deal of weight—even her nose had slimmed down—and there was a vague translucence to the skin around her eyes and, creepily, her two front teeth. Was she dying? She gave no other appearance of being unwell. Her once dark brown hair must have been colored, for it was now the lackluster brown of squirrel fur, lightened, like the rest of her, as if she weren't really herself, but what she'd been for Monica for the past twenty years: a fading photograph.

"Let me buy you some wine," Monica offered. "What would you like?"

When they'd settled on a bottle of something to split, Sonja said, "I don't know that I have much to tell you. It looks like *you're* the one with the story." This was a clear reference to Monica's apparent wealth, and Monica shook her head to play it down, so Sonja continued on. "Me? If you can believe it, I'm still with the Morandis, though I'm no longer an au pair, of course." She gestured at her clothes: a blue suit with a white scarf at her throat. "I'm Monsieur's personal secretary. We're on holiday, and I'm here to translate the 'impossible' Swiss-German. It's a good job now. I have the run of the place when they travel, and it's an easy work week, especially now that the little one is grown."

Monica laughed with Sonja and was about to say she thought she'd left the Morandis, when Sonja said, "Things look so good for you. I'm so glad you never responded to my postcards. You have no idea how good it was that you didn't come for a visit."

Monica smiled, because Sonja was grinning, but she shook her head. "But Sonja, I did visit. I . . . this is so odd. There was a maid there. She told me you had been dismissed."

"Oh, no, no," Sonja said. "You must be confused." She waved at the air, and the gesture, the slight flicking of the wrist, filled Monica with a quick rage. Sonja had used just this gesture when the two girls were young, when they were in public, and Sonja was telling some new acquaintance what a "silly girl" Monica was.

"I'm not at all confused," Monica insisted pleasantly. "There was a maid. I can see her as if it were yesterday. She was very kind. Véronique. She let me stay for a night and told me you'd been accused of stealing a ring." Monica was aware that Sonja might think she was putting her down, remembering something that wasn't flattering, and Sonja did look displeased, so Monica quickly added, "I remember telling her, 'How ridiculous. Sonja would never steal.'"

"Ah, but I did take that ring," Sonja said, her voice dropping. "I had no idea you'd come. I'm so sorry."

Monica shrugged, as if to say, "No need to apologize." "But you're still with the Morandis. I would think . . . "

"Oh, I gave it back. When they found me out, I said I'd found it under the dresser. Madame must have dropped it, and I expressed outrage at having been accused."

"But," Monica started, unwilling to believe Sonja had stolen despite the confession. "You never . . . I mean, I remember you. . . ."

Sonja interrupted her and said, "I was desperate for money. I was so desperate."

There was no question her voice was cracking, so Monica reached out and took her hand. "But you were a girl. The things we did as girls." She shook her head. "Young women seem so much wiser, today. Look at them." She gestured to the girls on the banks.

"Yes," Sonja said, willing to be cheered. "So you must have come when I went on my trip. I did have to go on a trip during those early months with the Morandis. And, anyway, I see I didn't mess up so badly, for here you are. You didn't end up in Paris, after all."

"Oh, no, I live in Paris actually. This is just a holiday."

"But," Sonja continued, "you didn't end up with some policeman."

Monica looked at her. "What are you talking about?"

"A joke," Sonja said quickly and tugged at the scarf at her neck. "A private joke. I'm just glad you didn't . . ."

"But what do you mean? I am. Well, he's no longer a policeman. . . ."

"Oh, good God," Sonja said, as if she'd suddenly remembered something unbearably painful. She looked, all of a sudden, as if she might cry. "How long have you been married?"

"Twenty years. This is actually an anniversary trip for Victor and me. We—" Monica didn't finish her sentence. "But what is it?"

"And you're happy?"

"Well, yes, I am," Monica said, defensive.

Sonja said, "Well, then, there it is. That's all that matters. Isn't it?"

"I suppose so," Monica said, and the two women sipped at their wine and moved on to other subjects, but then something occurred to Monica. She ordered a second bottle and said, "But how did you know that Victor was a policeman?"

"Oh, a dumb joke. I didn't mean a thing by it. Amédée Elevators. So impressive. I must have ridden them a thousand times."

Monica nodded. She had told Sonja what line of business her husband was in, but she hadn't mentioned her husband's—or her—surname yet. "My God," she said. It was, all of a sudden, completely clear. "You're having an affair with him, aren't you? Why else would you be in Lucerne and know his name and that . . . Oh, God."

"No, no," Sonja cried. "Don't be ridiculous."

"And you never married. Of course not," Monica said, bitterly. "A mistress, instead. Much more glamorous."

"No," Sonja said. "That's crazy."

"The whole Morandi thing. Ridiculous. Of course you don't still work there. You . . . Oh, God."

"No," Sonja said and reached across the table to take Monica's hands, but Monica flung her hands off hers. "It would be better if . . ."

"Better than . . ."

Sonja held up her hand. "Please," she said. "I was young. I was desperate for money. When they asked me to write you a postcard and tell you to come visit, I did it. I didn't think you'd come."

"But, of course, you knew I wanted to leave."

"Well, I guess, you're right. I *did* think you'd come, but I didn't think you'd stay. I never thought you'd meet Victor or end up with that couple—I don't remember their names— that horrible old man and the daughter, the one who Victor arrested." She lifted her hands to put quotation marks around the word *arrested*.

"Arrested?" Monica said.

"Yes. What was it?" Sonja said. "Did they say he had drugs or something? I can't even remember."

Monica felt she might cry, too. How did Sonja know about the old man and his daughter? And what was she talking about? Arrested?

"It was Véronique who arranged it. She always had crazy friends. And there was a man, a male prostitute, who she liked. He was part of a circle of artists she spent time with. I think she thought it was daring to count him as a friend. And Véronique, she was very beautiful. Perhaps you remember?"

Monica remembered no such thing. She said flatly, "That woman had the face of a ferret."

Sonja coughed and said, "This male prostitute told her to come to his flat—at an appointed hour—and sit in a chair. There were a few other men milling about. Then, Victor—

I'm sorry—then Victor rang the bell. She barked out some commands. You know: do this and do that, and the men did it to him, and when it was all done, she said, Victor was very polite, gave her a tip, and asked after her circumstances. He was educated, and she liked talking with him. They went out for drinks after, and that's when they hatched up the plan, for he couldn't help himself, he said, the thing with the men, but he needed to have a respectable life, needed both equally badly. He wanted Véronique to marry him, but she wouldn't do it. She said no woman in her right mind would. Which is how they got the idea of getting a farm girl, I mean, someone naive enough not to figure it out, his proclivities and all, and Véronique thought I'd know someone."

When Monica's mother was angry, her chin used to tremble, as if she had palsy, and Monica was aware that her jaw was shaking now. She didn't think it had ever happened to her before. She placed her chin in her palms, to steady her face, aware this made her look like an ingenue, fascinated by her friend's story.

"They knew, I mean, Véronique knew I was hardly a likely prospect."

Oh, yes, Monica thought, not you. Not clever you, but me, of course. Of course, me. "I . . . ," she started but found no words would come. She felt that speedy panic she associated with learning that a friend had died.

"I'm sorry. I'm so sorry. I thought you'd see how it was with him, as soon as you met him. His girlish looks, his . . ." Sonja stopped, as if finally aware that she was making it worse.

Victor, Monica thought, as if the word itself had a meaning that would resist what she was being told, but what she said was,

"Why me? Good God, in Paris you can always find someone to marry a rich man, whatever the terms of the marriage."

"But he didn't want someone like *that*. He wanted a true marriage, and then once I'd shown him your picture, he liked your looks. He wanted *you*. It wasn't just an anyone-willing sort of thing. And you were so brave. You'd done the Nice thing. I knew you'd be OK."

No one, Monica wanted to spit at her, no one has *ever* liked my looks.

"You always had that androgynous thing going on," Sonja said with what sounded like jealousy. Then she added, "And the dairy farm. He liked where you came from."

Monica studied her. Could she be lying? "It doesn't make sense. Why such an elaborate scheme? Why not just introduce us?"

Sonja laughed. "You must not remember what you were like then. You didn't date. It had to look like an accident."

Monica thought of an article she'd read—years earlier—about mail-order brides, pretty Southeast Asian girls who ended up with obese, American husbands.

Sonja tugged at the scarf at her neck and was quiet.

"So," Monica said, "Véronique sent me to the university and there Justine—who was an employee of Victor's anyway—sent me to the job, but how did . . . I mean, what if I'd never walked down into the subway. I could have done a thousand things that night."

Sonja looked at her. "What subway? He came to you, no? He met you when he came to arrest the couple for drug trafficking—not that they were really . . ."

Monica blinked. She repeated the story she had told so many times before, about how she had met Victor.

Sonja protested, "No, no, that wasn't how you were supposed to meet."

An elderly woman, with flesh that bagged like old socks at her ankles, jostled by Monica's table. In France, a waitress never seated strangers at the same table, but here it was different. The old woman was placed at the neighboring table—across from a middle-aged man who was spooning whipped cream into his mouth. He was alone and eating an ice cream sundae, crowned with a green cookie. He looked pitiful, and Monica had the sudden urge to lean over and ask him to marry her.

"They were," Sonja's voice called her back to her own table, "going to set up this fake drug bust. It really is an amazing coincidence about the subway. I mean that was his—what-do-they-say—his beat, but even so."

What kind of person would do this sort of thing? She'd trusted them all, every single one. Signposts on the way. That's how she came to think of them later. Directions: this is how you get out of your life.

"I . . ." Sonja looked like she might apologize again, so Monica quickly said, "Why did they?"

"Oh, that old man and that girl? They were so abominably poor. They were on the edge of starving. I don't know whether it was Claudia or Véronique who found them. Oh, I know. It was Véronique. She was in the market, and she overheard two women talking about wasn't it horrible that some people actually ate animal food, and then one woman admitted that she thought cat food made a decent meatloaf, and then the other laughed and confessed she made meat patties out of it. Véronique, why'd *she* do it? Well, you know—a lark. Anything like that, she went for. She left the Morandis shortly after. Became a photographer. For all I know, Victor set her up with a studio."

"He's not a bad man," Monica said, though she had no idea why. Surprised as she was, she was aware that she should be completely flabbergasted, that her willingness to believe what Sonja was saying about Victor must mean that she was aware that it could be true. Not that if you put her in a locked prison for a hundred years, gave her nothing to do but think, she'd ever have come up with this. Indeed, her husband had always been rather unforgiving on the subject of homosexuals, a tendency that had often embarrassed her as she moved—what with the museum and charitable work—in nominally liberal circles. Oh, God, Monica breathed, and thought of how infrequently they made love, how she'd slowly accommodated herself to Victor's relative lack of sexual enthusiasm.

"But, you," she said, at last. "We ... We were friends. You were my friend."

"I'm ... yes. I'm so sorry. But you must have known when I went away ..."

"Horrible," Monica interrupted before she finished. "A horrible thing to do." She *hadn't*—she told herself—she *hadn't* known such meanness before—not in her day-to-day life with Victor, who'd put this whole thing in motion. There was no meanness there. It was impossible to put it all together.

Sonja must have thought she was talking about Victor. "I don't think he can help it. I mean, it doesn't mean he's a bad husband."

Monica flinched at this, not at what Sonja was saying, but at the implication that she knew more about Victor than Monica did. After all, she thought, *I'm* married to him, though it seemed an idiotic thing to think in light of what she'd just learned.

"It's not just men," Sonja went on. Was the woman happy to be telling her all this? Was this her revenge for having lived as a servant while Monica, her husband's habits aside, had so much? "It's women, too. He likes women, I mean. You know, the story was that, as a boy, he'd been lovers with an orphaned cousin who lived with them, after her parents died in a train wreck— well, *you'd* know about that—and that was why—"

"Would you just shut up?" Monica said, and Sonja swallowed, sat up stiffly, and whispered, "Sorry." Did everyone know all this? Every time she'd told that dumb story of how they'd met, was everyone laughing? But, of course, that couldn't be. This was something Victor would have wanted to keep hidden from friends, too. They'd have been no more forgiving than his parents.

It was Sonja's meanness that was so impossible. She was the worst. Sonja whom she'd loved and admired so much. "And you?" It was clear Monica meant, "How could *you?*"

"But, of course, you knew. I mean, everyone in town knew," Sonja said, suddenly angry, as if Monica were to blame for what Sonja was about to say. "When I went away, I was pregnant. That Yugoslavian, if you must have every little fact."

Monica kicked her foot out, reflexively, as if a snail had suddenly crawled on it. She said, "Oh," a little insufficient word for all she was feeling. She had left Switzerland twenty years ago. Now, she was thirty-eight, which wasn't old. She knew that. But she didn't feel young, although—if the general longevity of women in her family continued into her generation—she would have time to live her years all over again. There was no telling what might happen next. And for the moment, she didn't care. She only wanted to dismiss this woman in front of her. An affectation, a phrase from her years as a wealthy woman rose to her lips, and she decided to say—with a detached disdain, as if she believed nothing of what she had just been told—"My, my." And she did just that, but the words sounded, to her ears—who knew or cared what Sonja heard?—like a baby goat's bleat. But she didn't care about that, either. Indeed, the tremulous notes of her own voice were so appealing that she said it a second time—"Ma-ma"—before standing to pay the bill.

LADY OF THE WILD BEASTS

First, her name was Jane, and if that wasn't bad enough, one day, while she was sitting in the dining hall and drawing her trademark Jews—tiny cartoon men with beards and wisdom who decorated the edges of all her notebooks—the men got up off the page, shimmied down a table leg, and bussed her cafeteria tray for her. That's right, a full-fledged schizophrenic break, and just when things were looking so rosy—her law school applications in and all. Normally, on Fridays, she volunteered at the raptor center just south of campus, offering her services as tree for any hawk who might want to have a go at her forearm. As she had been absentmindedly darkening a skullcap, she'd been wondering if she had enough gas for the round trip to the center, but now all such thoughts left her. She followed those little men to the wet conveyor belt by the dish room, then over to the college chapel—they seemed inclined for prayer—till she ended up, a few weeks later, at Claremont Psych. There was a great uncle somewhere who clenched his hand a lot—some mild form of Tourette's—but otherwise her family was pretty normal, or dead. (Dad was gone, the grandparents.) Well, sometimes the fates conspired against you. She'd gotten straight As, more or less, in college. A history major who took a lot of art classes. "All that pressure," her doctors said. Would she like to try something a bit more rote? Perhaps retail at a large clothing store?

Or, perhaps, a relevant family member could provide some sense of direction?

But there were no relevant family members. Mom was pretty helpless, even in the best of times. As for Sharon, Jane's twin sister, she aspired to housewifedom. "Housewiffledom," Sharon corrected Jane when she was feeling particularly accused. "I've always wanted to rule my own little housewiffle." At the hospital, Jane's roommate (undiagnosed by the doctors; diagnosed by Sharon and Jane as a real pill) said, "There's more than one person who'd bluff their way to the loony bin if they thought it meant permanent disability."

"Maybe," Jane said, to nobody's pleasure, "instead of retail, I'll go to art school?"

Hayden Smith finished typing the words *art school*, rolled his shoulders, and stood.

"Is this what you had in mind?" he asked, extending a piece of paper, still warm from the computer printer, to his boss, Jay Smart Tanner. Or Jay "They Don't Call Him Smart for Nothing" Tanner. The guy *was* pretty good at what he did. And mostly what he did was tell Hayden that he wasn't a very good writer. For weeks now, he'd been explaining that it wasn't enough to summarize plot. To write capsule reviews for *Cartoon Olympics*, you had to convey the *tone* of what you were synopsizing.

Which seemed odd, as if Hayden wasn't writing a summary for a marketing catalog, but Cliffs Notes for those who might find his publisher's products—adult-oriented comics, graphic novels, "Classics Illustrated"—too difficult to penetrate.

"I spoke to you," Jay Smart said, "about the word *paraphrase*, didn't I? It's got a lot of the same letters as the word *plagiarize*, but it means something entirely different."

Hayden hardened his face, a look his boss consistently misread as one of noncomprehension. Maybe he could transfer back to production. No one gave Hayden shit when he was still an inker, tracing over other people's pencil drawings. No one gave him shit, and he got to listen to the radio while he worked.

"Use your own words," Jay Smart said, with something like teacherly compassion. *How hard it must be to be an idiot.* "And get to the end of the story."

"Her story?"

"No, not her story, for Christ's sake. Just the story of the comic."

"Right-o," Hayden said, with a mock eagerness guaranteed to rankle his boss. "Will do." He headed back to his desk, Jane Berger's slim volume, *Becoming a Nutcase: A Training Manual,* tucked under his arm.

"Wow," Sharon Berger turns to say to her friend, "this doesn't look like any place I've ever been."

Tom lifts his hands off the steering wheel, as if in protest against her words. "I just drive here," he says.

"That so? That's not much of a defense."

"Sure it is. Haven't I introduced myself? Tom Solari, Hobo of the Road, famous underground persona, store my towels under the driver's seat, keep condiments in the glove compartment."

"Clever," Sharon allows.

"At least I'm all that, when I'm not driving home to see my wife in . . ." Tom stops, gives a mock shudder. "*Rochester, New York.*"

Since last summer, it has been Tom and Kathleen Solari's joke to say these three words—"Rochester, New York"—and then slap their hands to their cheeks in a silent open-mouthed shriek, à la the now-ubiquitous Munch painting "The Scream."

"It won't be so bad. It'll have its charms," Sharon has been saying all along, as they've complained about Tom's transfer. But, so far, Sharon thinks, she's been wrong. It's spring back home in Asheville, even highway embankments cluttered with wildflowers. Here, in Rochester, it seems to be no season. Not winter, not anything else. For miles now, the sky's been a fleecy blanket of gray. For color, there's only been the green of highway signs. Tom takes an exit, and Sharon forgoes the consoling tone she's adopted to smooth her friends through their move. "Oh, I see you've got a McDonald's here," she says. "That's nice. That's a very nice touch."

Tom gives her an oh-shut-up smile and then rubs his palm over a tuft of hair that (due to a bad haircut, another reason to hate Rochester) stands stiffly atop his head. Though Sharon likes Tom, she doesn't know him like Kathleen, pal for two decades, ever since college. She can't guess how much teasing is too much, thank you, when it comes to him, so she shifts gears, says, earnest as a diary entry, "I was a mapmaker in a former life. When I'm alone in a new town, I drive around and look at everything, so I know how things fit. Then I go back and look closely."

"Yeah, I'm the same way."

"Really? I guess I thought I was alone in that." ("Can't you *have* an experience without cataloging it?" Jane used to say.) "I always feel fairly hysterical as I'm racing about." She stops to mimic herself. "Yeah, so that's the Louvre. I got it, I got it. What's next?"

"Right," Tom says. "That's me to a T. At least when I was younger."

"Oh," says Sharon, vaguely confused, for she has always thought of Tom as someone like her sister Jane. He's involved in photography. Thus, quasi-arty. But he's married, of course, and has children. So he's nothing like Jane. Nothing at all. How disappointing, Sharon thinks. She has known him for years, but only as Kathleen's husband—a sidekick at dinner, a good-natured presence who watches the kids when Kathleen and Sharon go shopping. It's as if she is only really seeing Tom now, on this drive. How disappointing, she thinks again, and then, simultaneously, What a relief.

Tom Solari is making the lengthy trip, the endless drive from North Carolina to Rochester, because he has no choice. Kathleen and he have recently relocated—he works for Polaroid; she is an unemployed nurse—and this final bit of business, the driving of the car from North Carolina, is Tom's job. Kathleen was going to do it, but the night before last, her favorite great aunt, Lila, fell off a stepstool and broke her hip. So Kathleen has taken her two children and herself to Manhattan for a quick visit. They're to be back tonight, if they aren't home already.

Sharon is along for company. Sharon is along to help. But mostly Sharon is along to see Kathleen, to hear Kathleen say, "What can I do?" and "Do you want some tea?" and "Of course, you're not all right. No one expects you to be all right." She is here to hear Kathleen say, "You tell those lawyers to shove it."

Tom, for his part, seems relieved that the trip is almost

over and that Sharon hasn't mentioned Jane. He must have been afraid that this trip would be a litany of Sharon's woes or that, once they were moving, Sharon would fall catatonically silent, or that she would doze in depression, lolling her head against the passenger window and drooling rivers into the yoke of her sweater. But for the last hour—the final stretch of the journey—Sharon has been telling stories about her son, Tyler (recently he adopted a grape, insists it's his pet), and Tom's been answering in kind. Or just saying he remembers how sweet kids are when they're toddlers. Not adding, as so many of Sharon's friends, parents of older children, do, "Ah, just you wait." (She resents the wisdom of her contemporaries, which seems—even now that she has Tyler—like an insult, a reminder that it took her over a decade to carry a single pregnancy to term.)

Tom's hand wanders back to his crown. "I need gel or something. I look like someone plugged me into the wall."

Sharon laughs. "It's kind of punk. I like it." And then unbidden, like a chicken foot, floating up in the polluted bay of her memory comes this small fact. When Sharon was twelve, she and Jane got different haircuts. Sharon kept hers long; Jane cut hers in layers that ended at her ears. And then Jane cried and cried. No one would know they were twins now. They had never been the kind of twins who wore the same outfits or even did similar things. They had few friends in common. But with the haircut, Jane had panicked. If people didn't know they were twins, how would they know they were special?

Hayden typed: *College in Virginia, two years at Pratt Institute, one year in Lincoln, Nebraska, then back to Brooklyn, New York.*

Those were the facts of Jane Berger's life, but Hayden

knew the summary didn't convey the tone of Jane's cartoon autobiography. Plus it was too short. It left everything out.

His job wasn't half as interesting as he'd thought it would be when he started at the beginning of the year.

His job sucked.

"Hey," Tom says, slowing and then pulling the car to the curb. "We're here." They've stopped in front of a blue Victorian, a house that looks barny, outsized, and cramped, all at the same time. It is only an arm's-length away from the homes to its right and left. (Literally. Kathleen said her neighbor once passed the Yellow Pages through their respective kitchen windows.)

"What?" Sharon protests. "You were supposed to give me the tour as we got near. Say things like this is where Samuel and Jonathan go to school, this is where we buy Froot Loops, this is where the busybody at the corner lives, and this *is* the corner."

"OK, OK," Tom says as they get out of the car. He gestures grandly toward the road. "This is *my* street."

"Oh, really? This very street?" Sharon looks down the road, takes in the handful of detached wooden homes. Two-family dwellings, she guesses, with a family on the bottom floor, a single professional on top. In the evening dark, she can make out two "For Sale" signs. "OK." She stretches out the stiffness from the ride and imagines the great relief of collapsing into tears when she and Kathleen finally have a talk. "We're here. I'll mark it on my map. Center of the Universe."

When they enter the house, what they find, instead of Kathleen—armed with soap and her advice to take a bath, have some tea, and read a trashy magazine—is a slight, dark-haired woman, wearing black pants and an oversized blazer with a print of a Georgia O'Keefe skull on the back. "You," Tom says, in a deadpan and after an old Talking Heads song, "are not my beautiful wife."

"Alas," the woman smiles, sounding genuinely regretful. Then she drops the flirtatious tone and adds, "Well, I'm afraid I have bad news for you." Her mouth purses into a funny O of concern. "That slip that Kathleen's great aunt took? It was no slip at all. It was a heart attack. She lost consciousness, then she fell off the stepstool. Since she's been in the hospital, she's had a second and a third and now she's dead."

"Oh," Tom says.

"I'm so sorry, honey," the woman adds, reaching for Tom's arm.

Tom steps back from her fingers, turns to Sharon, and says, almost cheerfully, "Well, she was getting up there."

"Eighty-seven," the woman puts in. "At any rate, Kathleen's still in New York with the boys, and she'll need you to join her. She says you know where."

Tom nods. "OK."

"She's got to stay and do the funeral arrangements."

Tom continues to bob his head, and then his nod turns to self-reprimand, as if he means to say, "Where are my manners?" He coughs. "Sharon, this is Mariah, our down-the-street neighbor and . . ."

"As for you, Ms. Berger. I'm here to keep you company till Tom and Kathleen get back."

Tom grimaces. "Till we get back?"

"Like I said: she wants you to join her."

"I could go too?" Sharon offers, but Tom shakes his head.

"*You* know," he shrugs, suggesting the obvious: Kathleen, for all her virtues, isn't a great graveside schmoozer.

"Oh, crap. I'm going to miss her entirely." There's no way Sharon can extend her stay into Monday. Is it too much to admit she's jealous of the dead woman, for receiving Kathleen's care? Not that she goes uncared for back home, but she has Tyler, a built-in reason not to collapse into tears in the supermarket, though for some reason it is there, with the large aisles of pointless choices, that Sharon feels most desperate.

"I'm good company," Mariah says. "Don't worry."

"Oh. Of course, I didn't mean to suggest . . ."

But, then, just to disprove her claim, Mariah adds, her mouth again pursing into its Betty Boop O of sympathy, "I'm so sorry about *your* loss."

So Kathleen has already told her. Or maybe Mariah just saw it in the papers.

Jane Berger's best friend was Andy Meyers. She met him at the raptor center, where he worked for years, till he got a job at a Brooklyn aviary, which he didn't like that well, but which made (he had to admit) for a better social life. (There hadn't been that many people out of the closet in his particular pocket of Virginia.) He and Jane weren't alike really. Andy had never been to college. He wasn't comfortable around Jane's art-school friends, but he loved animals. Like Jane, he had a way with them—particularly young animals. He'd have been a veterinarian, he said, but he knew it would break his heart. He didn't like seeing animals in pain.

"Me neither," Jane said, back when they first met. And thus a friendship that lasted two decades. "He was her soul mate," people said at Jane's funeral. "There was nobody she loved more." And apparently he felt the same way. He'd listed Jane as the first and only benefactor on all his mutual funds. Jane— who'd drawn up a will only after her cartoon autobiography sold to the movies—had listed Andy first, too. And Sharon second.

Years ago, when Andy tried to come out of the closet, his mother said, "If you're trying to tell me you're gay, you've got another thing coming to you, young man."

"What're you going to do," Andy said, emboldened by her manner, "*hit* me?"

And now this very same mother, this mother who thought you could spank a person out of homosexuality, was suing Sharon Berger. To get the money that Jane had left Andy. Only the movie producers wanted their money back, since Jane had never finished her screenplay.

"You left out the whole thing about how he was a loner," Hayden's boss put in.

"Because he was such a fat guy. One of those gay guys who never actually does it."

"Where does it say that?"

"It doesn't," Hayden admitted. "But you can guess it from the way she's drawn him, right? He's openly gay, and he's a virgin."

Hayden's boss said, "We're not writing papers for our English class here. Just the summary. OK?"

"Well, see, if he was her best friend, she might not have wanted to say that. Might have hurt his feelings."

"Summary," his boss said and made a thumbs-up sign. "Invention," he said, then drew a circle in the air, and put a line through it. "This here," he pointed his finger downward to his cluttered desk, but it was clear he meant the office as a whole, "is a No Invention Zone."

Sharon Berger has heard a bit about Mariah, a neighbor with two little girls who regularly wander into Kathleen's house and remove all their clothes. Kathleen thinks it's sort of sweet—

their little bodies racing about her house—though they're in the habit of dropping to the floor for a yoga move (knees bent, legs flopping open and shut), which can be discomfiting. As Sharon makes her way up the stairs with her bag, she notes a few unfamiliar items. In the corner, a small, pink-sequined flapper dress. Over the banister, a deep-red flamenco dress with black lace.

Otherwise, it's the usual mess, Kathleen and Tom having achieved the look of a place just moved into and the look of a place ruined by lengthy occupancy. There are unpacked boxes in all the rooms, as well as half-packed boxes. Clearly, items are being removed as needed. Dresser drawers don't close, sweaters tumble from closet shelves. The walls must have been recently repainted, but at every corner and doorjamb there are finger smudges. Downstairs, cupboard doors swing open, and scraps of food decorate the kitchen. Someone has written *Shithead* in magnetic letters on the refrigerator.

Once when Sharon was visiting Jane in the city, she scrubbed Jane's toilet bowl—inside and out—thinking Jane would return to the apartment pleased for the favor. This was when they both were still in their twenties. Jane had been appalled. Of course, Sharon would understand the insult if she decided to spend a weekend straightening Kathleen's house, but back then she'd been surprised by Jane's reaction. They were sisters, after all. She'd actually hoped Jane would be impressed with how well she knew to clean a bathroom, a grown-up skill that (she only realized as Jane was yelling at her) she'd been proud of acquiring.

By six that evening, Tom is gone, and Mariah and Sharon are making their way to the living room, glasses of wine in hand. The house is chilly, Sharon's toes slightly numb. A Cheerio pops out of the couch's cushions as Sharon sits. Skinny Mariah plucks it from Sharon's hand and pops it into her own mouth.

"Stale," Mariah admits wryly. "But tasty."

Mariah won't devolve into a type Sharon recognizes. She has the dark hair and drawn face of a stricken Italian mother. Yet, when she slips off her funny-looking jacket, she is wearing—and this despite the weather—a white tank top. Her figure is good—which makes Sharon uneasy; people with good figures have always made her uneasy.

"Oh," Mariah says, before she sits. She goes back to the kitchen for some matches and then lights a candle on the table behind the sofa.

"I made this," she says. "It's a tea tree oil candle. Very healing. I make tea tree oil lip balm, too."

"For a living?"

Mariah laughs, as she circles back to the front of the couch. "For . . . like one-eighth of a living. And then my husband's superintendent of the schools, so that takes care of the other seven-eighths. More or less. I don't get too many weekends like this. Off from the kids."

Does this mean she plans on sleeping over? That they need to have dinner together?

"Now tell me about you," Mariah adds. Sharon feels a different question—"What happened to your sister?"—underneath this request, but she says, "Well, my husband's a corporate accountant, and I make cakes out of my home. For local restaurants, and I do some mail order."

"How long have you been married?" Mariah asks.

"It's been . . . fifteen years, I guess. Hard to believe," Sharon says, and it *is* hard to believe. Time has never made any sense to her.

"Me, just four. I got married when I got pregnant with

Clarissa, my oldest. I never thought I'd marry. I didn't really want to. I don't think I *get* marriage."

Sharon nods at this, but not in agreement exactly. What's to get?

"Every night this week, I've dreamed of divorce. Of course, I'm never divorcing my husband, but an old boyfriend of mine, from my twenties. But I've got the girls in my dream. So sometimes I wonder if it really is my husband."

Sharon smiles at this confession, more out of embarrassment than pleasure. "I just don't think about it all that much," she admits, and then imagines Jane scoffing. Interviewers were often surprised to learn that Jane had a twin, and when they asked the inevitable "What's she like?" Jane would say, "We're just really, *really* different."

"You spend so long thinking about how to attract a guy and then ... it's strange ... it's just hard to drop those habits. Like—" It occurs to Sharon that Mariah may be drunk. All these confidences to a relative stranger. "There's a man who owns a store that sells my candles, and he told me ..." Mariah interrupts herself. "Would you like another?" She points at Sharon's empty glass.

"Actually, I'll get it. Or some water."

"OK," says Mariah. When Sharon stands, Mariah lifts her seat cushion. "Hey, M&Ms!" She eats the single red candy she's found and then pokes at her own seat cushion. "I wonder if the kids left any mussels in here. I'm really in the mood for some mussels."

Jane Berger didn't marry. Jane Berger didn't date. Jane Berger didn't receive valentines. Jane Berger slept with a man at art school who said things like, "You're such a basket case. I'm the only one who will have you." He really said things like this; it wasn't just Jane making it up. Later, people—not women, but men who loved women who had known this guy—said it was so. The guy was a handsome psychopath. He knew what women to date. He was a hanger-on at Pratt. Even people who'd graduated decades apart knew him. He dressed like a banker—suits, a camel hair coat, sometimes a fedora—and he dated a woman with a strawberry wine stain over half her face, a girl who had lost her hands in a fire, and Jane Berger, of course.

"He sounds horrible," Sharon had said back then.

"He is," Jane admitted. She wasn't dumb. "But who else will have me?"

"Don't talk like that. That's crazy. If I can find someone, you can find someone."

"But you," Jane said—only it sounded like an indictment—"are normal."

"This isn't in the book," Jay Smart Tanner said, pointing to Hayden's latest effort.

"I know," Hayden smiled. "But I've been doing some research. I've been asking around. Don't worry. It's not invention. It's the truth."

His boss smiled back. "You're fired."

"You mean you're sending me back to production?" Hayden had actually been getting into this Jane Berger story—the little facts he'd dug up, Joe Reporter–style—but it'd be nice to be back with the other inkers.

"Nope, nope. They've replaced you down there."

"Well, wait a second, you mean you're just going to—?"

"Don't worry," Tanner said, checking the calendar, to see

exactly how long Hayden had been with *Cartoon Olympics*. "It's an unemployment check."

When Sharon opens the refrigerator, it barks. She closes the door and reopens it. To check her impression? To see if this time it might moo or cock-a-doodle-doo? The door barks again. Sharon turns to see a large brown puppy eyeing her from behind a corner gate. "They've got a dog," Sharon says, though Mariah is still in the living room and can't hear her.

Sharon doesn't know a thing about dogs—nothing about breeds or behaviors—except that she has always hated them. The dark dirty hole of their asses, their slobbery tongues, their hairy, eager bodies, plump with blood, and (most of all) their large, stalagmite teeth. This dog looks unaccountably *thick*, as if he (all dogs are he in Sharon's world; all cats she) were formed from the dirt that Kathleen's boys tracked in. Sharon can just see accommodating Kathleen trying to placate the kids by saying, "You want a dog? Let's see what we can do," and sweeping her arm across the floor, packing together broken leaves and wet dirt to make this animal.

"Hey," Mariah calls as she comes into the kitchen.

"Dog's new," Sharon says.

"Yup. Hairbrush. Jonathan named him." Mariah leans over the gate to scratch behind the dog's ears. "Here, I'll let him out."

"No, no, don't do that. I'm . . . I'm actually scared of dogs."

"Are you *really?*" Mariah asks, as if she's just encountered a highly unusual phobia. "Were you ever bit?"

"No, no. I just have this thing. I'm bad with animals. Don't like to feed carrots to horses, that sort of thing."

It occurs to Sharon that if Mariah has read about Jane, she's seen the photo that was running in all the papers: of Jane, arm crooked, smiling at a redtail hawk perched by her fist. The photo had originally been for the raptor center where Jane's friend Andy once worked. "Lady of the Wild Beasts," the bold part of the caption read—a reference, but who would know this, save the author and Sharon (who happened to have taken a college class in Greek mythology) to Artemis, Apollo's twin sister, virgin goddess of wild animals.

Mariah smiles at Hairbrush. "We'll have to keep him away from you."

"No, no, it's my job. To deal with it. And I am getting better." She leans over the gate to pat the dog lightly on the back, the quick warmth of his body under her palm—*Arrgh! It's alive!*—an unsurprising shock. "I can handle small dogs, and I'm getting better with dogs like this. He seems," she lies, she is always lying when she says something like this, "like a nice dog."

Jane Berger had a favorite review, of course, one she went back to when she was having trouble working. It said that she, Jane Berger, must be the love child of Will Eisner and Sylvia Plath. "It's not entirely a compliment," her psychiatrist once pointed out.

"But I never get the urge to put my head in an oven."

"Yes."

"Only . . . you know, to get the devil to leave my bedroom."

"You're feeling that way now?"

"Nooo. A joke," Jane had said in a tone that seemed to include the sentence, "You remember jokes, don't you?" She'd added, just to clarify—no reason to frighten the shrink—"You know, back when, back before the medicine . . ."

But the truth was: just last night, she woke with a fright. It felt like someone had stuck tweezers into her ear and pinched a bit—just a small bit—of her brain away.

The thing was, right now, everything *was* fine, save the buzzing, which she knew was just a side-effect of her medicine, but was still making it hard for her to do the screenplay. And that was why she was in such good (or bad) shape right now. Someone—why, it might be a schizophrenic's fantasy, but it was true—had deposited a quarter million dollars in her bank account, because she had agreed to write a screenplay about her own life. Based on her comic book. On the book that she had written and drawn (but she had yet to admit this to anyone) in a handful of months. Jane, just shy of forty, had never been very disciplined about her art. She called herself a comic strip artist and had the one book. (That one book was ten years old, and for most of the decade, it was something no one read, no one save for goony overweight boys with their trays of cinnamon rolls and wheezy enthusiasm for fantasy, all those over-eager boys with their heartbreaking, sweaty grips around their rolled-up comic books. What a life! To be drawing for those guys.) Jane had the one book and then, in more recent years, a few short pieces in *World War 3* comics, to her name. She'd been getting by—if you could call it that—teaching after-school art classes. Not much of a living. But now she had a contract and a deadline, too, for her screenplay. All because some movie producer picked up her tattered book from under a lopsided table in the john of some Starbucks. (Well, she had managed to get a quick strip out of that. The guy discovering her by reading about her on the john.) Next September. That was her deadline. They'd even started to cast. Only Jane couldn't figure out how to write without drawing.

It will all be fine, she told herself. It was really her medicine that made it so hard, that made her head so very buzzy.

Last week, she had called an old friend from college who was working as a political cartoonist. "You didn't see the *New York Times* article about me?"

The friend had hesitated.

"I've become," Jane had said—in her slow, studied voice; her medicated voice that prevented her from coughing up the laugh she wanted to cough up, so it would be clear that she was trying to be ironic, making fun of her own success—"something of a poster girl for schizophrenia. All praises to clozapine. You know: you can be schizophrenic and have a normal life. That sort of thing."

The friend had waited and waited for Jane to ask her how she was, what she was doing, and when she hadn't, she had finally asked, "So who are you hoping will play you in the film?"

Hayden couldn't help but note—and maybe because he was not doing this for money any longer, but for his own enjoyment or even "art," not that such pretensions had ever been part of his personal game plan—that writing about Jane *was* a form of . . . well, not schizophrenia, but multiple personality disorder. For the moment of the writing, Hayden got to "be" Jane. Not that that was in his personal game plan, either. Not that he had a personal game plan beyond employment in the relatively near future.

Employment, and not, please God, in a Xerox shop.

In the morning, there is a large man in Kathleen's kitchen, heavy work boots propped on the edge of the red Formica table, mug of coffee resting on his belly. His straight black hair and beard shimmer with cleanliness, and Sharon (who, unlike Kathleen, is super-neat) finds this cleanliness vaguely repulsive, coupled (as it is) with a general slovenliness of manner. The man's fleece shirt is misbuttoned, his lips too full and red, as if chafed from a recent spurt of sensual activity.

"This is my friend Mark," Mariah says with a smile. "The one I was telling you about."

Sharon looks at Mariah blankly. She cannot remember being told about any friend.

"At the Golden Buddha. The health food store?"

Sharon remembers a reference to him before the women finally went to bed, something about what he said or thought about marriage, but she can't quite recall if the discussion was ever finished. Since Mark is not—as Sharon first thought—a workman, she wonders what he's doing here. He can't possibly have stayed the night—surely Sharon would have heard him come in—though there is everything in his manner (at least his general comfort in the kitchen) to suggest he has.

"I've read that book of your sister's," Mark offers, in an offhand, almost disinterested way, as if he's not used to being generous in conversation. "I've always been into that comix scene."

Sharon smiles. She bites back the nonsensical "Thank you" that springs to her lips. There is nothing she can think to say that won't pain her.

Mariah turns from the sink, where she is rinsing dishes.

"After breakfast, will you come with me for a walk?"

"Sure," Sharon says. She *wants* a walk after yesterday's long hours of driving.

"Just the girls," Mariah says lightly to Mark.

"Time for work anyway." Mark stands and leans over to kiss Mariah on the cheek. It's the same sort of kiss that Sharon gave Tom last night. Entirely companionable and thus unreadable.

Jane would have asked. Jane would have said, "Who is he?" and gotten all the facts, but that's just not Sharon's way.

Once Mark is gone, Mariah reaches for the leash on the coatrack. "We've got to give the beast a chance to shit. I hope you don't mind."

"No, of course not," Sharon says, ever the good guest, though she notes her own silent reaction to Mariah's language. "Coarse." That's what people would have said in the old days. "That woman is too coarse."

Once the dog is leashed, the two women head out the back door and into the cool of the day, a small twister of broken leaves dusting up under their feet.

"This way." Mariah gestures with a shoulder and leads Sharon around the house and into the street. At the corner, they turn onto a busier street, and Sharon settles in for the luxury of a long walk.

"Hey," Mariah cries, almost immediately. Sharon turns to see Hairbrush jerking Mariah off the sidewalk and toward a poodle on somebody's front lawn. The owner, outside and painting the trim of her front door, says, "Oh, don't worry. They know each other. Your husband normally walks him, right?"

"Yes," Mariah says, seeming to enjoy the small lie. She pulls Hairbrush back to the sidewalk. "Have a nice . . ." On the word "day," Hairbrush yanks Mariah forward. Mariah's arm swings violently up, and Mariah herself is lifted, ever so slightly, off the ground. It happens again. And again. Before this walk is over, Sharon may be called upon to push a dislocated shoulder back into its socket. And yet, each time, the rise seems almost magical: Mariah skimming the earth; for however brief a moment, Mariah flying.

"HAIRBRUSH!" Mariah says with something like angry finality. She hauls the dog firmly back in line. "You dumb dog." As if he agrees with this assessment, Hairbrush settles down and starts trotting obediently down the road. There is half a block of peace, and then a child's voice calls from the upper window of a house, "Can I pat your dog? Can I pat your dog?" Moments later, a girl bangs through a screen door and calls from the front porch, "Can I pat your dog?"

She's not the only one who asks. By the time Sharon and Mariah have finished their walk—a few street blocks and then the perimeter of an open field—three men and one young woman have stopped to pet the dog.

"I should have had one of these back in college," Sharon says. "To meet men and all."

"It's no joke," Mariah allows. "I know men in the city who get puppies just so they can pick up women. As soon as the puppies stop being cute, they return them to the store, complain about un-get-over-able allergies. A big city like New York . . . there are enough pet stores to pull this off for years."

If you threw your copy of *Becoming a Nutcase* across the room, it would fall open (nine times out of ten, a quirk of the binding) to two pages titled "It's Hip to Be Square; It's Cool to Be Crazy." The left page features a vertical strip of Jane saying, in four identical panels, "Actually, I'm schizophrenic." Next to these four panels are four different people (Cocktail Party Acquaintance, Potential Employer, Possible Boyfriend, Old College Chum), each reacting to the news in words and a thought bubble.

The Cocktail Party Acquaintance says, "Oh." And thinks, "Time to go home."

The Potential Employer says, "We have an open hiring policy here." In the thought bubble, he tears up Jane's application letter.

The Possible Boyfriend nods. In thought, he dashes out of the scene.

There's a split frame for the Old College Chum's reaction. In the panel on the left, she says, "God, that must be hard." In the accompanying thought bubble, the Chum's head departs from her shoulders, rises six feet into the air, spins around several times. In the right panel, the Chum keeps nodding sympathetically, saying, "Really hard," as, in the thought bubble, her head descends and repositions itself on her neck.

So much for the left page.

On the right page, Jane says, her hand up in a flourish, "Dahhr-ling, I have to confess to you, I'm absolutely mad."

The four people all say the same thing they did when Jane confessed to being schizophrenic, but their thoughts are different. The Cocktail Party Acquaintance thinks, "Yeah? And who isn't?" The Potential Employer pictures a happy Friday afternoon, with Jane dancing on one of the desks at work. The Possible Boyfriend thinks, "Cool," and then imagines Jane looking at a book titled *Tantric Sex* and saying, "What if we try it like this?" The Old College Chum thinks, "Mad? You goof!"

Hayden heard they'd met only once: fat Sharon Berger, with her doughy accountant husband, and Andy Meyers, Jane's longtime best friend. This was at a café in the Village, a place with stained glass windows that faced onto old airshafts, so no light splashed into the room. Disdain all around. Or maybe love. After all, it was Andy who called Sharon and let her know Jane was giving away all the money from the film deal. (Loans to other comic artists, to the homeless guy who slept in the doorway of her apartment building.) It was Andy who offered up his city apartment for Jane's use, when she couldn't deal with the complications of finding a new place, once her sublet had run out. It was Andy who told Sharon that the whole screenplay thing was too much for Jane. It was Andy, after all, whom Jane always called.

"I did something stupid," she'd breathed into the phone, after the first attempt. "I kind of did something really, really stupid." Her voice rising into hysteria. She *was* fearless, in a lot of ways, but she had never been able to take the sight of her own blood.

The walk isn't that long—maybe two miles—but afterward Sharon is exhausted. The effort, she thinks, of making polite chitchat. Back at Kathleen's, she wants only to retreat to her room. She stacks up two news magazines, three fashion journals, and one cookbook, and excuses herself, so she can go upstairs to read in bed. Some time after 1:00, she sneaks downstairs for a sandwich, grabs another cookbook, and then heads back upstairs. The next thing she knows she's waking to a sky darkening behind the lace curtains of Kathleen's guest room. Through the floor, she can hear Mariah moving about the kitchen. She thinks of Kathleen's promise—"I got a lotta fancy bath products in my shower"—and rises to avail herself of some of this soap, only it's too chilly to undress, even for a warm shower. She pads downstairs.

"Can I give you a hand?" She asks as she walks into the kitchen.

"Shit," Mariah says. "It's just after 5:00, but I should have put this thing in the oven an hour ago."

What thing? Sharon wonders, because the kitchen is devoid of the smells of cooking food or, even, recently chopped food.

"I invited a few people over for dinner. I thought we could have a little party for you. They're a few of Kathleen's friends."

"Oh, gosh. Well, that's nice of you."

"The thing is the dog's supposed to go for another walk. You know what, if I wake up Mark . . . he's napping upstairs. You're both lazybones. The two of you could take the dog out."

"Oh, don't wake him, don't wake him," Sharon says with perhaps too much force. "I'll walk the dog. Or, I know! Let me take over in the kitchen!"

"Can't let you do that," Mariah says. "This dinner is my masterpiece."

Sharon wants to insist but doesn't.

"It would be great if you just keep Mark company, and I don't want to ask *you* to do it, since you're scared."

But she is a grown woman. She should be able to do this sort of thing. "He's a good dog," she says, half meaning it. She wouldn't do it if the dog were much bigger. "Really," she says now, "I wouldn't offer if I didn't want to." But, of course, she would. "I've got a strong sense," Sharon used to joke to Kathleen, after that college class she'd taken in Greek mythology, "of the guest-host relationship." It was the very line Sharon was going to use when she presented Kathleen with the jar of peach jam still weighing down her overnight bag.

Now Mariah says, "OK. Take the dog, but you'll need one of Kathleen's raincoats."

Sharon looks out the window. It's not just the relatively late hour; the sky has darkened with storm clouds. "Oh, it'll hold off."

"Take a jacket," Mariah insists. "And here, let me show you how this leash works." She demonstrates how to lengthen and shorten the line by pushing a button. "Here, and take these." She pushes a handful of dog biscuits roughly into Sharon's pocket. "Reward him when he takes a shit and all."

"Walking the dog," Sharon says, as if it is the title for the next chapter of her life. Then, theatrically, "I'm off to meet men."

"Well, if you meet any extras, bring me back one."

"Yeah, just what you need," Sharon says automatically, before she has a chance to consider her words, "*three* boys."

Mariah laughs. Has she heard Sharon? Or is she pleased to have been found out? Sharon imagines the strip that Jane would have drawn of this encounter.

"I make products from tea tree oil," says Mariah, and an expressionless listener nods.

"I'm having an affair."

"Oh," the listener's face lights up. "What's *that* all about?"

New York was too expensive before Jane got her screenplay deal, and then it was too expensive after she'd given her money away. But there was nowhere else Jane would live. Once she lost her rent-controlled sublet in Chelsea and had to stay with a cartoonist-friend in Brooklyn, she acted as though she'd been banished to the plains of Iowa. Everything was wrong. That was suicide attempt number one. ("Not a sincere attempt," her doctor had reassured Sharon; the cuts were so shallow, and she'd immediately picked up the phone for Andy's help.)

In *Understanding Comics*, Scott McCloud writes that "The cartoon is a VACUUM into which our IDENTITY and AWARENESS are PULLED." In Tan-Tan (as Jane always pronounced *Tintin*, since she said that was how the French said it), the abstract, relatively cartoony face of Tintin encourages viewer identification. Landscapes are drawn realistically, though, since one doesn't need to identify with a mountain. One needs to know what a mountain looks like. McCloud again: "ONE SET OF LINES TO SEE. ANOTHER SET OF LINES TO BE."

So what to make of the single strip Jane managed to produce

in her final months? In her last five-panel strip, Jane Berger is entirely particularized, not cartoony at all but portrayed in near-photographic detail. A frowning Jane sits in front of an old-fashioned typewriter, which is drawn (as bits of the bedroom background are drawn) in broad, oversimplified outline. She sits silently for four whole panels, and then, in the fifth panel, shoves the typewriter away from herself and cries, "Oh, I can't do this."

Of course, Hayden couldn't help but think of this sad scenario— "I can't do this"—when he fixed on the idea (late one night, none of his job queries having come to anything) of finishing Jane's screenplay for her. "Oh, I can't do this." How sad, Hayden thought. And then: But I can. After all, years and years ago, Hayden's own father had been given the same advice—no more drawing—upon entering a mental hospital. Of course, Hayden's father hadn't been schizophrenic. He'd been depressed and a drunk. (A jerk, too, Hayden's mother always added; that was the one problem that medical science hadn't managed to cure.) At the time, Hayden's dad had laughed at the injunction against art. Doctors! What did they understand about the creative temperament? A few years after his release (and divorce and move from Seattle to New York), the *New York Times* wrote an article on Hayden's dad's career. He was that much of a bigwig in the world of set designers.

"The doctors!" Hayden's father would say now, normally as he was refusing Hayden any support (material or practical) to get his own professional life in order. "Where would I be if I'd listened to them?"

Where *would* he be? If he'd been forced to give it all up? Back home with Mom? Back on the planet where you actually had to be nice to people to win them over? Or where he clearly thought he'd be: in a dusty cremation urn? Art sustained you. That was the lesson of his father's life. Art sustained you till it killed you. That was the lesson of Jane Berger's life.

Two lessons.

Unless, of course, the first lesson always became the second.

Sharon duplicates the morning walk. Down to the corner, right for a few blocks, and then right again for the field. All goes well till Sharon tries to make the second right turn. Sharon tugs the leash. Hairbrush tugs back. It's a repeat of the morning, only Sharon doesn't find herself jerked about as Mariah was. It's amazing what thirty pounds will do. She's at a standstill, tugging and being tugged, when a blue pickup materializes. Sharon doesn't hear it driving up, but all of a sudden there is a young man sticking his head out the window and saying, "How old's your dog?" He opens his door, so he can reach out and pat Hairbrush's head.

"Actually, I don't know. He's my friend's. I'm walking him for a friend." She shivers. Some cold drops of rain are in the air, not falling so much as suspended, the way water is right before a storm.

"I've got a golden retriever. Just got one a few months ago. Not much younger than this one," he says, as Hairbrush slips away from his hand.

"That's nice."

"Oh, yeah, they're great dogs." Hairbrush yanks at Sharon's arm.

"You live around here?" the man asks, as Sharon stumbles backward.

"Visiting, visiting around here." And then, because the dog

is so eager to get moving, "Well, bye." The man waits a moment and then closes his door and pulls back into the road.

Mission accomplished, Sharon thinks. She can tell Mariah that she has met a man. She can imagine making a joke of the interchange, of her reaction to a man trying to pick her up—though the man was, in fact, probably just being friendly. "Really," she'll say, all pretend earnestness, "this Rochester is a great city. A great, *great* city."

The dog lunges for a dirty kitchen sponge sticking out of a broken trash bag by the roadside. "No, Hairbrush," Sharon says firmly, replicating Mariah's tone from the morning. "No."

Eventually, they reach the park proper. On a softball diamond set back from the road, a few kids play Frisbee, but otherwise the place is empty. There's a large, barren stretch of land past the diamond. To the left, the park is fringed with willow trees. Behind the willow trees is the river. This is the world, Sharon thinks, as she looks at the border of willow trees, the wispy eyelashes of the park. This is the world that Jane no longer sees. For a few moments—perhaps the moments while she was talking with the man in the pickup—Sharon has let herself forget that her sister is dead. How unforgivable.

In the park, Hairbrush jumps about, exultant. All that open space, Sharon supposes, it makes a dog energetic. She handles him well enough, though she quickly exhausts her supply of dog biscuits, and this seems as dangerous as leaving home without a spare diaper. A few drops of rain fall from the sky, but it's still good to be out in the air, even if, at the end of the leash, the dog's body feels electric. *Play, play, play,* he seems to be insisting, though not as a child might, not as Tyler does, hoping that Sharon will enter his imaginative world. The puppy's desire is purely about energy and the chance to release it. "OK, dog," Sharon says. "We can run," and she starts to trot behind him. "Yes, yes," he might as well be barking in response, for he leaps up in delight and then rushes across the field. Sharon lets the leash out to accommodate him, and he picks up speed, going, really, too fast for her. He bounds off to the right, then left, cutting across Sharon's path and then making for a speck of blue over by the willow trees. Sharon has to twist her feet out of the leash and sprint to catch up. The bit of blue resolves itself into a muddy rag, which Hairbrush immediately starts to devour.

"No," Sharon says, but weakly. Who cares if he eats the dumb cloth? She's sure not going to pull the thing out of his mouth. The rain is more determined now, but it's not such a cold rain that Sharon minds. The dog seems oblivious. He turns from the blue rag for the baseball field, leaving Sharon quickly winded. How was it that the dog leash retracted? Sharon fumbles with the mechanism as she runs and then gives up, wrapping the leash around her wrist in an effort to make it shorter. There's a low level of fear in her, nothing too terrible, but she needs to master the leash by the time she turns for Kathleen's. Otherwise, it'll be an all-night frolic, under skies that have turned even darker, that charcoal gray of a dramatic storm.

As if in response to her concern, a tributary of lightning cracks from the clouds toward the willows. "OK," Sharon says to the dog. "We better go." It begins to pour, in that sudden way of storms, an angel finally spilling the entire pot of the sky onto the floor. Sharon turns for home, but the dog won't turn with her. Instead, he makes a high yelping sound and leaps up to yap the air. "No, it's OK. It's just water," Sharon pronounces as if Hairbrush were her son. ("You can be afraid. But you don't *have* to be afraid.") She gives the leash another pull. "Come on," she insists. "We have to go." But her tug only enrages him further. *"Now,"* she commands. Again in the tone she might use for Tyler. "I'm going to count to three and . . . ," but Sharon's failure as a mother is that she never comes up with a threat.

The dog barks angrily, his teeth fully bared, and then whimpers. Sharon looks past the messy windshield of her glasses to where his leash has tangled around his right front leg and neck. *Oh, Lord,* she breathes; she has been strangling him with each tug of the leash.

"Oh, OK, I see, I see. I'm sorry, I'm sorry," she says. "You're a good boy. I'll fix it." She reaches tentatively to unwind the leash, to take it back around his legs, under his body, and around his neck. But he jumps up and snaps at her approaching hand.

"Calm down," she says, though not insensible to the historical ineffectiveness of those two words. She works the leash away from his paw and then his neck. "Good, Hairbrush," she coos. But what she means is "Good, Sharon," for she has conquered one little fear, she has managed to touch the dog. When she has untangled Hairbrush, they start moving, but the leash is still too long. Within moments, Hairbrush is tangled again. He resumes yapping at the air just below her wrist. Sharon shudders once against his effort, feels her torso hollow out, her groin go cold. She's felt this way before— when out walking and a dog comes barking out of a house, and she realizes she can't continue in her path. *They feel your fear,* everyone says. *It's like an invitation.* God, what can she do? Tie Hairbrush to something and go get Mariah? But she is in the middle of an open field. The backboard of the baseball diamond is half an acre away. The trees even farther. Call for help? But the Frisbee players have disappeared. No one is out in this storm. Maybe she could . . . and then it comes to her with all the relief that accompanies giving up: she could just let the dog go.

Let it go, she thinks. Let it go. Call in sick. Cancel dinner plans. Fuck the guest-host relationship.

The rain is impossible now. The kind of drenching rain that makes it difficult to see too far in front of your face, as if the rain were not the rain but the dark. She might as well have jumped into a pool as stepped outside. It is raining *that* hard. Cats and dogs, whatever that expression originally referred to. Sharon imagines furry balls of all shapes and sizes, dropping down into the field. And for a moment, it is completely real for her. They all fall down, everything she's ever been worried about, and are joined by other animals. A horse, braying like a donkey, comes, spine first, and breaks his back over by second base. A big loping Irish red setter ready to smear her face with saliva. A pit bull—a biter of necks, a tabloid darling—smashes into the willows. There are buzzards and bats waiting to swoop into her hair, and things that don't even exist, like a manticore, that wriggles over the baseball backboard and heads toward Sharon's part of the field. Ancient mapmakers, Sharon knows, when they got to the edge of the known world, scribbled *Here Be Monsters*, in the territory beyond.

What might happen? she thinks. A dog might bite her. The injury is vivid and gory for a few moments—a large, ragged wound and teeth, long and thin, like a carpenter's nails suddenly turned to bone. There's no gushing of blood, because everything stops once those teeth pierce Sharon's skin. The dog is still yapping, and the leash is wound into its mouth like a horse's bit. Sharon will have to pull it out; she will have to put her hand in the animal's mouth. Then, trying to bully herself into a decision, she says, and she means the sentence to be a slap in her own face, her inner voice more vicious than it has ever been, *Your sister is dead. Your sister killed her best friend.* Sharon is the one with the reality problem now, for she will never, never believe that either of these things is true. Your sister is dead, she tells herself again. She stuck a knife into Andy Meyers' back. What do you have to be scared of now?

A WEDDING STORY

Her trip to London was purely for pleasure, but Rachel Rubenstein did have a goal. She wanted to buy presents for her nephews, something fun that wouldn't cost too much. She found what she was looking for at the grocers: chocolate eggs with prizes inside. They were from Germany. Or maybe it was Switzerland. Anyway, they were hollow chocolate eggs, lined with white, as if the shell were on the inside. Rachel cracked open a few, while she was still in London, to make sure they'd please. She found tiny puzzles, small one-toothed monsters, itty-bitty tops. Perfect. Only her eggs melted by the time she got home, so she gave the kids little misshapen brown lumps of . . .

"You know what I'm thinking those look like," her sister, Greta, began.

"I'd like that to be one of those thoughts you leave unexpressed."

"Gotcha," Greta said.

So, months later, Rachel wasn't surprised—not entirely—
by the foil-wrapped chocolate egg in Mamie Bess's effects.
She associated such items with Europe. Ditto Mamie, her
grandmother, who had come from Poland to New York City in
the 1930s and stayed there till earlier this morning, when burial
forced her removal to a Long Island cemetery. Not that Mamie
was actually on Long Island. She'd joined the Everlasting, if
Rabbi Cohen—he of the spittle-y lips and saggy cheeks—could
be trusted. Rachel wasn't sure she believed in such things, but it
was enough that Mamie did. The last time they'd spoken, it was
about a date Rachel had gone on.

"So?" Mamie had said. "You mind me asking what he's like?"

"I don't know," Rachel said. She was in her late twenties and
vague when it came to her personal life. It seemed altogether
possible that she might never have one. "A doctor and Jewish, so
it should be good, but I just couldn't get much of a conversation
going with him." The man had been the grandson of one of
Mamie's friends. Rachel was in a period of welcoming blind
dates, no matter what quarter they came from.

"He doesn't need to be perfect. Perfect isn't for here. That's
for the *yenne velt*. You know what that means? It's Jewish. It
means the other side."

Rachel smiled. She hadn't known that Mamie had notions
about the hereafter. She'd never mentioned it before. There was
definitely a life-is-for-the-living philosophy that ran through
the family. Rachel didn't really like talking about her nonexistent
romantic life with her grandmother, but she added, "He doesn't
need to be perfect. But I should be able to talk to him, don't you
think?"

"Mmm," Mamie mused. "Talking's overrated."

*   *   *

The chocolate egg made Rachel think of a jar that Mamie had kept in the pantry of her old house in Queens. Mamie lived there before moving to the condo in which Rachel was now boxing up her belongings. The jar had been full of candies that didn't exist anywhere save in Mamie's closets. Say "M&M" in the old Queens house, and you might be speaking a foreign tongue. But on Mamie's shelves, there were always containers stuffed full of hard candies that dissolved into soft cakey centers and strange mints that turned into chocolates the longer you sucked. Rachel didn't have any memory of chocolate eggs, but here was one now. She peeled it immediately. She was immoderately greedy for sweets, though dutifully embarrassed by this fact. The chocolate was old, dusty white, the way chocolate gets after many years. Rachel sniffed. It smelled only vaguely of cocoa; it might have been a chocolate egg from the old country. But it clearly wasn't solid. It felt, in her fingers, like those KinderEggs she'd found in London. There might even be a Cracker Jack–type prize inside. Age—when it came to candy—didn't worry her. She nibbled the top of the egg and imagined she heard someone cry, "*Gevult.*"

The egg didn't surprise Rachel, but the little rabbi inside the egg certainly did.

"Shalom," he called, half in warning, so she wouldn't bite further.

"Oh, my," Rachel cried and put the egg down, a little repulsed, as if it were a tiny mouse rather than a holy man crawling over a fence of chocolate to greet her. "Simon," he called. "Master of the Name."

"What?" she said. "*What?*" She felt momentarily dizzy and put her hand to her head. Had she had enough water today? Once, when she was in college, she'd gotten so dehydrated she'd started hallucinating.

"My name," he said. "I was just translating for you. Simon Baal Shem."

"A-ha," Rachel said, as if in assent. Could a figment of your imagination make up a name that would never occur to you? Probably not.

Rachel wasn't all that religious herself, but she'd had a bat mitzvah, way back when, and a few things had trickled down to her from visits with Mamie and her occasional foray into the synagogue in Maine, where she lived. "The Baal Shem?" she said now. "Wasn't he . . . ?" The founder of Chasidism, she was about to say, but the rabbi interrupted her.

"He was the Baal Shem *Tov.* The Holy One. I'm not him. In the Middle Ages, Baal Shem was a name given to any Jewish rabbi who might be a miracle worker."

"And you're one of them."

"I'm one of them," he said.

"But it's not the Middle Ages."

"Well," Simon said, brushing a shard of chocolate from his shoulders. "If you want to get stuck on details." He had a dark mustache and dark hair—both almost as black as the bit of fabric he wore as a skullcap—but his beard was flecked with white. His head of wooly hair discomfited her, resembling, as it did, the hair of one of the divorced parents at the daycare center where she worked. Rachel was always half hoping the man would ask her out.

"How long have you been in there?"

"What's time to someone inside an egg?"

"Oh," Rachel said earnestly. "I guess I don't know." He looked at her expectantly. The flat, mournful planes of his cheeks made her think of a Modigliani painting. Below them, his long beard hung like two separate pennants from his chin.

Rachel didn't know what to say. "What sort of miracles do you do?"

"I don't like to brag."

"No," she said. "I suppose you wouldn't." Rachel's mind was blank. She tried to call up an appropriate question, but everything she might ask—everything about which she was genuinely curious—struck her, for some reason, as off-limits. Or too silly. Who, for instance, had sewn the little dark suit he was wearing? Out of what ancient workshop came his mildly scuffed miniature shoes? She didn't ask. And yet she wasn't at ease with the quiet, though the rabbi sat peaceably looking at her, as if talk or no talk, it was all the same to him. At length, Rachel decided to treat him like any guest.

"Can I get you, maybe, something to eat?"

"That would be welcome."

"I don't know what's here." She opened Mamie's refrigerator, felt a stab of pain at the prune juice and cottage cheese there. The freezer had an iced-up bag of frozen ravioli. She turned for the cabinets, and in the end the rabbi contented himself with the better part of a garbanzo bean as a snack.

"So," Rachel said, as he chewed, "is there a . . . is there a reason why you're here?"

"Perhaps," the rabbi said but didn't elaborate.

Rachel knew which way was up. A miracle worker was no genie in the bottle, and even if he were, a rabbi required righteous behavior. Selflessness at the least, though she did have the urge to rub his head and ask if he could help her meet a nice guy.

Or lose a few pounds. Or reverse the state of the mutual fund into which she'd poured her meager retirement savings. A rush of shame came over her as the rabbi sat down, leaning his back against the pot of a jade plant and cooling himself in the shade of its leaves.

"Lovely," the rabbi said, tugging the dark gabardine of his suit over his hips and crossing his feet at the ankles. It looked like he intended to stay a while.

"In the morning, the men from the auction house will be coming to sell all this." Rachel gestured to what remained unpacked—a table full of cranberry glass on which dust had settled permanently, a coffee table cluttered with porcelain figurines, and a giant painting of three mermaids. Attached to various pieces of furniture and a large oval mirror in the hallway were name tags: Shira, Jenny, Greta, Samuel, Tova. Most of the bigger items were going to a grandchild or great grandchild. Rachel was supposed to take the grandfather clock, though there really wasn't enough room for it in her apartment. For the time being, it would be stored in Greta's basement. "If you don't mind, I have to . . ."

"Please . . . ," the rabbi said, gesturing as if to say she should continue doing what she'd been doing. "For the moment, I'd just like to watch."

The evening continued almost as if Rachel were alone. The rabbi stood only once to resettle himself into an old bag of white beans on the kitchen table, as if it were some giant throw pillow from the seventies. As he moved, he muttered in Yiddish, and when Rachel turned at the sound of his words, he looked up—his gaze was disarmingly direct—to say, "You speak Jewish?"

"No," Rachel admitted.

"Oh," the rabbi said and didn't translate his words.

For the rabbi, Rachel found a 250-count box of wooden matches, the contents of which she tossed into a trash bag already full with overstretched sweaters, worn slippers, and a disarming box of Depends undergarments. Probably no one knew what Mamie had suffered in the end. For the rabbi's mattress, Rachel dug a purse-size container of tissues from her handbag and added an old embroidered handkerchief of Mamie's late husband, for a blanket.

Rachel spent the night in Mamie's old bed, felt the discomfort of this acutely, though Mamie had lived a good, long life, and death at age ninety-two was no tragedy. (Who, if Rachel, didn't know this? A young woman who flinched at the evening news and fretted over tragedies near and far: an abduction in Florida, the cancer in her boss's breast, the bomb in Jerusalem. Oh, good Lord.) Still, she'd miss the old woman. Mamie had been a true friend.

On their second night in Mamie's apartment, the rabbi asked, "You want maybe to hear a story?" The place had been cleared of all belongings, save Rachel's suitcase and a sleeping bag and pillow that she'd brought from her apartment in South Portland, Maine. A cord snaked from the wall to a phone. In the morning, she would pack all this up and drop the key off with the president of the condo association.

"A story? Sure, I'd like that."

"But first a candle you must light."

Rachel looked around the empty condo. "But . . ."

The rabbi was insistent.

"I don't have a candle."

"Then we wait."

"Well, no," Rachel said, "let me go see if I can find a neighbor."

Once out in the dim hallway, though, Rachel realized she didn't really have the courage to bother a neighbor for something like this. A cup of milk for baking, yes, but a candle? It seemed too rude, and she'd have to ask for a holder as well.

When she came back empty-handed, the rabbi said, "A carved potato you could use for a candleholder."

Rachel nodded. She did have a jackknife.

"You should try maybe apartment 4F," the rabbi said sagely, and Rachel, thinking that perhaps miracle workers could see through walls, went up to the fourth floor and knocked.

An old man with a bristly gray-black mustache answered the door. His right side was partially paralyzed, and he leaned so dramatically into the strength of his left, Rachel thought he might tip over.

"I'm terribly sorry to bother you," she began. "I'm the granddaughter of Mamie Seidman. She lived in 2B?"

"Oh, *yeees*," the man said. "Come in. I'm so *sooor*-ry to *lose* her." Whatever had ruined the right portion of his body had given him a peculiar drawl. His voice had the cartoony sound of an audiotape played at the wrong speed. "*Yooouur* grandmother was a *good soul*."

Rachel's eyes teared up. "I know," she said. Fear had forestalled her own grief. If she gave into it, then what? All the grown-ups were gone now, and, Lord, they'd left her own idiot generation in charge.

"Everyone in the building loved her," the old man continued. "If someone got *saaad*, we always sent them *to her*. She could cheer anybody up. She knew how to look on the bright *side* of things. You know?"

Rachel did know, though she hadn't always loved her grandmother for this quality. When Rachel's pharmacist-father and homemaker-mother died (seven and eight years earlier, both of cancer, courtesy of the toxins that were the state of New Jersey), Rachel's grandmother had said, "They had their life. That was their life, and you have to feel blessed for it."

"Easy enough for Mamie to say," Rachel groused to her sister, Greta, "when she's been treated to eighty-five years." But then she'd tried to grow into the wisdom of her grandmother's words. She'd have to find a way to accept the loss of Mamie. She didn't—as Greta once pointed out—have any other choice.

"Come in and sit," the old man said. "I'm Howie Rosengren."

"I can't stay. I just needed to ask a favor."

"Anything," the man said. "And *ac-shually* I have something for you." He walked, dragging one foot, back into his apartment, and Rachel followed. He pulled a card from a wallet resting on top of a bookcase. "This here," he said, as he handed it to her, "is my *son's* business. Rosengren & Sons, though I don't do the work anymore. You go *down to* the shed . . . you don't even *both-er* with a *phone* call, but go straight there and ask for Jeremy. That's my little one's littlest one. You tell him you need a *marker* for your *grandma*, and he'll make *it* for you. Tell him I said to give you a *good discount*."

"Oh, that's OK," Rachel said. "I actually have a name from my grandmother's rabbi for the gravestone."

Mr. Rosengren made a contradictory farting sound with his lips. "Pfft, no," he said. "That rabbi is a fool. I don't *want* you *going* to him." Rachel was taken aback. Why did he suppose he could pronounce on such private business? "You *go* to *my grandson*."

"Well, thank you," she said reluctantly and asked for what she'd come for.

"Candle? Sure, we got candles." He limped further into the apartment and returned with a stub of a maroon candle and a box of matches. "I hope this will *do*."

"I'm sure it will." She paused. "You wouldn't happen to have a potato, too?"

"In my time," began Rabbi Simon, once Rachel was back in the apartment, "my days were the Lord's, but my hours were with horses." The rabbi and Rachel were seated cross-legged on the floor around the impromptu light of the guttering candle. "I took horses from the field and trained them for town and to make the runs from our city to the coast. One day, a man came to me with an untrainable horse. Me? What did I care? I had heard this before. *Nu?* I could tame a horse. But this horse. *Oy gut.* I worked for days, then weeks. Still the first time the horse draws a carriage, over it goes. The people inside were hurt. A young boy's legs . . . crushed." The rabbi shook his head gravely, his face glowing red in the candlelight. "'This horse is for the slaughterhouse,' I said. But the horse's owner said no, and so I worked on. What choice did I have? But you know how it goes. At the sight of me, the horse would stamp and kick. I lost hope. I went about my house with gloom. How could I rest knowing that through my failures, I had hurt a child? Then one day, a stranger he comes to my farm. 'I'll change your horse's ways,' he tells me. 'Who's stopping you?' I say. He goes out to my barn and within minutes, he's back. 'You will have no problem with him any longer,' he says. Well, this I didn't believe. But out I go and hitch the horse to a carriage to give the stranger a ride back to town. The horse trots happily. 'What did you do?' I asked.

"'I went to him with an open heart.'

"'And me too,' I said. 'Didn't I go to him with an open heart? For this is the way of the people of the Lord.'"

"'I went to him with an open heart and no desire for his learning,' the stranger said. 'And so he learned.'"

Rachel smiled. "That's a nice story."

"You were expecting something else?" The rabbi stood to shake his legs.

"Oh, no, no. It was a *great* story, a really *great* story." Was that too much. Mamie's nonstop praise, particularly in her later years, was invariably excessive and unfounded. "She's suffering," Greta once mused, "from dementia complimentia."

"Really great," Rachel couldn't stop herself from saying. "And really . . . terrific."

Rachel wasn't one to keep secrets, but the following week, back at the Busy Bees childcare center, where she had served as art instructor to the pre-K set for almost six years, she didn't feel quite ready to announce that she had a pocket-size rabbi living with her. The people at the center weren't Jewish—few people in Maine were. If they found her dreidl craft projects exotic, what would they make of this? Rachel didn't know herself what she thought of the circumstances, and after her first inquiry about the rabbi's purpose, she asked no further questions, supposing it best simply to attend to his needs. He had a fondness for "communing with nature," and she took him to the small strip of greenery that surrounded Country Creek Estates—the name for the complex that housed her one-bedroom apartment, all she could afford on her sparse salary. It wasn't a great place— the walls too thin, the cockroaches—in Maine, who knew?— likely to travel from a neighbor's apartment no matter how clean she kept her own cabinets. The other tenants all seemed broken in some way. There was a cab driver who'd been waiting ten years to save enough money to return to college, an angry blind woman who sometimes asked Rachel to read her the newspaper, and a born-again Christian who lived upstairs and who had the bland cheerfulness and dutiful work habits of a man who—in another country and at another time—might be inclined to kill her.

And there was another reason she didn't say anything: a reticence had fallen over her since her stay in New York. It might have been a delayed grief at Mamie's passing, or the curiousness of her situation, but she was having trouble talking to people. Real trouble, though ordinarily she thought of her easy manner with others as her greatest (well, actually, her only) gift. It had always been most pronounced with children—she could draw out the non-talkers, soothe the fussy, engage the frenetic—and around Christmas her mailbox was always the one most full of personal thanks. There were children who came back, even now that they were ten, just to say hi. Children and parents alike flushed with pleasure when they saw her in the grocery store. "Oh, Miss Rubenstein," they cried, as if shocked to find she lived outside the walls of the daycare center. Of course, her charms worked on the young and the married and seemed to elude the unmarried male. But now even those charms were gone, and she found herself with the same blankness of mind she had when first asking the rabbi about himself. It was as if she'd suddenly forgotten—but forgotten for all circumstances—what it was she meant to say.

Rachel called her old college roommate to chat. In Maine, she'd never developed the sort of fond friends she'd had in college or just after, when she lived with a bevy of roommates in Boston. She blamed the state itself. In Maine, people liked their privacy. You couldn't tell when they'd interpret friendliness as an intrusion.

"How's work?" Rachel asked Jessica.

"So-so."

"And George?"

"He's fine."

And then Rachel felt stumped. Did Jessica not like her phone calls? Maybe it wasn't Maine. Maybe she was the only one left, the only unattached person left who still needed friends.

"And you?" Jessica said.

But what could she say? That she had a kosher action figure living with her?

"*Feigele*," the rabbi said. Dear. He had quickly lapsed into terms of endearment for Rachel.

"Yes." Rachel finished washing her face and leaned down to where he was, his black shoes dampening in a small puddle at the sink's edge.

"I have for you another story. In fact, I have for you four stories."

"Four?"

"Yes, one I already told you. So three more. But all in good time."

"OK," Rachel said. She sat down on the edge of the bathtub. "Well?"

"Not now. Before you hear, you have to stop waiting to hear."

Back when she was in junior high school, in Elizabeth, New Jersey, some girls had been given the assignment of taking care of an egg for a week. They each had to have an egg with them at all times—or get a babysitter, if they wanted to go somewhere where it wouldn't be convenient to have a raw egg in tow. The idea, of course, was to frighten the girls out of pregnancy. Only it wasn't an assignment that girls like Rachel were given. You had to be fast—or fast in the mind of the teacher—to get an egg, and Rachel had always felt slighted at not being chosen for the exercise. Now, though, she had a sense of what those teenage girls had gone through, for Rabbi Simon could not be left at home. She'd tried it, on that first day of work after she returned from New York, and she'd come home to a terrified rabbi. The cockroaches had formed an ugly band and approached him where he sat, gnawing on a crouton at the kitchen table. He bowled one bug over with the stale bit of bread and then raced for the table's leg. He made it into Rachel's bedroom and hid there, behind the wheel of the bed, till Rachel returned. What portion in heaven for someone responsible for terrifying a man right out of worship and into the fearful muttering Rabbi Simon was doing when Rachel dropped her purse on her mattress? Who knew, but a week into his stay, Rachel was carrying him everywhere. Still, she kept him her secret, taking frequent breaks at work, if only so she could go to the bathroom and pull the rabbi out of her pocket. After a day or two, the routine made him moody and Rachel anxious. She couldn't miss work.

"From the time Rabbi Judea Lev was born," the rabbi began one night, and Rachel knew this was the start of his second story, "he was a serious child. His days he spent working the fields and his nights with books. But light or dark, he was always thinking about how to get closer to his God. One day, his family goes to the lake. It's hot, *nu?* and old times, new times, a hot man wants to cool down. But *oy gut!* A whirlpool pulls Lev under. At first for air he gasps but then he drinks the water, and darkness comes. After there is a light like no other, and Lev begins to ascend to it. His soul pines for the light like a schoolboy for his mother, and as he rises, he hears the fish and even the plants about him, each speaking in their secret tongue. But for the boy no language is secret. Everything he understands. Then he hears a voice say, 'Not yet.' A hand grabs his ankle, pulls him up through the water, and then he is in the arms of a strange man, and his mother is beside the man, crying and thanking him. Lev sees his mother's relief, but even so, he knows what he has lost, and as hard as he studied before, he promises himself he will study harder yet."

"You know what bugs me about that story?" Rachel began. The rabbi looked shocked, as if an objection to the story weren't possible. "It suggests getting closer to God is good, which I wouldn't argue with, but it also suggests death is the path. Doesn't it?"

The rabbi looked at her curiously and said, "No."

Rachel opened her mouth to protest, but the phone rang. It was Greta, calling to remind Rachel about the marker for Mamie's grave.

"Speaking of death," Rachel said.

"What?" Greta cried.

"Nothing. A dumb joke. Yeah, I'll do it. I didn't think there was any rush." The Jewish tradition was to unveil the stone on the first anniversary of the death. Rachel put her sister on speakerphone, so the rabbi could listen in on the conversation.

"No, but, let's just . . . Well, you don't know how long it will take for the stonecutter to do the work, and what if you forget when the time gets near and . . ."

"OK," Rachel said. Greta's inclination was to take care of a task before it was assigned, and Rachel's was to wait to the last minute. "I'll do it before the month is up."

"And the clock? When are you going to get it out of my basement?"

"Soon."

"When soon?"

"Ohhh," Rachel said. The truth was she had an uneasy relationship with things. She didn't like to be encumbered. She could fit almost everything she owned, minus a few pieces of furniture, into her Ford Escort. It was a point of pride.

"Your basement isn't going anywhere, is it? Can't you just keep it there?"

"Rachel," Greta said, aggrieved. "It's less room here than you think. Come on."

As the older of the two sisters, Greta seemed to feel that her three-year seniority and marriage gave her rights of authority. What this meant, most recently, was that Greta had controlled all aspects of Mamie's funeral, insisting on a catered reception, though Rachel's own way would have been homier. She'd have asked Mamie's friends to bring casseroles to the apartment. "A potluck funeral?" Greta was incredulous. But that's what Mamie would have preferred. Or so Rachel thought. After all, Mamie never liked being served by waiters or advised while in a department store, but then Rachel remembered that Mamie had taken her and Greta out for Chinese food after their father's funeral. It had seemed positively surreal, Mamie saying, "Girls, what do you want. Eggrolls? Spare ribs?" What they wanted was their father, but Mamie didn't let conversation turn to him. He was gone, they were here now, and they had to get on with things, so did they or didn't they want chicken with cashew nuts?

"OK," Rachel said now, hoping her vagueness about what she was assenting to would buy her more time. "Well, I've got to go." She clicked the phone off its speaker function and turned her back to the rabbi.

"You always say that when you want to hang up," Greta accused.

"No really," Rachel protested, and then because it wasn't truly a lie, she whispered, "I've got a guy here."

"Oooo," Greta said, interested. "I'll call tomorrow!"

"More important than Torah," the rabbi said as Rachel hung up, "is family happiness."

"Yes?" Rachel said, on the edge of being irritated.

"A trip to New York," he pressed his tiny palm to his chest, as if undone by a sudden fit of indigestion, "is what I'm suggesting."

The nature of the rabbi's awareness of history suggested he'd been interred in chocolate sometime after the Holocaust but before the fifties. So while computers, cell phones, and color TVs had to be explained to him, he knew his way around Manhattan and was disappointed only by what he didn't find. In the streets of the Lower East Side, where the rabbi had asked to go, no radios tuned themselves to WEDV. "I used to love that show, what's-it-called," the rabbi said when Rachel pulled him out of her purse and sat him down on her lunch table. ("Cool *doll*," the waitress had said, fingering the stud in her nose.) "I know!" the rabbi remembered. "*Yiddish Melodies in Swing.* That was a good one." The rabbi hadn't wanted to have lunch at a deli. He'd wanted a hot dog from Nathan's. But that chain was long gone, and the rabbi was put off by vegetarian Rachel's description of hot dogs as "cow cheeks and assholes."

"Very unladylike," he had said.

On the ascending ladder toward God, Rachel had clearly descended a rung. And yet she was aware of purposely having used the word *asshole* to test the limits of the rabbi's patience with . . . well, not her exactly, but her milieu, the world in which she lived.

They'd settled on a warren-like kosher deli, where they

shared a plate of potato pancakes and applesauce amid the lunchtime din. Rachel hid the rabbi behind a napkin dispenser and figured people could make their own guesses about why she seemed to be addressing the ketchup bottle. Outside, the stores were stuffed to bursting with imitation leather luggage, cheap jeans, and T-shirts with rude slogans. Here, waiters barely stopped to ask patrons what they wanted to eat before tucking their pads into their waistbands and racing for the kitchen.

"Do you like this place?" Rachel asked the rabbi. The wisdom of your stories won't work here, she wanted to say. I wish it would, but the world's just too complicated.

He wiped the corners of his mouth on a piece of a napkin, folded his hands neatly before him. He kept his air of decided calm no matter what was happening around him. "It'll do," he said.

"I have something to tell you about my brother-in-law."

"Yes?"

"He's kind of an asshole."

"Young lady," the rabbi began, but he seemed more entertained than disapproving.

"I'm not that young."

"Well, then, my old and decrepit friend, you've got quite a mouth on you."

After lunch and a brief tour of the lower part of the city—past the matzoh factory, by Gus's Pickles and the shul—Rachel joined her brother-in-law, Philip, for the trek from his downtown office back to Maplewood, New Jersey, where he and Greta lived with their two sons. All afternoon, a damp wind accompanied Rachel and the rabbi on their rounds. Now the sky began to unburden itself. Rachel and Philip skittered along the sidewalk to the garage where he parked his car, the day's newspaper serving as a makeshift umbrella for Philip, Rachel resigned to getting soaked.

"How was your day?" she asked, as they settled into the car, the wet strands of her hair whapping her cheeks like some sort of practical joke the day played on her.

"Fine."

Philip was a skinny tax lawyer, and even in the best of times, Rachel found him sour and overly obsessed with money.

"What's up with the kids?"

Philip glanced over at her. Was he annoyed?

"You know," Rachel said cajolingly, "I'm asking for the Cute Report. What new things are they doing or saying?" For each kid at the daycare, Rachel could find a thousand answers for this question. Max was talking about the way monsters made themselves skinny, so they could fit under his bedroom door at night. Jason had been looking at a book of trucks the other day, and when Rachel approached, he'd said matter-of-factly, "Hi, I'm just enjoying the fun." Little Sarah had looked up from the craft table just yesterday and said, "Miss Rubenstein, this Play-Doh is freaking me out."

"The boys?" said Philip. "The usual."

But there was no usual with little kids. That—Rachel thought, half-consciously bookmarking her notion to share with the rabbi later—was part of the fun. Normally, Rachel would have persisted in her effort to draw Philip out. She could usually get him to complain vociferously about some colleague at work, but she felt too irritated to open her mouth. He could ask her about *her* kids, couldn't he? The ones at the daycare? Or ask her something about art . . . or, well, anything, but that would mean he'd have to place just a teeny bit of value on one thing that she did. Which he couldn't. They'd crossed over the bridge, and Rachel turned to look back at Manhattan. Mamie always held that the rain cleaned the city off. From this distance, it did seem sparkly, though Rachel's few hours of wandering with the rabbi had left her feeling grubby. Occupying yourself in New York was exhausting; you had to bring so much vigilance to even a decision to rest on a bench. "Well," Rachel said, in a sort of sigh, and then settled into her own silence, a quiet that seemed to content Philip.

Over dinner, in Greta's small but neat ranch house with its mammoth leather sofa and chairs—forest green cushions stuffed beyond reason, as if for a giant's derrière—Rachel found new things to dislike about her brother-in-law, though it was six years into Greta's marriage, and Rachel thought she'd long completed the tally. Philip snapped at Greta for failing to pick up the dry cleaning and then reprimanded her as she went to eat a third chocolate-chip cookie. "Didn't the kids make those for Rachel?"

"Well, I wasn't planning on eating the whole plate," Rachel put in.

"Still," Philip said, his mouth tightening.

Little bastard. No wonder she hadn't been able to make conversation with him.

But perhaps the problem wasn't all with Philip. For after dinner, even Greta seemed beyond Rachel's reach. The sisters sat and watched the boys play a game that involved making and destroying a town that they had nicknamed "Big City Adventure." Ordinarily, Rachel and Greta would chatter on about books they'd read or old friends or their cousins. Now, Rachel was telling a story about their cousin Katrina. After ten years of marriage, she had finally met her husband's father. The man had been an alcoholic and homeless—a couch surfer, sleeping on friends' couches, and moving from apartment to apartment with his belongings in a single cardboard box. The man's history fascinated Rachel. At the very least, it explained some glitches in Katrina's husband's character, but Greta didn't seem to care. She was sitting heavily on a stepstool in the playroom, when normally she'd be bustling about, throwing trucks back into the play chest and stacking puzzle boxes on the bookshelf.

Rachel stopped her narrative, mid-sentence. "Are you all right?"

"Yeah. Just tired."

Of course, Rachel thought. But when her sister didn't ask her to continue her story, she wondered if she'd been talking too much.

"So," Rachel said, as if to start up again, but she didn't continue. A dark mood overtook her. She might be heading for one of those stretches (it had happened to her twice in the past) when she was visited by ruinous self-consciousness, and everything she said seemed strained and false.

Greta said, "I'll let David sleep in a sleeping bag in Matthew's room. That way you don't have to take the couch."

It wasn't yet 9:00, but Rachel turned in, relieved not to have to try anymore with her sister.

In David's bedroom, Rachel tried to sort her thoughts, but they merged with a general feeling of hopelessness. There was such a brief time of enjoying the fun before the years of ambition and unrealized ambition and then the suffering (whatever portion you were allotted) before you died. Everybody she knew wanted their life to be a stepping-stone to something else, and no one was happy where they landed. And what of it? That was life. It didn't matter really. Or it wouldn't matter if only there were someone to talk to about it.

Rachel put on her nightgown and then pulled the rabbi, sweaty and lint-covered, from her purse.

"Well, what do you think?" Rachel said dispiritedly.

"I couldn't hear!" he said, seeming to sense how her emotions had dimmed with the day.

Rachel had an urge to pick up a phone and call Mamie. "Hello. 1-800-THE-GREAT BEYOND?" Without fully realizing it, Rachel had relied on Mamie's authority—the wisdom of greater experience. Greta was family, but she couldn't fill Mamie's role. Greta was too much in the midst of life herself to offer any help with Rachel's.

"Maybe I'm just missing my grandma." She turned toward the wall, so the rabbi could dress for bed. He slept in some doll clothes Rachel had filched from the daycare: blue footsie pajamas patterned with red French horns. Complete with a matching cap.

"All set," the rabbi called. "You were saying?"

"My grandma." Rachel lay back in bed, an arm pressed against her left eye—she was allergic to something in the room. Above her head, a mobile of planes twirled and slowly settled. "Once, one of the teachers at the daycare said to me, 'You know what you have is a compassion disorder.' The morning paper had reported the death of a hundred and twelve people in a plane crash, and I couldn't get my head off the tragedy. 'You can't think about that stuff,' Mamie used to tell me. 'If you think about that stuff, you go crazy.' She wasn't trying to comfort me. She was telling me to stop it." And Rachel had liked it—Mamie's instructions, a reminder, however cruel: life isn't for the dead.

The rabbi didn't respond, and Rachel felt something—a clot of grief or loneliness—stick in her throat. Her thoughts were so natural to her; could it be that others really didn't share them;

that when she confessed what was closest to her heart, she was really being a pain in the neck? Rachel reached over and clicked off the lamp.

The light from the moon cut through the window, and the rabbi formed a shadow puppet of himself on the wall. "Well," he said at last, sitting up in his bed as he spoke, his pajama cap lopsided on his head, like a half-collapsed soufflé. "We're travelers, so I'll tell you the story of a traveler."

"Herschel Schtok wanted to learn the Law. He'd grown up in the country among peasants. Prayers he knew to recite, but Hebrew? He could not read a word. When he was old enough, he went to town and set himself up as a shopkeeper. Now began his studies. One day he hoped to visit the synagogue in Karyek. No one knows Karyek anymore, but in its day it was known for the holiness of its citizens. And the rabbi of Karyek was the holiest of them. There were rumors . . . things you wouldn't believe. That in his holiest of fervors, he left the earth entirely and flew through the air, though some said it wasn't flying really, but hopping, and that he did it when he was full of the joy of the Lord. A kind of a skip. What does it matter? Herschel wanted to meet this rabbi. Surely such a man could tell him how best to continue his studies. So Herschel wrote ahead and made for himself an appointment with the rabbi. Soon it was all set. The Sabbath hence Herschel would celebrate in Karyek. On Saturday after sundown, he'd go to the shul, when it was permitted to ask the rabbi questions.

"A peasant he knows how to wake up early, and so Herschel gets up before the sun on the day of his trip. He knows, too, about weather, so he gives himself three extra days for travel. Might not a rainstorm wash out his road? And how reliable is a horse anyway? Herschel rides as far as he can on his first night, and just when he fears he has traveled too far into the wilderness, that there will be no place for him to stay the night, he comes across a small inn at the foot of a mountain.

"The innkeeper comes to the door. He is a large man in a peasant blouse and tight boots and pants. He wipes his hands on his shirt, leaving two brown stains by his ribs, then holds out his palm to greet Herschel.

"'I'll just be staying the single night,' Herschel explains. 'I need to get to Karyek by Sabbath.'

"'And why not spend the Sabbath with me?'

"'I am going to see a very holy man,' Herschel explains. 'It is my life's journey.'

"'So be it,' the man says and shows him to his room.

"Herschel pays at once. He will be up before the innkeeper in the morning, as he intends to put as many miles between him and the mountain before nightfall. He travels all day, but he doesn't come across another inn, and at dusk, when he happens to turn his head around—strangeness of strangeness—he sees the inn in which he'd slept the previous night. Herschel, he doesn't know what to think, but he turns back and enters the inn for a second time. He explains again to the innkeeper that he needs a room, that he intends to meet a holy man by the next Sabbath. The innkeeper says, 'And you don't wish to spend your Sabbath with me?'

"'Don't joke with me, sir,' Herschel cries. 'Something has happened, and my senses are bedeviled, and I must keep to my true path.'

"Herschel departs early the next morning. Perhaps he took a circular road on the previous day? Today, he will pay more attention and make sure he does not double back. The Sabbath is drawing closer, and he does not think he will get a second chance, in this life, to speak to the Karyek rabbi. As Herschel travels, even the leaves seem to give voice to his fears, rustling about how little time each man has on earth. It is Friday, and Herschel's road goes through no towns. The day hurries past, and soon it's almost dusk. Finally, he sees a light in the distance. He pushes his horse forward. Again, he has arrived at the little inn.

"'I see you have chosen to spend the Sabbath with me after all,' the innkeeper says as he helps Herschel unsaddle his horse.

"Herschel, he is in despair, but he knows to respect an invitation, so he says, 'I'd be honored.'

"The innkeeper's wife—a girl whom Herschel had not seen during his previous visits—greets him before the hearth. She sprinkles salt on the table, brings out a challah, wine, and candles. The innkeeper's wife says the blessings, and Herschel joins in, his voice hoarse with grief over his failure. The Sabbath meal is a thick bean and bread soup, and despite himself, Herschel enjoys both it and the innkeeper's wife's quiet chatter.

"When he turns in for the evening, though, he cannot rest. His mind goes over all that has happened to him, and he can find no reason for the confusion that has led him in circles. He rises to walk outside, for, in the past, walking in the night air has calmed him. When he steps outside, he sees the innkeeper, holy book in hand, reading at the foot of the mountain, while from the sky comes a shaft of light. Looks, maybe, like a sunbeam and falls on the ground where the innkeeper stands, a soft gray at his ankles, but as the light travels up his body, it grows brighter and whiter, till his head and the blond curls there are in the purest of white light, so pure that it hurts Herschel's eyes, and he has to look down to the man's feet, which are no longer quite on the ground."

*   *   *

All through this long story, Rachel watched the rabbi's shadow and not the man himself. Then she turned to him and wished (out loud) that he'd stay with her forever. She supposed she felt a kind of love for him.

"Me?" the rabbi said. "I'm just a visitor with you. I won't stay much longer. That's the point of the story."

"It is?" Rachel said. She'd been an English major in college and knew a little bit about literary interpretation. She didn't see one bit of evidence for the rabbi's reading of his own tale.

"It is," the rabbi said. "Absolutely."

She slept heavily, and then woke in the middle of the night, wondering what the rabbi's story meant. She half expected to turn and see him floating above his matchbox bed, his head consumed with ethereal light, but when she peeked over, he was fast asleep, his forefinger pressed to his chin.

When she woke, the rabbi was gone.

"Oh, no," she cried. She hadn't thought he meant he was going to leave her so soon.

"Morning," Greta called and stuck her head into the bedroom. "Want some French toast? Is . . . What's the matter? You look upset."

"Nothing. Give me a few seconds, and I'll be out."

She showered and pulled on her clothes. As she went to get her lipstick from her bag, she heard a tiny "*Got mayner!*" Then a "Help!"

The rabbi was stuck in her wallet.

"What're you doing?"

"I was trying to get this," he said. He was pulling on a business card that she'd stuffed into her wallet. "The whole thing closed over on me."

Rachel freed the rabbi and then stuck him in her blouse pocket.

The card he'd been trying to get was for Rosengren & Sons. "Remember, you've got to go see this Jeremy fellow."

"What?" Rachel looked at the card. "Oh, that's right. The man in Mamie's apartment building. I'm pretty sure Greta's already got someone to make the marker."

But Greta didn't, and as they sat at breakfast, eating their French toast, Rachel passed the card over to Greta and said, "I know it's a schlep. But let's go over to Long Island and see what this guy's stuff looks like. I hear he does good work."

Greta shrugged an OK. "Oh," she cried, "I almost forgot. I have something for you." She went out of the room and came back with a big wrapped box.

"What is it?"

"It's a present. For you."

Rachel felt the lie of this instantly. Greta invariably gave presents because she liked to shop, not because she had divined something Rachel wanted.

Philip came in. "Morning," he said, taking a gulp of coffee. Everything about the man seemed parsimonious. Too selfish even to add a "good" to his "morning."

"So open it already," Greta said.

It was a toaster. But not just a toaster. It was a toaster that was more like a village, with a built-in clock, a mini oven, and a microwave.

"Greta," Rachel said, regretting the whine in her own voice, "I don't have room for this. You've seen my place."

"But you've been doing your toast in the oven. You told me yourself."

"I just don't need it. You're always getting me things I don't need."

Greta huffed. "You know the reason you're not married is you don't want to grow up. Grown-ups have toasters. It doesn't mean you've become a part of the capitalist patriarchy. It just means you can have some toast for breakfast."

"Say thank you," Philip said. "Why can't you just say thank you?"

Rachel stared at him with open dislike. He'd always felt optional—not like real family.

Rachel *didn't* say thank you. She turned from Philip and said evenly, "How am I going to be able to carry this on the train?"

"You never heard of the mail?" Greta said simply.

"You wanna drive?" Greta offered, as they headed for the car. It wasn't an apology, but it was something. Neither sister liked to be the passenger when the other was driving. Greta thought Rachel rode the brake too much. Rachel thought Greta was always about to plow into the car in front of her.

"No, thanks. You'll never be able to read this." Rachel lifted the paper onto which she had scribbled directions to the Rosengren & Sons shed. After the contretemps about the toaster, she'd gone to call Jeremy Rosengren.

"My granddad said to come down here?" Jeremy had asked affably. "That doesn't sound right. We've got a showroom in town. The number's 824-8120." But when Rachel called, an answering machine said they were closed for the week. Rachel called Jeremy back. "Closed?" he said, dumbfounded. "Well, you can come down here if you want. I've got a book of monuments—photos of the things we've done in the last few years—but it'd be better to wait the week." Rachel explained her situation—only in town for a few days. "Well, OK," Jeremy said cautiously, "though it's not the way we normally do it."

Greta navigated from New Jersey to Long Island, and then Rachel took over, consulting her directions and getting progressively more carsick as they drove. There was something impossibly hard to take about the way shops and chain stores were heaped up on the side of the roads here. And then there were the endless signs screaming about sales and bargains.

"Why is it Long Island always makes me want to barf?"

"You really *are* turning into a Maine girl."

"Should it say anything?"

"What?"

"The marker. Should it say anything, or should it just have Mamie's name and the dates."

"What would it say?"

"I don't know. 'She was loved.' Something like that."

"But we didn't write anything on our parents' markers. Or grandpa's. If hers says something, then it'll be like the others weren't loved."

"I suppose. But she was."

"Was what?"

"Loved."

"Well, I know *that*. Why are we arguing about *that*?"

"I don't know." Rachel felt like crying.

They found the dilapidated building that was Rosengren & Sons located behind a large office-supply store in Port Washington. At least, they found a big wooden shed with a chipping, rusty sign announcing *Monuments–Markers–Lettering–Repair.* Slabs of granite by the entrance door confirmed that they'd come to the right place.

They pushed through the door. Inside, there was some sort of shallow pit, surrounded by corrugated metal. Two giant cranes hovered above. A mechanical whirring came from somewhere deep within the room. There were three large stones in the pit, and to their left stood a few battered old wood chairs and a desk cluttered with Styrofoam cups and empty soda cans.

"They're supposed to do excellent work," Rachel added, half apologetic, though of course she didn't know if this was true. She called into the room, "Jeremy?"

"Un-huh," a voice answered, and a head stuck out from behind the largest of the three stones in the pit. "That's me. Are you Rachel?"

"Yes, you gave me directions this morning?"

"That was me."

Jeremy wiped his hands on an old gray rag and then came toward them, his hand extended. He was tall and slim, with a big grin that seemed less about his happiness to meet her than his amusement at something—perhaps his own ears, which stuck out of his head and made him look all the more goofily pleased by the world. "Normally people go to the sales office to see the markers, but I can show you stuff. Have a seat." He gestured to the chairs near them.

You wouldn't expect a man who deals in death all day to be so happy, Rachel thought.

As if he'd divined her thoughts, Jeremy smiled and said, "It's good to be in the business of helping people remember their loved ones. Let me show you some of your choices." He pulled a three-ring notebook out of a drawer. Greta held her arms out to receive the book, but he passed it into Rachel's hands.

"We'll look together," Rachel said and started flipping through the pages.

Greta explained, "We already have a family monument with the last name, so we're just looking for a marker with her name and dates." She sounded defensive, as if she expected Jeremy to try to talk her into more than what she wanted. "And she just died, so the unveiling is still a year away."

"Your grandfather told us to come to you. He lives in the same building with our grandmother. Where she used to live, I mean."

Jeremy scratched the back of his head contemplatively. "And did he say I should give you a *big discount?*" His voice took on his grandfather's inflections, and he gave two brief karate chops to the air, as if marking out a space in front of his chest where the words might hang.

Rachel had been wondering how she'd slip that piece of information into the conversation. She bobbed her head.

"Of course," Jeremy said. Rachel pictured the small business card that Philip always flashed at the crowded fish restaurant where he and Greta liked to eat. It said that he was a friend of the owner and should be seated right away. Philip always flipped the card out of his wallet rather grandly, and the waitress nodded at the card; probably the owner gave them to everyone he met.

"Well," Jeremy went on, "normally I just do the carving. I'm not in sales. But, sure, you can have a big discount." He smiled. "There's a reason I'm not in sales."

Greta looked at him uncertainly.

"Your grandma," Jeremy asked. "Was she the one who always made raisin kugel?"

The sisters shook their heads no.

"And she wasn't in the book group?"

"No, she was," Rachel said. "The Jewish book group?"

"Yeah, that always cracked me up. They would only read

biographies. 'What about a novel?' I'd say to my grandfather. 'There are lots of good Jewish novels out there.'

"'You never heard that truth is stranger than fiction?' he'd say. 'I stick to the strange stuff.'"

Greta cleared her throat and pointed to the book of monuments. "Maybe we should get back to . . ."

"Un-huh. Well, we can set the stone whenever. That's allowed. You'll see there are more formal and less formal things in there. We can do it as plain as you want, though normally there's a candelabra for the women. Sometimes words."

"Like what words?" Rachel said, quickening at this suggestion. She wanted something for Mamie.

"Normally we write—in Hebrew—'May her soul be bound with the bundle of light.'"

Rachel looked at Jeremy and smiled. "That's it. That's exactly what I want."

Greta looked at Rachel. She had never known her sister to make a quick decision. "Well, then," she said, "I can't disagree."

When people asked, and they inevitably did ask, "How did you meet your husband?" this was the story that Rachel told, the story of picking out the gravestone; the way she'd thrilled to Jeremy's suggestion about the words for Mamie. "May her soul be bound with the bundle of light." Yes, exactly, as if Mamie had resurrected herself, for one tiny moment, in the form of this stranger to remind Rachel that she wanted to comport herself in death as in life. By looking on the sunny side, and all that. But there was more to it, of course. There was the tentative way Jeremy called Rachel, later that day, and, apologizing profusely, asked if she wouldn't like to have dinner sometime. And the way she apologized in return, since she had to go back to work that Monday, and offered instead, "How about right now?" They had met halfway, he taking the train from Long Island and she from New Jersey. They ate at Grand Central's Oyster Bar, so they wouldn't have to waste any time walking around finding a place. He'd ordered French onion soup and spooned it onto his fettuccini. Rachel grimaced. "Sticking to the strange stuff runs in the family, I see."

Jeremy shrugged and put his spoon down. She shouldn't have been rude. Still, before their dinner was up, he took Rachel's hand and said, "Will you see me again? If you just say yes, then I don't have to worry about asking you later." They'd exchanged phone numbers and e-mail addresses, and Rachel had come back to the city the very next week. It wasn't so easy conducting a romance in front of a rabbi, and she left her friend tucked into a drawer at Greta's for that second date. Then Jeremy came to Maine. They went for a walk around the bay in Portland, Rachel pointing out the lighthouses and fireboats, Jeremy thrilling at the most ordinary things: the pile of lobster traps behind a restaurant, the friendliness of people on their path. Already they were writing their own history. "I just felt I had to see you again," Jeremy said about what had impelled him to call her, the night of their first meeting. He was usually quite shy with girls.

They married at a nature center in Maine. After the wedding ceremony, Rachel and Jeremy were conducted to a small room— it was normally some sort of administrative office—where they were expected to spend their first married moments relating to one another, before the onslaught of the party that Jeremy's family and Greta had planned.

Jeremy kissed Rachel. "Don't hold it against me that these are my first words to you as a husband."

"Yeah?"

"I really got to use the bathroom."

Rachel laughed. "Go down the back hall, then you can use the one upstairs without anyone seeing you."

Jeremy rolled his eyes at himself, hummed a line of "Isn't It Romantic?" and hurried out the door. All Rachel's clothes from the morning—her handbag and her summer dress—were piled on a filing cabinet. Outside, two goldfinches were perched on a bird feeder. She turned for her handbag and took out the little rabbi.

"It was beautiful. I'm sorry you couldn't have heard it. But it went so fast. I can't believe it's over." Jeremy's dad had tripped when he stood to read one of the seven marriage blessings, and there was an uneasy tittering until everyone realized he wasn't hurt. Her two nephews had made very cute flower boys, not scattering the petals, but throwing them over their heads like confetti.

"*Mazel tov*," the rabbi said. "Remember you once asked me what sort of miracles I do?"

"Yes?"

"I can make a man who doesn't have to go to the bathroom go to the bathroom."

"Oh," she said. "I think I can do that, too. I learned this trick at summer camp where you put a kid's hand in warm water, not that I'd ever—"

"I have a story to tell you."

"Now?" She had yet to be in the position of not wanting to hear the rabbi's words, but at the moment her mind was on other things.

He paid no attention to the incredulity in her voice and began in the same measured tones with which he'd begun all his stories. "*Feigele*, you will think this a strange story to tell you on your wedding day, for it is a terrible tale. You know, of course, the world is full of horrors, and for the Jews that has meant, at times, a pogrom. You know pogrom?"

"I know what it *is*, if that's what you're asking. I haven't, you know, myself, personally—knock wood and all—ever been subjected to a—"

"I'll tell you about Mendel Agar, who had a wife whom he loved beyond all reason. His hand was always in hers, if you came to call at the house. If she stood to do a chore, he would rise to help, and she would do the same for him."

"Oh, so this is going to be Mendel Agar's tips for the newly married?"

The rabbi held up a little finger, as if to indicate she shouldn't have interrupted. "But if you chanced to come on a Sabbath, you would see a very peculiar sight. They prayed together at home, but when they prayed, they looked like one who was dead. Their breathing became so slow it seemed to stop, and their skin turned cool. One day a visitor presumed them dead and sent for help, but when the help came, the couple was awake and blowing away the smoke of the Havdalah candle.

"Mendel he lives in Russia, and comes to Russia a terrible time for the Jews. One evening, a band of men arrive, and they give him this choice: You give to us the Jewish boys of your classroom, we want to have ourselves a little massacre, or we kill you. In the morning, the men will come for the boys."

"Mendel's a schoolteacher?"

"Yes, didn't I say?"

"Like me."

"No, not like you. Did I say like you? Listen. The next day the men come for Mendel, but they find him . . . already dead.

And his wife, too. Or so it seems, for the two are deep in prayer, sending up their soul's voices to God, so this terrible thing, it should not be. Into their prayers comes the knowledge that the boys will be killed no matter what Mendel chooses to do. Mendel and his wife pray for the souls of the boys. And for their own souls. They pray no one else will be hurt. They pray so long and so hard that their breath gets slower and slower and slower; their cheeks grow paler and paler and paler. Then they stop.

"It has never been done before, this thing that Mendel and his wife have done, but they have done it. They have prayed themselves into oblivion. Now when a neighbor chances by and thinks they are dead, they really are dead."

"You sound impressed," Rachel said.

"God gives burdens, also shoulders."

Dead shoulders, Rachel thought to say, but she hadn't planned for theological debate on her wedding day.

"So *bubele*," the rabbi said and then scurried up her arm and onto her shoulder, so he could reach over to pat her turned cheek with his dime-sized hand, "you let me finish, no?"

Rachel smiled a yes—she had routinely had his whole body in her hand, moving him from here to there, but this was the first time he had touched her with obvious affection. She returned him to the desk, and he sat himself on a stack of brochures that read *Nature Discovery Programs*. And then he continued with his story: "Mendel and his wife, their souls are not easy, and as good as they were in their days on earth, they do not enter into the Everlasting. First, Mendel is reborn into the home of a New York gravestone engraver, and his wife is reborn into the home of a pharmacist in New Jersey. As they grow, they feel as if they are looking for someone, but they never find this person. Other people marry and have children, and still they are alone, or talking with those who can never truly understand their words. It goes this way for some years. They once almost meet by the side of a lake in Maine, where the boy has gone with a friend for a week away from the city. They once almost meet in a subway car that grinds to a halt on a hot summer day. They once see each other in a sporting goods store, where she is buying sneakers, and he is purchasing a basketball. Then, but you know the end of the story yourself—"

Rachel turned to the sound of Jeremy coming back through the door. She was still half smiling at what the rabbi had to say and not yet thinking to hide him back in her purse. She planned to tell Jeremy about the rabbi sooner or later. But when she swiveled back to thank the rabbi for his story, he was gone, his little yarmulke and prayer shawl were gone, and it was time for the couple to go out to join their guests. They were having salmon for lunch. And roasted asparagus. And chocolate cake with white frosting.

—WITH DEBTS TO MARTIN BUBER'S *LEGENDS OF THE BAAL SHEM TOV*

ACKNOWLEDGMENTS

These stories previously appeared in the following periodicals: *Agni, Gingko Tree Review, The Massachusetts Review, narrativemagazine.com,* and *Ploughshares.* "Conservation" also appeared in *The Messy Self* (Jenny Rosner, ed., Paradigm Press, 2006). "Lady of the Wild Beasts" also appeared in *The Best Underground Fiction, vol.* 1 (Stolen Time Publishing, 2006). "A Wedding Story," also appeared in *Contemporary Maine Fiction* (Wes McNair, ed., Down East Books, 2005)

For their assistance (editorial and otherwise) during the writing of this book, warm thanks to Lan Samantha Chang, Susan Kenney, Bill Roorbach, Sue Sterling, Steve Stern, and Joan Wickersham.

I am grateful to Colby College, the Corporation of Yaddo, and the MacDowell Colony for their generous support during the writing of this book.

ABOUT THE AUTHOR

DEBRA SPARK is the author of four previous books, including the novels *Good for the Jews* and *Coconuts for the Saint*. She's been a fellow at Radcliffe College's Bunting Institute and a recipient of a National Endowment for the Arts Fellowship. Her articles, essays, stories, and reviews have appeared in *Esquire, Food and Wine, Maine Home+Design*, the *New York Times, Ploughshares*, and the *San Francisco Chronicle*, among other places. She is a professor at Colby College and teaches in the MFA Program for Writers at Warren Wilson College. She lives with her husband and son in North Yarmouth, Maine.